Home.

Was that how I thought of Mynaria now? I shouldn't let myself think of it that way, given that thanks to my Affinity, I might never be able to return. All I'd ever wanted, or thought I'd wanted, was to become queen of Mynaria, just like I'd been trained to. I thought I'd marry the prince and ascend the throne and use my power as a monarch to help the people of both our kingdoms. But that dream had gone up in smoke the day Thandi found out I was "dead." Or, if I was being honest with myself, the day I finally understood that my feelings for Mare ran far deeper than friendship.

Somehow, I had to find new dreams, but I had no idea where to start.

Also available by Audrey Coulthurst

Of Fire and Stars

Inkmistress

AUDREY COULTHURST

OF ICE
AND
SHADOWS

BALZER + BRAY
An Imprint of HarperCollins*Publishers*

Balzer + Bray is an imprint of HarperCollins Publishers.

Of Ice and Shadows
Copyright © 2019 by Audrey Coulthurst
All rights reserved. Printed in the United States of America.

ISBN 978-0-06-284123-0

Typography by Torborg Davern
20 21 22 23 24 PC/LSCH 10 9 8 7 6 5 4 3 2 1

❖

First paperback edition, 2020

For all the girls who love other girls—
you are as strong, fierce, and beautiful as Denna
and Mare, even if you don't know it yet.

THE NORTHERN KINGDOMS

HAVEMONT

OSMA

MT. VERITY

SPIRE CITY

ZIR CANYON

Northport Province

FAIRLOUGH

CIRALIS

COROVJA

Nax Province

ALMENDORN

ORZAL

LAKE VIERI

MYNARIA

LYRRA

ZUMORDA

PORT OF
KINGS

*Queenswood
Province*

VALENKO

EUSAVKA
RIVER

DUVEY

TAMERS FOREST

AMALSKA

NOBROSK

Trindor Province

KARTASHA

PORT JIRAE

ZEPHYR
LANDING

TRINDOR
CANAL

KRIANTZ'S
HOLDINGS

SONNENBORNE

✦ *Amaranthine*

WHEN MY MOTHER WAS ALIVE, I WAS A DIFFERENT PER-
son. That little girl wore simple clothes and wildflowers in her hair
and could sing any aria or tavern song known in the Northern Kingdoms. She believed in the Six Gods and trusted that they would
protect her and her family.

That little girl was a fool.

Winter's last rains and the spring's early sun battled for dominance over our city the day I took my last ride with Mother. Dressed
in my favorite breeches and a plain cloak, I met her in the gardens,
eagerly keeping pace with her all the way to the stables.

"Are we performing today?" I asked her, keeping my voice soft.

"I think we are," she said with a conspiratorial glint in her
eye. "Neilla sent a message saying they've missed us at the Bell and
Bridle."

Anticipation made me bounce on my toes. Neilla, the owner

of the alehouse, made rich, buttery cakes so delicious I could have sworn all Six Gods had blessed them. Mostly, though, I was glad that my mother felt well enough to leave the castle. Over the winter she'd become a thin shell of herself, her skin sallow, her face drawn. Even the flaming auburn of her hair seemed to have dimmed. Still, she was the queen, and everything I wanted to grow up to be.

"Is your stomach feeling better?" I asked. That was where her illness had started.

She took the reins of her horse, Lion, from a groom, and the big chestnut stallion nudged her shoulder fondly.

"I'm well enough," she said. "Don't you worry."

My heart sank. She said that when she didn't want me to know how much pain she was in. I may have been only ten summers old, but I was no fool. The gauntness of her face and the careful way she moved gave her away. More telling was that this was the first year since my little brother's birth that she hadn't taken on any horses to train herself. I whispered a prayer to the wind god, asking him to carry away her illness.

We mounted up and headed into the hills behind the castle. The air couldn't seem to decide if it wanted to be still or in motion, and every few minutes a cool gust blew raindrops off the trees into our hair. I sat tall in the saddle, still so proud to have my first horse after years of riding naughty ponies. Cinnamon wasn't a warhorse and I hadn't trained him myself, but he was a beautiful roan palfrey with floating gaits. Nothing gave me more satisfaction than being able to look down on my little brother and his pony from these new heights, or telling him to back off because Cinnamon had the temperament of an angry drunk when it came to other horses.

We rode under the budding trees down a barely visible trail to a secret gate. Mother had told me my father and brother had secrets too, but I couldn't imagine theirs were nearly as exciting. Did they leave the castle? Had they tasted the summer corn at Cataphract Square, blackened and coated in cheese and spices? Had they earned a hundred coins as musicians or played quat with friendly strangers in the pubs? Did they know where Mother and I went, or that we went at all?

The hidden gate opened onto a narrow cobbled lane that Mother and I followed into the city. Drops of water clung to every spring leaf and every tight bud, the sun making them glitter like a thousand tiny mirrors. Deep in the merchants' district, we rode into a small, quiet courtyard hidden from the bustling streets and busy shops. Planters bursting with greenery surrounded us on all sides, giving it the feeling of a garden in spite of the bricks under our feet and the buildings on all sides. We tied our horses in the simple run-in stalls, loosening their girths and tossing some hay into their shared manger.

"Let's go." My mother beckoned me into a servants' tunnel and through a secret door. Inside, we changed our clothes—me into a plain peasant dress with flowers stitched untidily along the hem, and my mother into short breeches and a tunic with sleeves gathered to the elbows. She brushed my hair with soot and tucked it into a snood to hide the coppery waves, then put on a vest and topped her ensemble with a flat cap that sported a large purple feather.

"How do I look?" she asked.

I giggled. The outfit made her look almost like a boy. "Like the most handsome musician in all of Lyrra."

She laughed. "Then I will need the most beautiful singer to accompany me." She produced a small sprig of cherry blossoms from behind her back. As she wove them into my snood with expert fingers, I closed my eyes and basked in her love.

When we emerged from the servants' tunnel into the back of the Bell & Bridle, we were no longer Queen Mirianna and Princess Amaranthine of Mynaria. We were Miri and Mara.

I loved being Mara. Mara didn't have to go to history lessons or balance books on her head or make polite conversation with boring courtiers. Mara walked with her mother through the city without a second glance from anyone. She sang to earn pennies and always got to keep a few to buy something from a vendor at the market. Mara was free.

Neilla stepped out from behind the bar and gave my mother a rocking hug that would have sent the noblewomen at court into vapors. A lively crowd had already gathered for the afternoon, filling the pub with a warm hum of conversation. While my mother spoke to Neilla, I opened the closet adjacent to the bar and pulled out a hide case. I laid it carefully on the floor and unclasped the fittings to reveal the instrument my mother had been forbidden to play since becoming queen. The burnished wood of the cello inside gleamed even in the dim tavern, the curves holding a promise of the beautiful music to come. "It's indecent!" the courtiers had whispered behind her back. "Spreading her legs to play a cello is far too crass for her station," my etiquette instructor had explained. Those dumpling-brained numbskulls had clearly never seen the raw joy on Mother's face when music came to life in her hands.

"Thank you, Mara." Mother picked up the cello. She tuned it

while I set the case out to receive coins and Neilla cranked open the pub windows, letting in a bracing early-spring breeze. My mother adjusted her stool one last time and, with a deep breath and a nod to me, set her bow to the strings.

The first notes resonated through the room, silencing all conversation. Mother's weakness vanished as she leaned into the music. Each phrase rang clearly as an orator's sentences, reaching inside those watching as if the gods themselves spoke through her. The music swept me away along with them, my heart so full I thought it might beat out of my chest.

But now was not the time for me to lose myself. I had to sing.

My soprano carried over the low notes of the cello, weaving its own spell on the audience. It was so easy to sway to the music, to feel each word as acutely as if I had written the lyrics myself. I'd already let go of being Princess Amaranthine, but now I shed the disguise of Mara, too, instead becoming the lonely spirit of a little girl who got lost in the forest after her mother sent her to fetch water. The song was at turns playful and mournful, carrying the audience through a tapestry of emotion that culminated in deep loss. When we finished, the room burst into applause. Tears glistened in the eyes of our listeners. I curtsied, then looked to my mother, whose gaze shone with pride. She sketched the symbol of the wind god before her, then blew me a kiss. Happiness burst in me like a crescendo. Perhaps the wind god had heard my prayer. How could my mother be dying when she played with such passion and life?

We played and sang on as people flowed into the pub, drawn by the music. They tossed coins into my mother's cello case and laughed, cried, and applauded for us until the afternoon waned. Little did I know that those were the last songs I'd sing with her. In less than a moon, she was gone. The gods had betrayed me.

After she died, I prayed and lit my vigil candles every evening, demanding that the Six bring her back to me. I sobbed myself to sleep every night until Father thundered down the hall and smacked me into silence for keeping him awake.

The only place I had to turn was the barn, and so the horses supported me through my grief. Between the amount of time I spent there and the surly personality I donned like a suit of armor, everyone started calling me Mare. As the years went on, I forgot the little girl who sang and danced and wanted nothing more than to be a good queen like her mother. That girl had been naive. She was gone, and Mare became the only version of myself I cared to be.

But some things require a person to be more than a name.

A kingdom in need of a fighter.

The threat of a war that could destroy everything.

Or a girl holding fire in her hands.

ONE   ✦ *Amaranthine*

WHEN I LEFT MY KINGDOM FOR THE FIRST TIME, IT WAS on a mission to serve the crown I'd never given half a damn about pleasing. My horse, Flicker, carried us at a brisk walk that quickly left the wide stone bridge and border guards behind. The red road we'd already been on for days stretched out ahead, flanked by evergreen trees identical to the thousands we'd already passed, and the chilly wind that had chased us out of Mynaria continued to gust relentlessly.

"I expected Zumorda to look different from home," I said to the girl riding behind me.

"Why?" Denna asked.

"I don't know," I said. "People talk about this place like it's some kind of mysterious death trap." I thought the landscape would reflect that somehow—or at least justify the uneasiness that knotted my shoulders. After all, I was a girl without magic who had entered a kingdom where nearly everyone else had it. Coming here willingly made me about as sharp as a bag of wet barn mice.

"People like to exaggerate," Denna said. "This is a trade road, and the horse merchants cross here all the time."

"It seems too quiet." My saddle creaked with the rhythm of my horse's strides as the wind whispered through the pines. All else was silent.

"After that fuss at the bridge, anywhere would seem quiet," Denna said.

"You're right." Perhaps the frustrating half-day struggle with the border guards to let us cross the bridge had made me forget the hush of the open road. Perhaps it was that we'd so recently left behind the steady rush of the river dividing my homeland from this place—a kingdom I'd grown up hearing was full of magic-using heretics. Or perhaps I was just waiting for something bad to happen.

The frigid late-autumn wind pushed us forward, sending a bone-deep chill through me. I urged Flicker to extend his walk, hoping to leave my anxieties behind. I focused on the press of Denna's body against mine, a reminder that I wasn't alone. Without question, she was the only thing that had made the long, cold ride to Zumorda tolerable. The way her eyes danced when she smiled lit me up like nothing else in the world. I loved her fierceness and her intelligence and her ability to find her way out of almost any situation with her wits.

I didn't love that everyone believed she was dead, or that her presence with me made both of us traitors.

"I'm starting to think going on a quest in winter wasn't my brightest idea," I said with a shiver.

"We should have run away moons ago and gone to Trindor and the sea," Denna replied.

I smiled at the thought, knowing it never would have happened. Denna had been much too concerned with doing her duty for both our kingdoms, and if I was being honest, I'd never especially wanted to leave Mynaria. "If I'd been the heir to the throne instead of my brother, we wouldn't have had to run away at all."

"True," she said. "But you would have hated that role."

"Also true," I said. Minding my manners and paying attention to my studies had never been my best skills, and expertise with horses would only take a princess so far, even in Mynaria, where horsemanship was a strong measure of rank. Still, I felt a little stab of guilt about the choices Denna and I had made that had ended her betrothal. In the past year my brother and I had lost our father and uncle, but at least I still had Denna. All Thandi had was a crown and the aftermath of a foreign coup to contend with.

"Either way, I'm sorry this is what it came to," she said.

"Don't apologize. It's not your fault I'm not used to the cold. Besides, I'm the chowderhead who got my brother to send me to Zumorda to open a dialogue with them. I should have said I was going to join the Sisters of the Holy Wineskin or some other made-up nonsense. If I'd told him I was off to run barefoot through the woods and become a vintner surrounded by other wild women, he'd probably have believed it with no questions asked." The thought amused me in spite of the accompanying twinge of guilt at the idea of lying to my brother. We'd rarely gotten along, but we'd mostly been honest with each other—usually to the point of brutality.

Denna laughed. "I'm glad you're with me instead." She tightened her arms.

"Me too," I said, lifting a gloved hand to squeeze her arm in return. Strangely enough, I was even a little bit glad to be doing something important for my kingdom. After years of being pushed to the sidelines by my father, who had only expected me to marry and run an estate somewhere, I'd managed to convince my brother to send me, the least diplomatic person in our kingdom, to lay the groundwork for an alliance. If we couldn't get Zumorda to work with us, war breaking out with Sonnenborne on our southern borders was all but inevitable.

Somehow I had to convince the Zumordan queen that Sonnenborne posed a threat to both our kingdoms. They'd assassinated my father and uncle, using magical means to throw suspicion on Zumorda. If I could just open a dialogue with the queen, then Thandi could send in the real ambassadors and I'd be free to focus on helping Denna find someone to educate her about how to use the magic she'd been hiding all her life. Getting it under control was our only hope of being able to have a normal life together, especially if we wanted to live in Mynaria, where those with magic were often punished or exiled. Even if my brother's reign helped make magic use more acceptable, attitudes would be slow to change.

Still, I questioned whether I was up to the task of engaging foreign queens and nobles. My rank as princess made me worthy of the assignment, but my background wasn't exactly in diplomacy—it was in training horses, sneaking out of the castle to spy in the city, and drinking cheap ale in seedy pubs. Moreover, Mynarians hardly ever went to Zumorda. The kingdom was full of magic users with the very powers we'd condemned—Affinities for fire, air, earth, water, and gods knew what else.

"We should be getting close to Duvey now," Denna said. "The trees are thinning, and the border guards seemed to think we'd reach it by sundown."

"The trees aren't just thinning—they look like they're mostly dead," I observed. Skeletons of evergreens stood everywhere amidst the live trees. They creaked against each other in the wind, and their bleached bones littered the forest floor.

"It does seem awfully dry here, which doesn't make much sense, given that there aren't any geological reasons for the climate to be different on this side of the border," Denna mused.

"I'll take your word for it." I'd studied the maps well enough to know which way to point my horse, but my knowledge ended there. "All I know is, when we get to Duvey I want five tankards of ale and to sleep past sunrise for once." We needed a refreshing stop to fortify ourselves for the rest of our journey. Traveling all the way to northeastern Zumorda, to the crown city of Corovja, wouldn't be easy with winter weather on the way.

"I could go for something with more kick than ale," Denna said. "I wonder if Zumordans have a Midwinter festival with liquor. In Havemont we have a competition for the distillers. Mother would never let me or my sister taste any spirits besides the winners, but the people-watching was always good." She spoke of home with a regretful fondness, a feeling I had a hard time understanding.

Home for me had never been somewhere I felt entirely comfortable. Not in the castle, anyway. In disguise out in the city?

Somewhat. The barn? Definitely. But my tendency to escape my maids and royal duties to do barn chores or play cards with liegemen meant I had fit in with the other nobles about as well as a jar of horse farts at a parfumerie.

"Well, I hope that by the time we visit Havemont, your sister is the one in charge of the festival. I doubt Ali will stop us from tasting all the spirits we want," I said, already picturing sitting in front of a roaring fire with Denna on a cold winter's night, both of us a little light-headed from good liquor and laughing too much. The thought of tasting sweet brandy on her lips instantly counteracted the chill of the crisp autumn wind.

"She'd encourage us for sure," Denna said, and I could hear the smile in her voice. "She's always had a mischievous streak. Did I tell you about the time she wrapped me up in furs and tried to convince a tradesman at a party that I was a cat he should purchase?"

I snorted. "That sounds like something I would've tried to do to Thandi. Although mostly I just threw him in the manure pile anytime he made me angry."

"If only his subjects knew he'd once been King of the Dung Heap." Denna laughed.

"More than a dozen times over." I smirked, but a twinge of unfamiliar regret needled me. My relationship with my brother had always been antagonistic, but maybe it hadn't needed to be. If we had tried harder to overcome our differences of opinion instead of taking opposite sides of every argument, would the rest of our family still be dead? It was pointless to think about, but the question still rose up in the back of my mind to taunt me.

The twilight shadows deepened as we rode over gently rolling hills past fallow fields carved out of the forest. All the houses we saw were closed and dark, their windows shuttered. There were no lanterns hung outside front doors, no other travelers on the road. It felt empty in a way it shouldn't have. Even Flicker seemed ill at ease, his head up and ears swiveling back and forth worriedly.

"The keep should be over the next rise. Where are the people?" Denna asked.

"Something definitely doesn't seem right," I said. "Let's get off and approach on foot through those trees over there." I pointed to a copse of evergreens at the top of the next hill. "We need to make sure it's safe."

When we reached the trees, I drew Flicker gently to a halt and braced my arm for Denna to use as an assist to dismount. We left Flicker tied to a tree and crept into the woods. On the other side of the copse we had a clear view down into Duvey Keep, a stone fortress inside a high wall.

"There are riders in there," Denna said, puzzled.

I squinted, trying to see enough in the fading daylight to make sense of the scene below. Several people on horseback were inside the walls of the keep. At first I thought they were doing skirmish drills, until one of the riders veered closer and I got a better look at his horse. It had the distinctive convex profile and high neck set typical of a Sonnenborne desert-bred. In one smooth motion the rider nocked an arrow and stood in the stirrups, preparing to let it fly. Fear twisted around my spine. It wasn't a drill—the keep was under attack.

My stomach heaved and I grabbed Denna by the sleeve, tugging her behind a thick tangle of bushes.

"What's going on?" she whispered, looking equally shaken.

"Sonnenbornes are attacking. Their horses look just like the ones Kriantz had with him in Mynaria. That snake had bigger plans all along." Grief rose to choke me. Speaking Kriantz's name consumed me with memories of the night my best friend Nils had died—the night I'd been abducted from the castle and Denna had chosen to forfeit her crown to come after me. In some ways, that night had broken us both forever. In others, it had made us both whole for the first time.

"His people must be more united than we thought," Denna said.

"But why in the Sixth Hell are they here?" It was true he'd given the impression that several tribes had only recently joined together beneath his banner—that they wouldn't do anything without his signal. But for the Sonnenbornes to be here now spoke of a plan far more complex and organized than he'd made it seem.

"They could be trying to take an outpost at the Mynarian border," Denna said, her voice grim. "The keep would make a perfect settlement to fortify for attack."

"Six Hells," I said.

"Perhaps they plan to retaliate for Lord Kriantz's death," Denna continued, fear making her voice rise. The Sonnenbornes didn't know who had killed their leader—only that it had happened on Mynarian soil. Denna had dealt him a swift and fiery death by calling down the stars with her magic. Though she'd saved my life, I knew that night still haunted her.

"Hey," I said, taking her hand. "You did what you had to. You saved me." I leaned over and softly kissed her cheek. The fear in her eyes eased a little bit, so I pressed my lips to hers just long enough to feel familiar warmth blossom in the pit of my stomach. The truth was that the terrifying memories haunted me, too. Sometimes the smoke of the campfires along our journey had reminded me of that night, the scent of forest and flesh burning, the way the earth had shaken as flaming stones rained down from above.

"Or what if their plans are more elaborate than we thought, and they're trying to cut off one of Mynaria's most lucrative trade routes?" she said, always ten steps ahead.

"You're right," I said. "They'd be positioned to do either of those things. We need to get out of here." Keeping Denna safe was the only thing that mattered to me, but I also doubted my brother would approve of his sister—or his envoy—getting murdered by Sonnenborne raiders. That would start the very war we'd set out to prevent.

Denna's brow furrowed. "If the Sonnenbornes are already this far into Zumorda, there are two things we have to do: tell Thandi, and get you to the queen as soon as possible." She spoke with the kind of authority I'd heard her use back when she'd still been my brother's intended consort.

"I like it when you talk queenly to me," I said with a flirtatious wink.

A brief smile broke through her distressed expression. "Truly, though. The queen will be on your side if they've attacked her people."

"Let's ride north," I said, already walking back toward Flicker. "I doubt they'll send scouts until they've secured the keep."

"We need to make sure the Zumordans win this battle first." She grabbed my hand to stop me. "I can use my magic to help them."

I looked at her like she'd lost her mind. "Walking into this fight could get us killed."

"What better way to win allies than to help the Zumordans?" she asked.

Fear flickered in my chest. "We can't. What if something goes wrong?" As much as I loved her, I'd be lying if I didn't admit that her magic sometimes scared me. Ever since she'd summoned the stars to save me from Lord Kriantz, her powers had become less predictable, and they'd only been steady as a green-broke colt in the first place. Less than a week ago we'd gone hungry one rainy night because Denna couldn't start a fire and it was too wet for the sparks from my flint and steel to catch. A few days later, she had a nightmare, and before I could wake her up she'd set her bedroll ablaze, charring it past salvation.

Frustratingly, Denna ignored my objection and carried on. "We could climb that tree by the wall. That first building looks like it might be the stables." She gestured toward a stone building just inside the keep. Half doors lined the side, and a second-story window stood wide open as though no one had gotten there to close up the barn for the night. "There should be a good view from the hayloft."

"Hay is flammable," I said. "Your Affinity is for fire."

"Then we'll make that useful," she said, and before I could stop her, she was on her feet, sprinting toward the stables.

I cursed and took off after her.

If I had an Affinity, it would definitely be for trouble.

TWO  *Dennaleia*

IN SPITE OF MARE'S OBJECTIONS, SHE FOLLOWED ME. She would never let me run into a dangerous situation alone. I just wished she trusted my Affinity half as much as I trusted her.

Even if getting involved in this fight was a terrible idea, part of me longed to try to use my magic again. While my powers had been erratic and hard to access for much of our journey, over the past few days I'd felt magic building. I worried that if I didn't let some of it out, it was going to spiral out of control like it used to in Mynaria. Now that I knew the scope of the destruction I could cause, the thought of losing control frightened me that much more. I didn't want to hurt anyone—especially Mare.

I hoisted myself clumsily into the tree next to the keep wall, and Mare followed with more grace. The distance between the tree and the wall was farther than I expected, and I had to swallow my fear as I scrambled from a flimsy branch onto the stone. The greenway between the wall and the barn seemed to be clear, so I wasted no time sliding awkwardly to the ground. Mare leaped down a few seconds later, hitting the ground in a controlled roll I envied and couldn't imitate.

Before we could move toward the building, an older man and a blond boy who looked about my age sprinted into the greenway with a rider at their heels. I stood frozen in horror as the horseman raised a thin metal javelin and plunged it through the man's neck from behind. He fell forward onto the protruding javelin, sliding down the weapon to leave a streak of gore on the bright metal.

"Father, no!" the boy screamed, whirling to face the Sonnen-borne rider. He held up his hands, and flames lit in his palms.

My breath caught. I'd never seen anyone wield magic like mine before, and it dispelled my secret fear that I was alone in the world.

The rider leaned down and blew a handful of powder into the boy's face. The flames sizzled out, and the boy collapsed to the ground. I couldn't help the anguished sound that escaped my lips.

Then the rider spotted me. Fear shot through me like lightning as he drew a thin, curved sword from a scabbard on his back and dug his heels into his mount to urge it forward.

"No!" Mare shouted.

I raised my hands and reached inside myself for my magic. The patches of numbness on my arms that had been there since I saved Mare stung with pins and needles, as though they were trying to come back to life. I gritted my teeth against the pain, grateful for the way it purged my fear. Blue flames engulfed my palms, and I tried to push the magic forward to form a wall. Instead, a fireball burst from my hands and swallowed the rider. His horse sat back and stopped hard, rearing up in fear and confusion. I dodged to the side with my heart in my throat, frightened for my life and for what I'd just unwittingly done. The horse whirled around and galloped back the way it had come, the burning rider flopping on its back until the horse dislodged him in front of the stables.

"Denna!" Mare ran toward me.

"I'm fine," I said, trying to keep my voice from shaking. This had been my foolish idea, and I had to see it through. "Inside. Now."

Grabbing Mare's hand and tugging her toward the back of the stables, I cast a worried glance at the boy we were leaving behind. My boots crunched over broken glass where a lantern had shattered inside the back door. Hoofbeats sounded nearby and shouts echoed from outside. We needed to find a hiding place. Mare darted past me up a hayloft ladder. I followed her, scrambling up the splintery wood. We ducked to avoid the ceiling beams, making our way past stacks of hay and alfalfa that still smelled sweet as summer.

A wide window on the wall over the barn's main entrance gave us a clear view of most of the keep. We crouched beneath the hay forks hung on either side of it, cautiously peering out at the battle below. Guilt consumed me when I saw another Sonnenborne riding up to the boy whose father had been killed in front of us. She dismounted, slung him onto her mare's back, and then used a tree stump to vault back into the saddle.

"Are they taking prisoners?" Mare whispered.

"It looks that way," I said. "I wish we'd done more to help him." The thought of the boy waking surrounded by strangers, knowing his father was gone—it cracked me in half.

The Sonnenborne urged her mount into a canter, guiding the

mare around a much larger band of her people engaged in battle with keep soldiers. The riders intermittently darted past heavily armored soldiers who were trying to fend them off on foot, but the fight was far from ordinary.

I clung to the edge of the window, terrified by everything I was seeing. An enormous hunting dog with a sleek brown coat pulled a Sonnenborne from his horse and tore out his throat. Farther away, a mountain lion leaped out of the underbrush and sank its teeth into a horse's jugular, instantly dropping the animal to the ground. The horse's rider flew off and was impaled with a keep soldier's spear before he could even try to stand up. The animals fought with the same precision as any mercenary.

"Why are the animals acting so strange?" Mare whispered, her frightened eyes meeting mine.

"Maybe they're controlling them with magic?" I speculated. The thought sent a little spark of wonder through me, even as my sorrow and revulsion over the bloodshed grew. I forced myself to look back outside. If I wanted to help stop this, I couldn't retreat into my own fear.

Another Sonnenborne rider charged for the soldier who had killed his comrade, but a blue glow engulfed the rider and he was liquefied like he was made of water. His horse bolted, scrambling over fallen bodies in its haste to escape. Seconds later, another of the Sonnenbornes was stopped in her tracks by some unseen force that made her clutch at her throat in a panic until she collapsed to the ground.

The Zumordans were definitely using magic. Energy crackled over the battlefield, creating an answering hum in my own body. Warning tingles sparked down my arms as though I'd stuck my hands in a patch of nettles. Power felt like it would burst out of my control if I didn't use it. As terrified as I was, part of me felt exhilarated—and that sickened me. I clutched handfuls of my cloak in an attempt to steady my shaking hands, trying to channel my fear into confidence. Surely it couldn't be that difficult to run off these people. All we needed were a few fires to create chaos and give the keep guards an advantage.

The only question was whether I could get my Affinity to cooperate.

"I'm going to try something," I said, cupping my palms and releasing just enough of my magic to make a small flame dance in my hands. It flickered erratically.

"Are you sure you can control it?" Mare watched me with wide eyes.

I tried to tamp down my worry that she was afraid of what I could do. Instead I turned my focus to a wooden cart that had overturned near the battle. My powers boiled up with the force of a geyser. The rush of magic pushed aside my fear, and I welcomed the pain that accompanied it. I shoved the energy toward the wagon, and the magic flooded out of me in a rush that made me dizzy.

Flames burst from the wagon with a roar. The Sonnenborne horses shied away from the fire with their eyes rolling in fear. One of the riders fell off, finding himself on the receiving end of a spear to the gut. My vision darkened at the edges as I struggled to rein the magic back in. I needed to calculate my next move even if the powers were telling me all I had to do was set them free.

I glanced over at Mare to see she'd pulled out her bow and nocked an arrow. Her first shot struck one of the Sonnenborne riders in the arm, disarming him enough for one of the keep soldiers to knock him out of the saddle. Shouts echoed from the courtyard as the foot soldiers did their best to take advantage of the opening they'd been given.

"They're in here!" a voice said in the Sonnenborne tongue.

They'd found us.

"I'll check out back," someone else replied. "If they're magic users, take them alive."

I whirled around, clamping down on my magic as hard as I could and sidestepping away from the window into the shadows.

The hayloft ladder creaked as someone ascended. I held my breath, terrified we were about to be discovered by the enemy. Footsteps drew closer until a Sonnenborne warrior appeared, the blade of her short sword glinting in the dim light. I shot a quick glance to Mare, who was frozen in place, eyes wide, her back against the wall next to the window. With our adversary's next step, Mare would be in the woman's line of sight. Mare's bow was useless against a sword at close range, and she knew it.

With a yell, the woman charged at Mare.

Mare screamed. There was no time to use my magic. I snatched a hay fork from the wall and thrust the handle into the swordswoman's path. She tripped over the tool, wrenching it from my hands as she pitched face-first out the window and landed with a sickening crunch on the flagstones below.

"By the Six, Denna . . ." Mare stepped toward me, and an arrow whizzed past, barely a handbreadth from her face. She shrank back.

Rage coursed through me, white hot with magic. I wouldn't let anyone hurt her. The last of my fear evaporated. I didn't care who saw me. I didn't care what I did. The direction of the wind shifted as I drew on more magic, reaching so deep inside myself I might as well have been hollowing out my own bones. I set flames on the wind and power spiraled out of me, twisting out of control. A gale rose, sweeping through the barn and jerking at my hair and cloak, loose pieces of hay providing fuel for the fire.

A wave of flaming debris undulated in front of the stables, waiting for my direction. The Sonnenbornes fell back, shouting and pointing at the fire seething overhead. Yes, that was what I wanted: to push them away. And they were giving me the perfect opportunity. I released some of the swirling gale toward the Sonnenbornes, trying to guide it above the keep soldiers so that no one on the defensive side would be harmed.

I might as well have tried to fence in a charging bull with embroidery string.

The swath of burning debris knocked down two keep soldiers and set them ablaze before slamming into the Sonnenbornes and surging higher. Horses bolted before the flames could reach them. I felt strangely detached from my emotions as riders fell and burned. Their bodies provided more fuel for my fires, which crept across the dead grass in search of more victims. Screams echoed through the keep grounds—not screams of bloodlust or battle, but of terror and death. The only thing holding back my horror was the overwhelming magic coursing through me. It drained me and it fed me at the same time, making me feel more full and alive than ever before. The bright blazes grew until a wall of flame arched across the courtyard, feeding on anything that might burn. Dimly, I became aware that Mare was screaming.

"Denna!" Her voice sounded as though it were coming from leagues away. "Stop!"

My whole body shook with the exertion of trying to keep my own powers from swallowing me. Tears leaked from my eyes with the effort, and with the knowledge that I had hurt and even killed people. It didn't matter which side of the fight those people had been on—that wasn't who I wanted to be. The magic had torn away my sense of self as it raced through me, making me do things too dreadful to comprehend. But the magic was as much a part of me as my beating heart, and that meant I had to shoulder the blame for the deaths. I tried to stop the flood pouring through me, tried to pull the magic back.

It wouldn't return.

My throat tightened with terror as the wind kicked up further, fanning the flames of my fire until it spread to the outer wall of the keep. The screams faded away until I couldn't hear anything but the frantic gallop of my pulse in my ears.

I tried to think of the earth, of something that could make me feel rooted to the ground. But instead I felt the stone of the wall inside my mind, like I had become part of the flames, like I was crawling over them and heating them with my own body. I saw nothing but fire.

The sound of rocks shattering split the air as the keep wall burst in an enormous explosion.

Then my world went dark.

THREE   ✦ *Amaranthine*

I FLEW TO DENNA'S SIDE THE MOMENT SHE COLLAPSED
and the firestorm stopped. Outside, the clash of weapons turned into
moans of pain and calls for help. I touched Denna's forehead with
trembling hands. Her skin felt cold and clammy to my touch, but her
chest still rose and fell with even breaths. She was the most precious
person to me in all the Northern Kingdoms, and I was closer to her
than I'd been to anyone, but when she'd stood in that window commanding a wave of fire large enough to destroy a small army, I'd felt
like I barely knew her at all. I shivered in the cold and held back the
tears that threatened.

"Denna?" I gently shook her shoulder. I didn't know whether
to be more afraid of what she'd done to the Sonnenbornes or of
what she might do to me by accident if she were startled awake. I
tried not to think about how many people she might have injured or
killed. Surely she hadn't done it on purpose—that wasn't like her.

The magic had to be taking over her mind as well as her body.

"Who's there?" someone shouted in Zumordan from the barn aisle.

I peered over the edge of the hayloft to see four soldiers, all of them dirty and battered with the marks of battle. The moment they caught sight of me, they started shouting in Zumordan spoken too rapidly for me to follow.

"I need help." I spoke in Tradespeech, my voice nearly breaking. There was no way I could get Denna down from the loft myself. I had no choice but to trust them, and to hope they could heal her. Maybe they would even know how to keep her magic contained.

"Surrender your weapons!" the leader shouted, now speaking Tradespeech as well.

"We don't want to hurt you." I held up my hands. "I only have a bow."

"Who are you?" the soldier demanded.

For once I was grateful for my rank. "I'm Princess Amaranthine of Mynaria, sent as an ambassador by King Thandilimon. And this is my maid, Lia, who seeks asylum and training for her magical gift." The lie about Denna's identity had become familiar on our journey, though never comfortable.

I couldn't see the soldier's expression in the shadows, but his stance shifted from aggressive to cautious.

"Princess, you said?" the soldier asked, his voice dubious.

"Yes, and I need help. Lia fell unconscious after the explosion." I was proud of myself for sounding authoritative even though fear had my hands shaking.

"That explosion almost killed half our fighters!" the soldier said.

"It also drove back the Sonnenbornes and saved your life," I snapped back. "We were trying to help. Now, can someone please get her a medic?"

The soldiers murmured among themselves for a moment.

"We'll see if we can spare a medic," the leader finally said to me. "There were a lot of injuries in the battle."

"I'm sorry," I said. "I'd hoped I would make it here in time to prevent anything like this from happening. King Thandilimon sent me to warn you of a threat from Sonnenborne."

The soldier seemed to relax a little bit at this overt display of allyship. "Let's get you both down from there and take a look at her," he said.

Denna's small frame made it easy for them to carry her down the ladder and settle her atop some clean horse blankets in the barn aisle.

"Her breathing is strong," one of the soldiers noted. "She probably overspent her gift." He shook his head. "Someone of her age and strength should know better."

I bristled. "She's untrained."

"What?" The soldier turned to me with a shocked expression.

"Magic users aren't welcome in Mynaria. She's had to hide her gift her whole life," I said. The facts somehow felt bigger than they had before, maybe because I now knew just how powerful her gifts were. My stomach turned, and I swallowed hard. She would never hurt anyone on purpose unless she had to. She wasn't that kind of person—at least not when her magic was under control.

"Tavi, please go see if the medics can make arrangements for this girl," the head soldier said. "We'll meet you at the main gate."

One of the soldiers gave him a sharp nod, then stepped back from the group. Her limbs curled in on themselves as she dropped to her hands and knees. A slender red fox stood where she'd been just a few heartbeats before. A chill crept down my spine as she turned to trot out of the stables. Magic that would get someone condemned in my homeland was performed so casually here.

"Let's get your maid to the keep," the lead soldier said. At his instruction, a muscular soldier picked up Denna, and the group of us trudged out of the stables. The body of the Sonnenborne woman Denna had tripped through the hayloft window lay splayed on the stone path just outside the front door. Her left leg jutted out from underneath her at an impossible angle that made my stomach heave. Denna had saved my life at the cost of another, and that death hadn't even been caused by magic. I didn't know how to feel about that but couldn't stop the wave of discomfort that crested within me at the thought. We stepped around the corpse, and I took deep breaths of the smoky night air to keep from gagging.

Closer to the keep, people carried injured soldiers past on litters while others directed foot traffic. Tavi, the fox woman, reappeared in human form a few moments later.

"We can't spare a medic," she said. "But they've sent for the herb witch, and a private room is being arranged."

"Why not put her in the medical ward with the others?" I asked. I wanted Denna where she could get the best care, not in a private room because the Zumordans were trying to respect me or honor what Denna had done for them.

"The herb witch will better be able to treat her," the lead soldier said, but a shifty look in his eyes betrayed him.

I looked around, noticing that our conversation had suddenly cleared out the area. What had been a hub of activity a few minutes before was quickly dissipating. Then I understood. They didn't want her in the medical ward with the other soldiers because they didn't trust her not to hurt anyone again. Besides, people she'd injured by mistake would likely be there under the care of the medics. Getting a room of her own was a defensive move, not an honor for the girl who'd saved their hides.

"Of course," I said. What choice did I have but to agree?

Inside the keep, the soldiers escorted us to a small room with rugged stone walls and a fire already blazing in the hearth. They laid Denna down on a cot with her head pillowed on a folded blanket.

"We'll leave you for now," the lead soldier said. "A guard will be posted outside your door. For safety."

I doubted Denna's safety or mine was what truly concerned them, but I couldn't blame them for not putting much faith in us. Our mistrust was mutual.

After the door closed behind them, I sat on the floor next to Denna's cot and took her hand in mine. Fears rushed in to consume me. What had she done to herself? What if she never woke up? She'd lost consciousness when she'd saved me from Kriantz, too. Surely this couldn't always be the cost of using her magic. Not for the first time, I wished she could somehow give her magic away and be free of it. That would make our lives so much less complicated. Guilt weighed on me for even thinking it. I knew her Affinity was part of her and that she'd be hurt if she knew I'd ever wished it away, but I didn't know how else to keep her—or us—safe.

A loud knock sounded at the door, startling me back to my feet.

I hadn't expected the herb witch to arrive so quickly. But the person waiting for me on the other side was no herbalist—he was a tall, bearded soldier still covered in the filth of battle.

"Lord Wymund, guardian of Duvey Keep, at your service," he said, extending a hand in greeting. His Tradespeech was barely accented, no doubt thanks to living in a border town.

"Thank you for your hospitality, my lord," I said, inviting him in.

"It isn't often we have a princess in our midst." He looked over my shoulder at Denna, who lay very still on the cot. "And we're grateful for your help turning back the attackers."

"You're welcome," I said. "Please just call me Mare."

"Like a horse?" He seemed amused.

"It's odd, I know—"

"Soldiers go by all kinds of names." He shrugged. "One fellow who used to fight for me went by Carmella Meatball. He was awfully handy with an ax."

I blinked.

"Anyway, we've been expecting you—we received a message for you from King Thandilimon yesterday. Glad you made it in one piece."

"What message?" I asked, startled. I hadn't expected to hear from my brother. It was almost impossible to get messages from Mynaria to Zumorda or vice versa, given how little fondness there was between our two kingdoms. It had been my expectation that I wouldn't be able to reach him from Zumorda at all—at least not until I'd managed to curry some favor with the queen and things were looking promising for an alliance. The only other option to reach him was to somehow communicate using magic. Even if I'd known who to ask about that, I had a lot of misgivings.

"A bird delivered this yesterday, along with a note asking me to hold it for you." Wymund handed me a small envelope. The message showed no signs of tampering—my brother's blue seal was still stamped in place.

"Thank you, my lord," I said, itching to open the note, but also worried about what I'd find inside. It couldn't be anything good.

"I must attend to my soldiers now," Wymund said. "Funeral rites will be held in the morning. After the dead have been properly honored, we'll have a victory feast in the evening. I hope you'll consider joining us."

"Thank you for the invitation. It would be an honor." It was the diplomatic thing to do, although the thought of leaving Denna for even a few sunlengths made fear prickle down my spine. Hopefully she'd be awake and well enough to attend with me.

I sat down at Denna's bedside, checking to make sure she was still breathing. Her stillness frightened me so much. I couldn't decide whether that or watching her use her powers was more terrifying. Both made me feel like I could lose her at any moment, and that was the scariest thought of all. As soon as I was assured her status hadn't changed, I turned my attention to Thandi's letter. I slipped my finger underneath the seal and opened the flap of the envelope. The date on the letter was only a few days past, making me wonder again how he'd gotten it to me so quickly. A bird wouldn't have been able to fly from Lyrra all the way over the Zumordan border in such a short time. Seeing my brother's swooping script on the page brought an unexpected swell of emotion. Given how contentious our relationship had always been, it surprised me to find that I missed him—at least until I began to read.

Dear Amaranthine,

Hopefully this letter will find you safe in Zumorda. Unfortunately, I have bad news. The riots between the fundamentalists and the Recusants on the Trindor Canal paved the way for an attack. The canal city of Zephyr Landing was overtaken by Sonnenbornes a few days ago. Many of our people were killed.

We've sent cavalry, but in the meantime, the Sonnenbornes have completely cut off inland trade and taken over canal trade from Port Jirae. The handoff was so smooth, they must have been planning it long before the riots began. As you can guess, this changes everything. I need you to do more than open a dialogue with the Zumordans—I need you to ask for their help reclaiming Zephyr Landing. I'm prepared to send another regiment of cavalry to Zumorda to help defend their cities in exchange—I'll station them just across the border for easy summons. Havemont has continued to be a supportive ally—Princess Alisendi has been a great help as my liaison while we attempt to renegotiate our alliance in light of Dennaleia's death.

This message was delivered with the help of the Recusants; surely you understand how dire things are for me to be working with them. I know your taking on a full ambassadorial role wasn't the plan, but from this point forward, you are my eyes, my ears, and my voice in

Zumorda. Please consider yourself an official ambassador
of the Mynarian crown, with all the power bestowed by the
office.

    Your kingdom and your brother are counting on you.

                             Yours,
                     King Thandilimon of Mynaria

I muttered a string of profanity colorful enough to get my title stripped. How could Thandi do this to me? An unfamiliar wash of guilt followed the typical rage. How *couldn't* he do this to me? People had died, and more battles were yet to come if what we'd found here in Duvey was any indication. He'd already been desperate enough to work with the Recusants, a group of magic users he hated and mistrusted.

The only contact he had in Zumorda with any power to help was me.

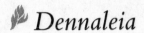 *Dennaleia*

THE SOUND OF SCREAMING STABBED THROUGH MY skull like a knife. I opened my eyes, but shadows lingered in my vision, slowly giving way to blinding light. Once they dissipated, the source of the brightness became clear: flames surged on all sides of me. I was on fire—and the screams were coming from my own throat.

Fear gripped me like a vise. Neither my magic nor my body was under my control.

Icy water cascaded over my head as an unfamiliar woman upended a bucket over me, cutting off my screams. She immediately followed the water with a wool blanket that snuffed the remaining flames. My teeth chattered from the sudden change in temperature as the room slowly came together—beamed ceiling overhead, stone walls to either side, wet cot beneath. Near the hearth, the unfamiliar brown-eyed woman stared at me curiously, waiting for me to respond. Her wild gray hair was barely contained in a knot at her neck, and a colorful cloak made of scrap cloth hung from her shoulders, the stitches tidy as a surgeon's.

"Mare?" My voice came out as barely more than a croak. Where was she?

"Mare is at supper with Lord Wymund." The woman spoke Tradespeech quite fluently. "I'm Sarika. Now tell me, how do you feel?"

"Head hurts," I mumbled. I sat up and my vision swam. Physically, I felt almost as terrible as I had after saving Mare from Kriantz. "What happened?"

"Apparently, you don't react kindly to smelling salts," Sarika said wryly. "Do you remember the battle?"

I nodded. Of course I did. Everything had been fine until I lost control. After that attacker had rushed at Mare, I'd let everything get out of hand. My stomach heaved as I remembered the look of surprise in the woman's eyes when she'd pitched out the open loft window and fallen to her death. I hadn't really meant to kill her, but there hadn't been time to think. After that, my memories were blurry. Still, I knew I'd hurt people—and it hadn't just been our enemies.

"That wave of flame was hard to miss," Sarika added, tucking an unruly spiral of gray hair behind her ear.

I cast my eyes to the floor, ashamed that I'd made such a dramatic scene and frightened to think that people were injured or dead because of me—again.

"How many on our side were burned?" I needed to know, even though fear rose in me at the thought.

"Five were injured," Sarika said. "I was supplying the medics with herbs to make burn compresses when they came to tell me about you."

She sounded so calm, but I couldn't even begin to conjure the same stoicism. My throat tightened and I blinked back tears. I set out to help people with my magic but always seemed to end up harming them instead. I didn't want this to keep happening. I'd come here to get training, to educate myself, and the first thing I'd done was hurt people. Even the Sonnenbornes hadn't deserved what I'd unleashed on them.

"Try not to fret. The fighters will heal in time," Sarika told me. "I may not be a master healer, but I have enough of the gift to help them start to mend. Besides, if you hadn't nearly blown this place to bits, they might have found themselves on the wrong end of a Sonnenborne spear. Because of you, they'll live to see the next battle."

"It doesn't make what I did right," I said. She couldn't possibly mean for me to think they might be grateful for what I'd done. If I hadn't felt so weak and unsteady, I would have gathered my things, found Mare, and fled as fast as my feet could carry me. The thought of facing people whose friends I'd hurt or killed was too much to bear. I already didn't know how I was going to live with myself.

"At least you kept them from taking any more prisoners." Sarika shook her head. "The parents who lost children are harder to help than the burn victims."

"The Sonnenbornes took children?" I asked, my heart dropping as I remembered the blond boy we'd failed to save.

"Not the smallest of them, but yes. Most of those who are missing seem to be between ten and twenty winters of age."

"But why?" I felt sick. How could that figure into the Sonnenbornes' master plan? Hostages meant more mouths to feed, so there would have to be a compelling reason to take them.

Sarika shrugged. "We don't know. Maybe the soldiers Wymund sent after them will come back with answers. Hopefully they'll at least come back with the children."

I wrapped my arms around myself and shivered.

"Let's get you into some dry clothes," Sarika said. She gestured in the direction of our packs. "May I?"

I nodded. Unless Sarika wanted to steal dirty clothes, she wasn't going to find much in there. Mare would have her coin purse on her. Sarika brought me the chamber pot and helped me change out of my soaked garments, then settled me near the hearth. The familiarity of having someone dress me was soothing. It gave me a pang of nostalgia for my life as a princess, a time when I'd known my purpose. Things had been so much less complicated then.

I stared into the flames. The worry and dread in the pit of my stomach kept me feeling cold in spite of the fire's heat. I wanted Mare to come back so I'd feel a little less unmoored, and so we could talk about where we were going next and how quickly we could leave.

"How long have I been here?" I asked.

"You slept all night and most of today," Sarika said, using a long hook to hang a kettle in the hearth. "I could have woken you sooner, but your body needed the time to heal. I'm brewing some tea that will help keep your magic under control. Do you think you can hold anything down right now?"

"I don't know," I said. My head felt fuzzy and my limbs held down by invisible weights. As I got warmer, the spots on my arms that had hurt so much when I first called on my magic danced with pins and needles that wouldn't ease. I wished the feeling would stop. The last thing I wanted was another physical reminder of my magic. Sometimes my gift made me feel possessed by an evil spirit. That was one of the Mynarian theories about magic—one I'd tried not to believe in too much. But maybe there was something to it if I could hurt people without meaning to.

I tried to push the dark thoughts away while Sarika prepared my tea. She moved with purposeful confidence that reminded me of Ryka, the captain of the guard back home in Mynaria.

Home.

Was that how I thought of Mynaria now? I shouldn't let myself think of it that way, given that thanks to my Affinity, I might never be able to return. All I'd ever wanted, or thought I'd wanted, was to become queen of Mynaria, just like I'd been trained to. I thought I'd marry the prince and ascend the throne and use my power as a monarch to help the people of both our kingdoms. But that dream had gone up in smoke the day Thandi found out I was "dead." Or, if I was being honest with myself, the day I finally understood that my feelings for Mare ran far deeper than friendship.

Somehow, I had to find new dreams, but I had no idea where to start.

Sarika held out a steaming mug of tea.

"What is it?" I took the mug.

"Willow bark and peaceroot," she said. "Have you had peaceroot before?"

"No." I shook my head, feeling sick all over again. Karov, a Zumordan I'd met in Mynaria, had told me about peaceroot—an herb used to quell Affinities. He'd told me the side effects of long-term use were awful: blinding headaches, and numbness in the hands and feet that would eventually make flesh necrotic.

"I see you know what it is," she said, deftly reading my expression. "You don't have to drink it, but it's the safest way to temporarily stop you from losing control of your gift. And it will keep you from being so easy to detect."

"Easy to detect?" I asked, confused.

"You haven't been shielding yourself, so every time you use your magic, it's like shooting off a beacon that most people with Affinities can feel from a hundred leagues away. Someone needs to teach you to rein in your powers—for your safety and everyone else's."

I swallowed hard. "What happens if no one does?"

"You could cause a catastrophic accident. Or lose control to the point where the magic consumes you from the inside out. And if the wrong people get their hands on you . . . they'll twist you into whatever shape they choose and use you as a weapon."

Dread sank deep into my bones. Sarika's tone was so matter-of-fact, as if she weren't talking about my life. Like I was a thing and not a person—a dangerous thing. Who might use me? How would they do it? How many people existed who might be powerful enough to do that, and how could I defend myself against them? It made my head spin trying to see around all the corners ahead.

I raised the mug to my nose. Coils of steam rose from it, astringent and herbal.

Sarika raised an eyebrow. "So you've decided?"

"I don't see how I have any choice," I said bitterly. "I set my own cot on fire without even realizing it. I hurt people on the good side of a battle, and I killed people without meaning to. How can anyone feel safe around me if this magic isn't under control?" There wasn't any point in indulging my fears about the peaceroot or wondering what would happen if I needed my magic and couldn't call on it. The possibility of hurting Mare felt like a greater risk every day, and if that happened, I would never be able to forgive myself.

I took a sip. The bitter tea wasn't pleasant going down, but I was thirsty enough that it wasn't so bad.

"This is the safest way for now," Sarika said, her voice more gentle. "I'll leave you a supply of peaceroot that should last a week or two. I don't recommend you take it longer than that."

"Can you teach me how to shield?" I asked Sarika. The sooner I learned the basics, the safer it would be for everyone—especially Mare.

She hesitated before answering, her sharp gaze falling away for a moment. "I don't think that's a good idea."

"Why?" My heart dropped even further.

"Your Affinity is not like mine," she said. "Someone much more powerful is going to have to train you, preferably someone with a fire Affinity like yours."

"But if shielding is a basic skill—" I started.

"No." Sarika's tone was firm, and I knew it would be futile to argue. "My magic is not nearly strong enough to hold yours back if something went wrong."

Her rejection stung, even if her reasons were sound. All I wanted was to learn, and no one had ever deprived me of that in my old life. After finishing my tea, I lay down on the cushions in front of the fire and closed my eyes. Numbness filled in the places inside me scorched raw by magic, and my gift receded into the distance. Not being able to sense it brought an uneasy peace. I was grateful for the calm, but all too aware of its falsity.

What a waste to have a gift I couldn't even use. I felt like I was drowning in it sometimes, like the magic was slowly rising into a tsunami. It didn't matter how far or how fast I ran, because the wave continued to grow, to loom, to tower over me until it blocked out the rest of the world and I was faced with something I could never fight back.

The only thing still keeping me afloat was Mare's love.

FIVE

✦ *Amaranthine*

THE DINING HALL AT DUVEY KEEP WAS MORE LIKE what we had for the liegemen's barracks in Mynaria than a proper feast room in a castle. My stomach lurched when I saw the trestle tables stretching the length of the hall, all with hard, backless benches instead of chairs. I used to sit at tables like these with my best friend, Nils, play games of dice or cards, hear the people gossip and tease each other about their latest conquests and failures in training and in the bedroom. Now Nils was dead, and the memories ached inside me. Pieces of melodies from the mourning songs echoing through the keep earlier in the day still resonated in my mind, making me think of him and everyone else I'd lost back in Mynaria.

I wove between the tables following my escort, a short but sturdy-looking swordswoman with a battered sheath belted around her waist. A few people were already seated, partaking of cheese, cured meats, and crackers laid out on trenchers. The only people at the keep who weren't dressed in wool clothes or leather armor were a couple of late-season trade families, and the fact that their formal garments looked worn or slightly outdated spoke volumes.

"Your seat, my lady," the swordswoman said in roughly accented Tradespeech, leading me up onto a dais at one end of the room and gesturing to a bench at the lone table there. Assuming Zumordan protocol was similar to Mynaria's, Lord Wymund had seated me as an honored guest.

"Thank you," I said, and took my seat. I should have been planning my next move as ambassador, introducing myself to anyone who seemed of suitably high rank, but instead I fidgeted, consumed with worry about Denna and wondering how long the meal would take. Even though Sarika had assured me after her first examination that Denna's condition was stable, I couldn't help worrying that something would change while I was away. Every time I'd had to step out to check on Flicker or use the bathroom, I felt like something terrible might happen. This meal was no exception.

Raucous laughter filled the hall as soldiers poured into the room. People seated themselves with no order I could discern, their sorrow from earlier chased away by the promise of celebrating the successful defense of the keep. The meats, cheeses, and crackers barely lasted three minutes, and then the volume of the conversations in the hall quickly began to rise.

I craned my neck to watch the largest entrance in hopes that Wymund would show up soon and set the servers into motion. But instead of a man, an enormous mountain cat stalked into the dining hall. It walked with its head low, amber eyes intent on the table where I was sitting. My eyes skittered across the room in search of some cue about how to react, but no one seemed to take notice at all. I was half up from the bench, about to bolt for the door, when the animal sinuously stretched and warped before my eyes. Seconds later, the towering, bearded figure of Lord Wymund himself stood before me in place of the cat.

I felt faint. Though I'd seen that female soldier turn into a fox the night before, it hadn't prepared me for this.

"Your Highness!" he bellowed in Tradespeech. "So glad you could join us for dinner tonight."

Servants hurried to serve the first course—a gamy-smelling soup.

"Thank you for your invitation, my lord." I sat down, gathering my wits. Even without the shock of Wymund's appearance, etiquette had never been my strength. I took a deep breath, reminding myself that in Zumorda, seeing a gigantic mountain cat turn into a man was apparently perfectly ordinary.

Wymund settled in at the table, his entourage following suit until soldiers surrounded me on all sides. They wore heavy leathers lined with wool, giving the whole dining room the faint reek of wet sheep.

"How's your maidservant doing? Better, I hope?" Wymund asked, raising his dark, bushy eyebrows. Before I answered, he proceeded to shovel some soup into his mouth. I grimaced as a sizeable amount of the watery broth ended up in his beard.

"Still resting." I tried to smile, but the look I got from the woman sitting across from me seemed to indicate that I hadn't succeeded.

"Perhaps you'd like some help coordinating somewhere safe

for her to recover?" Wymund asked. "There are some more remote places we could send her until she is healed and ready to apprentice to someone who can help her master her gift."

"I'm sure we could find you a new servant," the woman across from me added. Her voice was low and soft, much like the hoot of an owl. "There are young women here who would be honored to have the opportunity."

"Fewer than there were before the Sonnenbornes attacked," another soldier said bitterly.

The man next to him laid his hand on the soldier's arm. "The scouts will find your sister. Knowing her, she's already fighting back."

"How can she, if they dosed her with peaceroot?" The soldier shook off his comrade's touch.

"We're doing all we can to find them," Lord Wymund said, his tone stern. The table hushed as he made eye contact with everyone sitting around him. Then he turned back to me. "As Periline said, if you're willing to take on another maidservant, we could help get Lia the safety and training she needs. It's the least we can do after you helped us defend the keep."

Periline's cool gaze met mine, challenging me to go against her lord's suggestion. I tore my eyes away and surveyed the table, noticing that everyone was suddenly quite occupied with their food or wine. The silence held palpable tension, and I knew exactly what it meant—they wanted Denna gone.

"Your offer is so kind," I said, rattled. "But my kingdom is counting on me to speak with the queen as soon as possible. Hopefully Lia will wake soon so we can be on our way in the next day or two." Even if they hadn't been eager to get rid of Denna, with the news from my brother, it was more important than ever that we keep moving. "Are any trade or military caravans heading north from here?"

"Not this year," Wymund said, dashing my hopes. "We had some autumn flooding, and the north roads are already closed. Have been since just after harvest."

"That's terrible." My mind raced with worries. How were we going to get to the queen if the roads were closed? Taking a round-about way could add so much time to our journey that winter would make the roads farther north impassable on horseback.

"Yes, but we have plenty of soldiers. No better crew to move heavy rocks and resurface roads as long as the weather allows," Wymund said. "And we have Periline." He gestured to the woman across from me. "Her manifest is a snowy owl. She can check on the nearby farms, make sure everyone has what they need."

Then I put the pieces together. Tavi, the soldier who'd fetched Sarika, had been able to change to and from a fox. Wymund could take the form of a mountain cat. Periline apparently had the ability to become a snowy owl. Denna had told me that Karov, the Zumor-dan who had introduced himself to us in Mynaria, could change into a mountain bluebird. That meant manifests were the animal forms Zumordans could take. I swallowed a large mouthful of soup, scalding my tongue in an attempt to hide my discomfort with the strangeness of it all.

"So if we can't head north directly, what is the best way to get to Corovja?" I asked. "Our news for the queen is urgent."

"If you hurry, you might not need to travel all the way to

Corovja to meet with her," Wymund said. "Recruitment for her elite training program began a few weeks ago, and she's likely to be in Kartasha a little while longer."

"Wait—the queen is in Kartasha now?" I had assumed that like my brother, and my father before him, she would rarely leave the crown city. If she were in the southern city of Kartasha, only a week's ride away, I could be done with my duties in no time and free to focus on getting Denna the training she needed.

Wymund nodded. "She visits Kartasha for a week or so each year, usually traveling south with the nobles when they move to the Winter Court. This is a longer trip than her usual visit, thanks to its being a selection year for her training program."

"The Winter Court?" I asked, cursing my kingdom's lack of knowledge about Zumordan politics.

"It's where the nobles spend the winter," Periline said. "The seat of power switches between Corovja and Kartasha seasonally, though Queen Invasya usually remains in Corovja for most of the year. In the winter, the grand vizier serves as the queen's proxy at the Winter Court." She regarded me neutrally, waiting to see what I did with this information.

My mind reeled. I hadn't known there were two courts. How was I supposed to broker an alliance with the queen in one place and her court in another? The only answer seemed to be to catch her while she was still in Kartasha.

"What exactly is the queen's training program?" I asked.

"The same one I tried out for years ago," Wymund said. "I didn't get in, but I did get this scar in a bar fight in Kartasha." He pointed proudly to a gash that ran down the front of his neck and under the breastplate of his armor. "Every five years or so the queen selects a group of magic users to train with her personally before moving on to their apprenticeships. The selections are held in Kartasha in autumn, since it's the biggest city in Zumorda. Most of the queen's trainees will end up apprenticed to guardians and will follow in our footsteps."

"It is a great honor to be chosen," Periline said.

"And a rare one," Wymund said. "My gift wasn't strong enough to interest the queen, so I worked my way up to guardianship. Turns out a military strategist was more useful along this part of the border than a strong Affinity anyway." He tore a chunk of bread off the loaf in front of him and used it to mop up the last of his soup.

"How much longer will the queen be in Kartasha?" I asked, already itching to get on the road.

"The fighters we sent there for auxiliary security detail should be heading back sometime in the next two weeks, so I doubt she'll be there any longer than that," he said.

"How many soldiers did you send?" I frowned.

"Fifty of our best." He smiled, and even though sadness lingered in his expression, crow's-feet appeared at the corners of his eyes.

I sat back a little. No wonder the keep had been such an easy target for the Sonnenbornes. Fifty fighters had to be nearly 20 percent of their overall numbers, and if they'd sent their best to the queen . . . well. They'd been asking for an attack. The only question was how the Sonnenbornes had gotten word of their vulnerability—and what they'd ultimately been after.

"Lia and I will have to leave as soon as she's able," I said.

"Well, if I can't offer your maid any help or convince you to stay, is there anything else I can do to express our gratitude for your help protecting Duvey?"

I opened my mouth to tell him we didn't need anything, only to realize he'd given me an excellent opportunity. "Perhaps there's someone you could spare to guide us to Kartasha?" I asked. Traveling with a Zumordan would help us be more accepted by others on our journey and would give us a chance to prepare ourselves for our arrival in a bigger city. Learning more about Zumorda would hopefully prevent us from making any major social faux pas when we arrived at the Winter Court. My heart squeezed painfully at the thought of Denna back in our room. I was thinking like her. She'd be proud of me if she knew.

"That's not a bad idea," Wymund said, mopping at his beard with a rough-spun napkin. "The road to Kartasha isn't the safest. It skirts close to Tamer territory, and they've been roaming more than usual since the drought started. We've had trouble with them scaring people off the farmlands closest to the woods."

"Forgive my ignorance, but what's a Tamer?" I asked, starting to feel like there was no end to what I didn't know about Zumorda and its people.

"Odd folk, really," Wymund said. "Instead of taking manifests, they keep familiars—companion animals they're so closely bonded with that they can see through their eyes and hear with their ears. Tamers fancy themselves protectors of the natural land."

"And they can use their Affinities to turn the forest against anyone who dares to trespass in it," Periline added.

"They don't sound like people I want to meet," I said.

"No, definitely not," Wymund agreed. "A guide can make sure

you avoid them and also allow us to get word to the Winter Court about the attack. We could use the Court's help tracking the children who were taken. I'm afraid we may not have an extra horse to spare for your maidservant, though. The few stabled here are privately owned—Zumorda has no cavalry."

I didn't mind continuing to ride double with Denna, since it would allow me to keep her close, but a kingdom without any warriors who fought on horseback was unfathomable to me. However, it meant my brother's offer of cavalry might carry more weight.

"I hope we'll reach the Winter Court quickly enough," I said. "Or is there some other way to send word of the attack?" I trod carefully, not sure how permissible it was to talk openly about magic.

Wymund shook his head. "Communicating quickly across great distances takes an enchanted object or someone who can cast high magic. Farspeakers are rare. We lost our last one to a honeyshine addiction. He went freelance in Kartasha, last I heard."

"No one misses Hornblatt," an older female soldier said, her dry tone suggesting that there were a lot of stories behind the statement.

"I'm pretty sure there are still roaches in the east barracks," a man added.

I shuddered involuntarily.

"He always had cats." Periline sniffed haughtily, as though cat ownership was among the worst character flaws she could imagine.

"Yes, yes, Tum Hornblatt was a character," Wymund said, waving his hand dismissively. "It's a pity, though. I'd give the man a barrel of honeyshine to get word to the Winter Court before the queen leaves."

"Then we'll have to hurry if we can," I said. If Denna would just wake up. Worry made my stomach churn.

"I know exactly who to assign to you, and I'll speak to him tonight," Wymund said. "Can you pass the mutton salad?" He gestured to a plate sitting in front of me that held a large ring of something shiny and translucent in which chunks of meat and unidentifiable green vegetables were suspended. "Salad" was not the word I would have used to describe it. I gingerly picked up the plate and passed it to him.

"Thank you so much," I said. "We'll travel as quickly as possible. It's crucial to make sure Zumorda is fortified enough to prevent these kinds of attacks from happening again."

"Yes," Wymund agreed. "Hopefully the soldiers I sent there for the queen can return with the court's response." He didn't say anything more about our reasons for hurrying, but I knew instantly what the shifty look in his eyes meant. He wanted both of us gone as soon as Denna could stay upright in the saddle.

"Perhaps I should check on Lia," I said. I'd barely touched my food beyond the soup, but I was too worried about her to be hungry.

"Of course," Wymund said. "I'll have Alek meet you at the stables when you're ready to leave. He's a seasoned soldier, well traveled, and familiar with Kartasha even if he hasn't been back in a while. In the meantime, please feel free to attend meals as you need."

"Sir," Periline interrupted, "is it wise to send Alek away on the heels of an attack?"

"It's not ideal," Wymund admitted. "But we need to put safety first. Alek is the only one with enough strength to control things should they get out of hand."

They exchanged a glance that deflated me—they were talking about Denna.

"Besides, most of our energy will go into fortification," Wymund continued. "So far our scouts have been surveying in every direction and have seen no signs of the Sonnenbornes other than on the main trade road, and we have a force tracking them. It'll likely be a while before they try anything again, especially now that they think we have high magic on our side."

Periline deferred to her lord, but I could see that she wasn't as certain as he was.

"Thank you so much for your help and generosity," I said, extricating myself from the table and hurrying out of the dining area. My mind reeled with all the new information Wymund and his people had given me. Between Thandi bestowing me with the power of an official ambassador and how complicated the Zumordan political system seemed to be, I desperately needed Denna's wisdom.

When I opened the door to our shared room, I was surprised to see Denna lying on the cushions by the hearth instead of on the cot where she'd spent the last day. The herb witch sat beside her, filling sachets with dried herbs.

"Did she wake?" I asked softly.

Sarika nodded, and at the sound of my voice, Denna stirred.

Emotion welled up in me as her eyes opened, though she stayed lying down.

"Mare?" she said.

"I'm here." I sat down as close as I could without crowding her.

"Thank the Six." She laid a small hand on my thigh.

"I was so worried," I said, barely more than a whisper. Her eyes were already closing again. I wished I could hold her in the waking world just a few moments longer, but she needed to rest.

"She's had a tea of willow bark and peaceroot to help with her headache and quell her gift," Sarika said.

"How long until she's well enough to travel?" I asked.

"A few days, perhaps. But she can only take the herbs for so long. If you're planning on traveling while her powers are suppressed, you'll want to do that soon."

"We will," I said, gently tucking some loose pieces of hair behind Denna's ear.

"My work here is done, I think," Sarika said. "I'll be back to check on her each day."

"I can't thank you enough," I said, and meant every word.

"Of course." Sarika gathered her things and showed herself out of the room.

Denna's chest rose and fell evenly with her breaths. I stretched out beside her until I could feel all of her body pressed up against me. Comfort washed over me, pushing aside my fears and doubts. She was alive. She would be all right, and we had a plan to get to Kartasha. Tomorrow I would write to my brother, letting him know what had happened and where I was headed next.

For the first time since the attack, I felt something like hope.

Wymund's work on the fortifications began the day after my meal with him. Soldiers and servants worked side by side to clear the keep grounds of debris and repair the damage Denna had done. Inside, craftspeople studded huge split logs with wooden spikes to reinforce the keep's walls. Scouts returned each day with clean reports—no sign of Sonnenbornes. It was possible that the attack had been an isolated incident, though every time I tried to calm myself with that thought, my gut told me I was wrong. Even though the keep bustled with activity, the three days it took Denna to recover dragged on interminably.

On the day we departed, I'd just saddled Flicker when a bow-legged person more mountain than man strode into the barn leading an equally enormous dark bay horse with hooves the size of pie plates and a head like a battering ram. I'd assumed the horse was one of the keep's plow animals.

I approached the man with caution as he tossed a saddle onto the massive horse, wishing that Denna were well enough to do this instead. She was the personable one.

"Hello, you must be Alek," I said. "I'm Mare."

The gigantic man looked down at me with an expression as lively and readable as the face of a boulder. "We leave as soon as Wymund comes to see us off. Don't forget to tighten your girth."

"Right," I said, deeply annoyed by his tone. Who was this man to tell me to check my horse's girth? I'd been riding since before I could walk and training horses for eight years. Every first-year rider in Mynaria knew to check their girth. I stalked off before I could say something regrettable. Clearly I'd met the only person in the world worse than me at social pleasantries. I covertly scowled at him, then met Denna outside, where we could mount up.

"Mare!" Wymund's cheerful voice echoed across the stableyard.

I halted Flicker and turned toward Wymund, and my horse nudged my arm as if to ask why we we'd stopped. He seemed as eager to get going as I was.

"This is Sir Alek of the Misty Plains," Wymund introduced the man.

"We've met," I said, nodding curtly at the man, who stared down at me with the frown that was apparently permanently engraved in the stone of his face. Where Denna's eyes were clear as green sea glass, his were murky as stagnant water. A crooked scar zigzagged horizontally across his neck as though he'd once nearly been decapitated—probably by someone he'd been rude to.

"This is Lia, my maidservant." I gestured to Denna.

She curtsied prettily, and Alek gave her a short nod in return, then mounted his horse with more grace than I would have expected of someone his size. Astride the beast he looked even more imposing, in spite of the decidedly plug-like demeanor of the horse, who was already tugging on the reins to reach for a few blades of withered grass.

"Thank you for your hospitality, my lord," I said to Wymund.

"May our swords always meet on the same side of the battle-field," he said to all of us.

Alek stared at me, expecting me to respond on behalf of the group. My mind raced. Every ritual response I knew had to do with the Six Gods, because that was the custom in Mynaria. One of the few things I knew about Zumorda was that they didn't worship the Six. Denna whispered something in my ear, but I couldn't quite make out the words.

Alek sighed, apparently giving up on me. "And may our shields always be side by side."

My cheeks burned with shame. Every time I started to feel like I was doing something right as an ambassador, I managed to make a new mistake.

"Now get out of here," Wymund told us. "And stay out of trouble in Kartasha." He gave Alek's horse a few hearty smacks on the rump, to which the animal displayed no reaction.

"We will." I'd be perfectly happy to lie as low as possible until we reached the Winter Court. Until we got to Kartasha, the fewer people who knew I was in Zumorda, the better. The people of Sonnenborne probably wanted me dead as punishment for Lord Kriantz's death. If the tribes he'd united under his banner managed to stay organized, trouble was surely headed our way.

We rode out the gates of the keep and headed southeast on the dusty road with a dry, cold wind at our backs. I thought a weight would lift when we finally left Duvey, but Alek's presence made that difficult. I hadn't necessarily expected the person assigned to ride with us to be happy about it, but Alek seemed positively dour. Denna stayed silent behind me, focused on conserving her strength for the ride.

After the first day of travel, my worst fears had been realized: Alek's horse walked at the speed of a heavily burdened ox, Denna looked pale as a ghost by the time we made camp, and both Flicker and I were practically jumping out of our skins, feeling held back. I didn't want to push Denna too hard, but if we missed the opportunity to talk to the queen while she was still in Kartasha, it might set us back an entire season. We couldn't afford that—not with a

Mynarian city already under siege.

When the sun sank low enough to make the mountain in the southeast glow with amber light, the three of us dismounted near a stream to settle in for the night.

Alek hitched his stocky gelding to a tree.

"You, go gather some branches for lean-tos," he barked at me.

I stared at him, wondering if he was oblivious of the fact that I was a princess or if he usually ordered everyone around like hired help.

"We haven't untacked our horses," I said.

He stared back at me, unmoved. "Only a green soldier would untack his horse before making camp."

"It's cruel to leave your horse saddled when his comfort should come before your own." The pitch of my voice increased as my anger rose. My family raised the finest warhorses in the Northern Kingdoms. There was no way a Zumordan foot soldier who rode a plow horse knew more than I did about the animals I'd worked with my whole life.

"I can gather the wood while Mare untacks," Denna interjected.

"No," Alek and I both said, glaring at each other.

Denna sighed wearily.

"You sit down and rest," I said. "I'll take care of the horses, and then I'll gather the gods-damned wood."

"Leave my horse be," Alek said. "I'm going to go find us some dinner. If anyone attacks us before then, I'm not going to be the fool who gets caught with his mount unsaddled." He clomped off into the woods, leaving me seething.

I ranted to Denna as I took care of the horses. "What in the

Sixth Hell is his problem? 'I'm not going to be the fool who gets caught with his mount unsaddled,'" I mocked. "If he can't ride bareback well enough to outride an enemy, how can he even call himself a soldier?"

"The practices are just different here," Denna said. "Besides, even if he's a fighter, he's probably not cavalry." Her voice sounded weak, and I wondered if it was the peaceroot tea she'd continued drinking to quell her gift. She settled under a tree, sitting on the new bedroll she'd gotten in Duvey.

"I don't care if they're different. He shouldn't treat me like I'm five years old," I said.

"You're right, he shouldn't." She pulled her cloak tighter around her shoulders. "Can you try not to fight with him, though? We're lucky to have a guide."

"I know," I said. "I'm sorry. I just get this feeling he doesn't like me for some reason."

"He doesn't have a reason to like us," Denna pointed out. "Think about how most Mynarians feel about Zumordans. The same thing probably applies in reverse."

"Maybe," I said. But other people at the keep had mostly been curious or wary, not overtly hostile and rude like Alek.

"Or perhaps someone he cared about was injured during the attack at Duvey because of my magic," she said, her voice wavering.

"No. Don't blame yourself." I crouched beside her and gave her a gentle squeeze. "Wymund wouldn't have sent him with us if that had been the case." I didn't mention my other suspicions—that he'd sent Alek as a way to manage Denna, possibly even to spy on her. Alek hadn't shown any evidence of magical abilities, but if there was one thing I'd learned about Zumorda so far, it was that appearances could be deceptive.

Denna straightened her shoulders and took a deep breath, but I knew I hadn't convinced her.

"Hey." I sat down the rest of the way. "The important thing is that we're on this journey together." As harrowing as it had already been, I wouldn't trade anything for that.

"I'm grateful." She slipped her hand into mine, the connection reminding me that Alek had left us alone together. Her green eyes looked almost gray in the fading light and her cheeks pale in contrast to the soft pink of her lips. Just looking at her made my breath catch.

I leaned forward and whispered into her ear. "If you kiss me, I promise not to argue with Alek . . . at least until after dinner."

I felt her smile against my cheek as she turned her face toward me, and then her lips met mine in a kiss that made my pulse race. The feel of her in my arms made the rest of the world fall away, and for a few minutes, our problems seemed as distant as the stars.

"It's getting dark," she murmured between kisses.

"The damned wood, I know," I said, reluctantly rising back to my feet.

"Maybe I'll feel better about everything when we get to Kartasha," she said.

"I know I will. I just want to get the conversation started with the queen so Thandi can send a real ambassador and we can focus on finding someone to help you with your magic." The sooner we did that, the sooner we could have a real life together.

By the time Alek returned with a mesh bag filled with fresh fish,

I had both horses untacked and curried, two lean-tos built, and a fire started. It hadn't been hard work to find dry wood—a solid third of the trees seemed to be dead. The drought Wymund had mentioned was evident all around us. I'd had to clear a wide swath of ground to make it safe to start our fire.

Alek looked around the camp. "I told you not to untack my horse."

I fumed but stayed silent, remembering my promise to Denna.

"She was just trying to help," Denna said.

Alek sighed, then wordlessly started jamming gutted fish onto sticks in a way that suggested he'd like to be doing it to me instead.

"So what can we expect in Kartasha?" Denna asked, her tone light. She was clearly trying to reduce the tension before Alek or I decided to push the other into the fire.

"A lot of nonsense," Alek grumbled, positioning the fish near the fire's coals. "The guardian of Kartasha is not someone you want to trust." The firelight made the lines in his face even deeper. "As for the grand vizier, she's powerful, but don't underestimate the guardian's influence on her."

"How do you know the guardian of Kartasha?" Denna asked.

"Laurenna and I grew up in the same slum," he said. "Took different paths."

His tone made it clear that no further discussion was welcome. I sighed. Wymund had seemed to think Alek would be helpful to us, but given his lack of desire to share useful information, that didn't seem to be the case.

By the time we had finished dinner and Denna had drunk her nightly tea, she looked a little shaky.

"You should rest," I told her.

She nodded, not even arguing. She curled up on her bedroll, massaging her forearms, and I wondered if the peaceroot helped at all with her pain. Sarika had said she could take it for a week or two, but what if it stopped working before then? Denna's magic would be back in all its unpredictability. The thought made an involuntary shiver run through me. The creaking of the dry woods echoed my worries. It wouldn't take much to set them ablaze.

"I'll take first watch," Alek told me.

I scowled. "I've been taking first watch on this journey."

"And now I will, because we're in my kingdom, and the first watch is the most dangerous. You don't even carry a sword."

His comment stung. I had wanted to learn swordsmanship when I was younger, but Mynarian princesses weren't taught such things. I kept my mouth shut with all the force of will I possessed. Just because he planned to take the first turn guarding the camp didn't mean I couldn't also watch over Denna. Her eyes were already closed, her dark lashes casting shadows on her face that danced in the firelight.

"I'm at least going to stay up awhile to make sure she's all right," I said.

"Suit yourself," Alek said, and stalked off to walk the perimeter of our campsite.

I curled up with my back to Denna's, grateful for the small amount of insulation our closeness provided from the deepening chill. Still, by the time Alek came to hand the watch over to me, I felt frozen to the bone. I ended up pacing around the campsite, hoping that getting my blood moving would keep me warm and awake. The cold didn't relent, but I needn't have worried about wakefulness—not when it turned out Alek snores were like the sawing of a thousand logs.

By morning I was thoroughly exhausted. After a quick breakfast of bread and cheese packed from the keep, the three of us took to the road again. I let myself ease into Flicker's ground-covering walk, grateful for the warmth radiating from his sides into my legs. The farther southeast we traveled, the drier the terrain became. Our horses' hooves kicked up dust with every step, and the only visible snowpack was on the tallest mountains.

"Is it usually this dry here?" I asked.

"No," Alek said, a fountain of information as always.

"It doesn't seem like it should be," Denna mused. "Don't you get a lot of rain in Mynaria this time of year? Most autumn storms follow a southeastern track, and there is no geophysical barrier that would prevent them from traveling this way."

"It's just a drought," Alek said. "Happens every few years around these parts. Now, watch your horse's feet, because this trail is about to get rough."

He took the lead, and we guided our horses down a steep descent into a narrow valley, picking our way around boulders and a few fallen trees in the road. We'd barely reached the valley floor when Alek drew his mount to a sudden halt. I barely had time to sit back in the saddle and give a squeeze of the reins to stop Flicker from bumping into him.

"Sard me sideways," Alek said.

I shot him a surprised look. Surly as he was, he had a certain dignity, and the profanity startled me.

I nudged Flicker forward just far enough to see around Alek. A stream ahead of us raged through a riverbed filled with rocks of all shapes and sizes, and the bridge across it was no more than a few pieces of ragged, burned wood on either side. At first I thought that was what Alek had reacted to—until I saw the bodies of three Duvey Keep soldiers tangled in the middle of the road, their glassy eyes open to the sky.

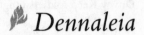 *Dennaleia*

MY STOMACH TURNED AT THE SIGHT OF THE CORPSES. Alek recovered first, dismounting and walking his horse to where the bodies lay. Flicker stood frozen in place by Mare's steady hands.

"Our scouts," Alek said tersely.

"The Sonnenbornes who attacked Duvey must have done this," Mare said, finally urging Flicker to take a few steps forward.

"They were smart about it, though," Alek noted, pointing to a wound in one man's abdomen. "Sonnenborne javelins don't leave ragged edges."

"And the other two?" I asked, trying not to let my voice shake.

"Blows to the head, it looks like. Some kind of polearm, maybe even a guisarme."

"Do the Sonnenbornes use those kinds of weapons?" Mare asked.

"Certainly," Alek said. "But the Tamers use more primitive polearms. At a glance, this looks like their handiwork."

"But you don't think it is?" I asked.

He nudged one soldier's shoulder with his boot and gestured to the rust-colored powder dusting the corpse's face and shoulders. "That's peaceroot powder. Tamers would never touch the stuff."

"I thought peaceroot had to be ingested as a tea." I had no idea peaceroot could be used as a weapon. The idea of it filled me with dread.

Alek shook his head. "There are skilled herbalists who mix it with nightshade and powder it. The stuff's expensive, but powerful enough to knock almost any magic user unconscious and suppress their Affinity."

"You said the Tamers wouldn't touch the stuff—but the Sonnenbornes would?" Mare asked.

"Sonnenbornes have no magic. Nothing for them to fear." Alek muttered what sounded like another curse. "Peaceroot is also a non-native plant. Tamers only use resources local to them."

"So the Tamers don't trade with outsiders?" I asked. It would have been the only way they'd be able to obtain peaceroot.

"Not usually." Alek looked across the burned bridge to the road on the other side.

"This just makes it that much more important to get to the queen," I said softly. Coupled with the information in the letter Mare had received from her brother, it was clear the Sonnenbornes were making aggressive strides into both Mynaria and Zumorda. We needed to at least reach an agreement to work together to stop them.

"You're right," Mare said. "Can we do anything for these soldiers? Give them a proper burial before we move on?"

Alek shook his head. "I saw the plans for the wingscouts before I left. They'll be here in no more than a day or two."

"Better to leave them some evidence to work with," I said, understanding Alek's line of thought.

He gave me a sharp look, and I cast my eyes to the ground, hoping I hadn't given away that I was more than Mare's maidservant. I tried to quell the ember of frustration smoldering in my chest. There was little I hated more in the world than playing the fool, and now that Mare and I were no longer alone, I knew I'd have to do it more and more often. My ability to survive and stay with Mare depended on keeping my true identity secret.

"How are we going to cross the river?" I asked Alek, hoping that deferring to his ideas would distract him from wondering how I might know anything about scouting patterns or crime scene investigation.

Alek stared pensively at the water but didn't respond. The rushing river formed an impassable barrier. Both sides were lined with wide swaths of muddy ground that indicated the water level was lower than usual, but that just meant it ran more fiercely over the rocks.

"We're going to have to find an alternate route," Mare said, already turning Flicker south. "This can't be the only place to cross. Or maybe there's a shallow spot? It's not that wide."

Alek held up a meaty hand to stop her. Mare tensed in my arms. I glanced worriedly between them. I couldn't expect Mare to be anyone other than who she was—the bold, brazen girl I'd fallen in love with—but I wished she could rein herself in a little to get along with Alek. He was intimidating, and though I didn't think it likely, he could kill us both and leave us in the woods if he felt like it. Besides, Mare needed the diplomacy practice before arriving in Kartasha or Corovja, both places where her ability to get along with people she disagreed with would matter that much more.

"Can you ride a bit closer to the water?" I asked Mare.

She complied, guiding Flicker toward the mud near the bank. Hoofprints heading the direction of the bridge marked the passing of many horses before us.

"The Sonnenbornes definitely came this way," I said, pointing to the hoofprints in the mud. "They must have burned the bridge so that no one would be able to follow."

Alek muttered something under his breath that was probably another curse. "Good eye, Lia," he said to me.

I shrugged diffidently, hoping he didn't make too much of it. Observation and deduction were key parts of any scholar's work, and it felt good to use those skills, even if I should have kept quiet.

"Isn't it odd that they came southeast instead of heading directly south back to their own lands?" Mare asked.

Alek shook his head. "No trade roads in that direction—just Tamer territory and hostile farmers. This is the fastest way south."

"I thought the Tamers lived in eastern Zumorda," I said. Geography had been one of my best subjects in my studies, and my recall of cartographic details had always been excellent.

"What makes you think that?" Alek asked, giving me a sharp look.

Inwardly, I cringed at dropping such an obvious hint about my true identity, but I managed to put on a confused and innocent expression. "I saw a map one time. Maybe it was wrong?"

"It must have been old. Another band of Tamers settled in the south more than fifty years ago," Alek said, his tone gruff.

"Are there any other bridges nearby?" I asked, hoping to keep him from overthinking anything I said by focusing on the present problem.

"No, and the water is deeper and swifter than it looks, even low," Alek said.

It already looked pretty swift to me, but I didn't say anything. I got the sense his comment was more for Mare's benefit.

We had rivers like this back in Havemont, where I'd grown up. I used to walk the mountain trails with my father and sister, learning how to test my footing, find good hiking sticks, and avoid crossing anything that looked like this river, because it was too easy to get swept away. The sadness I'd carried with me since leaving Havemont swelled, choking me with loneliness. As much as I loved Mare and knew I'd made the right choice being with her, I missed my family. Everyone but my mother thought I was dead, and I didn't know if she'd shared the truth with my father or sister. Part of me hoped she had told them. I couldn't bear the thought of my family grieving unnecessarily.

"What do you think we should do?" Mare asked me, urging Flicker a few strides south along the river's edge. A few horse lengths away from the destroyed bridge, the crescent of another partial hoofprint was visible. The rider must have kept close to the edge of the water—any other tracks had already been washed away.

"It looks like someone else tried to ride south to find another place to cross after the bridge was destroyed." I pointed at the hoofprint.

"That seems to be our only choice, too," Alek said, joining us. "There's only one problem. See those trees?" He pointed at some evergreens to the south. "That's where the Tamers' territory begins. Whoever left that southbound print is going to find that out the hard way."

"Based on what Wymund told me, I'd rather avoid them," Mare said.

"We could camp near here and I could skip my next dose of peaceroot," I said. "Perhaps fire magic could be used to temporarily stop the water, or maybe—"

"No," Alek and Mare said in vehement unison.

I cringed. Of course that had to be the only thing they agreed on. I wanted so badly to help, not to be this useless, dangerous person trapped by my own incompetence. Also, as grateful as I was for the peaceroot keeping anything bad from happening on our journey, the emptiness left by my magic's absence made me feel numb and off-kilter. The powers lingered just out of reach, like if I only tried hard enough, maybe I'd be able to reach them through the fog. And the peaceroot did nothing for the physical symptoms of overextending my gift—my arms still ached, and the numb spots persisted. I'd never felt less like myself.

"We'll have to ride south and take our chances," Alek said, not looking pleased. "If we stay near the river's edge away from the woods, there's a chance they won't feel threatened."

A tingle of nervousness ran through me. If anything did happen, my magic was useless. Alek had his sword, and Mare had her bow. I had no way to fight back.

We rode alongside the river for a few sunlengths, the pace of our horses slowed by having to pick our way around the rocks littering the banks. Trees grew larger as we rode farther south, though just as many were dead as they'd been in the sparser forests along the main road. I worried as the sun followed its westward path, wondering if we would be able to cross the river in time to make camp safely away from the Tamers.

"We should be getting close now," Alek said, his voice so soft I almost didn't hear him over the rush of the river.

We'd barely gone ten more horse lengths when Flicker shied so suddenly, I would have lost my seat if I hadn't been hanging on firmly to Mare. Two people had materialized seemingly out of nowhere and now stood blocking our path. Their clothes were made of well-fitted leather and furs, mottled to help them blend in with their surroundings. One stood half a head taller, but they otherwise had few defining characteristics to differentiate them from each other.

"Turn back," the taller man said in strangely accented Zumordan.

"We don't mean to trespass," Alek said. "The north bridge has been destroyed, and we'd be grateful to use the one on your lands. We won't linger."

"There is no passage for your kind here," the other man said, putting a hand on the hunting knife belted at his waist. A dog at his feet growled, making Flicker snort uneasily.

"You've done enough damage already," the first Tamer said, gesturing at the dead tree closest to us. "You city folk with your clear-cutting and farming—you're the reason this drought has fallen upon us."

I wondered why they thought that—if it was somehow

embedded in their belief system, or if there was any truth to what they were saying. Could magic, perhaps magic that the city people used and the Tamers didn't, somehow be behind the drought?

"We must respect their wishes," Alek said to me and Mare. "We'll have to look for a place to ford."

Instead of seeming mollified by Alek's directive that we abandon our plan to go farther, both Tamers drew their weapons. Flicker backed up as Mare tightened her hands on the reins.

"Cross here and you'll pollute our fishing grounds with your corpses," the taller man said, stepping forward aggressively.

Mare looked to Alek for direction, but his eyes were fixed on the Tamers' weapons as he backed his horse away.

"We'll go far enough north so as not to bother you," Alek said.

"We don't have time for that," Mare said in Tradespeech, undoubtedly hoping that the Tamers wouldn't understand. "We've already lost half a day riding due south!"

Alek never took his eyes from the Tamers, but his expression soured even further with Mare's words. Before he could respond to her, another pair of Tamers materialized from behind some nearby trees, and then two more behind us. We were surrounded. My mouth went dry, and I held even more tightly to Mare.

"Sarding Hells," Alek muttered.

"Alek?" Mare's voice quavered with uncertainty. If we were going to flee, we needed to do it now, before they closed in on us.

"Follow me and don't ask any stupid questions or waste any time," Alek said, turning his horse suddenly toward the river.

He lifted one hand from the reins and rapidly traced an intricate symbol that resembled that of the water god while murmuring something under his breath. The river water slowed and eddied, turning back on itself until it coalesced into a path that looked hard and smooth as glass.

The Tamers all started yelling, then tightened their circle around us. Alek dug his heels into his mount's sides, and the slow beast took a startled leap forward onto the transparent surface of the bridge. The horse's hooves kicked up a spray of water but didn't sink into the bridge. Somehow, Alek had used magic to make the water solid. I gasped in amazement. I'd figured he had an Affinity of some kind, but his grumpy demeanor hadn't made me want to ask any questions. I wished I could have sensed what he was doing, seen the magic, but the peaceroot kept me even more blind to it than I ordinarily would have been. He'd looked like a soldier saying a prayer, nothing more.

"Hurry!" Alek shouted back to us, his voice strained.

Mare urged Flicker toward the water bridge. He balked in the mud, prancing and snorting, rearing up when Mare nudged him with her heels. The Tamers' dogs seemed to have multiplied behind us, and an entire pack of them converged to bark and snap at Flicker's legs. He struck out at them and I clung to Mare, frightened of losing my seat.

"Go!" Mare shouted at Flicker, the usual calm she kept around her horse shattering. Startled, Flicker splashed through the water at the edge of the river and scrambled onto the bridge, walking as unsteadily as a newborn colt. Dogs leaped into the water to swim after us, only turning back when we reached the deeper part of the river. I made the mistake of looking down, and my stomach flipped over at the sight of white water foaming under the glassy surface of the bridge, which was quickly narrowing.

"Hold on tight!" Mare said to me, and I obeyed with all my strength as Flicker scrambled up the opposite bank and the last of the bridge disappeared back into the water. I cast a glance back to see the Tamers lined up on the shore, weapons still drawn should we be unwise enough to try to return. Alek swayed dangerously in the saddle and then slumped over his gelding's neck. We rode up alongside his horse to spot him in case he lost his balance, but he waved us off.

"What in the Sixth Hell was that?" Mare asked Alek.

Alek mumbled an unintelligible response.

"He must have an Affinity for water," I said.

"We have to keep riding," Alek said, clumsily righting himself and clucking at his horse to walk on. He lurched in the saddle like a drunk.

Mare and I exchanged a nervous glance but quickly urged Flicker to follow him and his horse as they plodded on toward our destination.

"The Tamers won't follow us?" I asked.

"Not likely," Alek said. "We're gone. That's all that matters to them."

Even though his words were reassuring, I couldn't help but cast glances back over my shoulder the rest of the day until we made camp back on the main road that night.

Alek recovered over the next few days, but it was a slow process. I continued to drink my peaceroot tea and let my magic recede into the background, trying not to let the increasing intensity of my headaches make me sluggish. Willowbark was no longer enough to quell the pain, but the peaceroot was the only key I had to safety, so I took it and pushed away worries about the dwindling amount I had left or what would come after that.

A few days before we reached Kartasha, Alek was finally well enough to take first watch again, leaving Mare and me huddled in front of our small campfire.

"How are you feeling?" Mare said. She asked the same question every day, sometimes more than once, but it carried more weight this time. I knew she was asking about what lay ahead in Kartasha, not just whether I was surviving the trip.

"I'm nervous," I admitted. Mare had a clear goal upon our arrival in Kartasha, but my own role left me feeling strangely uncertain.

"About what?" Mare asked.

"Pretending to be your maid seems relatively easy after the political deception I had to deal with as a princess," I said. "But what if someone figures out who I am and that I'm not dead? Kartasha is said to be full of swindlers and thieves. What if there are people there who want to return a lost princess to her betrothed or her parents in hopes of receiving a reward?"

"I won't let anyone take you from me." Mare's gray eyes were dark pools in the firelight. The fierceness in her expression lit a spark of desire in me. Until I met her, I'd never known what it was to be wanted or loved so much. I'd also never known just how much I had to lose.

"I know," I whispered. "I'm just scared." Giving voice to my fears made them that much more consuming. Worse, part of the problem was that I no longer had a sense of purpose. I didn't know what I was going to do after taming my powers. I couldn't see a path ahead that spelled out a simple life for Mare and me. Even if I could, would I be happy living a modest life somewhere, knowing that my Affinity was powerful enough to make a difference in the world?

"I understand. I'm worried, too. Even with you to guide me, I'm sure I'm going to find twenty ways to look like a bonehead at the Winter Court." Mare sighed. "And now that the Sonnenbornes are already invading Mynaria, I can't afford to."

"I know you can do this," I said. The key to success in any court was confidence more than knowledge. "Just remember the things we've talked about on the way here. Pause and think before you speak. Be active, not reactive. You're a princess and an ambassador— you are entitled to demand the respect of the highest-ranking nobles in any kingdom's court." At least reciting the lessons that had been drilled into me since childhood made me feel more like myself.

"You make it sound so easy. Why can't political dominance be determined with an ale-chugging contest?" she asked. "I could win at that."

I laughed, and a little of my tension melted away. "Well, when you're back in Mynaria, lauded for your exceptional ambassadorial skills, and Thandi bestows a massive estate in the hills on you, you can start your own court in which that is the preferred way for a newcomer to establish his or her standing." I spoke with the prim authority of the royal woman I'd once been, and Mare was laughing before I got halfway through.

"That would be perfect," she said.

"Wouldn't it?" I lay down with my head in her lap, and she stroked my hair absently. "We could have a stable full of fine horses that you could train and sell, and perhaps I'd start an artists' salon.

But it wouldn't be just for the nobles—we could invite local crafts-people and musicians. Turn it into a destination for the finest in the kingdom."

"Is that what you want?" she asked, her voice curious and tender.

"Honestly, I don't know." It was hard to think past the immediate concerns of stopping the Sonnenbornes and finding someone to help me learn to control my magic. Besides, even tamed, how would my fire magic fit into a simple life like the one we'd just fantasized for ourselves?

"Then we'll figure it out together," she said.

"That is something I know I want." I sat up for a kiss that quickly turned into several more, and then nestled closer to her. Wherever I ended up in life, next to Mare was the one place I knew I belonged.

SEVEN

✦ *Amaranthine*

KARTASHA WAS EVERYTHING WE'D BEEN PROMISED, and more. As the layer of dust on our clothes could attest, our journey had been dry, but snow still crowned the high mountain looming east of the city. The setting sun bathed the peak in shades of peach and coral. Unlike my hometown of Lyrra, Kartasha had no wall to mark the city's edge, and I wondered how the queen or the Winter Court regulated anyone coming in or out. No wonder Kartasha was said to be such a lawless place.

"We'll have to dismount to enter the city," Alek told us, and sure enough, a sign on the road we traveled indicated that we were to proceed on foot. I felt small on the ground next to Flicker after so many days in the saddle, and I missed having Denna pressed against me.

"Are you intending to go directly to the Winter Court?" Alek asked, tugging his mount out of the way of an oncoming ox wagon.

"There's no time to waste," I said. I hated to walk up to their front doors bedraggled from travel, but what choice did we have? It was late enough in the day that I didn't expect them to schedule an audience for us until morning.

"Then you'll want to head for the tower." Alek pointed at a tall white building that stood halfway up the mountain. "You take the lead."

I blinked, surprised. His directive had to be a matter of protocol—or because he didn't want to be the first person to lay eyes on Guardian Laurenna. Given what little he'd said about her, I gathered he'd rather never be in the same city as her again.

"What's the best way to get there?" I asked, hoping I sounded more confident than I felt.

"Follow the main road to the fountain and take a left," he said, pulling up the hood of his cloak.

The crush of people intensified the deeper we got into the city. Everyone walked around with weapons exposed—knives tucked into belts, swords buckled at waists, other blades strapped across chests. White flags seemed to decorate every building, and some people had even chalked ornate white dragons onto their storefronts. Magic sparkled all around us, as much a part of daily life as breathing. A broom swept the street in front of an inn by itself. A basin filled with laundry churned with no hand to guide it. I cast a glance at Denna, whose eyes were wide with wonder. By contrast, my feelings were more like those of my horse, who I could tell was barely managing not to spook like a green colt at every new thing he saw.

"Excuse me," a man said behind me in rough Tradespeech. I moved aside to let him pass, shocked when I saw his Sonnenborne garb. Two more people rushed after him, both carrying tall stacks of folded fabric.

"What the Sixth Hell are Sonnenbornes doing here?" I asked.

"Those are textile merchants." Alek shrugged.

"Sonnenbornes just attacked a city a week's ride from here!"

"Which is why it's doubtful that those textile merchants were involved in the attack." Alek spoke to me slowly, as if I were very stupid.

"Kartasha is neutral territory," Denna added.

"Its people will feel different after we share details of the attack," I said. Still, it didn't sit right with me. Rumors had to have made their way ahead of us, even if we came bearing the official message. Wouldn't that have made people suspicious of Sonnenbornes, especially if they knew that children had been abducted during the battle?

We passed a number of Zumordan drinking establishments, each one humming with conversation as it filled for the evening. I had a feeling that, like the alehouses in Mynaria, they were excellent places to pick up gossip and information—if one knew enough languages. Kartashans seemed to hail from all over the Northern Kingdoms. They wore a variety of fabrics, from the furs of the far north to the woven layers of the desert south. Pack animals varied from donkeys to horses to oxen, and I'd also never seen so many loose animals. It alarmed me at first until I realized that many of the roaming creatures had to be people in manifest form.

Would that be one of Denna's abilities once she mastered her magic? The thought unnerved me, though I could never let her know that. Her choices were hers alone, and her magic was hers to master. I tried to shake off my worries. Things like this were part of what had bred so much suspicion of Zumordans in my homeland—accusations that the people were less than people because they could turn into animals or because they didn't worship our gods.

As we got closer to the tower, we entered an enormous stone archway wide enough for ten warriors to ride through abreast. It felt wrong to walk through with my horse beside me instead of riding. My body hummed with nervous energy. The test of whether I could be the ambassador my kingdom needed lay just ahead, and it made me suddenly homesick. For the first time I thought I might understand how Denna had felt when she first came to Mynaria for her wedding. At least she'd spent her whole life preparing. Coming to Zumorda had been a harebrained plan on my part, developed in haste to make sure I could find a way for Denna and me to be together after she nearly died saving me.

I'd never had a long-term plan for my life, and my immediate future was too uncertain to make one. But now that I was so far from home, I knew Mynaria was where I ultimately belonged. My skill with horses gave me prestige there that I wouldn't have anywhere else. Maybe my childhood fantasy of running a remote horse breeding and training farm away from the watchful eyes of the crown was just that—a fantasy—but I knew in Mynaria I could have a future I loved, especially if Denna was with me. The knowledge that we couldn't go back until Denna had her magic under control was frightening enough, but knowing we would somehow have to explain that she was still alive or face hiding her true identity forever . . . it all left me feeling like the future I wanted might be impossible.

Past the archway, the sprawling collection of buildings at the base of the tower bustled with activity. Servants hurried about their business, and the smell of cooking food made my mouth water. People who had to be nobles moved at a slower pace, their jeweled robes catching the last of the sun's light.

We came to a halt outside a closed gate of heavy wood leading to the inner sanctum of the tower. Four guards eyed us, unimpressed.

"My sword is your sword," I said, greeting them in clumsy Zumordan as Alek had advised me to do.

Only the one closest to us reacted—by grabbing the hilt of her weapon. "Where are you from, foreigner?" she asked in Tradespeech.

Denna jumped in, performing the role of herald in much better Zumordan. "I present to you Her Royal Highness Amaranthine, princess of Mynaria and official ambassador of King Thandilimon. We wish everyone at the Winter Court strength and prosperity, and come to lend our swords for mutual success." The words poured from her mouth smooth as water. My cheeks burned. We hadn't even made it to anyone of rank and I'd already made a misstep. I was grateful to Denna for saving me but wished she hadn't needed to.

The guard looked Denna up and down, then took her hand off her sword.

"She's your mistress?" she asked Denna, jerking her chin in my direction.

"Yes," Denna said.

"Why?" The guard smirked. "She's *vakos*. Something's off about you, but you're clearly not."

Denna paused, and I could almost see her mind turning the foreign word over to decipher its meaning. I knew the moment she understood, because her expression went completely blank. I recognized that look—Denna had long ago mastered the mask of neutrality necessary to survive court life.

"She's a dignitary, and it is an honor to serve her." Denna's voice was so soft and deferential I barely recognized it.

The guard seemed confused by this response but turned back to me and spoke in Tradespeech.

"State your business with the Winter Court," she said.

"We come bearing news of recent attacks in Duvey and a siege in my homeland, and humbly request an audience with the queen."

"Attacks?" Another guard reached for his sword.

"The troubles of other kingdoms are not welcome here," the female guard said. "And the queen isn't holding audiences during her stay."

Alek stepped up beside me and pulled back his hood.

"Sir Alek!" The female guard sank to one knee. The others swiftly followed her example.

I shot him a confused look, but his face was as impassive as ever.

"Can't one of you idiots at least reach Guardian Laurenna or Grand Vizier Zhari?" Alek asked. "I have an urgent message from Lord Wymund, guardian of Duvey. And she's a princess of Mynaria, for sard's sake."

I glanced at Denna, who looked a little pale. So much for diplomacy—at least I hadn't been the one to sling manure all over protocol this time.

"Yes, of course, sir, I'll relay that to her right away and see if one of them can fit you in," the woman said, then shrank into a hound. I took a quick step back, startled, then mentally chastised myself. I couldn't let them see how unnerving I found their abilities.

A few minutes later, the wooden gate creaked open and we were ushered into the inner courtyard. One of the guards stayed close by, unsubtly keeping an eye on us. When the dog returned and transformed back into her human form midstride, I managed to hold myself steady.

"As an honored member of the Mynarian royal family, you have been offered a place to stay here at court," the woman said breathlessly. "Guardian Laurenna and Grand Vizier Zhari will see you tomorrow, and you are also cordially invited to attend the court's daily cocktail gathering this evening to meet some of the nobles."

"That's very kind," I managed, trying not to give in to the anxiety that flooded through me. A court function sounded like a great place for me to make a terrible first impression. Flicker sidestepped, keyed up by my tension. "Please extend our gratitude to Guardian Laurenna and Grand Vizier Zhari for their hospitality. We'll gladly accept their invitation to tonight's gathering."

Alek made a disgruntled sound, but the soldier visibly relaxed at my acceptance of the offer. "Your chambers will be prepared shortly. Speak to the attendant at the merchants' hall to the north and they'll be able to guide you to your rooms and draw you baths, if you'd like."

"Am I expected to attend?" Alek asked the guard.

"The court would be honored by your presence, Sir Alek," the soldier said, her gaze sparkling with admiration. "A room will be prepared for you as well."

"And our horses?" I asked.

"Quite welcome at the Winter Court's stables. You'll find them among the southmost buildings here at court. Would you like a page to guide you?"

I glanced at Alek, and he shook his head.

"No, thank you," I said.

With that, the guards bade us farewell and resumed their posts, leaving us to show ourselves to the barn.

We were barely out of the guards' earshot when Alek released a growl loud enough to scare a page hurrying past. "I can't believe Wymund sent me on this sarding errand."

"You can leave anytime," I said. I certainly wouldn't object if he turned around and left for Duvey immediately. He'd gotten us to Kartasha and into the Winter Court, so his purpose had already been served. Besides, the only thing that seemed more likely to ruin a court function than my presence was both of us being there.

"I was ordered to make sure news of the attack reached Laurenna personally. Never mind that she's about as likely to listen to me as a sarding icicle." Alek's jaw twitched.

"If you and Laurenna don't get along, why did she invite us to stay at court?" I asked.

"She's not stupid," Alek replied. "She'll want to know my news, and she wouldn't risk offending a member of another kingdom's royal family. She wants you close so she can watch you. Find out who you are, what you want, and what you're made of before she decides your worth."

"Great," I said. She sounded like all the worst qualities of the nobles in Mynaria rolled into one person.

"So what are we going to do?" Denna asked.

"Deal with it," I cut in before Alek could respond. "If she

wants to know what we are made of, we prove our worth." I met both of their eyes in turn, seeing doubt in Denna's and displeasure in Alek's.

"Unfortunately, it's the only thing we can do," Alek said, surprising me with his agreement.

We entered the stables, which seemed to be warmed with some kind of radiant heat. Outside the open rear doors of the stalls several large turnout fields sloped downhill, all enclosed within the Winter Court's walls. The barn wasn't terribly large, but only a few courtiers kept horses here—probably those who had estates outside Kartasha that they needed to ride to and from. From what I knew of Corovja, it was as inhospitable to riders as Denna's hometown of Spire City, so not many nobles were accomplished riders, given that they spent most of their time in the north.

A stablehand showed us to two empty stalls in the middle of the row, gesturing to the brush boxes hanging in front of each one while trying to explain in broken Tradespeech where the hay and grain were kept. Then he hurried to assist two other riders who had just entered from the door at the other end of the barn. When I got a closer look at them, I nearly dropped my reins in shock: they were Sonnenbornes.

I recognized their skirmish saddles and the cut of their clothing immediately. The woman's dark green split caftan fell almost clear to her ankles, the color a striking accompaniment to the black hair contained in a tight coil at the nape of her neck. The man's jerkin was the same style as the one I remembered Lord Kriantz's men wearing, and my stomach turned at the thought of my abductor. Sometimes I couldn't believe he was dead, and I expected to see him one day walking toward me, alive, with the same savage look he'd had on his face when he murdered my best friend.

"Guardian Laurenna said we'd find accommodations for the horses here?" the woman said to the stablehand. Her Tradespeech was smooth and practiced, as though she'd learned by studying it rather than immersion.

"Yes, yes," the stablehand said, and guided them toward the two empty stalls on the other side of Flicker's, inquiring about whether they'd prefer to care for the horses themselves or have him do it.

I pretended to be occupied with currying the dust and sweat from Flicker's coat as I felt the woman's gaze land on my horse.

"If your people are capable of taking care of that one, I will trust you with mine." She passed the split reins to the stablehand, and he led her light bay gelding into the stall alongside Flicker's.

I bristled. For all the respect her people had for our warhorses, they certainly hadn't shown any to our people.

With their horses handed off, the two riders left the barn. I put Flicker in his stall and tossed him some hay. For his part, my horse didn't seem perturbed by his new stablemate. He raised his head and then blew out a sigh before going back to his food. Traitor.

As soon as the stablehand finished with the Sonnenborne horses and had rushed away to his next task, I stepped over to the bars dividing Flicker's stall from the one occupied by Alek's horse.

"How can they be here?" I asked in a low voice. "Textile merchants in the city are one thing, but how can the Winter Court allow Sonnenbornes right now?"

"Everyone is judged on their own merits here," he said. "Something you should be grateful for."

I ignored his jab. "That doesn't make any sense!" I said, my voice rising. "How can anyone be sure these two weren't complicit in the attack on Duvey? How do you know they can be trusted?"

"I don't," Alek said. "It's Laurenna and Zhari's problem, not mine."

"This place makes no sense," I ranted, turning away from him and exiting Flicker's stall. Denna waited for me outside, casting a furtive look down the barn aisle, but no one else was around. "How does anyone stay safe here? How has the Winter Court not been taken over by whoever decides to waltz through the front door and just start murdering people?"

Alek chuckled as he exited his horse's stall, only fueling my anger. "Now you're starting to understand. Do you Mynarians even know how the Zumordan throne is passed on?"

I looked at Denna, but she only shrugged. If she knew anything, she wasn't going to risk saying so in front of Alek.

"Gladiatorial combat," Alek said. "The challenger must fight three of the reigning monarch's champions and then defeat the monarch herself."

"What?" That made Zumorda sound more like a dictatorship than a monarchy.

"Zumordans respect power—the power of an individual, their magic, and their manifest." Alek dropped brushes back into the box outside his horse's stall.

I stared at him. "So I'm powerless here."

"You're the one who will determine that," he said, and strode out of the barn to the north.

"Do you believe what he's saying?" I asked Denna, hoping she could make sense of everything and give me some hope that I wasn't doomed to failure.

"This place is definitely very different from Mynaria or Havemont," she said, ever the diplomat.

"But how in the Sixth Hell am I supposed to play social climber in a court where people allow the enemy to walk right in the front door and murder each other to prove their power?" I asked.

She met my eyes, and though I could see the exhaustion in hers, she radiated a quiet strength I wished I had. "You're no fool," she said. "Watch and listen. Take your cues from those around you and you'll find your way."

Denna and I hurried out of the barn and followed Alek to the merchants' hall. Inside, the building attendant, a tall, angular woman with bright blue eyes, showed us to Alek's room first. The chamber was barely larger than a closet and didn't have its own bathroom.

"Please thank Guardian Laurenna for this," he said to the attendant, then entered his room and shut the door harder than was necessary.

I covered my mouth, barely managing to hide a snicker. As rude as he was to me, it was rather amusing to see someone else get the best of him, even with something as subtle as a room.

There wasn't much to the chamber we'd been given at the other end of the hall—just a simply furnished room containing a bed, a vanity, a small wardrobe, and a chaise Denna was apparently intended to sleep on as my maid. A short rack of wine bottles sat alongside the vanity, with four glasses perched on the top. The only decoration was a gray rug on the floor that had clearly seen better days.

"Should we be insulted that they gave us rooms in the merchants' hall?" I asked Denna, tossing my pack on the floor near the bed. "We're nowhere near the rest of the court."

"I don't think so," she said. "Alek's room was clearly an insult, but there is some respect and caution in putting you here away from the other courtiers."

"But why?" I asked.

"Based on what we've seen and what Alek said, power here has to do with one's ability to use magic," I said. "Those with gifts naturally outrank those who have none." She stripped off her dirty cloak and sat down on the vanity stool.

"That clears up why the gate guard was confused that you worked for me instead of the other way around," I said.

"Putting you in a building with a large number of magic users would be dangerous. How would you defend yourself if something happened over there?" She stared at me with worried eyes.

"I hadn't thought of that," I said. "And I suppose it would also put me in a better position to go around killing important people, if that were my objective."

"That too," she said.

"Six Hells, I'm exhausted." I lay back on the bed, wishing I could go to sleep instead of to a cocktail party full of backstabbing and potentially murderous courtiers.

"You'd best take your bath before the water gets cold," Denna said, pointing to the tub that had been filled for me in the washing chamber.

I groaned but obediently got to my feet. "What am I even supposed to do at this thrice-damned party?"

"See if Alek can introduce you to anyone, and barring that, see what you can pick up," Denna said. "When one doesn't know what to say at court, the best thing to do is listen."

"You are the only reason I have any hope of not completely sarding this up." I smiled at Denna, grateful that we were once more somewhere we could speak as equals. In so many ways, she was my superior.

"You're picking up language from Alek. That can't be good," she teased.

"What would be good is if you came and shared the bath with me while it's still warm," I said, tugging off my boots and tossing them aside.

She smiled shyly, her cheeks turning pink.

I winked and walked to the washroom, confident she'd follow.

My first attempt to ingratiate myself at court went about as well as trying to train a horse to crap star-shaped road apples. The cocktail party was held at the residence of one of the Winter Court's respected nobles in a much larger building than the modest merchants' hall. Stepping through the door into the gilded ballroom immediately filled me with the familiar dread that came with attending any court function, even though the decor and sartorial splendor were of an entirely different variety than I'd seen back home. Tall columns wrapped with gold-leaf vines stood throughout the room, clusters of nobles mingling among them. Pastel colors seemed to dominate this season's fashion, and I could not have felt more out of place dressed in my dark blue formal Mynarian livery. It wasn't as if Alek was any help, either. His expression as the herald announced us together held all the joy of freshly flattened roadkill.

"I present Her Royal Highness, Princess Amaranthine of Mynaria, and Sir Alek of the Misty Plains," the herald shouted over the din of conversation in the room.

A few people cast curious glances at us. A much larger number glared at me with overt hostility. I smiled, trying not to let my uncertainty show. At least I was used to the disdainful looks, given what my reputation had been like back home.

I bolted for the beverage table past a rather hideous series of frescoes on the walls, ignoring whatever Alek was grumbling behind me. A pale green beverage with muddled citrus at the bottom was placed in my hand, and I took it without questioning the contents. The glass was filled to the brim with ice and topped with a sprig of mint. It smelled like bug repellent. I took a swig to discover it tasted about the same.

"Shit of the gods, what is this stuff?" I asked Alek, who had asked the bartender for a glass of water.

"Chartreuse Smash," he said, his tone dour.

"Well, it does have a sort of violence to it," I said. I took another sip, bracing myself for the drink to punch me in the throat. "Can you introduce me to some of your friends?" I asked. He had to know at least a few people from his days here prior to taking the post at Duvey, and talking to almost anyone in this viper pit might help me better understand the Winter Court.

"I don't have any friends," Alek said, as though the mere suggestion was repulsive.

"Acquaintances?" I asked.

"This isn't where I prefer to spend my time," he grumbled.

"Besides, there are a lot of outsiders here—spectacle seekers. Hoping the magic of the queen's selected trainees will rub off on them, no doubt."

"You know Laurenna," I pointed out.

His fingers reflexively searched for the hilt of a sword that wasn't there. "She's not here. You're the diplomat. Go talk to people."

I sighed. He clearly wanted my company about as much as a hoof to the face, and I didn't feel much different. Talking wasn't my strong suit, but listening I could do. What I really wanted to know was why there were Sonnenbornes at the Winter Court and how they might interfere with my agenda—which was, of course, to get done with this ambassadorial nonsense as quickly as possible and go back to figuring out what was next for me and Denna.

I slipped away to meander through the increasingly crowded room, hoping to catch a few snatches of conversation that might help me find out what the courtiers thought of the queen, her grand vizier, or the Sonnenbornes. Most people were speaking Tradespeech, so at least I didn't have to try to translate from Zumordan.

". . . she looks weaker than she did last year, I'm sure of it," a woman said, her voice barely above a whisper and dripping with false concern.

"Really, you're going to start underestimating her now?" the man standing beside her asked.

"Of course not!" the woman said, aghast at the suggestion. "But you have to admit, when the monarch has been challenged eight out of the past ten years, times are changing. She can't keep winning forever."

I frowned. While Alek had mentioned how the throne was

taken in Zumorda, he hadn't mentioned that there had been challenges for it recently.

One of the other men in the group noticed me lurking. "Maybe you're right, if the stance on Mynarians has become more lax." His voice was louder than the others, and his gaze even colder than Alek's usually was.

I kept walking, drinking fast. It was useless to try to engage with people who already held something against me. My drink was gone before I got halfway across the ballroom. I scanned the area for the quickest path back to the beverage table, only for two familiar figures to catch my eye: the Sonnenbornes I'd seen at the stables. They'd exchanged their riding clothes for formal garb in lighter colors more suited to court, but the woman's black hair was unmistakable. I pushed through the crowd, joining the drink line directly behind them. I meant only to eavesdrop on their conversation, but the woman took a step back and bumped into me almost immediately.

"Apologies," I said, flustered.

"The mistake was mine," the woman said. Her eyes were long-lashed and a warm hazel. "Forgive me, but I don't think we've been introduced."

"Princess Amaranthine of Mynaria," I said, standing straighter.

She smiled diplomatically. "Pleased to meet you, Your Highness. I am Eronit of Sonnenborne, and this is my husband, Varian."

"I'm surprised to meet a Mynarian here." Varian smiled thinly through his reddish beard.

"And I am equally surprised to meet you," I said, keeping my tone neutral. If either of them had a connection to the assassinations that had destroyed my family, it was going to take everything I had not to strangle them before we reached the front of the beverage line.

"We Sonnenbornes have always had a presence in Kartasha," Varian said.

"But I don't think you've made a habit of attacking Zumordan border cities," I countered.

Eronit's eyes widened. "What are you talking about?"

I didn't buy their innocent act. "Duvey Keep was attacked by Sonnenbornes. We had the misfortune of crossing paths with them at the wrong time on our way here."

"Which tribes?" Eronit said. "We don't all believe the same things. I doubt our own people would have been involved in such an attack."

We arrived at the front of the line and each accepted a mug of mulled wine from the harried servant tending the table.

"Perhaps we should take our drinks and continue this conversation elsewhere?" Varian suggested.

I nodded my reluctant agreement. While it felt like fraternizing with the enemy, I needed to find out whatever they knew about why Duvey had been attacked or what their kingdom's next move might be. The three of us moved aside so that others could receive their drinks.

"What is different about your tribe's beliefs from those who attacked Duvey?" I asked them, hoping a comparison might get to the root of Kriantz's master plan.

"Our people are dedicated to the desert," Eronit said. "We believe it is our true homeland, and our duty is to survive there as we have for hundreds of years. We oppose those who seek to expand our kingdom's borders to gain resources. The desert has all we need."

I was flummoxed. The entire reason Kriantz had tried to start a war between Zumorda and Mynaria was to steal land. He had implied that all the Sonnenbornes were starving in the desert and his people had no other way to ensure their survival. Eronit and Varian didn't look malnourished in any way—they were fit and strong.

"We rarely leave the desert, in fact," Varian said. "This is our first time outside the borders of our kingdom."

"Ours is a tribe with many scholars," Eronit said. "The merchants bring back much for us to learn and study."

"That's why we are visiting," Varian explained. "For our studies."

I looked back and forth between them. "What are you studying?"

"The intersection between climate, botany, and magic as it relates to successful horticultural models in the Sonnenborne desert," Eronit said.

"I didn't think the Sonnenbornes used magic," I said, hoping to hide my failure to understand most of the other words in her sentence.

"We don't." Eronit smiled. "Which is why we've come here—to study with those who do and learn more about why magic is absent from our homeland."

"I doubt the details would interest you," Varian said with a condescending smile.

I frowned. I probably wouldn't understand the details, but Denna might, if I shared them with her. And it seemed interesting that Eronit had said there was no magic in Sonnenborne. We had it in Mynaria—people just considered it heretical and dangerous. That was quite different from a kingdom where magic simply didn't exist.

Eronit's face suddenly lit up as she looked over my shoulder.

I turned around to see Alek looming behind me, creepily quiet like he always was. Of course he had to go and interrupt the conversation just as it was getting interesting.

"Sir Alek of the Misty Plains. It's an honor," Eronit said.

Alek gave her an acknowledging nod, his expression flat as ever. I looked back and forth between them with some suspicion. How did Eronit know who Alek was?

"It's a pleasure to meet you." Varian extended his hand to Alek and introduced himself and Eronit. "Is it true you're going to be offering training while you're in town?"

Alek shrugged. "I'll be at the salle in the afternoons if anyone cares to spar."

Varian looked as giddy as a first-year liegeman. "We've heard many stories of your heroics. It would be an honor to learn from you."

Heroics? It was hard to imagine Alek as a hero of any kind, unless he'd somehow managed to grouch his enemies to death.

"We'll look for you at the salle," Varian said.

"You'll have to excuse us," Eronit said. "The person we're meant to meet with has just arrived. It was a pleasure to make your acquaintance. Sir Alek. Your Highness." She nodded to each of us in turn.

The two of them walked away and joined a small group of Zumordans who had just entered the ballroom, integrating in a seamless way I wish I could have. How did two other foreigners make things look so easy their first time outside their kingdom? I scowled after them, and then turned that same expression on Alek.

"So you're a hero, eh?" I asked.

"I'm a fighter. I do what I'm told, when I'm told, where I'm told to do it." His tone implied that I was lacking in all those abilities. "If you care to introduce yourself to Grand Vizier Zhari, she's here." He gestured to a tall older woman bedecked in pale gold robes who stood near the windows. She carried herself with the quiet air of someone who had great power. Her hair was white as the snow on the mountaintop and cut very short, and though she carried an ornamental staff, she stood straight as any soldier. Poised between two of the gaudy columns, she looked far more like a work of art than any of the frescoes in the room. It surprised me to see that no one was toadying to her—in fact, most seemed to give her a wide berth other than a respectful bow or nod as they passed, almost as if they were afraid.

"Are people scared of the grand vizier?" I asked Alek.

"If they're smart," he said.

I took a fortifying gulp of wine, reminding myself that even out of my element, I technically outranked Zhari. I edged through the fringes of a group surrounding a young brunette noblewoman about my age who seemed to be holding her own small court in the center of the room. She wore a pale yellow dress that glittered with sparkling embroidery and swept low beneath her finely chiseled collarbones. The crowd seemed be actively thickening around her, and as I got closer, I could see why—she seemed to have had several drinks and was in the middle of telling a scandalous story.

"And then," the noblewoman said, "his pants fell off and I

knew why his manifest was a mouse!"

The other nobles lost their minds with laughter, while I blinked in confusion.

"Another drink, Lady Ikrie?" someone shouted over the crowd.

"Someone get me another glass of the bubbly stuff!" Ikrie waved clumsily at a nearby server, who hurried to her side.

"Better a mouse than a drunk idiot at a party," I muttered.

The noblewoman's blue eyes locked on me, taking in my livery. Her pretty face twisted into a sneer. "Unless I misheard, you insulted my character and my dignity, Mynarian."

She'd done an excellent job of that all on her own, but there was a dangerous edge to her gaze that told me I'd be better off not pointing that out.

"No, I just have a fondness for mice," I joked.

The crowd around us tittered nervously.

"Perhaps I should challenge you to a duel for insulting me." Ikrie flicked her fingers, and a gust of air thumped me in the chest, sending me stumbling backward. "It'll be good practice for when I take on the queen's other trainees at the Midwinter Revel."

A jolt of fear went through me. Apparently I'd accidentally insulted one of the magic users the queen had selected for her elite training program, and a noble one to boot. Would she really expect us to fight? I looked to Alek for guidance, but his unreadable scowl gave me none.

"But she doesn't have an Affinity, my lady," one of the other nobles said. "You can't duel someone who is *vakos*."

"I heard she's the Mynarian ambassador," someone else added.

Ikrie laughed. "If a *vakos* blunderer is the best Mynaria can do for an ambassador, perhaps we should do them the kindness of absorbing them into our empire."

"My people will defend our kingdom with our last breaths," I snapped.

"And my people will be happy to steal those breaths from you," the woman said. She raised a hand, and air rushed out of my lungs. I dropped my wine mug, which shattered on the floor, and clawed at my throat. Stars swam in front of my vision and darkness started to close in, and that was when she finally released the magic.

I fell to my knees, inhaling deep breaths.

"Perhaps think twice before insulting your betters," Ikrie said, turning on her heel and leaving me on the floor. Servants converged on the empty area to clean up the wine and shards of mug littering the tile. My cheeks burned with shame as the other nobles quickly dispersed. No one wanted to be seen consorting with the person who had just been publicly humiliated. Alek offered me a hand, and I grudgingly let him pull me back to my feet. Dark wine stains mottled the knees of my breeches.

"Most air users have a knack for Farhearing," he said.

That explained how she'd heard me over the din of the crowd. "How am I supposed to know what kind of magic someone has?" I asked. Fear was quickly taking over from my embarrassment. I couldn't know what kind of gifts the people around me might have or what risks they might pose. Anyone in the room could kill me with a flick of their fingers, and that was a terrifying thought. Not even my rank provided any protection—it was meaningless here.

Alek shrugged. "Pay attention."

"Well, that was an interesting way to introduce yourself to

court," a low female voice said beside me.

I turned, finding myself face-to-face with Grand Vizier Zhari. Her golden robes gave her the air of a religious official rather than a high-ranking courtier. Perhaps in Zumorda that was almost the same thing, since Zumordans didn't worship the gods. Age was evident in the lines on her face, but her gaze was as bright and clear as the gems glittering in the spiral at the top of her staff.

"My sword is your sword," I said haltingly, still trying to catch my breath.

"If what I know of Mynarian royal women is true, you have no sword to offer." She favored me with a small smile, but it was more kind than mocking.

I mentally cursed my father for never letting me train. It wasn't as though I'd never asked, especially after my mother died and I needed some way to fill the hours that had previously been spent making music.

"Regardless, I look forward to working together for the betterment of both our kingdoms," I said, hoping I sounded like the diplomat I was supposed to be.

"In which case I find it interesting that you were talking to our Sonnenborne visitors," Zhari said, her amber eyes curious. They seemed out of place in her lined face, too clear and catlike to fit the rest of her. "There isn't much love lost between your kingdoms as of late."

"I can only speak for my kingdom," I said, treading carefully. "I'm here in Zumorda hoping to help, not to bring trouble. When Duvey was attacked, we took the side of the keep to help push back the enemy."

"Perhaps the real question is why Duvey was attacked in the first place," Zhari said, looking at Alek. "Alek, your training gave you the skills to consider that, even if you turned your back on it."

I shot Alek a puzzled look. What training was she referring to?

"Can't say I know," Alek said, his tone cold enough to freeze every drink in the room.

"Then delight me with your theories," Zhari said, shifting her weight and setting the bells hanging from the spiraling top of her staff jangling like wind chimes. The soothing calm she projected made for a dramatic contrast with Alek, who set his water glass on the tray of a passing servant hard enough to rattle the poor girl's teeth.

"I suppose it looks like Mynaria killed a Sonnenborne ambassador, and the Sonnenbornes decided to take border cities in retaliation," he said. "Duvey is close enough to the Mynarian border to be a logical outpost to station fighters for that purpose."

"There's no evidence of that!" I sputtered. It hadn't occurred to me that the Zumordans might not see the battle at Duvey for exactly what it was—an attack on one of their own cities, not retaliation for something that was my kingdom's fault. Worse, the fact that a Mynarian border city actually had been taken only served to support Alek's theory.

"We will need to investigate to find out what the facts are," Zhari said.

"You're right, we do need to investigate," I said, trying to sound calmer than I felt.

"And so we shall. I look forward to speaking with you more tomorrow," Zhari said. "Enjoy your evening." She walked away slowly, chimes jingling.

"Why did you throw me under the carriage wheels like that?" I asked Alek, my frustration boiling over.

"I didn't do anything." He stared down at me, impassive as ever.

"You basically blamed Mynaria for what happened in Duvey. You have no reason to believe that."

"I didn't blame Mynaria. I said that was what it *looked* like."

I wanted to scream. "You made it look like the attack was my kingdom's fault."

"I was answering her question," he said, unmoved.

"I'm leaving." I turned around with my head held high. There was nothing to be gained by staying. Alek could stay or come with me—I didn't care. Disgusted expressions followed me all the way to the door. In spite of carrying myself with all the pride I could muster, I still felt a tremble starting in my lip as soon as I crossed the threshold out of the room. Back home, I had sometimes felt powerless, but I'd never felt weak. At the Winter Court, it had taken me less than a day to set myself up as completely ineffectual and, worse, an embarrassment. I'd barely gotten any information from the Sonnenbornes, one of the queen's hand-selected magic users had nearly suffocated me, Zhari had appeared just in time to witness my humiliation, and Alek had made me look like a fool. Denna was counting on me, as was my kingdom.

Tonight, I'd let everyone down.

 *Dennaleia*

I LAY DOWN TO TRY TO REST AFTER MARE DEPARTED to meet Alek for the party, but in spite of my exhaustion, attempting to nap was futile. My head pounded ceaselessly thanks to the peaceroot, to the point where I put off taking the dose that usually accompanied my evening meal. I needed to be doing something, not lying around in a room waiting for Mare to return from the party, which was how I ended up in the hot laundry room a few buildings away from the merchants' hall, scrubbing our travel-stained clothing.

I kept my head down and my ears open, hoping to catch some useful court gossip along with the basic techniques of washing clothes. After several inept attempts and some confusion about which herbs and soaps to use, an older woman took pity and showed me the correct techniques, clucking all the while about young people and their incompetence. My cheeks burned. I hated feeling unknowledgeable and hoped I hadn't given away that I'd never done laundry a day in my life.

The din of the laundry room was overwhelming, and what few snippets of conversation I caught were mostly complaints about all the work caused by the additional visitors to court due to the queen's presence. There wasn't much I expected to be of use to Mare in her diplomatic efforts, and by the time I left, exhausted, with our damp clothes in tow, I felt more defeated than ever. I didn't regret using my magic to save Mare's life, but I hated how small my life had become as a result. I'd never realized how much sociopolitical power I had, or how familiar and comforting it had been, until it was gone.

I hurried into the night and back toward the merchants' hall. The dry, frigid air made me shiver in spite of my cloak. The sun had barely set, bathing the courtyard in twilight hues of gray and purple. Overhead, the moon shone nearly full in the evening sky. Servants still bustled between the buildings, taking care of the last of the day's chores, and I merged into the flow of foot traffic to cross the courtyard.

"Out of the way!" someone yelled.

A sudden blast of wind hit me as I looked over my shoulder, barely stifling a scream. The wings of a white dragon blocked out the moon as it swooped in to land. I clumsily sprinted for the closest building as the dragon's wingbeats sent gusts overhead. A wide-eyed page stood already flattened against the wall, and I flipped around alongside her and clutched the laundry bag to my chest with my heart hammering in my ears. In Havemont, dragons were creatures of legend, not reality.

The magnificent creature folded its wings after landing, arching its neck and surveying the courtyard. Everyone stood perfectly still, prey frozen in the gaze of a predator. The beast paused when it looked at me, its sapphire eyes burning in a way that made my magic stir even through the fog of the peaceroot. My hands prickled with pins and needles as I tried to calm my breathing and resist the urge to run.

When the dragon finally looked away, I exhaled a rattling breath of relief and turned to the page to ask about proper protocol for this situation, but she'd already slipped away. I glanced back toward the dragon to find it gone as well. The servants were back in motion, and a few birds winged down from the sky and transformed into human form to follow a tall woman wearing a white cloak with the hood pulled up. They were all dressed in black from head to toe, barely visible as more than shadows. The woman in white strode purposefully out of the courtyard, her cloak billowing behind her like a flag.

I scampered back to the merchants' hall, more than happy to retreat to the safety of our room and the simple task of finding places to hang our laundry. After that was done, I found myself once again idle, pacing restlessly through the room as I awaited Mare's return. When I finally saw her approaching across the courtyard, I knew that something had gone wrong. She kept a quick pace, her posture stiff and unnatural. Alek was nowhere to be seen. I hurried to the door and stepped into the hall to wait for her. Her tight expression immediately softened when she got to the top of the stairs and met my eyes. As soon as we entered our room, she put her arms around me and exhaled a long, shaky breath.

"How did it go?" I asked after she pulled away, afraid I already knew the answer.

"It was a disaster," she said, collapsing into the chaise facing the windows. "What a day this has been. I can't believe how composed you were when you first came to Mynaria, if this is what it feels like to be away from home and tasked with a diplomatic mission for the first time."

"What happened?" I sat down beside her.

"Without killing someone's kindly old relative, I couldn't have made a worse impression." She gave me more details of the evening's events, leaving me more dismayed by each interaction she'd had.

"Perhaps things will go better when you meet with Zhari and Laurenna tomorrow," I said. "Zhari at least sounds interested in the facts."

"Only if Alek can resist undermining me every step of the way." Mare growled with frustration. "I don't understand why he seems to have it in for me. He wasn't half as rude to the Sonnenbornes, and he didn't do a damn thing to help me out of that altercation with the woman who nearly killed me with her magic."

"He's rather inscrutable." I took a deep breath and then asked the question pressing most urgently on my mind. "But what are you going to do if someone else tries to use magic against you?" Fear hummed in my bones at the thought. She had no way to protect herself.

"I don't know," she said, her voice grim. "My title isn't enough to protect me here. Normally I'd just avoid court and anyone who might want to hurt me . . . but that isn't a choice in my current position."

That was what I'd been afraid of. Worse, there wasn't much I could do to protect her with my magic still out of control. As much as I hated to admit it, she'd probably been right to leave when she did. This was quite a setback from a political standpoint, but I didn't need to voice that. Mare wasn't a fool. She knew.

"You made the right choice to leave early," I said.

"I hope so." She rubbed her temples. "Gods, I miss Cas."

"Me too." I squeezed her arm. Her uncle had possessed a silver tongue and the keenest diplomatic sensibilities of anyone I'd met in Mynaria. He would have been the perfect ambassador, able to read any room, able to forge connections among courtiers and commoners alike. He'd been the first one murdered at Kriantz's hands.

"Cas would have already had the Winter Court wrapped around his finger, and a spy network in place to boot." The pain in her voice made me ache with sympathy. "And I miss Nils," Mare said more softly. "I hate that sarding snake Kriantz, his people, and everything they stand for."

"I know." I leaned into her, aching with the memory of everything she'd lost.

"If I didn't have you . . ." She trailed off.

"You'll always have me," I said, hugging her close until she relaxed in my arms. "Even if I'm doomed to be your laundress."

"Is that what you did tonight?" she asked.

"That, and reorganized the other things we brought. Tried to rest but didn't have much luck."

"I'm sorry you couldn't be with me instead," Mare said. "The Six know you would have kept me out of more trouble than Alek managed to."

"Perhaps I could have talked Alek into helping me find a mentor here in Kartasha, too," I said, unable to hide the sadness in my voice.

I hated feeling so detached from all the important things that were happening.

"I'm sorry," Mare said, standing up and taking my hands. "I've been so selfish. We came here to get you magic training and I've done nothing about it. What can I do to help?"

I squeezed her hands in return. "I'm not sure there is much. Perhaps you can ask Laurenna and Zhari about finding me an instructor when you meet with them tomorrow? Or we can determine whether there might be someone available in Corovja if we go there to stay close to the queen?"

"Of course," Mare said. "Both cities are among the largest in Zumorda. There will have to be someone willing to take you on. How has your head been?" She gently tucked a loose strand of hair behind my ear.

"The headache hasn't been too bad tonight," I said, releasing her hands. I stood up and stepped closer to one of the lights in the room, a luminous ball that sat on a stand atop the vanity. Power radiated from it in a way that made my hands tingle. I touched the ball, and the light shut off. With another touch, it came back on. There were several similar balls throughout the room—some in sconces on the walls and others on stands like this one.

"Did you notice these mage lights earlier?" I asked. "Things like this amaze me." I wished I could help her understand how much it meant to be somewhere that magic was all around and how much I wanted my powers back. I could tell the Zumordans' casual use of magic made her nervous, but seeing magic in everyday objects made me feel like there was somewhere I could belong—a place my gift might be ordinary.

"Magic truly is everywhere here," Mare said, looking more unsettled than awed as she sat back down.

I turned back to the light and flicked it on and off again, trying not to let her see how much her anxiousness about magic stung me. It wasn't her fault, especially after someone had nearly killed her with their powers tonight. Still, every time I saw the worry in her eyes, it felt like rejection. Somehow, I needed to reassure her—and myself—that things would be all right.

"Do you think being here is a terrible mistake?" She unbuttoned her jacket and leaned back against the chaise.

I shook my head. "Your kingdom needs you." I stepped in front of Mare, letting my hands alight on her shoulders. I climbed my fingers up to the nape of her neck as she exhaled, then pulled out her braid, burying my hands in her chestnut hair. "I need you."

She reached for me, beckoning me closer. When I sat down beside her, she put her lips on my cheek, brushing a tingling line to my mouth. No matter how many times we kissed, it felt like an impossible gift. The curves of her body were a source of endless magic—a territory that I wanted to spend my whole life mapping.

Our lips met and parted, exploring each other as jolts of desire sang through my body. She lay back and pulled me on top of her, slipping her hands under my shirt to run them up my back. Her smile against my neck made me weak. Then she bit lightly. A shock ran down to my shoulder, raising goose bumps in its wake.

I wanted her to touch me everywhere she could reach, and some places she couldn't without our clothes coming off. Our kisses deepened and she raised her thigh between my legs in a way that sent sparks racing through me. My magic surged with my emotions, consuming me with energy. I no longer had a body; I was only sensation, pulsing, sparkling, the glow of feeling obliterating everything.

I pulled her up so we were both upright, then skimmed my fingers under her shirt, down her ribs, and over the soft curve of her waist. Pressure built, and my magic uncoiled like an animal waking from sleep. Mare pulled the shoulder of my shirt aside and pressed her mouth into the soft hollow above my collarbone, teasing me with her teeth. My arms tingled and sparked, and a rushing sound filled my ears.

The lights in the room flickered all at once and then burst in a storm of shattering glass.

Mare and I jerked apart. The light from the hearth was all that remained.

"Ouch," Mare said, standing up and brushing a few shards of glass off her pants. "I think a piece of glass might have gotten me."

"Oh gods." I scrambled to my feet. "Let me look and see."

"No, wait—first, what in the Sixth Hell just happened?" she asked.

"I'm not sure," I said, but the way my magic felt quiet again made my stomach sink.

She stood up, wincing and putting a hand to her side. "Did you feel anything magical happen? Do you think the peaceroot is losing its effectiveness?"

I hung my head. "I didn't take it tonight."

"Denna." Her eyes grew large and worried. "Why?"

"The headaches were getting bad. It's been nearly a week. We're finally in Kartasha. . . . I just thought . . ." I trailed off, not sure how to explain to her how much I needed to feel like myself again when everything else about my life had changed.

"I'm sorry," she said, her voice softer. "Do you think your magic was the cause of this?"

"I wasn't trying to use it just now, but I felt some sort of energy, and then everything exploded." Guilt weighed me down. If it wasn't me, what else could it have been? It figured that before my powers were even fully back, they'd already be out of control.

Then Mare smiled a little. "Honestly, if you hadn't felt anything while we were kissing like that, I'd be worried."

"What if I blow out the lights every time we . . . do something?" And what if I did something worse? Mare had no way to protect herself from my magic. If I hadn't fallen so selfishly in love with her, she could have had a normal life with someone who didn't have uncontrollable magic. I felt guilty for stealing that future from her.

"That seems unlikely," Mare said, pressing another quick kiss to my lips. "It never happened before."

Her words comforted me in spite of my misgivings. Maybe she could have a normal life with someone else, but I couldn't imagine my life without her. I went to put my arms around her waist, but she flinched.

"Sorry," she said. "Whatever got me in the side hurts."

"We need to find better light so I can take a look," I said.

"Hello?" a woman's voice said from the other side of the door.

We stood up, stumbling in the near dark and smoothing our clothing back into some appearance of normalcy.

"Come in," Mare called.

The building attendant appeared in the doorway. She carried a lantern that cast long shadows, accentuating her narrow features and deep-set eyes. "Everyone all right in here?"

"Yes, we're all right," Mare answered.

I hung back in the shadows, playing the part of demure maid.

"The lights have failed in the building," the attendant said. "Please don't leave this floor until we find the source of the problem. Take this lantern to see by for now. And mind the glass."

"Is this unusual?" Mare asked. "Should we be concerned?"

"No, no, we'll get to the bottom of it quickly," the woman said. "We've called for Guardian Laurenna. She'll be here as soon as she can."

"Do guardians usually come by to investigate blown-out lights?" Mare asked incredulously.

The attendant nodded vigorously. "Guardian Laurenna's water Affinity allows her to trace magical disturbances back to their source."

I swallowed hard. This was my fault, and Mare was going to end up suffering for it. My magic was most likely the source of the problem, and no doubt it would take Laurenna only moments to figure that out.

As soon as the attendant left, my worries came flooding out. "Oh gods, I'm going to ruin everything for you," I said. "I'm so, so sorry."

"No, you won't," Mare said. "I did a fine enough job of ruining this evening already."

I wrung my hands, not convinced. Political missteps were one thing. Blowing out the infrastructure of a building with magic was entirely another.

"Can you take a look at my side?" Mare lifted her shirt just above her waist.

I picked up the lantern and held it aloft, then nearly dropped it when I saw Mare's waist.

"What is it?" she asked, frowning and craning her neck to try to see around the fabric. She pulled her shirt farther to the side, catching a glimpse of herself in the mirror over the vanity. I knew the moment she saw what I had, because she froze in place.

Blisters were rising on her skin in the shape of a small red handprint.

I backed away from her, the lantern light cast on her injury dimming as I retreated. "I'm so sorry," I said, my voice shaking. But it was so much more than that. My every fear had just come to fruition, and after only one missed dose of peaceroot. For the first time, I wondered if the Mynarians were right—maybe I was too dangerous to live.

"It's not your fault," Mare said, dropping her shirt and stepping closer.

I shied away again. "I don't want to hurt you."

"You won't." She caught my hand and held it. "I'll be fine. It's like a little sunburn." She kept her tone light, but I could see in her eyes that she was trying to mask the pain.

"You need a medic," I said frantically. The lantern rocked in my hand as I turned quickly toward the door. There had to be something

I could do to help her, even if it was never enough to atone for the damage I'd done.

"No, I'm all right." Mare caught my arm to stop me. "The attendant told us not to leave. She'll be back any moment with Laurenna."

As if on cue, a knock sounded at the door.

"Permission to enter?" the attendant's voice said tentatively from the hall.

Mare opened the door while I retreated and tried to gather my shattered nerves. Beside the building attendant stood a tall, middle-aged woman. The attendant's lantern cast a cold glow on the sharp angles of her nose and jaw. Ash-brown hair streaked with gray hung straight to just above her shoulders, and her dark eyes were already scrutinizing us. Sensible gray trousers and a pale blue shirt that crisscrossed in the front hugged her lean frame, her outfit surprising me with its simplicity. Her expression was sharp and unreadable, while the attendant looked as though she were about to have a nervous episode of some kind.

"Please be welcome," Mare said, then introduced us both and gestured for them to enter.

The attendant, seeming to remember that she should introduce Laurenna, said, "I present to you Guardian Laurenna, born of Kartasha, final apprentice of legendary Guardian Nalon, and most powerful water user of the—"

"Enough." Laurenna cut off the attendant and strode into the room, stepping over to examine one of the shattered lights.

To my surprise, a girl about twelve or thirteen years old followed on Laurenna's heels, wearing a mischievous expression that suggested she was nothing but trouble. In spite of her rounder face, curly hair, and darker complexion, there was no mistaking that the girl's eyes and high cheekbones mirrored Laurenna's. A pendant shaped like a seven-pointed star glittered around her neck.

"I'm Fadeyka," she said, and extended her hand to Mare the way I'd seen many Zumordans greet each other.

Mare introduced herself.

"Oh, are you the princess from Mynaria?" Fadeyka's expression grew abruptly cunning. "Do you know how to ride?"

"Faye, that's enough," Laurenna said, glancing back at her daughter.

Fadeyka pouted, then rolled her eyes once Laurenna's back was turned.

"It appears there was a magical surge in the building that destabilized the enchanted lights. And it seems to have originated in this room." She looked curiously at me and came a few paces closer. "May I touch your hand?" she asked.

"Of course, my lady," I said, even as a tingle of fear crept down the back of my neck.

Laurenna gently took my hand the way she might have if she'd been planning to raise it to her lips for a kiss, but instead pressed her thumb on my knuckles. Sharp tingles raced through my arm, as if my magic were being tugged toward my fingertips.

"Oh!" I gasped, pulling away and taking a step back. My arm still smarted, and I felt telltale warmth blooming in my palm. I clenched my fist tightly and forced the magic away.

"Well," Laurenna said, her gaze frightfully keen. "That question is answered. Lia, you are much more than you seem."

Goose bumps rose on my skin. I stared at the floor, wishing I could disappear and frightened of what she'd sensed.

"How can you tell that by touching her?" Mare asked, her expression frightened.

"Some of us have strong Sight, and some have other ways of seeing magic," Laurenna said. "My ability to sense magic works best when I am close enough to feel the movement of a person's blood, and it is not bound by the limitations of Sight."

Mare's expression clearly showed that she was sorry to have asked. Guilt washed over me again. All this was my fault. I'd broken things. I'd scared Mare. I'd brought Laurenna to us under all the wrong circumstances.

"I'll need to question your maidservant," Laurenna said to Mare.

A chill ran through me.

"Of course," Mare agreed, casting a worried look at me.

"The mage lights are easy enough to replace, but we need to confirm that the power in this area is stable and that the source is identified," Laurenna said. "Lia, you'll come with me. And Princess Amaranthine, you are welcome to rest in my study while we clean up and investigate further."

"Thank you, Guardian," Mare said.

"Take Princess Amaranthine to the study." Laurenna gestured to the building attendant, who looked relieved to have a task and somewhere else to be. "Fadeyka, you go with them."

The girl looked back and forth between us and her mother, seemingly torn between wanting to know more about what the magical problem in the building was and wanting to pepper Mare with more questions about horses and gods knew what else.

My fear rose at the thought of being separated from Mare. I hadn't even had a chance to attend to her injury, and I didn't know what kind of coercion techniques they might use on me to get me to talk about my history and my magic.

For Mare's sake, all I could do was try to stay strong and make sure she came out of this looking better than I did.

NINE

✦ *Amaranthine*

I FOLLOWED THE ATTENDANT THROUGH SEVERAL PAS-
sages and across a second-story outdoor bridge into an adjacent
building. With every step, the handprint on my waist burned, but I
didn't dare say anything. Honestly, I didn't even want to think about
it. I couldn't bear the idea of Denna feeling guilty over accidentally
hurting me any more than I could hide how much it frightened me
that she had. Eventually we arrived at a room lined from floor
to ceiling with books, most of which seemed to be about natural
history and agriculture. Fadeyka immediately darted over to the
shelves.

"Please stay here until we return for you," the building attendant said.

"We will," I reassured her, and she dashed off to her next task,
which was probably to continue hovering around Laurenna.

I turned to find somewhere to sit, only to see Fadeyka clinging precariously to a bookshelf several feet above the floor.

"Six Hells, what are you doing?" Letting a guardian's daughter fall and crack her head open didn't seem likely to help me earn good standing at the Winter Court. I dashed over to where Fadeyka was and held up my arms to catch her. The pain in my side flared in protest, and I bit back a cry. She ignored my question, continuing to rummage around behind the books, the tip of her tongue sticking out in concentration.

"Got them," she finally said. "Here, catch." She tossed a bag down to me that I barely managed to grab before it hit the floor. Seconds later she had both feet on the ground and took it back.

"What is that?" I asked, my heart rate finally slowing now that she was safely back on the ground.

"Cookies," she said matter-of-factly. "The court cook gave them to me. Want one?" She pulled out an oddly shaped cookie that looked more like a narrow piece of toast filled with nuts and shoved it into her mouth. The crunching was loud enough to spook a dead horse back to life.

"All right," I said, taking the cookie she offered and holding it to my nose to sniff. It had a sharp smell, both earthy and herbal.

"It's anise," Fadeyka explained around a mouthful of cookie, then shoved a second one into her mouth before she'd finished swallowing the last of the first.

I bit into it, surprised when it didn't just crunch but actually shattered between my teeth. It was like no cookie I'd ever tasted— nuttier, more brittle, and ending with a burst of flavor that stopped me cold. I gagged.

"What in the Sixth Hell is that horrific taste?" I asked.

"Maybe the anise?" Fadeyka continued to crunch happily.

"It . . . it tastes like death. Like sadness. Like something that in any other form would have the texture of a deceased bat." I wanted to spit the rest of the cookie into one of the ornamental pots and scrape my tongue.

Fadeyka giggled. "More for me!" She held out her hand for the rest of my cookie.

"Gods. I wouldn't even feed that to my horse," I said. At least the flavor had been foul enough to provide a temporary distraction from my burning side.

Fadeyka stopped chewing abruptly. "Does that Mynarian war steed in the visitors' stables belong to you?"

"Yes. That's Flicker," I said, still grimacing over the foul taste of Fadeyka's "cookie."

Fadeyka's eyes got big as saucers. "Can you teach me how to ride like a Mynarian warrior?" she asked. "Mother hasn't let me learn. She says riding's only useful in southern Zumorda, and she expects me to go to Corovja for my studies when I'm older."

"Maybe it's not that useful in Corovja, but what if you want to go somewhere else?" I asked.

"Exactly!" Fadeyka bounced on her toes. "I need to know how to do everything. I want to learn to ride." She said it with the confidence of someone who hadn't yet found many things she couldn't do.

Nostalgia swept through me. I used to give riding lessons back in Mynaria. If not for that, Denna and I never would have become friends, or lovers.

"Will your mother allow it?" I asked.

Fadeyka snorted. "She doesn't care what I do as long as I do well at my studies."

"And do you do well at your studies?" I asked.

"Obviously," she said, with a roll of her eyes, then launched into a monologue about some book she was currently reading as part of her geography lessons. It involved a bunch of incomprehensible nonsense about alpine farming techniques that made my eyes cross almost immediately. I slumped into a chair and let Fadeyka continue to talk my ear off. She didn't require much prompting—just the occasional nod or grunt of acknowledgment.

". . . it's just maddening that I'm not even allowed to study magic yet beyond the basics, and now it's pointless to ask for anything else because Mother is so grumpy thanks to Alek showing up." Fadeyka paused to crunch on another cookie.

I sat up straighter. "I heard your mother and Alek don't get along. Do you know why?" I could think of plenty of reasons not to like Alek, but there seemed to be some particularly bitter history between him and Laurenna that I might be able to find a use for—especially if it was somehow tied to why the Sonnenbornes had been so friendly to him.

"Well, according to my mother, he was too weak to make the hard choices required to finish guardian training," Fadeyka said.

"As in, his magic was too weak?" I asked.

"No, the opposite." Fadeyka set down the cookie bag and flopped onto a nearby chaise, putting her boots up on the arm in a way I had a feeling her mother wouldn't like. "Alek's weakness was that as an apprentice, he initially refused to use his gift on behalf of his kingdom when his mentor asked him to. Not long after that, he broke his apprenticeship. No one does that, especially not someone who's training to be a guardian."

"When did this happen?" I asked.

"Years ago." Fadeyka flung her arm dramatically. "It was during a battle in the west. My mother and Alek were there with Nalon, the guardian they were apprenticed to. Nalon asked them to use their powers to help with the battle, but Alek didn't like Nalon's plan. He felt it wasn't going to be a fair fight for the enemy."

"Moral superiority and deciding his way is the only way— sounds about right," I said.

"But if they didn't act, it would've hurt the farmers farther south. So my mother convinced him to use his powers. They won the battle, but Alek felt deceived. So he turned his back on his training, my mother, and everything else. I think he spent a few years working as a hiresword at Misty Plains near the Sonnenborne border after that."

"So that's how he got his title." I'd wondered about that ever since he'd said that he'd grown up in the slums.

Fadeyka nodded. "The people of the Misty Plains bestowed the title on him for his acts of heroism in protecting them from bandits or something."

"And your mother never forgave him for leaving?"

"Never," Fadeyka said. "If you see me at the salle training with him, don't tell her," she added furtively.

I almost laughed. "Why would you want to train with someone your mother hates?"

"He's one of the best swordsmen in the kingdom." She shrugged. "It would be foolish to turn down the opportunity to learn from someone who is the best at something."

"Gods, you and Den—" I barely stopped myself from saying Denna's name and making a comparison that would have revealed her identity.

"Who?" Fadeyka asked.

"A friend back home who was a scholar," I said hastily. "She would have appreciated your dedication to learning from the best."

"Sensible." Fadeyka shook the cookie bag, seemingly disappointed by its dwindling contents.

When the doorknob turned moments later, Fadeyka's cookies mysteriously vanished into some crevice of the chaise or gods knew where else. Laurenna entered the study, alone.

"Where's Lia?" I asked, immediately alarmed.

"Having some tea and still in questioning," Laurenna reassured me. "She'll be escorted back to your room as soon as she's done. Did Fadeyka mind her manners?"

Fadeyka smiled widely, her dark eyes innocent and the cookies nowhere to be seen.

"Yes, of course," I said.

"Well, it appears we found the source of the problem with the lights," Laurenna said. "Your handmaiden seems to have a rather volatile gift."

"I apologize for the damage," I said, cringing. "If there's anything I can do to repay you for the trouble—"

Laurenna waved me off, stepping closer. "The damage was minor, all things considered. I admit I expected a bit of trouble from a Mynarian envoy, but I didn't expect her to be accompanied by a rogue magic user."

"I was hoping to talk to you about her tomorrow," I said. I'd more urgently been thinking about asking if I could get some medical attention for my burn but now knew it would be the wrong move. I couldn't let Laurenna see Denna as a danger—only as someone who needed help.

"Perhaps now is a better time," Laurenna said, taking a seat. "Tell me about Lia."

"She's my maidservant," I said. "Having grown up outside Zumorda, she hasn't had any training for her Affinity, which we discovered earlier this year. When my brother, King Thandilimon of Mynaria, sent me here as an envoy, I chose Lia to accompany me in hopes of getting her the sanctuary and training she so desperately needs."

"That was generous of you," Laurenna said, eyebrows raised.

Fadeyka looked at me with confusion. "If she's the magic user, why are you the envoy?"

"Things are different in Mynaria," I said carefully.

"But power is inarguable," Fadeyka said, not comprehending.

"That definitely seems to be the case here in Zumorda," I said.

"Your people have never been fond of magic users," Laurenna said to me. "What makes you different?"

"You're right that many of my people are suspicious of magic," I admitted. "But I think it's time for that to change. We have nothing to lose by learning to work together, and potentially everything to gain." I was grateful for having rehearsed my response to this predictable question. The words came out easily in spite of the uncertainty churning in my stomach. It was hard to still believe what I was saying after everything that had happened since we crossed the border.

"In what way?" Laurenna stared at me intently.

"On our way here, the city of Duvey was attacked by Sonnenborne skirmishers," I told her. "The soldiers there were at a disadvantage because they had no cavalry. If there'd been a regiment of Mynarian cavalry there, the battle could have been ended much sooner and with less loss. Moreover, Sonnenborne has made it clear through their actions over the past year that they want Zumordans and Mynarians to fight each other. I'm here in hopes of preventing that and making sure we work together to uncover their master plan."

"You think the Sonnenbornes have a master plan?" Laurenna said, seemingly amused by this idea. "They don't have a ruler, or even a government."

"I know it seems like they're just a bunch of disorganized tribes." I soldiered on. "But many of them banded together and tried to start a war between Mynaria and Zumorda by killing members of my family—the royal family—and framing Zumorda." I hoped Alek's theory hadn't made it to Laurenna by way of Zhari yet.

Laurenna listened and Fadeyka sat riveted as I told the story of my father's and uncle's assassinations and how we'd nearly made the mistake of retaliating against the wrong kingdom.

"This Lord Kriantz you mention—his ring interests me. Most enchanted objects originated in Zumorda, and those of us who have them are often reluctant to part with them." Laurenna's eyes flicked to Fadeyka, whose hand closed around her pendant. A little shiver of unease traveled down my neck at the thought that the necklace might be something as dangerous as Kriantz's ring.

"My brother has the ring," I said. "There's a fringe group of magic users in Mynaria who might be able to help him unravel its secrets, but I'm sure they have nowhere near the expertise Zumordans do." Maybe flattery would get me where straightforwardness hadn't.

"Well, regardless of what's in the past, we are going to have to decide what to do with Lia," Laurenna said. "As for your rooms, conventional lanterns will be provided for now. I'm afraid it may be a bit cold. The enchantment maintaining the heated floors also blew out. I don't want it reenchanted until we've confirmed the nature of the failure, but servants are stoking up the hearths in the meantime."

"What do you mean by 'what to do' with Lia?" I asked hesitantly. "We hoped to find her training—"

"We'll talk about it more tomorrow," Laurenna said. "Zhari is one of the most powerful magic users in Zumorda. Her insight will be helpful."

"And what of the queen?" I asked. The queen was the one I needed to win over—at least to get permission to send in a more formal ambassadorial entourage. "Will she be present tomorrow? We traveled here with Sir Alek, who has a message of his own from Duvey."

Out of the corner of my eye, I caught Fadeyka making a wide-eyed face and a neck-slicing motion. But it was too late—I'd already said Alek's name. Laurenna no doubt knew that he was in Kartasha, but bringing him up had apparently been a mistake.

"Wymund always did have a tendency to choose interesting messengers," Laurenna said, her expression darkening. "I'll see that the queen is also notified of tonight's events. I imagine she'll want to join us tomorrow, and Lia will also be expected to attend. The page outside the door will escort you back to your rooms." Laurenna stood up, and Fadeyka followed suit. Clearly the conversation was over.

"Good night, Mare. I'll look for you at the stables!" Fadeyka called as her mother dragged her off down the hallway. I had a feeling she wasn't going to let up about the riding lessons.

I trudged after the page, feeling defeated by the day, wishing that I felt the future held more hope. Tomorrow we would see what we could do to find a mentor for Denna. Her path was laid out, but I couldn't help feeling as if mine was uncertain. If not for her powers, we never would have met Laurenna tonight and I wouldn't have had the chance to talk to her in a less formal setting. We never would have ended up getting to meet the queen so soon after arriving in Kartasha. Even as a servant, Denna was the driving force behind every bit of progress we'd made since arriving in Zumorda.

Where did that leave me?

TEN 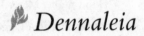 *Dennaleia*

I EXPECTED LAURENNA'S QUESTIONING TO BEGIN AS she led me out of the merchants' hall, but instead we walked in eerie silence that only served to increase my anxiety. As soon as we set foot in the courtyard, a huge black raven swept silently from the dark sky and transformed into a person as she landed in front of us. Her hair was as dark as the raven's wings.

"The captain of the Nightswifts will escort you to your questioning," Laurenna said, and handed me over to the woman, who didn't even bother giving me her name before turning on her heel to lead me across the courtyard. Her height made her strides nearly twice as long as mine, and I had to hurry to keep up.

"Where are we going?" I asked timidly.

"The library," the woman answered in a clipped tone.

Normally I might have been thrilled to visit a foreign library, but my fears were much too consuming. Who was going to be questioning me? What did they want to know? How was I going to balance truth and lies to keep to a story that made sense leading up to where I found myself now?

Soon we entered a two-story building adjacent to the tower at the center of the Winter Court. Intricate carvings of plants and animals decorated the doors, which swung open on silent hinges. My escort seemed to know her way, weaving between the shelves with a thoughtless grace that made me feel clumsy by comparison. Unlike those of Havemont and Mynaria, the Kartashan library was arranged like a maze instead of in tidy rows. Cozy sections for every kind of book connected to each other through narrow walkways with no order I could discern.

An open doorframe in the back led into a small alcove. A reading desk took up the center of the room, and a few cushioned chairs were tucked around the outside. A woman was waiting in one, and she stood up when we entered the room, her white cloak pristine as fresh snow. Silvery-gray hair twisted back from her temples to an ornate knot on one side. Her lips, painted bloodred, quirked into something almost like a smile. In spite of her relatively simple clothing, it was abundantly clear that she was of high rank.

"Thank you, Karina—you may take your leave," the woman said in Zumordan. "Please make sure the contingent of Swifts attending tomorrow's meeting with Count Ulak are among the best. He's likely to resist what's in store for him." Her voice was cool and lovely as a winter sunset.

The raven-haired woman bowed and left the library as quickly as she'd appeared from the night sky.

"What's your name, girl?" the woman in white asked me.

"Lia, my lady." I curtsied deeply, figuring it could not hurt to be gratuitous with my respect, since I was unsure of the woman's rank or role.

The woman smiled, as if privy to a secret, and I immediately got the sense it would be unwise to say anything else before she spoke. She came a few steps closer, moving with catlike grace.

"You truly don't know who I am, do you?" She stood close enough now that she was looking down at me. She was much older than I would have thought from how she carried herself, with spiderwebs of lines crisscrossing her face.

I shook my head, even as realization started to dawn.

"My name is Invasya."

I went cold and then hot in the space of a heartbeat. The woman standing before me was the queen of Zumorda. While at one time I might have felt fully at ease in the presence of another royal, now I felt only terror—that my identity would be discovered, or that I'd get myself killed for making a misstep no servant would ever be foolish enough to take.

"Apologies, Your Majesty." I curtsied again deferentially, half wondering if I ought to be on my knees instead. Her presence was so intimidating, it would have felt perfectly natural, even to someone like me, who had been royal from the day I was born.

"Don't apologize. Sit." She pointed to one of the chairs in the corner of the room.

I obeyed her, sitting gingerly on the overstuffed chair. She folded herself into the one she'd been seated in before. A flick of her hand made a servant materialize as if from nowhere. The girl carried in a tea tray and set it down between us, silently fixing each of us a cup and vanishing as quickly as she'd come.

The queen picked up her cup and considered me with her piercing blue eyes. "Drink," she ordered, and sipped from her own cup.

I took mine, keeping my eyes downcast. The tea had the verdant smell of fresh mint, familiar and soothing. I took a sip. Seconds later, a sensation hit me like ice running through my veins. Trembling took over my body so powerfully that I could barely speak. My teacup rattled on its saucer, and I barely managed to keep hold of it.

"What . . . what's happening?" I said, frightened by the loss of physical control.

The queen watched, a half smile on her face. "It's all right. Take another sip, dear. The tea is purging the last of the peaceroot from your body."

I tried to do as she said, barely able to bring the cup to my lips. When I swallowed, another flood of ice ran through me, but then the trembling began to subside. Even my headache receded until it was no more than the dull ache I sometimes had after a long day of reading. Without the haze of the peaceroot, everything felt sharpened—including my fear.

"May I ask what is in the tea, Your Majesty?" I asked.

"It's mint tea with a drop of verium added," the queen said. When my face did not reveal any understanding, she added, "A purification tincture."

"Of course, Your Majesty," I said, clutching my cup tightly to still the unsteadiness of my hands.

"You're much more interesting to look at now," the queen said, tilting her head.

"What do you mean?" I asked, frightened of what exactly she could see.

"Your Affinity," she said, and my magic stirred softly as if to answer her. I felt it all now—every tingle prickling my skin, every swirl of my powers as they shifted restlessly inside me. I tried to quell them, but under the queen's gaze I found it impossible.

"Stop fighting yourself," the queen said.

"I just don't want to hurt anyone," I said, my voice small and choked. But it was too late. I had already hurt the person I cared about most.

"Whether or not you hurt anyone, people will come looking for you soon. You can't blow up a section of a major trade road and expect people not to notice. Something like that star fall hasn't been seen since before my rule." She paused, smiling to herself as though amused by a private joke.

I swallowed hard. How did she know about that, much less that I'd been responsible? I opened my mouth to deny it and then thought better of it. If she knew what had happened, lying wasn't likely to do anything but make me look like a fool or a criminal.

"Wise girl," she said, as though she'd read my thoughts. Perhaps she had. "Do you know why I'm here in Kartasha?"

"It was mentioned that you've been recruiting a special group of trainees," I said.

"That's right," she said. "Only the best—the most powerful magic users, who will be the next generation of leaders in Zumorda and beyond. They'll go on to become guardians, spies, the heads of elite magic schools, or perhaps even my top advisers. But there is a problem I've been investigating as well. Young people with

Affinities have been disappearing in unusual numbers, especially from this region. I find that suspicious, especially given that it's a recruiting year." She took another sip of her own tea, waiting for my response.

Fear rose in me as I remembered the boy who had been abducted in front of us in Duvey, and my magic swiftly rose with the emotions. A few sparks dripped from the fingertips of my left hand before I could hold them back.

"Let's not do that," she said. With a flick of her fingers, the sparks went out, and the smolder of my magic receded into the background.

I blinked rapidly, surprised by the sudden peace of my magic fading. "I'm sorry, Your Majesty—I didn't mean—"

The queen held up a hand to silence me. "Don't apologize for what you are. Because I can See that is the very least of what you can do."

"Yes, Your Majesty." I looked down at the floor. She was right, but I'd spent a lifetime trying to hold back my powers, to keep my Affinity as small and polite as I was. I had needed to do that to make sure it wouldn't ruin the plans for my future—and then it had anyway. Could I possibly rebuild my life around a new paradigm in which my magic wasn't the enemy?

"Kartasha is not a particularly safe place for someone of your abilities—not with young magic users vanishing and plenty of powerful people who would be eager to use you as a pawn." The queen held out her hand, and a flame bloomed to life in her palm. "As you can see, our gifts are similar. Perhaps you'd be interested in training with me."

My breath caught in my throat. Was she offering what I thought she was?

"The rest of my trainees have already been selected, but there is room for one more," the queen said. "Would you like to join them? I depart for Corovja in two days' time."

"I'm not Zumordan, Your Majesty," I said softly. It felt wrong to sign on for a future in a kingdom that wasn't my own, even if it would be the finest training available anywhere. But my not being Zumordan wasn't the whole truth. My magic had indeed come from Zumordan blood that I hadn't known about until just before I'd left Mynaria. My mother's parentage was the best-kept secret in Havemont—her mother's Zumordan maidservant had served as a surrogate to bear her. The queen saw through everything else I'd been hiding. Perhaps she could see that, too.

The queen continued on as if I hadn't spoken at all. "Since you're new to Zumorda, you may not know that magic users generally apprentice to another with their same Affinity. But for those who are unusually strong, it pays to learn about multiple kinds of gifts and how to defend oneself from them. I used to have my guardians choose apprentices on their own, but now I prefer to have the elites train in Corovja first, especially those who hope to serve as future guardians. It exposes them to more kinds of magic and motivates them to compete for the best apprenticeships. Most important, it gives me a chance to build personal relationships with those tasked with defending my kingdom."

"That seems very wise, Your Majesty," I said.

She smiled. "Of course it is. I've had a long time to learn what works and what doesn't in ruling this kingdom."

I tried to do some mental math to figure out how long she'd ruled here, but I had no idea. In Havemont, Zumordan history was taught only as it related to that of my kingdom or Mynaria. Zumorda was neither ally nor foe—simply a place to avoid unless you were a magic user. Either way, I remembered no reference in my studies to any ruler of Zumorda besides the queen. She had to be older than any of my grandparents had been when they passed.

"My reign has been long and prosperous," the queen said. "Making sure I have the best advisers and the strongest guardians watching over my cities and protecting my kingdom will ensure that my legacy continues even if I one day step down as monarch. It's especially important now with the unrest that seems to be surrounding us on all sides."

"Isn't the throne usually taken in combat?" I asked tentatively. Zumordan tradition didn't seem to suggest any room for stepping down from the throne—only for defeat at someone else's hands.

"Yes," the queen said. "But perhaps we should consider modernizing Zumorda and leaving the bloody rituals of our past behind."

Uncertainty gripped me. Having trained most of my life to be a ruler, I respected the idea that the queen was trying to create a situation that would involve less bloodshed, but I feared the way others would react. One didn't go against hundreds of years of tradition and expect people to agree without question.

"If you choose to accept my offer, most of your time would be spent training under Saia, the guardian of Corovja, and Brynan, her second-in-command. Neither of them has fire Affinities, so the remainder of your training would be with me."

A battle warred in my heart. She was offering me the opportunity of a lifetime, but I didn't know how that would figure in with what Mare needed to accomplish.

"I'm not Zumordan," I repeated. "I have no manifest."

"That doesn't mean you can't take one if you wish," she said. "I came to my manifest late—at seventeen winters."

My skin crawled, even though my curiosity was piqued. As much as I wanted to learn how to master my magic, taking the form of an animal wasn't something I'd considered. I tried to imagine how my family would react, how Mare might see me differently. All I could picture was horror in their eyes. I drew on my diplomacy skills and did my best to respond in a way that precluded any promises.

"Your Majesty, this is a great honor," I said. "I'll have to discuss it with my mistress." It had occurred to me that as improbable as the queen's offer was, it might be an opportunity to get Mare closer to the queen and accomplish what she needed to. I didn't want to destroy the hope of that if it was a possibility.

The queen's eyes flashed. "With a gift like yours, you are your own mistress, Lia. Never let anyone tell you otherwise."

"Yes, Your Majesty." Outwardly, I agreed, but inside, I felt only turmoil and resentment. I'd never been in charge of my own fate, and somehow, even now, it didn't feel like that had changed. If it wasn't people determining what I was to do with my life, it was my magic.

"With your consent, until you make your decision, I can shield you from the casual Sight of other magic users. It won't stop you from being able to access your magic—just prevent your unshielded powers from being a beacon to every other magic user in southern

Zumorda. We wouldn't want anyone with bad intentions to get their hands on you."

I didn't have to think about my answer to that. "That would be most kind and generous of you, Your Majesty."

A gentle glow emanated from her fingertips. A tingle passed over me as she waved her hand in my direction. "You are now under my protection. I expect your response in two days' time. You're dismissed."

"Thank you, Your Majesty," I said, then fled the library.

The chilly air was a balm after the gauntlet of emotions she'd led me through. My gift swirled inside me, alive once again. Part of me hated how good it felt, because life had been easier when I didn't have my magic to worry about. Even Mare had seemed more at ease around me while I was on the peaceroot, more comfortable and secure that it was tamed. I'd loved her ease around me during that time, but I'd sometimes silently resented that my misery led to her comfort. Before we'd left Mynaria, she'd accepted my magic as part of me, said it didn't change anything between us, but that was before the star fall, before I'd rained death down on Kriantz, before I'd killed and injured so many others in Duvey. How could I be surprised that there was sometimes fear in her eyes when she looked at me? What was I supposed to tell her? I had too many questions and no answers, and only two days to decide what to do.

If I accepted the queen's offer, perhaps we could both go to Corovja. Especially with the ongoing border attacks and people like me disappearing here, Corovja felt like a safe choice. But Mare hadn't even met with Laurenna and Zhari yet. Politically, she was still in new territory on a very uncertain path. Neither she nor her kingdom could afford for us to make decisions in haste. I felt hopelessly trapped in the midst of it all.

When I got back to the room, Mare was already there waiting for me. A merry fire burned in the hearth, filling the room with gentle light.

"Wine?" she asked, gesturing to an empty glass beside the half-full one she'd poured for herself.

"Wine would be good," I said, crossing the room and sitting down on the chaise.

Mare joined me there, handing me the glass I'd requested. The liquid was a translucent garnet red, much lighter bodied than the wines I'd had back home.

"How did your questioning with Laurenna go?" she asked.

"It wasn't Laurenna," I said, taking a deep breath and trying to gather my jangling nerves to tell her what had happened. "Outside she handed me off to the captain of the Nightswifts."

"Who are they?" Mare asked.

"The queen's personal guards, apparently," I said. "Then I was dosed with verium, a tincture to purge the peaceroot from my body."

Mare's posture stiffened, and any hopes I'd had that I could tell her the rest of what had happened died away.

"Your magic is back? Your full powers? Did they do anything else to get them under control?" she asked, her voice rising.

I shook my head, feeling more and more crushed by the fear in her expression. My magic stirred along with my worries, tingling down my arms in the familiar way it often had back in Mynaria.

"What did you tell them?"

"The same lies and truths we've told everyone else," I said.

"There was nothing more I could say. You saw what happened when Laurenna touched me. She knows more than I do. Everyone does. I don't know anything, really. I hate it."

"You're not alone," Mare said. "It seems we both have a lot of learning to do. But it's going to need to happen fast." She stared out the window with a brooding expression on her face.

I wanted to lean over and kiss her. I wanted her arms around me, and her voice murmuring in my ear that everything would be all right. But the expression on her face and the way she'd put a little distance between us told me what I needed to know. My magic frightened her, and now that it was back in full force, she didn't trust me.

I couldn't tell her about the queen's offer tonight. It would only confuse her objectives for the meeting with Laurenna, Zhari, and the queen tomorrow. I'd have to handle it on my own and hope the next two days provided some clarity about what to do.

The next morning, I jolted awake with my heart racing and my mouth parched. The room was still nearly dark, with only the faintest hint of silvery light peeking in between the curtains. In my dream, Mare had been drowning in a river. I kept reaching into the water to save her, but she slipped out of my grasp over and over again. Everywhere I touched, her skin burned and blistered, turning black and peeling away to reveal the bone and sinew underneath. The current swept away bits and pieces of her, and the harder I held on, the more she fell apart.

Even once the reality of the waking world had set in, I couldn't let go of the consuming guilt. The damage was already done. I'd hurt her without meaning to. How could I ever trust myself again?

Mare lay on the bed, her breathing deep and even. It took several minutes of watching her to reassure myself that she was all right. There was no way I was going back to sleep after that nightmare. Guilt followed me like a lost dog, staying with me as I used the washroom and then returned to the bedroom. I peeked outside the curtains and saw only a few servants crossing the courtyard at this early hour. However, I had a feeling I knew of one other person who would already be up and might be able to help me.

I pulled on my cloak and walked down the hall, then knocked softly on Alek's door. He opened it quickly, as if he'd been standing on the other side waiting for me. Unsurprisingly, he was already dressed in full leathers and had packs slung over both shoulders. The room behind him was immaculate.

"What do you want?" he asked.

"To talk—just for a moment." I swallowed hard, suddenly nervous. Maybe it was foolish to ask him for help. "Were you on your way out? I can come back later."

"I'm moving to Wymund's quarters in the court proper," he said.

"I could help you carry your things," I said hastily, eager to offer some help in exchange for the enormous favor I was about to ask.

"If it's all the same to you." He shrugged, handing me the smaller of his two packs. "We walk, you talk."

I followed him down the stairs and into the crisp morning air. The dry cold bit at my cheeks and crept under my cloak, making me wish I'd put on another layer.

"The peaceroot is gone," I said, dispensing with formalities.

Alek gave me a startled look. "But you still don't—" His eyes narrowed. "Wait. Something is different."

"The queen gave me a temporary shield," I said, understanding that his Sight wasn't allowing him to see my powers. She'd blocked them somehow.

His gaze grew sharper. "The queen?"

I nodded. "Look, I need to find a mentor, and quickly. I hoped you might help—if there was someone here who trained you, or another person they might know who would be willing to take me on. The queen's protection is temporary. She's leaving tomorrow." I needed other options. Unless Mare's meeting with the queen resulted in us heading to Corovja as well, I didn't know how I could accept the queen's offer. Being separated from Mare was unthinkable.

Alek frowned and walked faster, so I had to rush to keep up with him. "If the queen's laid a claim on you, I won't interfere with that."

"She hasn't," I said, though his words filled me with doubt. It had only been an offer, not a claim, hadn't it? "I just want to find the best person to learn from. Training with the queen comes with a lot of obligations to the kingdom—obligations I don't know if I can fulfill, since I'm foreign-born." I hoped appealing to his morality and loyalty to his kingdom might sway him to my side.

"There's Zhari's program. Try that. No better way to get connected in Kartasha," he said.

"That's something different from the queen's training program?" I asked tentatively.

"Zhari has a program meant to identify those of lesser means who have stronger magical gifts. Something similar existed when I was young—it's how I got out of the slums. Mynarians." He snorted. "I forget you know nothing."

"I'm not Mynarian." I wouldn't have admitted it, but he seemed to have particularly strong feelings about them that weren't helping me get what I needed. And in a way, it felt good to say something about myself that wasn't a lie.

He gave me a sharp look, though his feelings remained unreadable.

"I'm originally from Havemont," I explained.

He exhaled a long sigh. "That makes sense. And in that case, you should absolutely sign up for Zhari's program. Plenty of Havemontians come down for training in Zumorda. You wouldn't be the only one."

"Do you think they'd be able to find me a mentor quickly enough?" I asked, hopeful.

"The waiting lists can be long," Alek admitted, frowning. "And likely longer than usual right now—many of the young people who came here hoping to be signed on for the queen's training but didn't get in are signing up for Zhari's program instead."

"I'm not sure it can wait." I hated the worried tremor that crept into my voice.

"Neither am I," he said. "I suppose I'll have to see what I can do. I'll look into it this afternoon."

"Thank you," I said, relieved to have even a tiny shred of hope to hold on to.

I stopped by the medics' hall on the way back from Alek's new quarters and picked up some salve and bandages for Mare's burn. Her gratitude for the salve was almost too much to bear, as was seeing the scorched flesh when I helped her apply it.

In spite of knowing I had Alek's help, my stomach was still a tight ball of nerves by the time Mare and I were dressed to meet Laurenna, Zhari, and the queen. When we arrived at the base of the tower, Alek was waiting for us. He stood there with his arms crossed, frowning as always.

"What are you doing here?" Mare asked him.

"You told Laurenna about Duvey last night," he said tersely. "That's what I'm doing here."

Mare gave him a look of mistrust as the three of us followed a page into the tower. The bottom floor was a vast receiving room the size of a great hall, decorated with overwhelming detail. Gilded arches circled the room, with intricate plasterwork twining from those up to the ceiling, which displayed a fresco of a great white dragon. We followed the page up a narrow spiral staircase that curved along the edge of the room and went to the next floor. The second room was smaller, but no less fantastic. An arched window looked out over the courtyard we'd walked through to get here, and on the opposite wall a mirror of the same size and shape reflected everything back at us. A wide table, large enough to accommodate about ten people comfortably, sat at the center. Beyond that stood an adjacent door through which two servants entered the room to bring hot water and herbs for tea. As soon as the place settings were finished, a herald entered the room. I stayed two steps behind Mare, doing my best to appear inconsequential.

"I present Lady Laurenna, guardian of Kartasha; Grand Vizier

Zhari of Corovja; and Her Majesty Invasya, the dragon queen of Zumorda, Bearer of Flame and Ruler of Generations." The herald bowed and quickly took his leave.

Mare executed a deep curtsy, and I followed suit as the three women filed into the room with the queen in the lead. Her height was as impressive as I remembered; she even towered over Mare, who had several inches on me. Again she wore white, this time a dress that managed to flatter her elegant form in spite of being made up of dozens of fine layers. She favored me with an almost invisible nod that made me shiver with nerves. What if she said something about our conversation last night before I could tell Mare myself?

Laurenna stepped over to the table, the silky skirts of her pale gray dress swirling around her legs. Plunging necklines both in front and back revealed more skin than I would have expected to see at a morning tea. Zhari's simple robes, a darker gray, were a sharp contrast to both of the other women's garb in design if not in color. She was just as Mare had described, with a calming presence that seemed to balance the intensity of the other two women.

I glanced at Alek, whose mask seemed more thoroughly in place than ever. If he had any feelings about seeing Laurenna, they weren't showing.

"To Her Majesty Invasya, the dragon queen of Zumorda, Bearer of Flame and Ruler of Generations, I present Her Royal Highness Princess Amaranthine, ambassador from Mynaria; her maidservant, Lia; and Sir Alek of the Misty Plains," Laurenna said.

"Thank you, Laurenna," the queen said. Her voice was as smooth and sharp as it had been the night before, a sword that always followed the swiftest path to an enemy's heart.

We settled at the table and Laurenna gestured for the servants to begin their duties. Hot water was provided to each of us in individual pots, and then the servants came by with a selection of teas.

"I hear you made quite the entrance to court last night," the queen said to Mare. There was no trace of mockery in her tone, only a statement of fact.

"I apologize for any missteps I made," Mare said.

"It's easier to make good impressions when one isn't saddled with poor company," Laurenna said, shooting a humorless smile at Alek, who stiffened in his chair.

Everyone pretended to be quite interested in the steeping status of their tea in the awkward silence that followed.

"And it also seems last night there was a bit of a problem in the merchants' hall," the queen said, looking at Mare rather than me. I knew exactly what she was doing—she was checking to see how our explanations lined up and how much I'd told Mare. Worry flooded me, accompanied by regret that I hadn't told Mare about my conversation with the queen. I'd wanted to spare her the burden, but it seemed I might have not done her any favors.

"I apologize," Mare said. "It was an accident."

"It's so interesting that someone with an uncontrolled fire Affinity would show up here on the heels of several large-scale acts of magic along the trade road between here and Mynaria's crown city," Laurenna commented.

"The star fall in Mynaria was brought on by Lord Kriantz of Sonnenborne," Mare quickly said. "He betrayed my kingdom and tried to send us to war with Zumorda. Mynarians mostly seem to be of the opinion that he was punished by the gods."

Laurenna smiled just the slightest bit. "Ah, yes, you Mynarians are still gods worshippers. Much easier to attribute things to powers outside your control than to take command of what you can."

"We shouldn't be too hasty to judge them," Zhari said. "We can't expect people to be comfortable with things they don't understand."

"Hopefully we can start to change the hearts of those opposed to magic use," Mare said, her eyes flicking to me.

Laurenna shook her head. "Mynarians. I suppose with their exposure to magic largely being thanks to those like Alek, it's no surprise they're leery of it."

Everyone turned to look at Alek.

"You were there, too," he said through clenched teeth.

"Of course." She smiled. "Nalon wouldn't have left one of his apprentices behind. But I wasn't the one who crossed the border."

"Because you tricked me," Alek snapped back.

They stared at each other with overt hostility, the tension between them thick enough to cut.

Mare looked like she wanted to say something but knew better than to interject.

"The past is the past," the queen interrupted, giving both Laurenna and Alek sharp looks. "What interests me are the present and the future. Why did the king of Mynaria chose to send his only living relative on a diplomatic mission when the family is already so weakened?"

"It is a show of trust, Your Majesty," Mare said. "My brother is committed to opening positive lines of communication with Zumorda."

"It's a pity the Havemont princess died," Zhari said, shaking her head sadly as she removed the infuser from her tea and stirred in a spoonful of honey. "Mynaria would surely be more stable with a queen to share the duties of the throne."

I swallowed hard, preoccupying myself with my own tea and hoping the trembling in my hands didn't give me away.

"Perhaps," Mare said. "But that's why I'm here—in hopes of creating a more stable future for our kingdoms. With the threat of Sonnenborne looming, it's crucial that Zumorda and Mynaria help each other. The Sonnenbornes already tried once to turn us against each other—we can't let that happen again."

"What exactly does the Mynarian crown perceive the Sonnenborne threat to be?" the queen asked.

"From what we know, Lord Kriantz of Sonnenborne united several tribes under his banner, then came to Mynaria under the pretense of forming an alliance," Mare said. "What he was really doing was sowing mistrust and rumors to try to get us to attack Zumorda, to help him take land."

The queen laughed. "Attack Zumorda? Our counterattack would devastate them. King Thandilimon might as well usher in the Zumordan empire."

"There are some who wouldn't be opposed to that," Laurenna said.

Mare ignored their comments and continued on. "Kriantz tried to abduct me and then died in the star fall."

"So he was stopped in the end, and you shouldn't have anything else to worry about," the queen said.

"That's what we'd hoped, but the attacks on Duvey and Zephyr

Landing show that the Sonnenbornes' plans run much deeper than we originally thought," Mare said. "We saw them taking prisoners in Duvey." She looked to Alek, gesturing for him to take up the discussion.

"Many of our young people were missing after we drove off the Sonnenbornes," he said. "Scouts were sent to investigate, but on our way here we passed a band of them who had been killed."

Zhari frowned. "We've had some disappearances here as well, but no attacks. Our relationships with the Sonnenborne merchants who trade here are good. If the Duvey attackers you speak of came to Kartasha after burning the bridge, we haven't seen or heard from them."

"Is there any way to track them?" Mare asked.

"They're *vakos*. No magic. No manifests," Laurenna said. "It makes them a bit harder for us to trace by magic. Though you Mynarians are equally empty. There are just fewer of you here."

"We need to fortify Duvey and locate the Sonnenbornes who attacked us," Alek cut in. "Wymund assigned me to stay here until we determine the origin of the attacks and track down the missing children."

"The warriors we borrowed will be on their way back to Duvey in a few days' time. Perhaps they'll provide the additional fortification Guardian Wymund needs." Laurenna's voice dripped with condescension.

"That's putting us back at net zero," he said, his voice rising. "Don't punish the people in Duvey because you hate me."

"Don't forget who started this," Laurenna said. "You're the one who walked away when things got hard."

Alek stood up. "Your Majesty, Lady Zhari, thank you for the tea." He strode out of the room without looking at Laurenna or saying another word.

"Some things never change," Laurenna said, looking rather smug.

"You shouldn't bait him, Laurenna," Zhari said, sounding mildly amused in spite of her chiding words.

"He makes it too easy," Laurenna said. "And he deserves to be reminded that he chose himself over his kingdom."

"An unfortunate choice," the queen said, taking a sip of her tea.

"Your Highness, perhaps you could do me a favor," Laurenna said, turning her attention to Mare.

"What did you have in mind?" Mare looked dubious.

"Since Alek plans to stay here, I'd like someone to keep an eye on him and report back to me. There's probably nothing to be concerned about." Laurenna waved her hand dismissively. "But his history does concern me. With the time he spent near Sonnenborne, I suspect he knows more than he's letting on, and I don't trust that he'll make choices that are in the best interest of Kartasha or the kingdom."

"That assumes we'll be staying here for the time being," Mare said. "Would it not be wise to consider accompanying the queen to Corovja to continue discussions about a potential alliance?"

Inwardly, I winced. Mare had overplayed her hand. It would have been better to try to shape the conversation to let the queen make that suggestion herself.

"There's no need for you to be in Corovja. Laurenna and Zhari are the first line of defense in the south, and I trust them and the

Winter Court to manage any issues affecting this part of the kingdom," the queen said. "Zhari will be here through the end of next year, likely taking on a guardian trainee from my elites after they complete their initial training. Whether Laurenna and Zhari choose to act upon your news or ally with your people will be at their discretion."

"Excuse me, Your Majesty, but what the Sonnenbornes did to my family poses a direct threat to Zumorda," Mare said. "They attacked a city in your kingdom. They took over one in mine. There is no confirmation that they've given up. The tribes that united to cause this problem are most likely the ones that attacked Duvey, which suggests they have a plan. It's only a matter of time before something worse happens."

"And if they try anything, they will die, just like everyone else who has ever challenged me during my rule," the queen said. Her voice was quiet but chilling. "Just last year a fool from this very town thought she would take my throne from me. Do you know what happened to her?"

Mare sat tall and defiant, refusing to back down, but I could see the uncertainty in her eyes.

"The coliseum in Corovja was painted with her blood," the queen said. "I tore out her heart with my teeth and swallowed it whole."

From anyone else, it would have sounded like an exaggeration. From the queen, it sounded like the unembellished truth. My throat constricted with anxiety. Though I had once been destined to be a queen myself, I couldn't imagine this kind of monarchy—one dictated by blood and death.

"I am not here to challenge you," Mare said.

The queen laughed. "That's fortunate for you." She turned back to me. "And I suppose it's fortunate for me that you aren't Zumordan, manifested, or trained. Yet."

Was she implying that I could be a threat to her? I felt sick at the thought. Killing was one way to earn a throne, but not one that held any appeal to me. What did pique my interest was the thought of apprenticing with Zhari. She seemed steady and kind, a strong contrast to the queen. What if I accepted the queen's offer and then made it my objective to come back to Zhari as an apprentice? That would put me back in Kartasha and back with Mare, with my powers under control. But even if that were what I wanted, I'd have to work with the queen in the meantime to make it happen.

"I would never challenge you, Your Highness," I said. Even though in another life I would not have had to defer to her, the words still would have held true.

"Respect is the sign of a wise subject," the queen said.

"And action is the sign of a wise ruler," Mare added. Her voice was calm, but the barb hit its mark.

The queen's expression darkened. "It is unwise to fight with fire when your opponent has an Affinity for it." She held out her hand, and a burst of flame erupted in her palm.

Mare and I both jumped.

"The Winter Court will be monitoring tariffs and trade with Sonnenborne as they always do. Sir Alek can do as he pleases, but Laurenna and Zhari are also responsible for following up on the Duvey attack to ensure that the threat is gone, though I expect Wymund has already fortified accordingly. I will return to Corovja tomorrow and leave these duties in their hands." She turned her ice-blue gaze on me. "Lia, I expect you'll make a choice about your training no later than tomorrow."

Mare shot me a confused look. I kept my expression neutral even as guilt and worry lurched in my chest. Time was running out to accept the queen's offer, but she'd told Mare to work with Laurenna and Zhari. They would be here in Kartasha. I felt torn between two worlds and two versions of myself—the queen I should have become and the magic-using maidservant I was now. I didn't exactly miss my old life, but I missed knowing my place and my purpose. I'd had the knowledge I needed and the research expertise to explore anything I needed to know more about. My life had been planned out in advance, from the schooling I would receive to the marriage I would make and the children I was supposed to bear for the throne of Mynaria.

Now all those dreams other people had for me were dust, and still, my fate didn't feel like it was in my own hands.

ELEVEN

✦ *Amaranthine*

I FUMED ALL THE WAY BACK TO THE MERCHANTS' HALL.

"I can't believe the nerve of that woman!" I said as soon as the door of our room closed behind us. "I tell her what happened and she behaves like it's inconsequential, shoving me off on her minions. Six be damned, I'm only one rank beneath her, and she treated me like I was nothing!"

"It seems like Kartasha is where things would normally be handled in the winter," Denna said, trying to soothe me.

"And why did she have such an attitude about your training? We get warned that young magic users are disappearing all over southern Zumorda, and then the queen tells you that you have to figure out what to do about your training in the next day, without even doing anything to help!" I flung my jacket down on the bed in frustration.

"Alek will help me," Denna said. "I asked him to reach out to some contacts in the city to see about a mentor for me. We can visit him tonight."

"It figures that Alek would be the only one making himself more useful than tits on a biscuit," I grumbled. "And now Laurenna wants me to keep an eye on him, which I suppose I'll be able to do since we're stuck here in Kartasha for the foreseeable future."

"Maybe these weren't the first steps we hoped for," Denna said, "but things will work out as they are meant to." She tugged me over to the chaise and down onto it.

"You are the only good thing I have," I said, drawing her closer. I breathed in, reveling in her warmth and the sweet smell of floral soap lingering on her skin.

She kissed me, and I immediately lost myself in the softness of her lips and the comfort of her arms. But as I let my fingers trace over the bare skin above the top of her bodice, she suddenly pulled away.

"What's wrong?" I asked.

"What if I hurt you again?" she asked, barely able to get the words out.

"You won't," I whispered, my voice gentle. "You won't." But the handprint on my side told another story, and we both knew it.

Denna and I finally managed to track Alek down after dinner. As much as I wasn't looking forward to spending more time in his company, Denna had a good reason to see him, and at least Laurenna might be pleased that I was doing what she'd asked as far as finding out more about what he'd been up to.

We headed back to the same residential court building where

the ill-fated party had been held, and my anxiety rose immediately upon crossing the threshold. I hoped we wouldn't run into Ikrie or anyone else who'd witnessed my humiliation. The polished granite of the foyer floors contained pearlescent flecks that reflected the illuminated globes suspended in ornate iron wall sconces. Dark beams arched across the high white ceilings, lending the interior a sense of formality that provided the perfect backdrop for the nobles passing through—one of whom happened to be Fadeyka. She was wandering through the room at an unhurried pace, using one hand to support the book she had her nose buried in and the other to pop candies into her mouth.

Her eyes lit up when she saw us, and she snapped her book shut as she rushed over.

"Where are you going?" she asked, crunching on a piece of hard candy.

"Guardian Wymund's quarters," I said. "We're looking for Alek."

"That way." She pointed to a hallway opposite the one the building attendant at the merchants' hall had told us to take. I sighed. If Fadeyka was anything like the noble brats I'd known growing up, she knew her way around every inch of the court and its buildings. That attendant was rubbish at giving directions.

"Can you show us the way?" I asked.

"Sure," she said, skipping off in the direction she'd pointed. "Just don't tell my mother!"

"Six Hells," I muttered. The last thing I needed was more trouble. I'd gotten in enough since arriving in Kartasha.

The girl led us up several flights of stairs at a speed that left both Denna and me out of breath.

"It's down here at the end of the hall." She knocked on the door without pausing to consult us, and a few moments later it swung open.

"Faye!" Alek said, clearly surprised to see her. He was out of his armor for once, wearing a simple shirt and trousers that somehow looked all wrong on him.

"Brought you something," Fadeyka said, and pointed back at us.

I braced for a snide remark to fly out of his mouth.

"Thanks, kid. Have you been practicing your parry?" he said. His voice was uncharacteristically kind. It figured he'd be nicer to Fadeyka than he ever was to me, but I couldn't really begrudge her that. She was just a child.

"Yes, sir!" she said.

"What do you two want?" he asked, regarding Denna neutrally and me with the usual hostility.

I gave Denna a look indicating that she should take the lead. If I started the conversation, it was bound to go poorly.

"We came by to see if you'd had any luck talking to anyone about an apprenticeship for me," Denna said.

"Come in," he said, waving us into his chambers. Fadeyka took that as an invitation to her, too, covertly passing Denna a lemon candy as we settled ourselves in Alek's receiving room. While the rooms were as well kept as any other noble's chambers, they lacked the gaudy opulence so pervasive at the Winter Court. Simple wool rugs in soothing tones of blue and gray covered unpolished stone, and the heavy wooden furniture looked as though it would have been at home back in the keep at Duvey.

"This morning Mare was told she'll need to stay here in Karta-sha to work with Laurenna and Zhari, so if there's someone local who could train me, that would be ideal." Denna folded her hands neatly in her lap, looking much too formal for the casual setting. I bumped my knee into hers, subtly startling her off-balance. She straightened her skirts, confused by my behavior.

Alek sighed, muttering something I couldn't quite make out that sounded like an insult directed at Laurenna. "You'll want wine for this conversation."

"I'll have some, too," Fadeyka said.

Alek gave her a withering look. "Your mother would kill me. Happily."

Fadeyka giggled. "She lets me have wine sometimes."

"Then you can have wine with her," Alek said. "Not me."

Fadeyka rolled her eyes and ate another candy instead, making a point of crunching on it loudly. Alek shook his head and poured me and Denna each a glass of wine, shortchanging me by a noticeable amount.

"If wine has to go with this news, it can't be good," I said.

"It's been difficult to get any answers." He spoke to Denna, ignoring me. "There's a respected teacher who runs a school in the south of town who initially she said she'd be happy to evaluate you, but I received a message just a short while ago saying she's full for the winter."

"She can't be the only option, though, right?" I asked.

Denna sat perched on the edge of the couch, her shoulders tense. "What did the others say?"

"The other three said no when I told them your name," Alek

said. "They already knew who you were."

"That doesn't make any sense." I didn't understand. How could anyone have heard of Denna when she was disguised as Lia the maid-servant? "Are you sure you've asked everyone who is an option?"

Alek looked at me like I was a smear of manure on his shoe. "I've only had one afternoon, and I don't have as many connections here as I used to."

"We completely understand," Denna said. "I so very much appreciate you asking them."

"I've also asked around at the salle, but most of the warriors training there have weaker gifts and were trained at home," Alek said. "A lot of people choose to master either the sword or magic, not both."

"I want to do both, too," Fadeyka declared.

"Well, you're on the right track, spending every afternoon in the salle." Alek took a sip of his wine. "Build the muscle memory now and it will still be there even if you have to devote several years to a magic apprenticeship."

I couldn't decide whether the patience and encouragement he had for Fadeyka were charming or annoying. At least that con-firmed where Alek was spending his time. I recalled him telling the Sonnenbornes he planned to spend his afternoons in the salle, and apparently he'd followed through on that. Perhaps I could catch all three of them there—if I could find some excuse to be there without it seeming suspicious.

"It's more interesting with you there," Fadeyka said. "You let me spar with people other than Kerrick."

"A fighter needs to know how to battle more than one opponent," Alek said.

"Why take up the sword at all if you have magic on your side?" I asked. I understood why Wymund had done it, given that his Affinity wasn't very strong. But even without knowing much about magic, I knew that bridge Alek had built to help us escape the Tamers was no small feat.

"Mother says he took up the sword in earnest after failing guardian training," Fadeyka helpfully supplied.

"Your mother only knows her side of the story and only tells the parts that suit her," Alek said sourly. "My father was a bladesmith in his youth. I took up sword work a long time before my magic or my manifest. And I quit guardian training. I didn't fail."

"Why?" Fadeyka asked.

"It's not important," Alek said. "Besides, Lia's training is the problem at hand."

"Is there anyone else at court who might have helpful connections to find Lia an apprenticeship?" I asked.

"With the queen's claim on her, I doubt it." Alek knocked back the last of his wine.

"Claim?" A jolt of alarm went through me. I looked at Denna, whose wide-eyed look of guilt and fear scared me even more. "What is he talking about?"

"There's something I didn't tell you about yesterday," Denna said, her voice shaky with nerves. "When Laurenna took me for questioning, the Nightswift delivered me to the queen."

"What?" I couldn't believe she hadn't told me. Finding out

thanks to an offhand comment from Alek felt like a slap. I thought we trusted each other.

"She offered me training—in Corovja," Denna said.

Fadeyka's eyes widened. "As one of the elites?"

Denna nodded. "I didn't say anything because I didn't want to burden you before the tea this morning. I talked to Alek right away, hoping he'd be able to find a local placement, or at least some options to choose from."

Now I was the one with a stomach turned inside out. If other people were refusing to take Denna as an apprentice, I had no doubt the queen was behind it. If she'd hand-selected Denna as one of her trainees, of course she'd remove all other options but for Denna to accompany her to Corovja.

"Were you even going to tell me?" I asked, standing up. I didn't want to have the rest of this conversation in Alek's presence. I wasn't honestly sure I wanted to have it at all.

"Of course, but there's been no time." Denna followed me to the door as I stormed out and down the stairs without even bidding farewell to Alek and Fadeyka.

"Let's talk about this back at the merchants' hall," I said, for once heeding the curious glances of servants and nobles alike as we passed back through the foyer of the building. It wouldn't look good to have a fight with my supposed handmaiden in the middle of one of the Winter Court's largest residences.

When we got back to the merchants' hall, Denna shut the door to our room so softly and in such contrast to my feelings that I almost wanted to walk back over to it and slam it. Instead I paced restlessly in front of the windows.

"You said there was no time to tell me, but we had last night. We had this afternoon." She had to understand how it felt that she'd withheld something so significant from me.

"Last night I hurt you." Her voice was small. "How could I tell you the queen wanted to take me to Corovja after that? What if you wanted me to go?"

"Of course I don't want you to go!" Had she gone mad? Even if I hadn't been wildly in love with her, there was no way I could survive the Winter Court without her. Today's meeting hadn't been a complete disaster, but it also hadn't been particularly productive as far as getting help taking back Zephyr Landing or starting talks about an alliance. Laurenna and Zhari barely seemed to believe me that Mynaria wasn't somehow to blame for Sonnenborne attacking Duvey.

"Then I'll find a way to get training here. Maybe after the queen leaves, after it's clear I'm not going, someone will be willing to take me." She took a tentative step closer.

"There are no guarantees of that," I said. "And what if they won't? You're going to just run around here with your magic out of control, blowing up buildings?"

Denna froze. "You know I wouldn't." Her voice was soft and wounded.

"How can you be sure?" So many things had happened that were beyond her control. Perhaps she'd meant to call down the stars to save me from Kriantz, but had she meant to destroy that wall in Duvey with a storm of fire? I knew she hadn't meant to burn me.

She blinked back tears. "I'm doing the best I can."

Guilt ached in my chest. "I know you are, but I still need you to be honest with me. I don't understand why you didn't tell me about meeting the queen or about her offer. Gods, I hate this place." I slumped onto the chaise. "I wish we'd never come here."

"We came here because of me," Denna said, her lip trembling. "Because of my Affinity."

"Well, I wish you didn't have it. I wish it could be taken away." I wanted a simple life with the girl I loved, not to play political games and worry that the person I loved most in the world was going to burn me if I kissed her too passionately.

"You can't wish away the parts of me you don't like," Denna said, her voice stronger. She came closer, standing between me and the window. "Do you even know what you're saying? It's like you're asking me to cut off a limb because it would make things easier for you."

"That's not what I meant," I said. Wanting things to be easier didn't mean I wanted her to be someone else or to hurt herself to make my life better.

"Isn't it?" she asked, her voice rising. "Would you be happier living our lives together with me always pretending to be your maid, even though this isn't who I am, or who I was raised to be?"

"No, of course not. I just want you to be safe. I want us to be safe. Nothing about living with magic all around is safe!" I begged her to understand.

"It seems to work out fine for everyone in this kingdom," she said.

"Sure, and the throne is taken in bloody combat and the queen brags about tearing out the hearts of her challengers. Perfectly ordinary and safe," I said, making no effort to hide my sarcasm.

"It's not safe for me to hurt you, either!" she said.

"So the answer is going to Corovja and putting an entire kingdom between us?" I asked.

"I'm not going to leave you!" Denna said, her voice impassioned. "Can you just let me be who I'm meant to be?"

Somehow, her declaration stung instead of comforting me. Was her insistence that she wasn't going to leave supposed to make it better that she'd hidden things from me?

"Maybe you should go," I said, and regretted the words the moment I uttered them.

Denna looked as though I'd struck her, and her eyes filled with tears. "That isn't what I want, but I will if it's what you do."

"All I want is an ordinary life for us together," I said.

"What's an ordinary life?" she asked. "We were both royalty. Our lives were never destined to be ordinary or small."

It struck me for the first time that I'd never asked Denna exactly how she pictured our future together beyond the silly fantasies we joked about.

"Then what, you go to Corovja for training and become a bloodthirsty Zumordan overlord like the rest of these people?" I asked.

"Or I could work hard in training and earn my choice of apprenticeships and ask to be placed back here with Zhari so I'm close to you. If you want that."

My throat tightened. As upset as I was, the thought of losing her was unbearable. We'd had so little time together. What was I going to do without her to guide me, to help me, to make sure I didn't offend the other half of the court or get myself killed? I'd barely even begun to explore the Winter Court, and I couldn't imagine navigating it without her by my side.

I finally risked a look at her face. The fear in her eyes crushed me, but I didn't know whether she was more afraid to stay here or to go to Corovja.

"You have to do what's right for you," I finally said. "What I want doesn't matter. It never has." My whole life, my family had always tried to bend me into a different shape than the one I'd chosen for myself. I couldn't do that to Denna, even if it broke my heart.

TWELVE 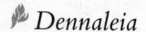 *Dennaleia*

AFTER OUR ARGUMENT, MARE SPENT SO LONG AT THE stables that I fell into a fitful sleep on the chaise, tormented by her words and my own thoughts. She wanted me to stay small and tame. Maybe that version of me was the one she'd fallen in love with, but my magic wouldn't allow me to continue to be that person. If I stayed in Kartasha and tried to, I was bound to fail without the proper training, and the best potential mentors in Kartasha had already rejected me. Every day would be another chance for me to hurt Mare again. That left me only one option.

Short on sleep and long on fear, I dressed in the predawn darkness and stuffed a few books Alek had given me into my travel bag. Mare slept soundly as I crept quietly through the room and finally settled at the vanity with a piece of parchment and a writing implement. Part of me hoped she would wake up and stop me—pull the pen from my hand before I even dipped it in the ink, kiss my fingers as she had so many times before, tell me she was sorry and that she loved me and that we could find a way to make things work. But it would only make things harder.

I dipped the pen in the ink and began to write.

> *Mare,*
>
> *You won't like the choice I've made, but I hope you'll try to understand. The only path forward I can see for us together right now holds both of us back. Like Alek said, the queen's claim would make it impossible for me to find an apprenticeship in Kartasha. You said that what you wanted didn't matter—of course it does. It's the only thing that matters to me. So if you want to be safe, and you want me to be safe, I have to leave. If I can't keep you safe from those who would harm you—worse, if I'm the source of that harm—I don't deserve a place by your side.*
>
> *I've accepted the queen's offer to train in Corovja. Please take care of yourself and your kingdom. When we meet again, I hope it will be as equals, and I hope you will forgive me for the distance I've put between us.*
>
>

All my love,

D
>

My throat constricted so that I could barely get out the breath necessary to blow the ink dry. I left the note on the vanity and gathered my few things with shaking hands, blinking back tears as I stood at the door and looked at Mare one last time. She lay on her side with her hair spread out over the pillow, and my fingers clenched reflexively at the thought of its soft mahogany waves. I wished I could take a map of her freckles with me, a reminder of the stars that had guided me here and that I had hoped I would never leave behind. My memories would be a poor substitute for the reality of her kisses. Every muscle in my body wanted to cross the room and curl up beside her. Instead, I forced one foot in front of the other to exit the room and then the building.

Outside, I huddled beneath an archway in the courtyard after sending a page to deliver my acceptance to the queen. The wind blew in short gusts, biting my cheeks and chilling me to the bone. The queen's caravan, while modest in size, still took up most of the courtyard, and servants scuttled back and forth, packing the last of the supplies for the journey to Corovja under the watchful eyes of a number of the queen's Nightswifts. Some of them hovered around the caravan in human form while others circled overhead as birds.

At the center of the chaos, a great barge waited. It hovered above the ground with seemingly nothing but air to hold it up. There were no wheels, just a smooth underside that curled up in the front like a sleigh. Intricate woodwork in dark mahogany decorated the exterior. Behind it, several smaller sleds waited, also floating above the ground. If I hadn't been so preoccupied, I might have gaped in wonder. I had never seen anything like them.

An imposing black-haired figure appeared in my peripheral vision, boots clomping over the cobblestones, and I recognized Karina, the captain of the Nightswifts. Behind her, the queen swept into the courtyard in her white cloak, casting a glance in my direction. A small smile danced over her ruby lips before she turned away and disappeared through a door in the side of the largest barge. Karina continued toward me, stopping a few paces away.

"Lia," she said, "time to go."

Fear twisted in my belly, and for just a moment, I considered backing out. How could I leave Mare, after everything that had happened? We had fled Lyrra so that we could be together. But the memory of her burned flesh filled my mind, the way my hand had branded her and the pain in her eyes each time she had to change the poultice. I'd thought I could protect her. Instead, I'd hurt her. I could have killed her. No matter how much it hurt to leave, I had to go.

I followed Karina past the queen's barge to the smaller one just behind it, which was made of the same rich mahogany, but not quite as ornate. The footman pulled open the door and said, "Your bag, miss?" reaching for my small leather satchel. My hand tightened around the strap.

"I'll keep it with me. Thank you," I said, and climbed into the barge. The inside was pillowed with soft white cushioning. Feeling intimidated and alone, I settled into a seat.

Three trainees sat across from me, a girl and a boy in green travel cloaks a few shades lighter than mine, both with dark curly hair and striking aquiline profiles, and another boy dressed in faded black from head to toe. The only other passenger was a sandy-haired man in a Nightswift uniform who leaned against the window on the right-hand side of my bench, eyes closed, snoring softly.

When the footman shut the door, the noise of the court abruptly cut off. We began to move, drifting across the courtyard, slowly at first but picking up speed as the caravan approached the gates, our barge moving so smoothly that it could have been gliding across ice. A prickle came over my skin, making the numb places on my arms ache. Hidden beneath my cloak, my hands twisted together in my lap, and I clenched my jaw as tightly as I could, trying to shove the magic away.

"You're the fire user, right?" the boy in green asked in Zumordan. There was a sharpness to his expression that made me wary.

"Yes. I'm Lia," I introduced myself, trying to regain what little composure I had.

"Eryk," he said. "This is my sister, Evie." He gestured to the girl also wearing green.

"Were you acquired through Zhari's program as well?" Evie asked, her expression friendly and curious.

"Don't tell people that," Eryk admonished his sister. "Our rank has changed now that we've been chosen."

I shook my head. "Were all of you?"

"Not me," the boy in black said. "Tristan." He extended his hand and I shook it, hoping I performed the gesture correctly. As a maid, I'd barely had to introduce myself to anyone, and as a princess, everything had been far more formal—no one ever would have touched me except another royal. His grip was warm and strong.

"How did you get selected?" I asked Tristan, my curiosity getting the best of me. I knew better than to judge people by appearances, but his disheveled looks were a sharp contrast to Eryk, who was groomed to fit in with nobles, and Evie, whose simpler look was equally as tidy as her brother's.

"My Affinity isn't very common," Tristan said. "Most of the bigger magic schools are in Kartasha, but when I came down to enroll in one, the headmaster turned me over to the queen. What's your story?"

"Same thing," I lied, "though I don't think my gift is very rare." It was close enough to the truth.

"Fire Affinities are quite common," Eryk said, the disdain in his voice clear.

"Did you see that the others have private sleds?" Evie asked the group, her eyes wide.

"They should have put us all together," Eryk, looking sulky.

"Just because we were selected doesn't suddenly make us nobles," Evie said.

"It might someday," Eryk retorted.

Tristan and I exchanged a glance and shrugged. Worry crept down my spine. I wondered what they would think if they knew who I'd been in my old life.

I detached myself from the conversation and stared out the window, scarcely able to take in the scenery. Mare's words haunted me—that she wished my magic would disappear, that what she wanted didn't matter. Of course what she wanted mattered; that was why it hurt so much that she wanted me to be something I couldn't be. I knew I'd done the right thing by leaving, and I'd known it was going to hurt. I just couldn't have imagined how much.

The caravan traveled along at a surprising speed, as fast as a cantering horse, except without the rocking movement or the sound of hooves thundering in the dirt. Occasionally, I caught glimpses of Nightswifts in bird form swooping past the window, circling in the air above us as they searched for any obstacles or threats. The chatter of the other trainees eventually died off, and the Swift never opened his eyes, though he did grunt and roll to the side once. He had to be a guard assigned to night duty. In an effort to calm myself, I dug in my satchel and took out a volume on Zumordan language that Alek had given me, and I passed the next few sunlengths memorizing as many words as I could. My command of the language was already good, but it wouldn't hurt to brush up, since I'd never used it regularly outside my studies.

Around midday, the caravan drew to a halt, pulling off the road so that the servants could unpack food. A rapping on the sled's door made me jump, and I turned to see it already opening to reveal Karina.

"One of you will join the queen for lunch each day," she said. "Lia, you're first." I hurriedly gathered my books and satchel, shoved them into a shelf beneath the seat, and followed Karina outside into the cold afternoon.

Karina escorted me to the queen's barge and ushered me inside ahead of her. Its spacious seats were wide enough for the tallest Swift to stretch out on. A narrow table was attached to the floor, and laid out upon it was a feast the likes of which I hadn't seen since fleeing Mynaria. A plate of roasted venison, a number of vegetable dishes, and a bowl of plump, red raspberries waited, untouched. A crystal decanter of wine completed the spread, catching the sunlight and displaying a brilliant diamond pattern on the table. Seated on a plush rear-facing bench in the barge, the queen waited, her eyes seeming to stare right through me. I swallowed.

"Lia," the queen said.

"Good afternoon, Your Majesty," I said, hovering awkwardly in the doorway.

"Sit."

I hurried to obey as Karina slid onto the seat next to me. The queen began serving herself, and after a moment, Karina and I followed suit. Though the food was delicious, nervousness fluttered in my stomach, and I couldn't eat much. Maybe the servant disguise was starting to become part of who I was. I no longer felt like a princess. I barely knew who I was at all.

"I want to see the reports on Tilium," the queen said to Karina. "We should arrive there by midafternoon."

A brief look of surprise crossed Karina's face, but she quelled it immediately and produced a finely made leather document case from beneath her seat. She opened the gold dragon's-claw clasp and removed a neat stack of vellum.

A pang of longing went through me. Back in my old life, I might have been the one helping to look over the kingdom's reports. It would have been up to me to know everything about my people and my land, to help make decisions that would best protect and help them. Those duties would most likely never be my concern again, and something about that made me feel ill. I'd spent my whole life building up to that role, preparing to be queen of Mynaria. Now it all felt like a waste.

The queen began leafing through the vellum, a faint crease appearing between her eyebrows. Her hands trembled the tiniest bit, the only sign of age I'd seen her display.

"Where are the latest intelligence reports?" she asked.

"We have none, Your Majesty," Karina said. "The last scouts we sent never returned."

I watched them, my curiosity piqued in spite of my anguish over leaving Mare. The queen looked up and fixed her gaze on me again.

"Perhaps Lia may have some insight to offer." She held several reports out to me, and I had to untangle my clasped fingers to take the thin vellum from her. "Consider this an assessment to establish a baseline for the nonmagical aspects of your training. Karina, tell her about Tilium."

My stomach dropped. What if she'd already seen through my disguise? And what nonmagical training? The queen hadn't said anything about that in her original offer.

"Tilium is a small village north of Kartasha," Karina told me. "A man has started some kind of cult there."

"A cult?" I repeated. I wasn't aware of any kind of religion being practiced in Zumorda.

"It started with a man named Sigvar who has a spirit Affinity," Karina continued. "Seems he brainwashed the village into following him, and hardly anyone paid their tithes this year."

The queen's expression darkened. "I need to know how he's doing it. And why." She looked at me again. "What do you think, Lia?"

I paused, caught off guard by her question.

"I—I'm not sure, Your Majesty." Of course I had theories about the why, if not the how. Years of studying politics and religion had given me a great deal of insight that I might put to use. But I wasn't Dennaleia anymore. I was Lia, a simple handmaiden who shouldn't know much about politics or the theology behind other kingdoms' worship of the Six and how that might tie into a Zumordan cult. I wasn't sure why the queen would even ask me.

Still, she stared at me, waiting for some kind of answer.

"Do you often have problems with cults in Zumorda?" I finally asked.

Karina answered. "No, although we've had several more than usual over the last few years. Mostly just fools trying to get people to start worshipping gods again, often because they've spent too much time in Mynaria and have been deluded into thinking the gods will give their magic more power. Most of these groups are harmless."

"But this one isn't?" I needed to know whether it was just their failure to pay the tithe that was the concern, or if it was something worse.

"The last reports we received described the town in a state of disrepair. Most of the crops failed because no one tended them, and the few shops have closed down. Several residents fled and brought us news of what had happened, but that was some weeks ago now. Everyone we've sent to investigate has yet to return."

"And . . . we're headed there now?" I was confused. Monarchs didn't walk straight into danger—at least not the ones who had raised me. We had spies and soldiers and specialists who could be deployed to deal with things specific to their areas of expertise.

"Yes," the queen said. "Threats to Zumorda must be dealt with swiftly."

Fear prickled over my skin. Why would a monarch risk her own life to investigate something like this instead of sending guards? Surely they would be better trained to handle such a situation. The queen, for her part, didn't seem worried at all. She and Karina moved on to discussing reports from other towns, but my mind kept churning with questions. What did the queen think of the war Mynaria had nearly declared? Did she consider the Mynarians threatening? And if a cult was a concern, why wasn't the attack on Duvey also a threat? Was it because Wymund and his fighters had already defeated them? I didn't know anything about this cult or even what a spirit Affinity entailed, but it all sounded dangerous. Prickling magic spread down my arms and into my hands. I balled them into fists and closed my eyes, but all I could think of was Mare. What would she do now that I was gone? Would she find her footing in court? Win over some nobles who would take her concerns seriously? What if they ignored her because Zumorda was already planning to attack Mynaria? Or even Havemont? We knew nothing of what kind of forces they might be able to send. Most of all, I worried that she must hate me for leaving and see it only as me choosing my magic over her rather than what it really was—me choosing her safety and some hope of us having a future as equals.

"Lia," the queen said, her tone sharp. I jumped, and before I could stop the magic, my hands uncurled and flames burst from my open palms. The blaze leaped to the ceiling, alighting on the intricate mahogany. Karina let out a shout of alarm. Fire continued to pour out of my hands in a torrent I couldn't hold back.

"Stop!" The queen's voice boomed, and something slammed me back in my seat, an invisible force so strong that it felt like ten people were holding me in place. Before me, the queen had her arms outstretched, palms open and fingers splayed. Though I saw nothing, I felt my magic being pulled into her hands. Her gaze fixed on me, face twisted into a focused expression.

She was taking my magic. Somehow, she was drawing it out of me.

Fear gathered in my belly, and I struggled, trying to escape, but it was useless. I tried to move but could barely twitch my fingers. The flames around us dissipated, drawn away by the queen. Then the pressure abruptly vanished, and I lurched forward, catching myself hard against the edge of the table with my elbows.

"Sarding Hell," Karina snapped, glaring at me. Her face was white, one hand resting on the hilt of a dagger strapped to her waist.

"I'm so sorry," I tried to say, but the words barely whispered past my throat.

The queen tightened both hands into fists, and for a moment, her eyelids fluttered closed. A strange expression crossed her face, almost calm, but with a flush blooming in her cheeks. She took a long breath in before opening her eyes to look directly at me. She smiled, a predatory expression that chilled me to the bone.

"You lost control," she said, her voice calm and measured.

I struggled to push myself upright, leaning back against the seat, breathing as quickly as if I'd just sprinted down a mountain. "What just happened?" I managed to ask between breaths.

"Your magic was too great for you to handle," she said, "so I took some of it from you."

"What do you mean?" I suppressed a shudder as I remembered the way her powers had trapped me against my seat.

The queen looked a little impatient, but she answered my question. "Magic users can give power to one another, if they so choose. It is a common occurrence. But only a few of us are strong enough to borrow magic from others, especially without their consent. Your Affinity will replenish itself in time. I had to remove your powers for our safety, and yours."

I shivered despite the warm air inside the barge. I searched for my magic, trying to call it to my fingertips, but when before a rush of tingling power would have danced across my skin, now I felt nothing but a light prickle in the tips of my fingers. It was frightening, but peaceful. I couldn't hurt anyone now. I leaned back in my seat, heavy with relief and exhaustion.

Learning had always come easily to me. Geography, politics, mathematics, the harp . . . anything I studied, I eventually mastered, even the subjects that I struggled with at first.

I knew already that magic wasn't going to be the same.

The queen dismissed me to my own sled to resume the journey. Eryk had vanished, leaving just Evie, Tristan, and the sleeping Swift as my companions. When I asked where Eryk had gone, Evie rolled her eyes and told me he'd managed to get himself invited to ride with Aela, one of the noble trainees.

Several hours past midday, our small caravan pulled away from the main road. The smaller road we turned onto was rocky and uneven. Shiny patches of ice had collected in potholes that could easily break a horse's leg with one wrong step, making me especially grateful for the luxury of our floating barges. Clearly, the town of Tilium either wasn't expecting any visitors or didn't want them.

We halted after several more minutes of travel, near some trees with branches bare of leaves. Some distance farther down the road, the town of Tilium stood, a small collection of humble buildings, many of which looked abandoned. Overhead, heavy-looking clouds blanketed the sky, and when I stepped outside the sled with the other trainees, the air seemed even chillier than before. I pulled my cloak tightly around me and shivered.

The door to the queen's barge opened. Karina appeared, wearing a plain pair of brown trousers and a work shirt in place of her Swift uniform. She moved to the side and strapped a sheathed sword to her waist as the queen exited behind her.

"Trainees," Karina called, and the three of us hurried over. "You will accompany us into Tilium."

Eryk and a tall blond girl who had to be Aela joined us, as did a blue-eyed brunette with a haughty expression. She looked me up and down.

"You're the servant of that *vakos* ambassador from Mynaria, aren't you?" the brunette said.

"Not anymore," I replied, sensing danger.

"Doesn't seem like she lost too much," the girl commented. "You look like you could hardly light a candle." She flicked her fingers at me and a puff of air thumped me in the chest.

I shrank away from her, wrapping my arms tightly around myself.

"Don't pick on weaklings, Ikrie," Aela said, smirking.

Shame made my cheeks burn. With a start I recognized Ikrie's name—she was the one who had threatened to challenge Mare to a duel at the party in Zumorda and nearly suffocated her in front of everyone. Anger gathered in me like storm clouds, and it was lucky for Ikrie that the queen had taken my magic so that I felt only the barest stir of it rise with my emotions. Ikrie had given Mare another reason to fear Affinities, provided another hammer blow to the wedge that had driven us apart. My stomach tightened uncomfortably, and I swallowed hard as I glanced at the village, then back to the people around me. A party of six guards had gathered on foot, and four more circled us overhead in bird form.

"Karina, explain the situation to our trainees," the queen said.

Karina told the others what I'd learned over lunch and added, "The mayor of the city never sent reports, so we can assume she's been absorbed into the cult. The guardian of Valenko hasn't been able to check on this place in a while due to her ill health, so we should proceed carefully."

"Thank you, Karina," the queen said. "Lead on."

Karina commanded the guards to fall into formation. They surrounded her and the queen, and I fell into step behind them along with the other trainees. We approached the town on the narrow dirt road, our boots gathering mud with every step. Around us, the farmers' fields lay half fallow and half sown with crops that had been ill tended and allowed to rot in the ground after harvest.

The queen dropped back to walk alongside us momentarily, and her eyes flashed over to me as we drew closer to the town. "Lia, tell me what you See."

I knew she meant something more than what I saw with my eyes, but even if my powers had been working, I wouldn't have had the faintest idea how to see magic. The other trainees stared at me, waiting to see what I was capable of. I cast my eyes toward the small village ahead of us, then glanced past it to the surrounding hills and forest. I saw nothing beyond the ordinary, aside from the stillness and eerie silence. Not a single person was in sight.

"There's smoke rising from a chimney in the center of town," I said. "Since many of the residences seem to be abandoned, my guess is that it's someone who hasn't been taken in by the cultist. Chances are also good that it's someone who does have the ability to use magic." I knew that those without gifts tended to live on the fringes of Zumordan society, even in villages as small as this one. A *vakos* Zumordan wouldn't live in the middle of town.

"What makes you think that's not the cultist's home?" the queen asked, tilting her head.

"A cult leader needs a place of spiritual significance to his followers. And it needs to be somewhere large enough to hold gatherings as his flock grows." I paused, my eyes roaming over the landscape. "Like that barn up there." I pointed to a large stone building. "Look how well the area around it is tended—that's quite a contrast to everything else we see here."

The queen gave me an approving nod, and I exhaled a sigh of relief.

"There's also magic pooling on that hill," Evie said, drawing the queen's attention to her.

"Anyone can See that," Ikrie said.

"So what would you do next, Ikrie?" the queen asked.

Ikrie's expression changed swiftly from condescension toward me and Evie to complete obsequiousness. "Drain off as much of the power as I could and prepare to use it for offense."

I frowned. Attacking without even knowing the details of what was going on didn't seem like a good idea to me.

"And Lia, what would you do?" the queen asked.

"I'd speak to whoever is tending that fire." I gestured toward the solitary column of smoke in the center of town. "If they haven't been taken in by the cultist, they'll be able to tell us more. We should gather as much information as we can before confronting him, especially if we don't know what kind of powers he has."

"In that case, onward." The queen moved back up to rejoin

Karina and lifted a hand to command the Swifts into a new formation.

"We do know what powers he has," Eryk said. "A spirit Affinity, like mine."

"Then why does that power pool up there feel like earth magic?" Evie snapped back.

"Who cares, if it's there for the taking?" Ikrie said.

A few minutes later, Karina knocked on the door of the house with the smoking chimney. The door creaked open promptly, revealing a woman wearing a leather apron and an annoyed expression.

"He's on the hill," she said. "Path's past the granary." She started to shut the door, but Karina blocked it with her boot.

"Pardon the intrusion, ma'am," she said. "We need to speak to you first about what's going on here. Queen's orders."

The woman squinted at us, finally taking a closer look at our party. The Swifts flanked us on either side, though a few more of them had transformed into birds and perched on nearby rooftops to watch from above with the others. The woman's gaze moved from Karina to the queen. Her eyes widened.

"Queen's orders. Of course," she babbled, opening the door wide. "I'm so sorry, Your Majesty, I didn't mean any disrespect. It's just that everyone who's come through here lately ends up on the hill and—"

"Enough," the queen said. "We're here to handle it."

The woman nodded and ushered her in.

"Lia, this was your idea—you'll come to observe." To my surprise, the queen indicated that I should enter with her and Karina, leaving the other trainees outside. The house was a rickety affair of wood, with clay patching the spaces between the slats, but there was an organic order to it all. A tidily made bed stood in the back corner. Closer to the entrance, two bright lanterns surrounded a worktable covered with wire coils, beads, and semiprecious gems sorted into small containers. Small pottery vessels and cruets lined the shelves overhead. A small anvil stood beside the table with a toothed saw and several sizes of tongs, hammers, and chisels hanging on the wall above it.

"When did Sigvar start gaining followers?" the queen asked.

"A bit more than a winter ago, if memory serves," the woman said. "He came into town with claims of restoring the old Mecklen farm on the hill. Which I suppose he's done."

"And why haven't you been drawn in by his magic, if it's powerful enough to destroy the economy of an entire region?" the queen asked.

The jeweler smirked a little. "Men have never interested me."

A little hum of recognition went through me. I'd never known what attraction was—what love was—until I'd met Mare.

"I'm not without an Affinity," the woman added. She wrapped her palm around the pinecone-shaped charm necklace she wore, and when she removed it, the pinecone had transformed into an ornate flower.

"An earth user, then," the queen said. "A lot of you seem to come from this region."

The jeweler nodded. "The Mecklen farm is on a site that is reputed to have once been an earth temple in the days before your reign, Your Majesty."

My curiosity was piqued. They'd had temples here? Zumorda

hadn't always been a godless place? Zumordans often made summer pilgrimages to the High Adytum in my homeland, but they did that because the Adytum was an ideal place to cast powerful enchantments, not because they worshipped our gods. I thought they journeyed to Havemont because they'd never had temples of their own. Apparently, that wasn't true.

"So what you're saying is that he's built a shrine on top of what used to be an earth temple, and anyone with an attraction to men is susceptible to his gifts?" I asked.

"Mostly," the jeweler said. "My resistance certainly isn't due to my earth magic—plenty of the others up there are earth users. How else do you think they have that garden looking so nice on the edge of winter? But most men are susceptible, too. If you're attracted to him or you want to be like him, might as well sign away your soul before you look into his eyes."

"So as one of the few exempt from his powers, why haven't you tried to stop him?" Karina asked.

"I paid my tithe to the crown," the jeweler said, pointing to a piece of wood by the door with notches carved into it. "My success or failure does not depend on him, and I'll be damned if I'm going to let some young buck come in here and uproot me from the town I've lived in all fifty-three winters of my life."

"Then I suppose we'd best uproot him instead," the queen said, the predatory expression back on her face.

We bade the jeweler farewell and exited her cabin to climb the hill to the Mecklen farm.

"That was indeed useful information," the queen said. "Wise choice to inquire there, Lia."

Ikrie scowled, and the other trainees regarded me suspiciously, making me want to shrink away from everyone. I hadn't meant to attract attention or gain any special treatment. Karina shared what we'd learned with the other trainees as we ascended the hill. A few of the Swifts flew overhead, swooping from tree to tree ahead of us to scout out the place. They were quieter than ordinary birds, and something about the silence of the woods alongside the trail unnerved me.

As we drew closer to the barn on the hill, men and women paused in their chores to wave to us in friendly greeting. Only when I got close did I notice the similarities among them. Although their eyes were bold shades of brown and green and blue, even in the weak light of the winter sun their pupils were hardly larger than pinpoints. The people seemed to look through us, unseeing, their expressions empty. It made my skin crawl.

We found the man who had to be Sigvar at the farm's well, hauling buckets of water up to pass to men carrying them into the barn. His rolled-up sleeves revealed muscular forearms marked with inked symbols I didn't recognize. Our party drew to a halt, the Swifts moving into a protective semicircle around us. When Sigvar turned to face us, Karina's stern expression morphed into an unfamiliar smile, and then she proceeded toward him at a slower pace. My heart lurched into my throat. Karina was supposed to be the most powerful of all the Nightswifts. If he could effectively disarm our best fighter in a few heartbeats, there was no hope for anyone else. Every instinct screamed at me to run.

Sigvar's warm brown eyes invited all of us to come closer, his grin genuine and framed by a neatly groomed beard. His fitted shirt, partly unbuttoned at the top like an unwelcome invitation, clung to his strong physique. The other trainees stared, their eyes glazing over. Even the guards we'd brought with us lost focus, their limbs going slack. A few even dropped their weapons. I braced myself, waiting for something, for whatever magic it was, to affect me. But I felt nothing.

"Welcome!" He gestured to the farm. "Have you come to join us here? We accept those from all walks of life to serve the earth god by tending to the land and its animals and people."

"I've come to find out why Tilium was unable to pay its tithe this year," the queen said. There was a tightness in her jaw that betrayed her use of magic—she was protecting herself from his influence, but it was taking its toll.

"My queen!" Sigvar said. He fell to one knee but kept his gaze fixed on her. "What an honor to have you in our humble town."

"Your gift does not burn brightly in my Sight," the queen observed, staring him down. "But I can See pieces of it in everyone here. How exactly did you manage that?"

"An initiation spell, my queen. It binds us all together, allows us to share a consciousness and a community," Sigvar said.

I looked around, realizing that the other people had closed in around us, all of them staring at us blankly. Above us, the flying Swifts soared to land on the ground, their forms elongating, feathers and talons and beaks dissolving into human skin, clothing, mouths. I recognized one of them—the sandy-haired man who'd slept in my sled. As they took human form, their pupils shrank and their expressions grew slack.

Fear made a small surge of magic flow through my arms, and

for once I was grateful for its presence.

Sigvar beckoned with one finger, and I watched with growing horror as Karina stepped toward him. Tension warped the queen's face, but she was frozen in place by Sigvar's magic, the blue in her eyes slowly swallowing the dark centers.

My panic rose. Was Sigvar going to kill Karina? The queen?

The queen lifted a hand, holding it palm up, and a flame sparked to life in it. But her hand trembled and the fire guttered and went out. A small gasp escaped her lips. Beneath my feet, a strange rumbling welled up from the ground, as if the earth itself were joining the fight. I frantically looked around, trying to find the earth user responsible, but only Sigvar seemed to be wielding magic.

"I think you should come with me," Sigvar said. "I can show you all that we've built." He gestured, and Karina moved easily to the side as he took a step toward the queen. All around us, the rumbling intensified, and small pebbles rose off the ground.

"No!" The shout came from in front of me, from one of the queen's guards. The sandy-haired Swift lunged at Sigvar, clumsily attempting to draw his sword. Sigvar stepped back in surprise, the friendly expression on his face dropping like a discarded mask. But before the Swift could get close, a female Swift swept the sandy-haired Swift's legs out from under him. He fell to the ground, and the woman drew her sword.

I lunged forward without thinking, slamming myself into the attacking guard's side. The beginnings of flames sparked in my hands, and I grabbed her arm.

The woman yelped when I touched her, but she shoved me away easily, and I tumbled to the ground. The guard stood over me, sword drawn, her eyes widening, her pupils growing, confusion on her face. She hesitated just long enough for the sandy-haired Swift to scramble off the ground and punch her in the side of her face. She crumpled.

My legs shook, and I rolled backward toward the queen, scraping my palm on a sharp rock and lurching to my feet just in time to see the queen launch a fireball at Sigvar.

His shriek echoed through the hills as flames engulfed one of his arms. It was enough to break his hold on the queen's guards and the other trainees. His people surged toward us, but Karina, alert again, swept them aside with a powerful gust of wind that knocked them flat.

"Take his breath!" the queen shouted.

Ikrie stepped up to join Karina, and they both lifted their arms to jerk the air out of Sigvar's lungs. He fell to his knees, clutching his neck, and then his eyes rolled back in his head and he hit the ground. As soon as he lost consciousness, his followers collapsed around him.

"For traitors, there is no mercy." The queen knelt beside him and rested her hand on his chest, which rose and fell with breath once more. She closed her eyes, and her jaw tightened with concentration that slowly turned to euphoria. Smoke rose and his skin blistered, but that wasn't the only damage she was doing. His body convulsed as though he was being burned from the inside out, and his veins pulsed black everywhere they showed through his skin.

A collective scream went up from his followers like some kind of unholy chorus, a sound that made goose bumps rise all over my body.

When the queen removed her hand from Sigvar's chest, he lay

very still, his breathing so slight it took me several long moments to be sure he was still alive. The queen's cheeks glowed with a healthy flush that made her look many years younger. In her palm, a silvery flame lingered, and she closed her fingers around it before feeding it into a vial she pulled out of her cloak pocket.

"His form," the queen said, turning to the dazed Swift behind her. He rushed to follow her order, kneeling beside Sigvar and blowing a breath of air into the man's face. Sigvar's body rippled and shifted until instead of a man, a buck lay on the ground before us, his head crowned with arching antlers.

I watched in horror as the queen beckoned another Swift forward. The guard removed a hammer from his belt and struck the antlers until they snapped free of Sigvar's skull, leaving bloody holes behind. But she didn't stop there—she pulled a knife from her pocket and held it in her hand until it blazed red hot, then seared the wounds with the blade. Two blackened pits were all that remained when she was done.

Behind her, Evie clutched her stomach like she was about to vomit, while Tristan watched with detached curiosity.

All around us, Sigvar's people had begun to rise, stumbling toward the queen. They were weak but clear-eyed, their faces full of confusion. Among them was a boy with a familiar face—the same blond boy I'd seen taken by the Sonnenbornes in Duvey after his father was killed. How in the Hells had he ended up here? I got to my feet.

"His hold on them is gone," the queen said, satisfied.

"What did you do to him?" I asked, not sure I wanted to know.

"I burned away his gift." A savage smile cut through her face.

I shuddered. Having my gift torn away was the most violating thing I could imagine, even if it would have made my life easier in countless ways. A little flicker of anger burned in my breast as I looked at Sigvar and wondered if his fate was what Mare would want for me. She'd said as much.

The queen turned to her guards and gestured to Sigvar's crumpled manifest form. "Take him prisoner," she said. Two Swifts moved forward, lifting the buck roughly off the ground and carrying him down the path.

"Will he change back?" I asked Tristan.

"Eventually," he said, his tone grim. "It involves more than taking someone's gift to part them from their manifest."

As the Swifts took names from the cult members and organized everyone to go back down to town, I approached the boy from Duvey.

"Hello," I said.

He looked up from under his unruly mop of blond hair, confusion still evident in his eyes. "Who are you?"

"I'm Lia," I said. "I saw you in Duvey. How did you get here?"

The boy looked around as if searching for a familiar face and finding none. "I don't remember. I want to go home."

My heart went out to him. I knew how he felt. "Do you remember leaving Duvey?"

He shook his head. "There was a battle, and then I woke up here. Sigvar kept us safe."

"The Swifts will help you get back to Duvey," I reassured him, but I was troubled. Somehow he'd gotten from Sonnenborne hands into Sigvar's, which made no sense at all. We were far northeast of where he'd been taken, and the Sonnebornes surely would not have ridden this far north just to drop a boy off with a random cult. None of it made any sense, and I had a bad feeling that the only way to untangle it would be to talk to Sigvar himself, who was unconscious and a prisoner of the queen. Even though the trainees had been expected to help with this mission, it would raise a lot of suspicion for me to ask to speak with him. I'd have to tell the queen and hope she'd look into it.

When we made camp that night, I kept to the shadows, hiding between two of the barges to eat my meal of fresh bread, farm cheese, and apple preserves from the last town we'd passed through. Evie and Tristan had both mysteriously vanished; the servants looked at me askance if I got too near; I would rather have walked into a pit of angry vipers than go anywhere near Ikrie, Aela, and Eryk; and I didn't dare try to approach the queen or her cohort without an invitation. I did my best to blend into the background and listened to the conversations going on around me. Much of it was typical— talk of family and children, crops, past adventures. The off-duty Swifts often broke into song, laughing and teasing one another until someone's feelings got hurt and that person fled the gathering in bird form.

As I finished up the last of my meal, someone approached—the sandy-haired Swift from my sled. His face was covered in scrapes, and his left cheek bore a large bruise, made all the more spectacular in the jumping shadows cast by the nearest campfire.

"Hey," he said, "you're Lia, right?"

"Yes," I said, remembering just in time not to curtsy.

He smiled and stuck out his hand. I took it, shaking it cautiously.

"My name is Aster. And I want to thank you. I think you saved my life today."

"Oh," I said. "Well, I just did what made sense."

"You have good instincts. With a little training, you could put up a formidable defense."

I suppressed a laugh, surprised that I even felt like laughing at all. "That's kind of you to say." And it was funny, too, given that the top of my head put me barely at eye level with his chest. Physical skills hadn't been part of my education as a princess.

"I mean it." He grinned again. "If you ever want a lesson, all you have to do is ask. Everyone should know how to throw a punch."

I was about to tell him no, but then I thought better of it. There was no one here to defend me now, and my magic was notoriously unreliable. It couldn't hurt to learn.

"Can you show me now?" I asked.

"Of course!" He seemed delighted and, a few minutes later, had me making a proper fist with my thumb on the outside.

"Like this?" I said, holding up my hand for inspection.

"Yes, but keep your hand aligned with your wrist." He corrected the angle between my hand and wrist. "Now, hold up your fists in front of your face. When you punch, do it from your shoulder."

I swung wildly, and he laughed.

"Here, like this." He showed me in slow motion how to rotate my arm into a straight line as I punched, making impact with my first two knuckles.

"Where do I punch?" I asked.

"Well, that depends on where you can reach, short stuff."

"Hey!" I laughed.

"The face is a bad idea—you're likely to hurt your hand. Try for the neck or the sternum to knock the wind out of someone. And remember, the point is to hurt someone enough to get away. The longer you engage in a fight, the better your chances are of losing."

He ran me through the punches a few more times, showing me how to follow through.

"I'd best get back to the others," he said, once he was confident that I had the basics down.

"Thanks," I said, feeling a little surge of gratitude.

He nodded and headed off, joining a few other Swifts at the edge of the campfire. For the first time since I'd left Mare behind, a little bit of hope glimmered on the horizon. At least someone besides Karina and the queen had shown me some kindness.

And now I knew how to punch someone in the throat.

THIRTEEN ✦ *Amaranthine*

MUFFLED SHOUTS FROM OUTSIDE WOKE ME TO A ROOM
that was too cold without Denna pressed against me. My guilt grew
heavier as I searched for her. She wasn't in the chaise or the washroom, and I assumed she'd gotten up early, perhaps to run errands,
or perhaps to avoid me. I shouldn't have fought with her about her
magic or what to do. It was her choice, and her choice alone, and I
knew that. My fear didn't give me the right to dictate what she did
with her life.

I threw on my cloak over my nightclothes and peered out the
window. The courtyard bustled with activity as the queen's caravan
departed for Corovja. A great barge was the first out of the gate. It
hovered above the ground, eerily steady in spite of the cold breeze
that sent leaves swirling across the flagstones. Four smaller floating
sleds filed out behind it.

I sat down in front of the mirror with a sigh, but as I lifted a brush to my hair, I saw a letter sitting on the vanity. Denna's unmistakably tidy penmanship decorated the front. My breath caught as I unfolded it and began to read.

"No," I whispered, crumpling it in my hand.

I dropped the letter on the floor and bolted from the room. It felt as though my heart was being ripped out of my chest. I flew down the stairs out into the courtyard, shoving my way through the remnants of the crowds that had gathered to see off the queen's caravan. Angry curses followed me, but I didn't care. By the time I got a clear line of sight to the barges, the last one had already left the courtyard.

"Lia!" I shouted, but my voice was lost in the din of the crowds as they sent off their queen. I ran out the gates after the final barge as it picked up speed, only to be caught by a man dressed in black, a Nightswift, one of the queen's elite guards. He hauled me to the sidelines as I thrashed in his grip, depositing me just outside the gates of the Winter Court. Traffic had already swept the barges away, and there was no way I could catch them on foot. The wind blew in short gusts, biting my cheeks, and I pulled up the hood of my cloak so no one could see the hot tears as they began to fall.

How could she leave me without even saying good-bye? Every choice I'd made since she'd rescued me from Kriantz had been for her. Her happiness and safety were all I wanted, and she'd barely heard me out before deciding we were better off apart. I walked slowly back to my room, half convinced by the time I got there that her letter had been a mistake, that I would find her waiting for me, ready to kiss my tears away. But when I returned to the room, it was as empty as I'd left it.

The unfairness of her choice hit me twice as hard with the full magnitude of my aloneness upon me. She could have talked to me, given me a chance to apologize for the previous night, to explain to her that my need for her outweighed everything else. Alek could have tried harder to find her an apprenticeship—he'd only asked a few people. How was that enough? Instead she'd accepted the offer of a bloodthirsty monarch I didn't trust at all, cut off all communication, and put most of a kingdom between us. She'd left me alone with a diplomatic mission that was doomed to failure without her wisdom to help me.

I paced my room the rest of the morning with no idea what to do with myself, eventually tugging on a cloak and heading to the stables to see Flicker. I would have given anything to talk to Denna one last time—to try to talk her out of this senseless plan, to explain again how much I needed her, to tell her that I trusted and loved her. The burn on my side was temporary. I wanted her to be permanent, and for the first time since leaving Mynaria, I was faced with wondering if she actually wanted the same thing. She was about to be surrounded by people with gifts like hers, people with powers and abilities I couldn't even fathom. How could I ever compete with that? I no longer knew what she'd even seen in me that had drawn her to me in the first place. All I knew how to do was work with horses. I had no magic, no diplomatic skills, no friends, and almost no family. Perhaps my father was right that I'd always been a disgrace, and Denna was finally seeing that, too.

The icy air cut through me like a sword as I walked to the stables. The bare branches of the trees lining the footpaths clacked against each other like closing teeth. Heavy clouds had swallowed the top of Mount Prakov to the east, making it seem like the sky was far too close to the earth. Unlike the orderly gardens of the palace where I was raised, the interconnected areas here flowed, like water, from one into the next. I had to trudge uphill and down through a maze I hadn't yet figured out just to get to the stables, and if there was a better way, I didn't know it.

Unfortunately, my hopes of seeking refuge at the barn were dashed before I even got out of the gardens. As I passed through one of the stone arches between gardens, Fadeyka popped out from behind a bush.

I spooked like a green horse. "Six Hells. Don't jump out at people like that."

"Alek says it's useful to practice stealth," she said.

"Sard Alek," I muttered under my breath. It was partly his fault that Denna had left me.

"You look terrible. Are you going to the barn?"

"I was thinking about it," I said.

"Everyone is talking about how you almost got killed at that party the other night," Fadeyka said.

"I'm shocked," I said, my tone flat. It figured that even Fadeyka had heard. Shame reddened my cheeks. How was I supposed to make allies at the Winter Court after a scene like that? I hadn't been prepared for everything my brother was trusting me with, and I didn't know what to do about it. Now, without Denna, I would be even more lost.

"At least Ikrie's gone now with the other trainees," Fadeyka said.

"Delightful," I said. Images flashed through my mind of Ikrie attacking Denna, suffocating her to death like she'd nearly done to me. Then I remembered how pretty Ikrie had been with her perfectly coiffed brown hair and big blue eyes, and the way that yellow dress had hugged her slender curves. Worse than the thought of Ikrie hurting Denna was the thought of the two of them together—of Denna falling for someone who could give her all the things I couldn't.

"Want a lemon drop?" Fadeyka offered me a candy that seemed to have picked up some lint from the inside of her cloak along the way.

"No thanks," I said, and kept walking.

Fadeyka skipped alongside me, crunching on her candy. "Are you going to ride today?"

"I don't know," I said.

"Is Flicker inside or outside?"

"I don't know."

"Can I watch you saddle him?"

"Do you always have so many questions?" I asked, exasperated.

"Yes," she replied, her voice resolute. "It's how I know so much."

I sighed.

We entered the stables, and I let myself into Flicker's stall, pleased to see that he'd been groomed and rugged. Thankfully Fadeyka had the common sense to stay outside. Flicker's ears pricked, but he didn't move as I walked over and leaned against his shoulder. His warmth quickly traveled through my cloak and back into my bones where I needed it. I breathed deeply, feeling the knots of tension in me slowly unwind.

"Are you going to ride?" Fadeyka asked again.

I sighed. "I think I'm just going to clean stalls today." Ambassadors of the Mynarian crown probably weren't supposed to clean stalls, but it was where I used to do my best thinking back home. Besides, I felt about as good as what I'd be tossing into the wheelbarrow. "It's too gods-damned cold to ride anyway."

"Not *that* cold. It hasn't even snowed yet," Fadeyka said.

I shivered at the thought. "I am definitely not riding in the snow."

"There's an indoor arena," she pointed out. "Usually we'd already have had half a dozen snows by now. The drought's just been bad this year."

"Ugh." I grabbed a manure fork from the wall and pushed a wheelbarrow over to Flicker's stall.

"If I help clean stalls, can I ask more questions about horses?" Fadeyka asked hopefully.

"Why not?" I said, resigned. It wasn't like I had anything better to do. As we scooped stalls, she peppered me with detailed questions: what grains the horses ate, how old they had to be for weaning, how to tell different kinds of hay apart or what regions those grasses grew in back in Mynaria. Then she rattled off all the current trade rates for agricultural-related commodities, after I made the mistake of asking how much the winter hay supply cost here. I had a headache before we were halfway done.

"What kind of sword drills can you do on horseback?" she asked. We'd already discussed jousting and mounted archery, but the questions had not stopped.

"Don't know," I said. "They never let me learn."

Fadeyka slung a forkful of manure with extra force, nearly missing the wheelbarrow. "What? Why not?" The idea seemed to deeply offend her.

"'A princess doesn't need a sword,'" I said, quoting my father.

Fadeyka snorted. "That's the silliest thing I've ever heard."

"I always thought so, too," I said. Swordsmanship had always been a sore point for me—one of the things my brother was allowed to learn and I wasn't. I got embroidery lessons. Or at least they'd tried to give me embroidery lessons; I'd sneaked off to the barn instead.

"So why don't you learn now?" She asked the question with such guileless curiosity that it took me off guard.

I'd been so used to my father telling me what to do and ignoring him to forge my own path that I'd forgotten about the things I could do for reasons other than rebellion.

"I don't know," I said.

"That's a silly reason."

I hated to admit it, but I was inclined to agree with her. And as I thought it over, I realized the answer to how to find out more about what Alek was up to and keep an eye on him for Laurenna was right in front of me.

"You're right. I should learn to use a sword," I said, though secretly, the idea made me a little nervous. If the training here was anything like what my brother had received, it started early. I'd be more than ten years late to learning, and I doubted the clumsy practice I'd done on my own after watching my brother was going to be much of a foundation. But there were other reasons to do it even beyond digging up potential links between Alek and the Sonnenbornes. While I wasn't privy yet to the details of what Laurenna or Zhari were doing about the Sonnenbornes, their soldiers would have thoughts and opinions—and be more forthcoming with them.

Fighters tended to be less interested in politics and more interested in solutions, which was a perspective I could appreciate. Plus, it would be a diplomatic gesture to show I cared enough to learn a skill that was a bigger part of life here than in my homeland.

"I was going to the salle before dinner anyway, if you want to come," Fadeyka said.

"All right," I agreed.

Fadeyka bounced on her toes in excitement.

After bidding Flicker and the other horses good-bye, we walked back toward the tower, Fadeyka's litany of questions continuing the entire way.

"How old is Flicker?" Fadeyka asked.

"Five," I said.

"Have you had him his whole life?"

"Pretty much."

"Where did you buy him?"

I sighed. "I bribed the royal stablemaster to give him to me." It wasn't entirely a lie.

"Really?" This seemed to impress her. "Who else have you bribed?"

The questioning continued like that all the way to the salle, interspersed with declarations of her opinions—that the high-collared dresses coming into fashion were terribly itchy, that the castle cook's assistant wasn't bad-looking when he bothered to wipe the soot off his face, that she could draw the seal of the Winter Court perfectly, even with her eyes closed, that the best route to the salle or the stables when the snow got deep was through the servants' tunnel at the back of the kitchen, and that Queen

Invasya was pretty for an old lady, but terrifying.

It figured that the only person interested in befriending me here was a precocious thirteen-year-old who asked too many questions. Still, I'd warmed to Fadeyka. She was rather like a cross between me and Denna—my interest in horses and fighting and Denna's absurd intellectualism all rolled into one person—and she was a desperately needed distraction during a time when I knew I couldn't face the reality of my life.

She led me past the merchants' hall and another building that looked more like soldiers' barracks, and then through a door into a long room that functioned more like a hallway. Foot traffic split to walk around a fountain that served as a median through the length of the room. The brilliant shades of green used to decorate the walls gave the illusion of springtime in spite of winter looming.

At the end of the hall, we pushed through a heavy door of transparent material. The room inside had a worn wooden floor, heavily scarred by warriors' boots and dropped blades. Fadeyka immediately dashed off to the trunks lining the wall and was donning a light set of practice leathers and snatching a short blade off the wall before I had a chance to take it all in. Now that I stood in the salle, I had to work hard not to second-guess my confident decision at the barn. These people all seemed skilled, and some, like Fadeyka, had been training since they were barely able to walk. The last thing I needed was something else to prove I was terrible at. I felt bad enough about myself already.

Several pairs of people sparred with various shapes and sizes of practice blades. In a far corner, Eronit and Varian went through an intricate series of exercises with staves. Across the room, Alek was putting a pair of trainees through some particularly challenging drills. He was relentless, making them repeat the exercise over and over until their muscles trembled but every step was just as he instructed. I skirted the edges of the room, but before I could take a seat on one of the benches along the far wall, Fadeyka had pulled a light sword off the wall and was offering it to me.

"Alek's the best coach, and he's about to finish with those two," Fadeyka said. "You'd better hurry up if you want your chance with him."

"Who said anything about training with him?" I asked. Watching him was one thing. Getting thrown on my arse by him was entirely another.

"You want to get good fast, don't you?" Fadeyka gestured with her free hand. "Don't pass up the chance."

I hated to admit it, but the kid was right, and I did actually want to learn. Maybe if I did well, Alek would stop looking at me like I was as useful as a sweat-soaked saddle blanket. I steeled myself. There had been a time when I didn't know how to shoot a bow, climb over the castle wall, or search for information at the pubs. This was just another new thing to learn.

I reached out and took the sword.

"Like this," Fadeyka said, correcting my grip. "But let's make sure you have just the right one."

Fadeyka helped fit me with practice leathers, then showed me several weights of swords, giving me a chance to heft each one and feel the difference in balance. I expected laughter or disdainful looks for letting someone Fadeyka's age tell me what to do, but no one paid any attention. Some of the swords were so heavy I could barely lift them, and others felt off to one side or the other. In the end, I wound up with the first one she'd handed me, and she smiled knowingly.

Once I was appropriately dressed, I waited until Alek was finished with the first set of trainees and then approached him.

"Winter Court costume party tonight?" he asked.

I stood up straighter. "I'm here to learn," I said, ignoring his jab.

He looked at Fadeyka and back to me.

"All right, then. But we do this my way." Soon he had me out on the practice floor, and I forgot everything that had preoccupied my mind before that. The agony of Denna's loss faded into a dull ache that was almost tolerable. The drills were simple, but hard to execute well, and gave me enough to focus on that I barely stopped to think other than of my next step or move. I didn't even care when Alek barked at us both about our form—not when the adjustments he suggested made my strikes feel twice as strong. Any worries I had about hurting Fadeyka were banished immediately. She had twice my speed and many more times my skill.

When Alek finally called us to a halt, I was sweating and exhausted.

"Not too bad for your first time out," Fadeyka said.

I eyed her balefully. "I'm going to feel this in at least ten unmentionable places tomorrow."

"It's a start," Alek said, then turned to Fadeyka. "Do you want to try the evasive move we practiced the other day?"

Her whole face lit up.

"Only a few times," he said.

I stepped out of the way as they took their positions across from each other. Alek came at her with a straightforward thrust of his blade, but instead of parrying the way I'd been learning to, Fadeyka managed to bend herself out of the way in an unnatural motion. Then fog gathered in a wall to obscure her from Alek. Other fighters stopped to watch.

"You have to be faster," Alek said. "Use the fog first, so that your opponent can't see where you move."

"It's hard to think when there's a sword coming at me," Fadeyka complained.

"If you practice enough, you won't have to think," Alek said.

The fog dissipated and Fadeyka got back into her guard position. They repeated the exercise, but this time she pulled the fog in more quickly, vanishing into it as she dodged. It would have been the perfect escape, except that she suddenly appeared on the wrong side of the fog wall, nearly impaling herself on Alek's sword.

I gasped, but when Alek lowered his sword and reached for her, another person who looked identical to Fadeyka had appeared closer to me. Then, suddenly, there were four more, all of them moving erratically and without any clear purpose.

"Faye!" Alek shouted. He hastily sketched a symbol and the fog dissipated, revealing what had to be the original Fadeyka, who had collapsed to the floor.

I watched in horror as another duplicate separated itself from her body and staggered away.

Alek dropped to his knees beside her and shook her shoulder, but she was unresponsive. He muttered something under his breath and gestured as if to gather up the other Fadeykas, but they only flickered. For the first time since I'd known him, I saw something almost like concern wash over his stonelike face.

Most people backed away, and a few even headed for the doors of the salle. Following them might have been smarter, but I felt rooted in place. It didn't seem to matter where I went or who I was with. Magic was always all around me, affecting my life in ways I couldn't predict or make any sense of.

I took a step closer to Fadeyka, and one of her clones stumbled into me. I flinched, but the mirage passed through me, making my body flash with heat where we touched. Without warning, the doppelgängers swept toward Fadeyka's body and poured back into her, and she convulsed as each one joined her. When the salle returned to silence and peace, a female fighter was standing over Fadeyka, who sat up, wincing.

"Is that a trick you know, Shazi?" Alek asked the dark-haired woman.

"No, but I've seen it before," she said, confusion in her pale blue eyes. "I didn't think Faye had an air Affinity."

"She doesn't." Alek stood up, frowning.

"Did someone curse her?" I asked.

Alek and Shazi both looked at me like I had the brains of a pitchfork. Fadeyka laughed, which quickly devolved into a coughing fit.

"Mynarian," Alek explained to Shazi, waving his hand disgustedly.

I tensed, but Shazi's expression softened. "Ah. You're *vakos*, then. No, the magic was definitely coming from Faye, but that's odd. She's only shown signs of a water Affinity, from what little I know."

"Magic users can't use more than one type of magic?" I asked. That didn't line up with what I'd seen Denna do. Her powers seemed to always have some new form they were taking. It might always start with fire, but it ended with so much more destruction than that.

"Not without a multi-Affinity," Alek grumbled.

"Zhari would surely know if Faye had a multi-Affinity," Shazi said to Alek, her eyebrows raised.

"Could be she's still developing it." Alek shrugged. "No manifest yet."

"Is a multi-Affinity . . . bad?" I asked. "And why would Zhari know?"

"It's rare," Shazi said. "They tend to be harder to control. Zhari is the only guardian who has one, and she's mentored most of the apprentices who've turned up with them."

Cold dread wormed its way down my back. Perhaps that was why the queen had such an interest in Denna. My heart squeezed painfully. Now there was no way to know or find out.

"Don't talk about me like I'm not here," Fadeyka mumbled, reaching for my hand. I hoisted her to her feet, letting her hang on until I was sure she wouldn't keel over.

"Take her to Laurenna," Alek barked at me, already turning away.

I scowled at his back, knowing full well why he didn't want to do it. I bit back the sharp retort on the tip of my tongue. If nothing else, perhaps it would come off as a favor to Laurenna. I didn't have to tell her that Alek told me to do it.

"Do you know where your mother is?" I asked Fadeyka.

She nodded. "Merchants' Guild hearing. I just need to put away my sword."

I took off my gear and then hovered around her anxiously as

she clumsily put away her weapon and practice leathers. She walked much more slowly than usual as we left the salle, without the customary slew of questions that characterized our conversations.

I expected some kind of commotion when we reached the guild meeting, but instead we were told to wait outside on a hard bench. Fadeyka was uncharacteristically quiet, slumping against the wall, exhausted.

"Are you all right?" I asked.

"Tired," she said. "And Mother isn't going to be pleased."

Fadeyka's words proved correct, when Laurenna finally emerged from the guild meeting and strode over to her daughter with purpose. Zhari came behind her more slowly, gliding effortlessly over the floor with the help of her long staff.

"What happened?" Laurenna asked, then proceeded to frown as Fadeyka explained what had transpired at the salle. I couldn't help but admire the girl's storytelling, particularly her ability to omit Alek from the tale entirely.

"Zhari, what do you make of this?" Laurenna asked.

"It's hard to say," Zhari said. "Her gift is still developing."

"Someone said it could be a multi-Affinity," I said, catching a glimpse of Fadeyka's look of relief that I hadn't mentioned Alek by name.

Laurenna and Zhari both gave me looks of deep scrutiny.

"It's more common for those to develop after an initial Affinity has settled," Zhari finally said. "But not impossible." She turned her amber eyes on Fadeyka.

"Could the charm have caused it?" Laurenna asked Zhari, pitching her voice more softly.

Fadeyka protectively gripped the seven-pointed star hanging around her neck.

"I doubt it," Zhari said. "That's not really what it was intended for."

I glanced back at the charm with a creeping sense of unease, wondering if it was capable of anything on a par with the ring Kriantz had used to kill my father.

"Let's talk about this more back at my quarters," Laurenna said to Zhari, putting her hand on Fadeyka's forehead. "Thank you for bringing my daughter to me," she added to me in polite dismissal.

"It was no trouble," I said. "Please let me know if I can do anything else to help."

I bade them farewell and walked back to the merchants' hall, my legs feeling more leaden with every step. I barely had the energy to slip through the door of my room. As I rinsed off the dirt and grime of the day, I pondered what to do next. I still had my brother's offer of cavalry on the table, but I needed to save it for the right moment. Getting some information of value to Laurenna took priority for now, as it seemed like that was the best way to win her over and invest her in my concerns.

I also wanted her and Zhari to grow more comfortable around me, so that conversations about Fadeyka's magic or anything else wouldn't have to happen behind closed doors. Even if I couldn't use or sense magic, I still needed to know what to watch out for if I expected to survive in Zumorda. In the meantime, now that I'd been to the salle, I knew it could be a place for me to make apolitical connections that would help me much more than ineptly trying to curry favor with nobles at the Winter Court. If I wanted to know more about Alek's history with the Sonnenbornes, other soldiers were the place to start. They'd have stories, and if they were anything like the liegemen in Mynaria, a few drinks would be more than enough to get them talking. Perhaps I was doomed to be a disaster at court, especially without Denna's help, but I had no shortage of confidence in my ability to keep up with the drinking habits of fighters.

Not for the first time in my life, I was going to have to play spy.

FOURTEEN 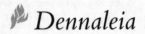 *Dennaleia*

A JOURNEY THAT SHOULD HAVE TAKEN WEEKS PASSED
in only a matter of days, our caravan never slowing its impossibly
fast pace. Evidence of the drought quickly faded as we continued
north. I lost myself in books and distanced myself from Evie and
Tristan's conversations, which wasn't difficult, as they seemed more
interested in talking to each other than to me. I hoped to talk to
the queen about the boy from Duvey who had been in Tilium,
but she didn't summon me for a private session again. Instead, the
other trainees were called to her one by one, always standing a little
straighter when they returned, always with a little more fight and
fire in their eyes.

We made a few other stops, but there were no further scenes
like what we'd experienced in Tilium. The queen dealt quieter justice to those who deserved it and delivered gifts to the towns that
had tithed well. The trainees were rarely asked to help, but we were

always invited to bear witness—invitations that were clearly orders. For a town nestled in a valley where the rain seemed ceaseless, the queen provided a magical sconce enchanted to contain a flame that could never be extinguished. In a small mountain village, she had Karina use her wind magic to clear sheep pastures that were already thigh-deep in snow. I'd had to back away as Karina pulled the wind from the sky, feeling prickles in my own arms. In Orzai, a massive town of stone and mist, one of the queen's soldiers carved a new canal out of solid rock to deliver water to a poorer district.

It wasn't the kind of monarchy I was used to seeing. The queen didn't just rule her kingdom. She acted within it. She herself was the one making a difference for her people—not passing down decrees, making decisions with a group like the Directorate, or sending minions to do her bidding. Even though the regional guardians had governance of their sections of the kingdom, the queen was the one they relied on to make the most dramatic changes for them and their people. Neither Mynaria nor Havemont was run this way. The monarchs of those kingdoms had absolute power in theory, but not in practice. Here it was clear that the queen was worshipped almost like a god, and her power was absolute. I admired the way she took personal action to help her people, but her sense of justice was frighteningly ruthless.

After Orzai, we passed other towns but didn't stop, continuing until we reached foothills and then mountains as magnificent as the ones I'd known back home. The weather kept getting colder until I couldn't stop shivering, even wrapped in my fur-lined cloak inside the floating sled. Clouds hung among the snowy peaks like veils, and a part of me reawakened at the sight of them. I'd forgotten what comfort it gave me to see peaks on the horizon, almost as if they were a shield from the rest of the world. After growing up in Spire City, I would always feel like the mountains were home to me.

Parts of our caravan broke away as night fell, the few riders with horses either departing with their mounts or leaving them in the valley farms. Much like my hometown of Spire City, it seemed Corovja was inhospitable for horses thanks to the steep grades. The road grew until it was wider and more winding than any of the others we'd traversed so far. Snow had been pushed to the sides, already piled as high as my knees. Evie, Tristan, and I pressed our faces to the windows of the sled, curious about our new surroundings. The farmland was long gone by the time we reached buildings, which quickly became tall and imposing. Their strange roofs came to sharp peaks at the top, most of them angled in one direction, some extending all the way to the ground. Windows were lit, but the streets were mostly empty. Moonlight occasionally broke through scudding clouds to make the piles of snow gleam with otherworldly light.

When our barge finally drew to a halt and we joined the queen and her attendants outside, my eyes widened. I'd expected something like the castle in Spire City, which was a warren of narrow passages and tall towers. Instead, a huge palace stood before us on the other side of a thick wall, its heavy iron gates being hauled open by ten guards about a hundred paces ahead. The building behind the gate was staggeringly large, easily four times the size of the Mynarian castle just based on the dimensions of the front. The whole thing was made of polished white marble as cold and austere as the snow.

It took us twenty paces to walk through the tunnel past the gate before emerging on the other side. I followed Karina, the queen, and the other trainees up to a set of huge wooden doors at the entrance of the building. Illuminated globes adorned the path, the cool blue light clearly magical in nature. Guards swung the doors to the castle open as we stepped near, bowing in deference to the queen.

A welcome wave of heat greeted us when we walked into the building. I did what I could not to stare, but if the castle was impressive from the outside, it was far more so once we'd walked through the doors. The smooth, polished marble of the floor reflected the light of intricate iron sconces holding orbs like the ones I'd destroyed in the merchants' hall back in Kartasha. The ceiling was so high, I felt as though it might as well be in the clouds if not for the hundreds, maybe even thousands, of glowing balls that hung from the ceiling at different heights.

Ikrie looked back at me, smirking when she saw my awestruck expression. At least it meant my disguise was probably working—someone who had grown up a servant would certainly gawk at a building like this. The queen immediately dismissed Ikrie and Aela, both of whom looked at home, no doubt because they had grown up noble and their families spent most of the year in Corovja, only wintering in the south. The two girls headed for a hallway leading out of the room, leaving servants to shoulder their packs. Eryk looked after them longingly, fidgeting uncomfortably at being left behind with the rest of us.

"Welcome to Corovja, the crown city of Zumorda," the queen said to me and the other remaining trainees. "Guards will escort you to your rooms. For your safety, you are not to leave the castle grounds without my permission."

"Thank you, Your Majesty." I curtsied, realizing too late that

Eryk, Evie, and Tristan were looking at me with confusion. The queen just seemed mildly amused. Mare always told me my manners and my technique were too good for a commoner. It was time for me to let those lessons go to make room for new ones. My adherence to protocol was too reflexive, too automatic, and the rules in Zumorda were clearly very different from those in my homeland. I kept forgetting that powerful magic users tended to be less formal around each other than etiquette would normally require. I purposely wobbled coming out of the curtsy. Hopefully everyone would write off my behavior as Mynarian.

"I have high expectations for you," the queen said, meeting each of our eyes in turn. Her sapphire eyes burned when she looked at me. "Your training begins tomorrow. Expect competition."

Ice spread through my veins. "Competition?" I said, my mouth dry. I'd hoped for collaboration, not a fight from the first day.

"Yes," she said. "See that you don't disappoint me." She turned and swept away before any of us could respond. The others dispersed with their escorts, leaving me frightened and alone with mine.

The guard who took me to my rooms looked barely older than me, and talked so fast and so much that I didn't have any obligation to hold up the other end of the conversation. He pointed out many features of the castle, but I was so weary and preoccupied that I took in almost nothing. The only thing that struck me was how empty the halls seemed. The castle I'd grown up in had always been bustling with activity, even during the coldest, darkest days of winter. I supposed most of the nobles were at the Winter Court. Even so, the emptiness was unsettling and made me that much more aware of how distant I was from everyone I knew and loved. Mare was still in Kartasha, and my family was even farther north than Corovja, in Spire City, probably still assuming I was dead. How was I supposed to survive this strange place without them for support? Without any knowledge of what I'd gotten myself into?

My rooms were finer than I ever could have expected, far outstripping Mare's quarters in Kartasha. All four of my interconnected rooms had windows looking over the palace grounds, and though I couldn't see anything in the dark, I knew the views would be spectacular come morning. Sitting down on the curtained bed, I almost felt like a princess again, except that now I was aware of everything I lacked in a way I hadn't been before. The rooms were too silent, the bed too wide, and the chill seeping into my bones a fitting accompaniment to my loneliness rather than the familiar kiss of winter beginning.

By the time a page arrived to escort me to training the next morning, I had long since been dressed, having found my wardrobe already supplied with several pairs of pants and shirts, all in an unflattering shade of rust. The clothing I'd worn for my disguise as a servant apparently wasn't appropriate for training.

"Here you are, my lady," the page said, after leading me on a convoluted path through the castle. "You'll find the training center through there and down the hall." He gestured. When I hesitated, he added, "Only students and teachers are allowed inside."

"Oh." Nerves made my stomach toss, and I suddenly regretted the small portion of oatmeal and preserves I'd had for breakfast. "Thank you very much."

The page nodded and disappeared back the way we'd come. The

guards stood aside, one of them opening the heavy door.

I didn't know what to expect from the training area, so I was surprised when the room I entered looked like a reception hall. Somehow I'd been thinking it would be more like a place where guards might practice—a salle or an outdoor arena, somewhere that looked fit for a battle. White walls with intricate plasterwork covering the supporting beams provided a bright contrast to the ceiling, which had been painted black and adorned with sparkling stars that spelled out the constellations I'd learned as a child. The floor was made of common dark gray stone, polished smooth. A strange but welcome feeling of calm washed over me as I entered the space. I could sense ambient magic all around, as if the walls and ceiling were imbued with it, and my arms tingled.

Finally, I was taking the first steps to mastering my powers. If I could do that, perhaps I could get my life back under control, too. All I wanted was some semblance of normalcy—whatever that looked like here. A set of useful skills that would allow me to use my powers without hurting anyone and maybe even to do some good in the world. I tried to quell my doubts that gaining those skills would be enough for Mare. Part of me worried that she'd never truly be able to be comfortable around me again.

The room wasn't the only source of magic. Evie and Eryk stood near the center of the floor within easy striking distance of each other, wearing uniforms similar to mine but in green and gray, respectively. Evie's brows knitted together in concentration, and she held her hands out in front of her, moving them slowly, as if she were tracing symbols in the air—but if she was, they weren't any symbols I recognized. Eryk's arms hung at his sides, but his palms were turned forward, facing his sister. Apparently they'd decided to practice without guidance. I clenched and unclenched my fists to try to dispel my anxiety, reminding myself they'd probably been training together their entire lives.

A row of simple wooden chairs stood against the wall, and Tristan sat slumped in one of them. His black shirt was tight on his wiry frame, and I noticed a hole in his pants, which ended in black work boots worn thin from use. His eyes flicked to me as I took a few cautious steps into the room.

"Hello." I smiled, hoping maybe our travels together had allowed for some sort of camaraderie to bloom, even if we hadn't talked much.

He paused for so long that my confidence started to fade. I should have tried harder to make friends with the other trainees along the journey.

A shout echoed through the room before he could respond. Eryk had collapsed onto the floor, and Evie stood over him with a triumphant expression on her face.

"Enough!" Eryk gasped.

"Say it," Evie demanded.

He hesitated for only a moment before choking out, "I yield."

She smirked and dropped her hands. Eryk rolled onto his back, letting out a frustrated groan and staring at the ceiling.

The door to the training room creaked open, allowing Aela and Ikrie to enter. Both of them looked at me, their stares lingering much longer than was comfortable. Ikrie whispered something to Aela and they both laughed. Before I could attempt to greet them, they turned away, dropping bags on the floor and kicking them underneath two of the chairs against the wall.

The door had barely fallen shut behind them before it opened again, and this time an older man and woman strode through. The woman's salt-and-pepper hair was done in a neat braid coiled into a bun at the base of her neck, and she carried herself with the confidence of authority. If memory served, she was probably Saia, the guardian of Corovja. Her companion followed half a step behind her. He looked somewhat younger, with a bare slash of skin at the base of his jaw cutting through his brown beard.

Eryk quickly jumped to his feet, and Aela and Ikrie turned to face the pair. The man stopped in the center of the room, but the woman continued walking until she'd disappeared through a door in the opposite wall.

"Pair off, everyone," the man said, apparently unconcerned with pleasantries. "Let's see what you know about shielding."

Ikrie rolled up the sleeves of her yellow tunic and approached me with a smirk on her face. Nausea gripped me. I thought there would be some kind of instruction, not just a command to do something I didn't even understand. I wanted to disappear into the floor.

"Do you even know how to shield yourself?" Ikrie asked, scorn in her voice.

"I—no," I admitted.

She rolled her eyes. "Fine. You can be on offense first."

"What?" I asked.

She didn't answer. Instead, a bubble of hazy air formed around her.

"Hit me," she said. "Your mistress wasn't brave enough to take me on. Maybe you'll be different."

Anger flared in my breast. She didn't know what I'd sacrificed to stand in front of her, and she certainly didn't know what Mare had sacrificed to be with me. I took a deep breath, then struck hard and fast, just as Aster had shown me.

Ikrie's shield of air parted around my arm as my fist rose toward her throat. Her eyes registered surprise for only half a second before my fist connected with her neck.

She stumbled back from me, choking, and the shield around her fell away.

"By the Six!" I cursed, and clutched my fist. Aster hadn't warned me that punching someone would hurt quite that much.

"What the sarding Hell!?" Ikrie finally coughed out as she caught her breath.

"You said to hit you!" I said, still clutching my hand.

"With magic, you lowborn fool, not your fist!" Ikrie said. She coughed again, and the sound reverberated through the room.

The instructor approached, a smirk on his face. "Pause your exercises, class. Lia here has just reminded us of an important lesson. Magical defense isn't everything. Make sure that you shield against physical blows as well as magical ones."

"That's not the point of this exercise, Brynan," Ikrie snapped. "This is what happens when untrained peasants sard up our routine."

I couldn't believe the way Ikrie spoke to him. There was no respect in it at all—though surely she didn't consider her instructor an equal.

"Which is apparently exactly what you need in order to be at peak performance," Brynan replied. "If you want your choice of apprenticeships, you need to be at the top of this class."

"I'm very sorry," I said.

"Don't be sorry." Brynan whirled to face me. "Never be sorry when you've found and exploited an enemy's weakness. Those in power are never sorry when they mete out justice to those who deserve it."

I shut my mouth, biting back the words I wanted to say. The memories of what had happened to Sigvar were still fresh—I knew what Zumordan justice looked like. But I *was* sorry. I didn't consider Ikrie an enemy, even if I hated the way she'd treated Mare and had been insulted by her jabs at me. If anything, I wanted the other trainees to be my friends. This was the first time I'd ever been around other magic users. I had so many questions that only they would be able to answer.

"Lia is behind all of you in training," Brynan explained.

A fresh wave of embarrassment rose in me. Of course I was. This wasn't what I'd spent my life training to do. I hadn't learned to use the Sight before I could read or had anyone to teach me what to do with my fire magic. I'd been hiding that part of myself and trying to become a queen—not a fighter, not a magic user.

"What that means is that you should expect some fumbles, yes, but also expect the unexpected. You aren't going to always be able to predict what she's going to do, because she hasn't had the same kind of practice drilled in as you have. She'll get there in time, but in the meantime, she'll keep you all on your toes."

Five sets of eyes ranging from darkest brown to lightest blue stared at me—with distrust at best and loathing at worst.

"Back to practice," the instructor said. "And switch partners. Lia, Eryk, and Tristan, move over to the next person."

I hurried to my next opponent, Evie. She gave me a pitying smile, her tightly curled hair framing her pixie-like face and amber eyes like a halo.

"You shield first," she said.

Before I could say anything in response, a chunk of rock broke loose from the floor and hurtled toward my head. I ducked and yelped, but it still clipped me in the temple. A bolt of shock and pain lanced through me. A warm trickle ran down my face, and when I wiped at it, my hand came away red.

These people were completely insane. It didn't matter who I fought with—any one of them could destroy me in a second. Panic started to rise, and with it, my power. Evie continued to hurl rocks at me that I was barely able to dodge.

In desperation, I reached for my own power. Fire burst out of my hands and formed a burning whirlwind around me. Still, Evie's missiles flew right through, only slightly deflected by the twisting flames. Fear whispered in my ear, telling me that I needed more power. Sigvar had used mind magic to control his cult, but he'd also been able to make the earth obey. Perhaps I could do the same and turn Evie's magic back on her—I'd had to use more than one kind of magic when I summoned the star fall. I opened myself fully to my power, bracing for the pain that rippled up my arms. The stones Evie had hurled at me rose from the ground, joining the swirling maelstrom of fire.

In spite of the chaos racing around me, I felt strangely at peace. No one could hurt me at the center of this storm. Shouting from others in the room was little more than vague noise. I didn't care what they were yelling about. I had the magic, and it was doing what I wanted.

Before I could fully revel in the power, the draining started—my limbs growing heavy as energy was sucked out of them to feed the fire. I had to let go of the magic or it would consume me. I balled my hands into fists and shoved the whirlwind away from me with a scream of anger that tore through the room along with my magic.

When the dust settled, I was the only one standing. I blinked in confusion, breathing heavily, trying to make sense of the bodies lying flat around me. As the last of the magic slipped away, fear edged back in. My whole body shook with sudden fatigue. Around me, a few of the trainees pushed themselves up, coughing on dusty, smoky air, but others lay still. A cold horror washed through me. What if I'd killed them? Hazy memories of blackened corpses flashed behind my eyes. I couldn't tell if the smell of burning flesh was real or a fabrication of my mind. Was I remembering Duvey or hallucinating something far worse?

I staggered toward the edge of the room, hoping to make it to one of the chairs along the wall. The edges of my vision turned red, then black, and my legs gave out. I crashed onto the stone floor, breaking my fall painfully with one arm before the darkness closed in.

A pounding ache in my head woke me, accompanied by a strange but comforting feeling in my right arm, as if warmth were flowing into it.

"That should be enough," a voice said nearby. "She's coming around."

I opened my eyes to see Evie touching my arm. Brynan and the woman with salt-and-pepper hair stood over me on my other side.

"Thank you, Evie," the woman said. "You can go."

I pushed myself upright, watching Evie vanish through a nearby door. I was on the floor in a small room with a desk on the far side and bright light streaming in through the window behind it. By the slant of the light, I'd been unconscious for at least three sunlengths.

"Lia," the woman said, her voice stern. "What happened?"

I blinked at her, still feeling disoriented and confused. What *had* happened? "Who are you?" I asked.

"My name is Saia," the woman said. "I'm the guardian of Corovja and head instructor here. Tell me what you did in the training room."

I sat up cautiously, not trusting my legs just yet. My head spun as soon as I was upright, and it took a moment for my vision to clear again.

"I . . . protected myself," I said.

"Did you take power from others?" Saia's eyes were narrow and fierce, and I shrank away from her. "Did anyone help you?"

"No," I said. None of those people would have helped me, and it was baffling that she might think otherwise. "It was just me."

Saia and Brynan looked at each other. Brynan appeared wary, while Saia's face was impossible to read. If the queen's best trainers didn't know how I'd knocked everyone out earlier, getting my magic under control would be even harder than I'd thought. How was I supposed to learn if they couldn't explain my powers to me? There didn't seem to be a classroom component to the instruction here, which would have made everything so much easier.

"But fire is your only Affinity," Saia said. "Correct?"

"As far as I know." But how was I supposed to be sure? It was the first gift to come to me. Whatever ability I had to pull on other magic was probably just caused by my lack of control.

"You came from Mynaria, yes?"

I nodded.

"It might be hard for her to articulate her powers," Brynan said. "She's had no formal training. Ikrie said she doesn't even have the Sight."

He knew I was untrained and he'd thrown me into fighting exercises with the other trainees. How did he expect me to learn anything that way?

Saia looked at me for a moment. "It hardly matters right now." She shot an annoyed look at Brynan. "You should never have been sparring with the others when you don't know how to See or shield yourself." She spoke to me, but her words were clearly a rebuke of Brynan, and I felt a pinprick of vindication.

"What should she do, then?" Brynan said. "If she doesn't learn to fight, she'll never be prepared for the Revel."

"What is the Revel?" I asked.

"The Midwinter Revel is an exhibition and a competition for the trainees," Brynan explained, clearly exasperated by my lack of knowledge. "The winner has first choice of apprenticeship and so on down the line."

A wave of fear crashed over me. "But I don't want to fight." There had to be other things to learn. I'd caused enough harm with my powers already.

"Fighting is the whole point." He spoke as though I were stupid. "We fight to defend our kingdom."

"But . . . Evie is a healer," I said, remembering the warmth that had spread through my arm and shoulder before she left. "Isn't she?"

"Among other things," Saia said.

"Maybe there are things I can learn from the other trainees if—"

"You're not here to make friends," Brynan said, his voice sharp.

"You're here to compete," Saia said.

Before I could ask any more questions, the queen swept into the room. Both Saia and Brynan nodded to acknowledge her.

"Accidents already on the first day of training don't speak well for your instruction," the queen commented.

Brynan's jaw tightened. "No one told us she didn't have the Sight until—"

"If you had read the briefing papers I provided you with yesterday, I think you would have found that information enclosed." The queen took a step closer to him, her white robes whispering over the rug.

"Of course, Your Majesty," he said, flinching as she drew closer.

"Lia—come with me," the queen said.

"Yes, Your Majesty," I said, fearful of becoming the next source of her displeasure.

Her guards moved in to flank us as soon as we exited Saia's small room. She led me through the halls until we reached the throne room, which was in a part of the castle that seemed much older based on its architectural details. The queen turned to face me as her guards quietly dispersed to the perimeter of the room. It felt empty of magical power, except what I sensed from the queen and, strangely enough, a patch of the marble floor that was red as blood.

"Please show me what you know of shielding," she said.

"Here?" I looked around, suddenly aware of how many burnable and breakable things there were in the throne room. Vases perched on stone pillars, tapestries hanging on the walls, and wooden beams that looked several centuries older than me. "Well, we didn't get much time to work—"

"Show, not tell." Her hands lit up in the space of a heartbeat, glowing with brilliant white light. Magic gathered in her hands, and the flame grew until she flung a fireball at me with absolutely no change in expression. I screamed and leaped to the side but wasn't nearly quick enough to evade her. The ball of flame smashed into my chest and knocked me to my knees, the stone floor rattling my teeth. My breaths came raggedly, and I skittered away on all fours like a frightened animal.

"Evidently Saia and Brynan haven't taught you anything today." Queen Invasya sighed. "Come along." She held out her hand and stepped toward me.

My hand shook with nerves as I reached up. Her grip was cool as marble, a strange contrast to the fire she'd held in her hands just moments before. As soon as I was on my feet, she paced away from me toward the middle of the room.

"Try again," she said. "Try to engage your Sight to anticipate my next move."

Her hands began to glow again, and my throat immediately constricted with fear. The queen's magic slammed into my chest. I stumbled a little, and the edges of my sleeves smoldered. Before I could recover, a second fireball hit me, and I fell over backward with a grunt of pain. I now lay over the line where the white marble met the bloody red. I crawled back to my feet, trying to hold back the tears stinging the corners of my eyes.

"No one has ever knocked you down, have they?" the queen asked, her tone and expression puzzled. "I wouldn't have expected that of a commoner."

I took several steps back, my arms held out defensively in front of me. She wasn't wrong. In my life as a princess, no one had ever tried to physically harm me. Fighting had never been in my purview. I held her gaze this time, scared to look away.

"Are you afraid?" She stepped forward and flicked her fingers at me. I recoiled, expecting another blast of power. Instead there was nothing, and I looked like a fool. A traitorous tear slipped down my left cheek and my lip trembled.

"You are," she said. "You'll have to get over that."

My head buzzed like a hive of bees. She knew I wasn't trained enough to hold off the kind of attacks she was throwing at me. My anger and my magic swirled inside me, and I felt the familiar wave of rising power that meant bad things were about to happen. I no longer cared about trying to stop them.

Queen Invasya raised a hand.

"No!" I balled my hands into fists. The emotions churning through me shot out of me at once and in every direction. A wall of fire bloomed from my fingertips, expanding to twice my height in mere seconds. I shoved it away from me with a feral yell. Invasya's fireball dissipated against the shield, which swept toward her. My heart stayed in my throat as the flames parted harmlessly around her and then hissed out with a flick of her hand.

The queen's surprise quickly turned to a small, knowing smile.

"No," I said again, more softly this time. I took a few steps back. I didn't want this. I didn't want to be pushed to lose control.

"That was interesting." She stepped toward me, this time keeping her arms by her sides.

I moved back in even time with her, breathing hard and still on high alert.

"Stop trying to run from your abilities," she said, her voice commanding. "Those thrice-damned Mynarians have made you afraid of your own power."

"I don't know how not to be afraid," I said. It wasn't the Mynarians' or my family's fault that they hadn't known what to do with me and my powers.

"Be afraid if you must," the queen said, "but fight anyway."

"Yes, Your Majesty." I didn't know how to do what she asked.

"First you need to find your Sight," she said. "Do you play an instrument?"

I lost focus, caught off guard by the random question. "Yes, the harp."

"Then I might have a technique for you to try," she said. "Come with me."

She led me into an adjacent room that appeared to be her study, then released a mechanism in the wall to reveal a narrow corridor. I followed her in, uncertain. The corridor was dim, though there was light at its end. When we reached the end, it opened into another chamber. In one corner of the room stood the most magnificent pedal harp I'd ever seen. It towered over me, standing even taller than the queen. Flower-covered vines climbed the column of the harp, the crown glittering with gold leaf and inlaid sapphires. Similar designs had been wrought in gold filigree that had undoubtedly been inlaid in the sides of the soundbox by magic.

"Play for me," the queen said.

"What?" I stared at her with wide eyes.

"I want to hear you play." She settled herself in a broad leather chair and gestured for me to go to the corner.

"All right," I said, swallowing hard. There was no way to back out of it now. I pulled the harp out of the corner and found a matching stool tucked behind the shelf. After a few minutes of adjustment, I managed to get the stool to a comfortable height. The instrument was still going to be a challenge to play—I was more accustomed to playing on a semi-grand due to my small stature.

"Do you play as well?" I asked. The instrument was in such fine shape and so carefully and lovingly maintained that it would surprise me if she didn't.

"No," she said. "It was a gift."

"What do you want to hear?" I asked. The fact that she didn't play meant I could probably get away with playing something that wasn't too basic, but I was fearful of giving away how much I knew of the instrument. I'd spent hours in daily lessons from the time I was big enough to reach the strings on a smaller harp as part of my royal education. It wasn't a maidservant's instrument.

"Something simple," she said. "Something that you can play without thinking about it too much."

I nodded, relieved. That was easy enough. Slowly, I began to play a lullaby—one of the very first songs I had learned. I kept the first verse very simple but began to ornament the melody the second time through. The instrument was powerful and resonant, and

I wished for a room several times larger to take true advantage of it.

"Don't stop playing," the queen said, "but I want you open yourself to your magic right now. Imagine that you can See the music with your Sight. Look around you as though you're reading an audience, but keep your attention on your playing."

I did as she asked, relaxing my gaze and letting my fingers find the strings by memory. The sensation was entirely familiar and comforting, and my mind quieted as my focus narrowed to the music. All around me, objects took on a luminous sheen that grew into a brilliant glow. The queen was most radiant of all, haloed in blinding red light. My hands faltered on the strings.

"Don't stop." The queen smiled, her expression so warm and encouraging that it looked foreign on her face.

I slowly adjusted my focus a little more back to the music and kept playing, not wanting to lose my sudden ability to See. On top of the mantel, a sword hung, and it burned with a fire I sensed I could touch if I wanted to. A shining orb of silver metal sitting on one of the bookshelves also glowed with a different kind of energy, one that wasn't familiar but felt a little bit like Eryk's, who I'd learned had an Affinity for spirit. Excitement hummed through me. Finally, I felt like a fundamental piece I needed to master my magic was falling into place.

When the lullaby came to a close and I let the last notes resonate in the study, my Sight faded away. Seeing the world with ordinary eyes seemed dull in comparison.

"See, it's not so hard if you approach it correctly," the queen said.

"But how did that happen?" I asked, still awestruck.

"Most of the time you're trying too hard. Magic is all around us, in every living thing, in all enchanted objects. You have to look beyond the ordinary to see it, but it's not so much activating Sight you don't have as it is using the sight you do have differently."

I tilted my head, unsure of her explanation.

"Try looking at me."

I obeyed her.

"Now look through me. Not with intent, just casually, like you're more interested in the space around me. Now listen to your breath, and imagine that you are on a stage, about to play. The world is your audience, silent and waiting. Think about the notes you just played, and imagine how they felt, how they resonated, in this room." When she wasn't leveling fireballs at me, her voice was actually quite soothing.

I had to stop my fingers from reflexively reaching for the strings in front of me. Calm slowly made my breathing deepen. It was surprisingly easy to listen to the world in this way.

"Now, shut your eyes and inhale deeply. At my command you'll open them again. You will do so slowly. But I do not want you to look at anything in this room. Look in my direction, but look through me, not at me. Be aware of all, and let all be aware of you."

She gave me several more breaths, after which I felt as though there was a strange hum in my head. Nothing irritating, but simply a presence in the back of my mind that I hadn't noticed before. Magic tingled in my arms and hands, the same familiar sensation I'd felt since childhood.

"Open your eyes slowly," she said.

I obeyed, letting my eyes open in the sluggish way that they did as I woke from sleep. The world came into semi-focus as a blinding riot of colors glowed and swirled and moved before my eyes.

"I can See," I said, then exhaled a deep sigh of relief and let the Sight slip away. For the first time, I believed I could do this. Now I knew what I was looking for.

"So now you must practice," she said. "Practice until the Sight is second nature, until it's always around you and visible at the strength of your choosing. Play your instrument until you See clearly. Then practice without it until it comes just as easily."

"Of course, yes, I will," I said. Maybe I could get better—it seemed as though hope finally existed.

"I'll have the harp sent to your rooms," she said. "You'll find more use for it than I do."

"Thank you, Your Majesty." I felt strangely touched, like someone wanted to see me succeed instead of fail and was giving me one of the tools I needed most.

"Do you have any further questions?" she asked.

I could sense the dismissal coming, but there were still things bothering me that raised questions only she could answer.

"About Tilium," I said. "One of the cult members was a boy I recognized as having been abducted from Duvey. I heard that young magic users are disappearing in the south, and at first I thought the Sonnenbornes were to blame. But then he turned up in Sigvar's hands and it didn't make any sense."

"Yes, the disappearances are a very high priority at the Winter

Court," the queen said, her voice grim. "But I sent Laurenna and Zhari a message after we dealt with Tilium. They've been made aware of Sigvar and are actively searching for others like him."

"But how did the boy get from Sonnenborne hands into Sigvar's?" I asked. That was the component that puzzled me most.

"It's impossible to say. Sigvar was quite thorough with his mind magic. None of the cultists had memories of the weeks leading up to being absorbed into the cult."

"That's frustrating," I said, disappointed that she didn't have more information.

"It is. But having stopped him, we've armed Laurenna and Zhari with the information they need to make sure others like him are caught and punished more quickly."

I left her study somewhat reassured, but other worries descended again as soon as I returned to my rooms and had time to think. I ached to talk to Mare, to share my worries about protecting myself and my identity in Corovja. Somehow I'd expected my training to be more scholarly in nature—not a frightening series of battles leading up to a competition that would determine my apprenticeship. If Mare had come with me and it had been a choice we'd made together, maybe there would have been at least one thing in my life that felt like solid ground to stand on.

I paced in front of the windows both from restlessness and to stay warm. Someone had built a small fire in my fireplace while I was at training that morning, but it had burned down to a few glowing coals. It would have been so simple to reach out and turn the coals to flame, but I didn't dare. Even thinking about it sent a shiver of fear through me. My magic was so volatile that I was afraid to use it again today. Besides, it was becoming clear that I would need every last bit of it to protect myself.

FIFTEEN ✦ *Amaranthine*

EVERY MORNING IT TOOK A FEW MINUTES OF WAKE-
fulness to remember that Denna was gone. I hadn't allowed the
court to assign me another maidservant, so I always woke alone to
the sounds of the merchants' hall: footsteps up and down the hallway, the muffled conversations of other residents as they departed
for early breakfasts or business meetings, and the clatter of wood
being delivered outside my door. In those sleep-fogged moments, it
felt and sounded like the world was going on without me, especially
as Denna's absence reasserted itself. In many ways it was. My incre-
mental progress as an ambassador was surely nothing compared to
what Denna was experiencing in Corovja. A whole new magical life
was opening up to her, while my existence felt like it was closing in
on me.

Other than the occasional morning spent at the stables teaching Fadeyka to ride, I trained with the sword until I was so sore I

could barely move by dinner each evening. The intensity of training provided a welcome distraction from missing Denna, and also allowed me to keep an eye on Alek. I most frequently sparred with Kerrick, one of the few trainees junior enough to fight me without being bored out of his skull. Every day I made it my goal to challenge him enough to wipe the ever-present smirk off his face, which wasn't easy since he fought dirty and used his short, wiry stature to dodge me with grace. Regardless, it was nice to be in company that didn't treat me like a princess or a leper—just an opponent. The salle was a simple place, and I liked that.

"Want to come have a dram before dinner?" Kerrick asked as we wiped down our swords. "A few of us are going to Morwen's."

I weighed the invitation against stalking Alek the rest of the evening, which was what I usually did after training—not that it had led to much. The man led a life as dull as his blade was sharp. After training he usually went to an early dinner, sometimes met up with other fighter types, and then retired to his chambers. The few times I'd followed him out of the Winter Court and into the city, it turned out he was going to buy scrap leather for armor repair or to get his blades sharpened.

I watched as Alek stepped back from correcting the stance of one of the more advanced trainees. The woman executed her pattern with such swiftness and grace that I could barely see her blade. I sighed. As hard as I was trying, it would take me years to get that good. And I didn't want to imagine the horror of still being in this hellsmouth years from now.

"A dram sounds good," I said, hoping I could get more insight about Alek from the other soldiers. Even though I wanted to retreat to my room and my brooding thoughts, there was more I could learn from the fighters.

Four of us left the salle together, with Kerrick in the lead. Shazi was one of the other fighters who'd joined us, and who I'd since learned could reliably take down opponents in a few quick blows. Kerrick also introduced me to Harian, a tall man with wide shoulders who fought with a broadsword so big I doubted I'd be able to lift it. In spite of his imposing size, he had a sweet and innocent demeanor I couldn't help but find charming. Seeing him and Kerrick walk together was like watching a stoat trot to keep up with a gigantic hunting dog.

"So what's with this intense training?" Kerrick asked me. "You're later to this game than I am, and I can tell you from experience that overworking yourself won't help you catch up."

"Why were you late to it?" I asked, ignoring his question.

"My father expected me to take up the family business providing loans to merchants," Kerrick said. "I always wanted to be a fighter, though. Never had the head for figures. Took him till last year to stop trying to make me into something I'm not."

"I never did what my father wanted, either," I said. If he'd had his way, I would have been a proper princess like Denna, stepping in to help run the castle's administrative and social functions until I was properly married off to someone of suitable nobility. I'd rather have eaten my saddle. Still, I felt some guilt now for going against him. He was dead, and there would never be an opportunity to prove to him that I could do something of value for the kingdom.

"Nice that the streets are still clear," Shazi said from behind me.

"Sure, Shazi. Nice if you aren't worried about the land," Harian said. "Without more snowfall, irrigation is going to be a problem in Nobrosk next spring. My parents' crop was poor last year."

"I didn't think of that," Shazi admitted. "I'm sorry. Maybe the queen will send some weather workers to help if things continue on this way."

As it turned out, we didn't have to go far. Morwen's, the drinking house the fighters favored, was just a few streets outside the residential district alongside the court. Shazi held the door, and we entered a room filled with a mix of round and trestle tables with stools. A musician tuned his lap harp in the corner as we found somewhere to sit in the back. I'd barely taken my seat when something brushed against my legs and made me jump.

I peered under the table to see a large tabby cat making the rounds amongst everyone's legs.

"Is there supposed to be a cat in here?" I asked.

"Oh yes," Harian said. "Morwen's always has cats." He glanced under the table and started talking in a baby voice. "Who's under our table? Sir Basil, is that you?"

I covered my mouth to hide a laugh.

Kerrick raised his arm to flag down a server, who quickly returned with a round of small glasses filled with clear liquid that looked like water and smelled like it could easily catch fire.

"To the health of the queen." Kerrick raised his glass in a toast. The others followed suit, and I copied them, trying not to think too hard as I swallowed the liquid. It burned its way down my throat in a trail of fire that tasted like the compounds I used to polish the metal fittings on my tack. I was still choking on it when the server came around for our next order.

"Does this place have any ale?" I asked the server, my eyes still watering.

She looked at me as though I'd asked her to take off her skirt without so much as buying her a drink first.

"Do you like barleywine?" Kerrick interjected.

"Does it taste like that?" I pointed to my empty glass.

He smiled. "No."

"Then yes, I do," I said. In spite of its foulness, the drink had sent warmth spreading through my body far more swiftly than ale could have. It would probably be the bottom-ranked beverage in the Havemont distillers' competition, but it did the job. Thinking of Denna and her homeland abruptly crushed me with sadness. Barely a moon ago I'd been dreaming of tasting spirits with her, so confident that nothing could ever separate us. How wrong I'd been.

The server hurried off to fetch our next round.

"Mare, you're from Mynaria, right?" Shazi asked, her pale blue eyes curious.

I nodded.

"Shouldn't you be spending your evening with the court?" Shazi retwisted her dark brown hair into its knot at the nape of her neck.

"Well, my first night at a court party, I got challenged to a duel by one of the queen's elite trainees." I launched into the explanation, playing it for laughs instead of the humiliation it had really been. If I didn't laugh at myself, I'd have to face all the ways in which I was failing as an ambassador. I hadn't been able to make myself go to the few court functions I'd been invited to attend, and I hadn't made a single ally among the nobility.

"No wonder you ended up here with all the riffraff," Kerrick said, chuckling as he sipped from his next drink. It was a deep caramel color, but the smell of it was still enough to singe my nostrils.

"At least we'll probably all be eligible for better posts after having trained with Alek," Harian said.

"Why is that?" I asked. "Indulge the stupid Mynarian." I wanted to know why they all regarded him so worshipfully. He was a good instructor, sure, but it had to be more than that.

"He was such a hero in my childhood. The tales we used to hear . . . ," Harian said, his voice growing wistful.

"A hero?" I looked at him like he'd shit a bird into his hand. Though it wasn't the first time I'd heard the word applied to Alek, I didn't understand. Alek was an accomplished swordsman and obviously had some powerful magic on his side, but he didn't strike me as the heroic type. More the sort to let you fall on your own sword and then tell your dead body how to do it differently afterward.

"Definitely in the south," Shazi said. "We had songs about him. My mother taught me one when I was a child." She hummed a few bars of what sounded like a drinking song. "And my father fought alongside him in the Battle of Eusavka River."

I tensed. "You mean the Sawmill Massacre." That had been a battle on the Mynarian border that killed hundreds of our people. Before I was born, my father had wanted to build a sawmill on the Eusavka at the border of Mynaria and Zumorda. He'd sent a group of craftsmen to begin construction, but just a few days after they'd broken ground, all but a handful were murdered in their tents as they slept.

"Is that what they call it in Mynaria?" Kerrick asked, his tone curious.

"It wasn't a massacre," Shazi interjected. "The Mynarians shouldn't have been there in the first place. If they'd been able to build their sawmill on the Eusavka and dammed the river the way they wanted to, it would have cut off most of the water my village relies on for irrigation. Our valley is one of the most fertile areas in Zumorda, with a much longer growing season than the north. The kingdom relies on us."

"Leading a group of warriors over the river and murdering our people in their camp while they slept fits the definition of a massacre," I said, doing my best to keep calm. The innocent craftsmen assigned to the project hadn't deserved death for being in the wrong place at the wrong time.

"It was a last resort," Shazi said. "Mynaria didn't seek permission to build the sawmill. They'd already begun construction when our soldiers came to ask them to stop. They weren't receptive to negotiations—I know, because my father was the one tasked with that."

"After the Mynarians refused to draw up an agreement or desist with their building, King Aturnicus sent horse archers to shoot at our soldiers from across the river," Harian said. "There was no other way to stop them."

"So Alek used his gift to help his fighters cross the river," Kerrick said.

That part of the story at least seemed to be consistent with the stories as I'd heard them in Mynaria. "The Mynarian survivors believed that the water god had turned against them," I said. If Alek was the kind of person who would wipe out nearly an entire camp of innocent workers, maybe Laurenna was right to hate him.

Harian laughed. "Sounds like Mynarians."

"We aren't all fools," I said, defensively.

"Of course not," Harian said. "You're here now, taking ownership of your own fate. Those are Zumordan sensibilities through and through."

I pondered his words. Was I owning my fate? The only reason I'd come here in the first place was to help Denna, and she'd left me. I hadn't meant to end up with the other things on my shoulders that weighed on me now. My best didn't seem good enough to cope, but maybe Harian had a point that taking ownership of my own fate was what mattered. What I needed to do was figure out how Alek was connected to the Sonnenbornes and what their next move was. It still didn't make sense to me that he'd supposedly been sent here to investigate the disappearance of Duvey's adolescents at the hands of Sonnenbornes, yet was so friendly with Eronit and Varian. Also, from what I could tell, he spent a lot more time in the salle training than he did investigating, unless he was doing it in the middle of the night.

"Well, we can't change the past," I said. "After the massacre, my people built a sawmill near Almendorn instead. The whole situation could have been avoided if Mynaria and Zumorda had conversed about the project instead of making assumptions on both sides that blew up into a fight. That's what I'm here to do now—make sure we prevent any misunderstandings and reduce the chance of causing each other harm."

"Work with magic users?" Kerrick waggled his eyebrows. "Out of the question!"

"Better than getting a lot of people killed for no reason," I said. "But King Aturnicus never was very keen to make allies here."

"Well, you certainly sound a bit more reasonable than he was," Shazi said. "I'm glad to know not all Mynarians hate us as much as we are led to believe."

"And I'm glad Zumordans were willing to teach me how to use a sword." I smiled, even as a pang went through me. Shazi couldn't have known my father was probably banging on the walls of his tomb over someone describing me as "reasonable."

"Now, if only the Sonnenbornes could prove themselves something other than their reputation," Kerrick muttered.

"What do you mean?" My interest sharpened.

"They're sneaky and secretive," Kerrick said. "Every merchant knows it."

"Don't generalize about entire groups of people," Shazi chided. "Every person is worth consideration by their own merits."

"Yes, yes," Kerrick said. "And usually I agree, even if they don't have any magic by which to determine their strength. It's not as if my Affinity is especially strong. But all these disappearances don't sit well with me. How do we know they aren't related to so many more Sonnenbornes appearing in Kartasha lately?"

"I heard a lot of people who came to the city in hopes of being chosen for the queen's elite never made it home," Harian said.

"Don't you think that's because a lot of them are signing up for the low-income magic training program?" Shazi asked.

Harian snorted. "The waiting lists are long. They might as well

• 243 •

wait at home—there's no reason to vanish into the city."

"What exactly is the program?" I asked.

"Guardian Zhari developed a new program this past year for young Zumordans with lower incomes to access better training for their Affinities. A lot of people have applied—my father lost two bookkeepers this year. He ended up hiring a *vakos* Sonnenborne just so he wouldn't have to go through it a third time."

"Pity she doesn't expand the program to some of the smaller villages," Harian added. "Almost no one leaves Nobrosk, but there's talent there if someone would nurture it."

"Who is responsible for testing them, though?" I asked. If the program had any relationship to the disappearances, someone actually seeing the magic users had to be involved.

"At present, Guardian Laurenna," Kerrick said. "Zhari handed over the testing to her not long after establishing the program. Her ability to sense magic beyond the Sight is useful in assessing people's gifts."

I tensed involuntarily at her name, probably a sign I'd been spending too much time around Alek. On the other hand, if Laurenna was the one doing the testing, there had to be official court records. It would be easy enough to check those against the names of people who'd been reporting missing to see if there was any overlap. I thought about bringing it up but decided it was best to keep to myself.

"Personally," Kerrick continued, "I find it odd that even though we've had an influx of Zumordans from all over the kingdom, my father's seen twice as many loan applications for Sonnenbornes to start new businesses here this winter as last. That's never happened before in all his thirty years in business. The Sonnenbornes are *vakos*. It's not as if they are coming here in hopes of finding magic training."

"Does he grant the loans?" I asked.

"Sure, if they meet his qualifications and provide collateral." Kerrick shrugged. "A lot of them don't, though."

"I heard what they did on the Trindor Canal and how it affected trade," Shazi said. "Honestly, that was when I started having my doubts."

"You mean Zephyr Landing?" I asked, surprised the fighters knew or cared. Merchants must have brought the news with them in the last few weeks.

Shazi nodded. "Mynaria is no concern of ours, but taking over a city in a coup like that with almost no warning . . . I just don't trust that that's the only time they'll attempt it, especially after they succeeded once."

"If they're thinking like strategists, they'll use the trade money to fortify their stronghold there, and then move on to another city. Maybe make a second attempt on Duvey?" Harian said.

"That's exactly what I'm worried about." I leaned forward. These people made sense to me—they were thinking like I did, and actually listening. "We need to make sure they aren't planning something like that. What if they're rallying forces here in Kartasha now to make another move on Duvey? That could be what the loans are really for—not for businesses, but for weapons."

"Sard me backward," Kerrick said. "I hadn't even thought of that. I told you I don't have a head for financial things."

"But you have at least half a clue about military strategy." Shazi rolled her eyes. "It's not like you've never played Commander's Choice with the rest of us."

"He's never beaten me, though." Harian's voice was smug.

"Shut up," Kerrick said, mock-punching him.

"I think the question is what we are going to do about the Sonnenbornes," I said.

"What can we do about them?" Shazi asked. "It's not really our problem. It's the court's. Guardian Zhari is already doing a lot to make sure that our people's powers are maximized. Our fighters are as well trained as theirs or better, and we have magic on our side."

"It will be your problem if something happens and you get sent to the front lines to fight against them," I pointed out.

"True," Shazi admitted.

"And during the attack on Duvey I saw magic users taken down with peaceroot powder," I added. "They've found a way to make it airborne and quick-acting, and they don't hesitate to use it, since it has no effect on them."

"Well, I can ask my father about the loans," Kerrick said. "Maybe there's some documentation about what they were for."

"Now you're using that pinhead of yours," Harian said.

"I have some friends who are Zumordan merchants." Shazi's expression took on a calculating air. "I'll ask them if anything has changed for them lately."

"And what about you, Mare?" Harian asked.

"If we gather enough evidence, I'll take it to the Winter Court. Guardian Laurenna and Grand Vizier Zhari have to listen to us if there's enough, and then the queen will have to step in and do something," I said. I also had every intention of keeping an eye on Alek, but I doubted that aspect of the plan would go over as well with them.

"I'll drink to that," Harian said, raising his glass. We all toasted and downed another sip of our drinks. The barleywine was much richer than ale on my tongue, dark and bittersweet.

Conversation grew looser as the drinks continued to flow, turning from politics and swordsmanship to magic. I learned that Harian had an earth Affinity and that Shazi's was for air, which made sense based on how she'd helped Fadeyka when her magic slipped out of control. None of them had strong gifts, which was part of why they'd taken up the sword. I wondered if perhaps they still had ambitions that might land them positions like Wymund's—guardian in spite of a less powerful Affinity. Sometimes at the salle I thought of him, and it gave me hope that I didn't need to have magic to be respected and powerful in my own way.

"So none of you wanted to try out for the queen's program?" I asked, trying to ignore the swelling ache in my chest. It was what Denna had chosen over me. I had to believe it was worth it.

"Not even if I was eligible," Shazi said. "Not that I would have had much choice, I suppose."

Her vehemence piqued my curiosity. "Why not? Isn't it a great honor to be chosen?"

"Yes, if you can survive the training." Shazi swallowed the dregs of her drink.

"My aunt was apprenticed to become a guardian," Harian said softly. "She didn't make it."

"You mean she died?" My eyes widened.

"Not right away," Harian said. "I was small when it happened, but I remember her coming home for midsummer holiday a few months after she started. She used to be the first to tell a joke or to laugh, and was always chasing us kids around to give my mother a break, but she came back a completely different person. I barely saw her leave her room. She never smiled. Four moons later, she came home permanently, stripped of her gift, with only her manifest remaining. By Midwinter, she chose to take her manifest permanently and left us to live the rest of her days as a wolf."

Kerrick shuddered. "Sometimes I'm glad not to have a greater gift."

Worry consumed me. Was this what Denna was going to be put through by the queen? If she didn't succeed, would she end up broken, without even a manifest to retreat to? Another, darker thought followed—that perhaps it would be a blessing for Denna to be stripped of her gift if there was a way to do it without harming her. The longer we were apart, the more I resented her magic for being the force that had driven her away from me. Our lives would be so much less complicated without it. If not for her gift, she would have stayed. Then I felt guilty for even letting the thought cross my mind. Me wanting to rid her of her gift was why she'd left. How could I even still consider it a possibility? She'd made her feelings clear.

"Even those who survive the training and get good placements are different from the people they were," Harian said. "My aunt's closest friend ended up completing the training and becoming our guardian. She still is, in fact. But it's amazing to see a woman who used to tend rare flowers with the greatest delicacy turn into someone who won't hesitate to spill her own neighbor's blood at the order of her queen."

All the drinks in the world weren't enough to warm me now. Denna's training—and her life—were in the hands of the queen. If she even wanted to return to me someday, would she come back whole?

SIXTEEN  *Dennaleia*

A FEW EVENINGS AFTER MY FIRST DISASTROUS INTRO-
duction to training, I set out to find the castle library. If my instructors
weren't going to give me any books to study, I'd find them myself.
It seemed like my only hope of catching up with the other trainees,
all of whom had demonstrated over the past days that their mastery
of their Affinities exceeded mine in every way. I wished there were
a sanctuary or temple I could pray in to steady my nerves and calm
my magic, but for now the library would have to do. The sky outside
was night-dark when I sought out a page and asked her for directions. She gave me an odd look but nodded, explaining in Zumordan
so quickly I could barely follow.

Books on magic had been rare in my homeland and forbidden
in Mynaria, so this was the best opportunity to learn in exactly the
way I did best: by reading. Book research and taking study notes
were things I actually knew how to do. I needed to find a book that

would explain my powers to me in a way I could understand and apply. I thought it would be straightforward—until I actually saw the library. A set of heavy double doors awaited me at the end of a narrow hallway, just as the page had described. I set down my lantern and tugged on the handle of one of the doors, surprised when it opened only a finger's length. It wasn't locked—just stuck. I battled the door for a solid five minutes before finally getting it open enough to slip inside.

When I held the lantern aloft, my heart sank. The library must have once been a beautiful room. It took up one of the castle's turrets that overlooked a valley, and had rounded walls lined on all sides with shelves. Tall, arching windows made up most of the south wall, and a staircase spiraled away from the door up to a balcony and more shelves above. In the dark, I couldn't tell how many floors there were. With the strong light from the south, the room must have once been perfect for reading during the day. Now a thick coat of dust covered its tables and chairs as well as the books stacked haphazardly on every piece of furniture. The place looked like it hadn't been touched in years, even by the castle servants. No wonder the page had looked at me so strangely for inquiring about it.

I paced through the room. There was no order to anything. Open trunks were stuffed with so many scrolls that they overflowed onto the floor, the edges of some yellowing from exposure to light. I pawed through a few and found mostly architectural drawings of the castle, plus a recipe for fig sauce randomly tucked between them. Nothing in the library was cataloged or in order of any kind. Before I had any chance of finding a book that would help me with my magic, I was going to have to organize everything.

I sighed, then rolled up the sleeves of my shirt and got to work.

By the time dawn started to glow on the horizon, I felt like a failure. I'd found only one book that looked like it might be helpful—a biography of someone who'd also had a fire Affinity. Of course it was in Zumordan, which meant my usual reading speed would be slowed by having to translate. Organizing the library hadn't gone well, either. It was hopeless to try to catalog it all without some kind of ledger, and I couldn't find any blank paper or writing utensils in the room. So I'd started making piles categorized by subject, which got me through only a small section of the ground-floor room.

Perhaps looking for answers in books had been foolish of me. Not only had I stayed up all night, ensuring I'd be exhausted at my next lesson, but I'd apparently done it for no reason. It felt like the latest in a series of mistakes, and I wasn't even sure what the first one had been. Was it letting everyone believe I'd died in the star fall? Was it the morning I'd gotten up before dawn to leave Mare behind? Or, the darkest part of my heart asked, was it the night I'd chosen to flee from the man I was betrothed to in order to save his sister instead? I couldn't go back in time, which made it pointless to think about, but my mind still chewed on the questions as insatiably as a dog with a piece of cured hide. Sometimes I felt like if I could pinpoint when I'd made mistakes, I could avoid making them again, but instead I just kept fumbling into new ones.

I paced over to the windows and looked out at the castle grounds. The snow outside amplified the golden light of the rising sun, which had begun to filter into the room in long beams. Walls below seemed to indicate a garden laid out in a mazelike pattern. Trees with ice-crusted branches were scattered among them. Beyond the farthest wall of the garden, a bridge led to a large, flat area that looked like the floor of a ruined building, the rest of which seemed to have slid off the side of the mountain. All that remained of it was half the floor crumbling into broken edges and a few pieces of wall with empty holes where windows had once been. I followed the outlines of the ruin, noticing four curved edges as though the building had once had alcoves. If the building had been symmetrical, two had collapsed.

Considering how pristine the rest of the castle was kept, it seemed odd that a ruin of that magnitude would be part of it. Even more strange, the empty windows looked similar to those that were such a defining characteristic of the High Adytum—the holiest temple in the Northern Kingdoms. In Tilium I'd learned that Zumorda had once had temples. Could this ruin be one of them?

I rooted through a pile of religious texts I'd found and skimmed the pages. Most of the content was familiar, even though the volumes were older than the ones I'd studied back home. All six gods were mentioned, though there were confusing references to the children of the gods, which may have just been a poor translation on my part, given that I'd never studied ancient Zumordan. I also figured that since Zumordans didn't worship the gods, the texts might have been translated from ancient Mynarian or Havemontian into Zumordan, which would make for even messier interpretations of meaning. Strangest of all, a few books also included an illustration of a seven-pointed star like Fadeyka's pendant and talked about its being a representation of all six gods working together with the help of a seventh god. I'd never heard of such a thing or seen the symbol in a temple or sanctuary before.

I returned to the trunk of architectural scrolls and sat cross-legged next to it. Halfway through examining the contents, I unrolled a scroll that made me pause. It was yellow with age and moth-chewed at the edges, the ink lines faded to nothing in some places. I spread it out on the floor and pinned it down with a couple of heavy books to get a better look. The version of the castle in the drawing was slightly smaller than the one now, but the central buildings were all the same. The most notable difference was a bridge leading to a huge building labeled *Grand Temple*. According to the map, it was located in the same spot as the ruin I could see outside the library window.

I sat back, reeling. Why would the Zumordans have had a temple on a par with the High Adytum unless they had once worshipped the gods? Perhaps they had. What had happened to change everything, and why was the ruin still here?

I dug through the rest of the scrolls in the trunk, unrolling them all in turn until I found another, newer set of drawings from just fifty years ago. The temple was no longer labeled, but while there were notes about the construction of a new wing of the castle that hadn't existed in the previous drawing, the architect's notes on the temple area merely read *Leave untouched*.

But why? Why wouldn't they have removed any physical sign of connection to gods they didn't worship? And why did so many Zumordans come to the High Adytum in Havemont every summer to do their magical workings if they had a temple here that could be equally grand if they restored it? My parents had always told me the Zumordans traveled to Spire City because the High Adytum had special properties that made it a powerful place to work magic.

But in a kingdom where magic ruled and the gods were no longer worshipped, why not rebuild their old temple for the same purpose instead of traveling all the way to our kingdom? Rebuilding it would have solved so many of the tensions among Zumorda, Havemont, and Mynaria. Mynarians didn't like Havemontians allowing Zumordans to visit the High Adytum, since the Zumordans would then in theory be able to cross into Mynaria from the Havemont side with less trouble—at least if they managed to pass themselves off as Havemontian. If Zumordans had their own temple, they could pilgrimage to Corovja instead of Spire City.

But there had to be a reason the queen hadn't had it restored. What was it?

I stood up and brushed the dust from my clothes. My powers had always felt calmer in sacred spaces. Perhaps it was that I'd been raised with the ritual and comfort of religion rather than a belief only in the power of myself and my magic. I wanted to test and see if the ruins of the Grand Temple provided me the control I couldn't seem to find elsewhere, and I wanted to look for evidence of the strange seven-pointed star symbol I'd seen in the religious texts. There was still time to get down there before the day's lessons if I hurried.

Back at my room, I bundled up heavily and then slipped out through a side door I'd noticed the servants using. The maze of the castle gardens didn't take too long to navigate, and soon I was crossing the long bridge over to the temple. I stopped as soon as I passed through the broken sides of the wall. Instantly after crossing the threshold, I felt a little calmer. It didn't have the same feel as being inside the High Adytum, but there was something familiar about it nonetheless. I exhaled deeply and sketched the symbol of the fire god, and was rewarded with a soothing heat that spread through my body like warm honey. If I closed my eyes, I could almost imagine I was home in Havemont, where my magic had never felt so wild or dangerous and where I'd known exactly what my path forward in life was.

"Mind the edge. It's crumbling," a voice said beside me.

I jumped, barely stifling a scream.

Tristan sat slumped just inside one of the walls of the ruin, his dark clothes making him stand out like a raven against the snow.

"Six Hells, you startled me," I said.

"Sorry," he said. "It happens a lot." He stood up, brushing the snow from his backside. He ran a hand through the dark shoulder-length waves of his hair.

"I didn't know this was your place. I can leave," I said.

He laughed. "It's as much mine as the sky or the snow. Spend all the time you want."

I eyed him mistrustfully.

"I'm not going to push you off the edge or anything," he said.

"That would be one way to get an advantage for the Revel," I said, unable to keep the bitterness out of my tone.

"Is that what you were trying to do on the first day of training when you nearly incinerated the place?" He looked more amused than upset about it.

"Of course not," I said. "And so you know, all I want is to learn to control my magic. I don't care about winning competitions or putting on shows. I didn't sign up for the Revel. I didn't even know it was happening. I thought this was going to be an opportunity to learn from each other, to study."

"Huh. Evie said she thought you were different. I guess she was right."

"Not Zumordan, no manifest, no idea what's happening here," I said. Exhaustion had done some serious damage to my diplomacy skills.

"That's not what I meant," Tristan said. "Besides, I'm not Zumordan, either."

"You're not?" I looked at him more critically. He spoke perfect Zumordan, and his Tradespeech was just as good. "Then where are you from?"

"Havemont," he said. "Just across the border. It's rather ironic that I had to journey all the way to Kartasha only to end up this close to home in the end."

My heart skipped a beat. He was from my homeland, and for some reason, knowing that made a pang of longing for my family grip me.

"I thought everyone here was Zumordan."

"Maybe by blood if not homeland," Tristan said. "Ikrie's the only one originally from Corovja, though—her parents are nobles. I'm pretty sure Aela's family runs a cartel of some kind out of Kartasha. She's awfully cagey about what it is they actually do."

"Your Zumordan is quite good," I said. "How did you learn?"

"Hard to avoid it living in a border town. Besides, my parents are Zumordan, so we spoke it at home." He shrugged.

"And they taught you to use your Affinity?" I asked.

He nodded. "What happened with yours?"

"My parents didn't know anything of magic," I said. He didn't need to know that I'd spent most of my life training to become a queen, or that I'd been betrothed to a prince whose kingdom reviled magic. Those pieces of my history were so distant now that they felt as if they belonged to someone else—certainly not to Lia, the innocent servant girl from Mynaria.

"Ah. That must have been difficult," he said.

He had no idea.

I paced around the half-moon of remaining floor, staying clear of the edge that plunged to the valley below. Tristan followed me, quiet as a shadow. Curious, I kicked away the snow and dug in with the toe of my boot until I found patterned tile underneath. It was worn and faded from years of exposure to the elements, but the red was unmistakable. Farther along were spans of tile in blue, white, black, yellow, and green. The order of the colors was different from those in the High Adytum, but they were the same as those of the gods we worshipped. I looked for any sign of the seven-pointed star I'd seen in the library books, but there was nothing of the kind left in the ruins. The only unexplained design elements in the ruins were the silvery threads of mirror woven amidst the other colors to tie everything together. The books had speculated that the symbol represented the gods working together. Maybe the mirrors formed a larger pattern I couldn't see because of all the snow.

"The gods must have once been worshipped here," I mused. I'd thought I would come to Zumorda to find answers, but instead, I was finding only more questions. "But when did the people of Zumorda stop?"

"When the dragon queen took her throne," Tristan answered.

I looked up, startled. The question had been rhetorical—I hadn't expected an answer.

"What do you know about it?" I asked.

"My mother told me the story." He smiled a little, as though at a fond memory.

"So how did the start of the queen's reign affect the worship of the gods?" I asked. "I thought the throne was always taken the same way, through combat." I started walking back toward the bridge to the castle, moving to stay warm. Even with the calming presence the ruins seemed to provide, I didn't trust myself to use my magic again with another person nearby.

"It is, and that hasn't changed," Tristan said. "What changed was the distribution of power. Before the dragon queen's rise to the throne, the monarch was the only person in Zumorda capable of using magic. That magic was granted to the monarch through a bond with the gods. Common people could still take manifests, but it was done by aligning oneself with a god and performing a bonding ritual rather than the blood ritual that is most commonly used now."

"Is the blood ritual how you gained your manifest?" I asked, hoping I wasn't overstepping with the question.

"No, my mother showed me a more passive way to do it," he said. "When the queen took her manifest, she did it through a blood rite and therefore had no bond to a god. She broke the rules and gained her own magic in the process. So when she challenged the boar king for his throne and won, the gods deserted Zumorda."

"If the gods were the source of magic and they deserted Zumorda, why didn't it become a wasteland like Sonnenborne?" I asked.

Tristan shrugged. "Because the magic is in the people, I suppose."

"Why *is* Sonnenborne the way it is?" I wondered. I'd never thought to ask the question before, but Tristan's story had my mind racing at top speed. Had they once angered the gods, too? Was that what had brought about the fractures between all our kingdoms?

"I don't know much about Sonnenborne," Tristan said.

"No one really does." For the first time, I realized Sonnenborne was in many ways even more mysterious than Zumorda. No one really went there, but why would they, when it was no more than a wasteland? An even larger question loomed in my mind now. If the gods had something to do with Sonnenborne becoming a desert, did that mean there was a way to restore the kingdom? And if we could do so, might it stop them from attacking us?

SEVENTEEN

✦ *Amaranthine*

WITH THE NEW INSIGHT I HAD GAINED FROM KERRICK, Shazi, and Harian, over the next week I turned my focus to finding out more about the disappearances of magic users. I hoped it might give me some indication of what the Sonnenbornes were truly plotting and why they'd abducted the children in Duvey. It didn't hurt that this would also provide an excellent opportunity to one-up Alek if I could get to the information before he did. The easiest way to do that was of course to start with the last person he'd ever deign to talk to—Laurenna. The only downside was having to attend a court function, because trying to get a proper audience would have taken days. I talked myself into it grudgingly, reminding myself that it was the best way to get the information I needed, and that it was far past time I stopped shirking my duties to my brother and Mynaria.

I chose an unassuming luncheon—a celebration meant to honor a prominent Kartashan horse trader. At least horses were one thing I knew something about, and therefore it wouldn't seem suspicious for me to attend. It also meant the gathering was small and there were several Sonnenbornes in attendance, including Eronit and Varian.

To my surprise, the luncheon was held out on an open balcony high in the Winter Court's tower. I expected it to be cold, but the temperature didn't change as I stepped outside. When I looked more closely, I could see a faint, shimmering barrier between the balcony and the outside air, and that was what made me shiver. Magic everywhere, as usual. Buffet tables laden with heavy platters of food overlooked the city, and servants moved purposefully through the room with additional trays of small bites to tempt the guests.

I reached for a wafer smeared with cheese and topped with thin-sliced pickled vegetables, and was surprised when a familiar pair of brown eyes appeared on the other side of the servant's tray.

"What are you doing here?" Fadeyka asked.

"I got hungry," I said, popping the bite into my mouth. The crunch of the vegetables and crispness of the cracker were the perfect contrast to the creamy cheese. As much as I hated making small talk and being surrounded by toadying, I had to admit I'd missed the food that came along with life in court.

"Then make sure to get some pears before they're gone. The custard is brandied." Fadeyka pointed to a platter on one of the tables. Halved pears with rich purple skin glistened atop pastry shells made of countless layers. Tiny crystal pitchers sat in neat rows beside them, kept warm on some kind of magical tray.

"Isn't that dessert?" I asked. No one else had touched the platter yet.

She smiled rather evilly. "Dessert . . . appetizer . . . it's open to interpretation."

"Lead on," I said, and followed her to the pears. If someone saw me eating the wrong thing, it wouldn't seem like a surprise that I'd broken protocol, given how little they all seemed to think of Mynarians anyway.

I cast my eyes around the room, spotting Laurenna with a flute of sparkling wine in one hand. A glacier-blue dress hugged her willowy frame, cascading down to her feet in heavy waves. As I got closer, I saw it wasn't as simple as it appeared; impossibly small glass beads were sewn onto the fabric in intricate patterns that swirled like water when she moved.

"Your Highness," she said as I approached. "How thoughtful of you to join us today."

Fadeyka hid behind me, shoveling the remaining half of her pear into her mouth.

"I wouldn't have wanted to miss the opportunity to congratulate Lord Olivieri on a successful trade season," I said, hoping I'd gotten his name right.

Laurenna set her glass on a nearby table and smiled. "I suppose horses are always of interest to the Mynarians." She grabbed Fadeyka by the wrist as the girl reached for a glass of sparkling wine.

"Just one," Fadeyka said, whining.

"No," Laurenna said firmly. "You're not allowed to drink at

parties. Besides, don't you remember what Zhari said?"

"That I shouldn't eat or drink anything that might interfere with my magic until we know what's going on," Fadeyka recited, punctuating her words with a melodramatic eye roll.

"Speaking of Zhari and young magic users," I said, "I heard she has a program that helps find apprenticeships for those of lesser means."

Laurenna nodded. "It's been quite successful so far. The very enchantment that keeps us warm right now was cast by a young man discovered in the program."

"A lot of magic users came here recently to try to get a place with the queen or to sign up for Zhari's program, didn't they?" I said, treading carefully. "I've heard rumors that some people who signed up for those programs have since vanished."

"That seems unlikely." Laurenna frowned, taking a small salad from a passing server and handing it to Fadeyka. "Eat your vegetables," she told her daughter.

Fadeyka made a face, earning herself an even sterner look from her mother.

"What makes you say it's unlikely anyone is disappearing?" I asked. They couldn't possibly be in such denial about what was going on in their part of the kingdom.

"I didn't say it was unlikely that people were disappearing," Laurenna said. "It's only unlikely that people would be disappearing who had signed up for Zhari's program. Anyone who signs up is documented in official court records. The list is kept safe and secure with court clerks."

"How accessible are those records?" I asked.

"Not especially," Laurenna said. "They're restricted to members of the court. As an ambassador, you are entitled to view them, but it's not as if anyone can walk in off the street to look. Some of the people who sign up for the program are looking to escape dark pasts that would all too easily follow them."

"That makes sense," I said, the gears already turning in my mind. If the list was being used to target people, that meant that someone inside the court had to be leaking the information.

"If you talk to the records master, just don't bring up ice fishing," Fadeyka warned me.

"Why?" I asked.

"Because you'll die in that records room listening to him talk about it," she said.

On the other side of the balcony, Eronit and Varian were helping themselves to soup served in tiny hollowed-out gourds. My eyes narrowed. They'd said they were scholars, but they were also serving as ambassadors of sorts, which meant they had access to the records. Given that Denna and I had seen a boy abducted by Sonnenbornes right before our eyes, it made sense that they might somehow be involved.

"Is it just a list of names, or is there personal information on the list as well?" I asked.

"Their names, ages, Affinities, and where they're staying in town so we know how to reach them if they're chosen," Laurenna said. "If you know of someone specific who went missing, the clerks can check the list for their name. And please do report any such disappearances to Zhari—she's very proud of the program and cares very much about its success."

In spite of the false warmth created by the enchantment on the balcony, a chill crept over me. The information Laurenna said was cataloged on the list was more than enough to find people to target for abduction.

"If the lists are kept secure, it sounds like people are just making up rumors." I didn't want her to know that I had any further plans to investigate or that I suspected the Sonnenbornes might be involved. It would be much better to come to her once I had evidence in hand.

"There is always a great deal of talk that goes on at court," Laurenna acknowledged.

"As there was back home," I said, deciding to omit the fact that as often as not, the gossip had been about me and whatever inappropriate nonsense the courtiers thought I'd been up to. Most of the time it had been only half as bad as reality. I wondered what they said about me now, or if I'd been forgotten now that I was a kingdom away. Did they remember the princess who'd spent all her time in the barn? Or had more recent scandals overwritten memories of things like the feast night before Denna's wedding, when I'd kissed her on my way out the door, telling her it would be something to remember me by?

My heart clenched at the thought of her. That night I'd been prepared to give her up—it had been my choice, and the only path to follow, since I couldn't bear to watch her marry my brother. But now she was gone on her terms, and I hadn't even had a chance to talk her out of it. She hadn't even kissed me good-bye.

"Let's go get more food," Fadeyka said, tugging me away from her mother and breaking my reverie. The ache stayed in my chest as she led me along the buffet. I let her help stack my plate with anything she thought I should try. Tiny fried fish with flecks of gold sparkling in the breading. Apples sliced to nearly transparent thinness, mixed with herbs and a rich, creamy sauce and delicately spiced. Saddle of venison laden with dark purple berries I didn't recognize. A scoop of potatoes whipped with garlic and local cheese.

All the while I kept an eye on Eronit and Varian as they filled their own plates and claimed a table in the middle of the room. I'd have to try to talk to them if I wanted any answers. I took my plate, which was piled dangerously high thanks to Fadeyka, and meandered toward their table.

"You're not subtle," Fadeyka commented around a mouthful of raisin-studded bread that I'd fortunately managed to avoid.

"I'm not trying to be." I scowled at her.

Infuriatingly, she laughed. "When someone who is direct tries to be indirect, it rarely goes well."

"At least I'm not the one eating bread full of sad, shriveled grape corpses," I said.

She took another bite and smiled blissfully, utterly unbothered by my insult.

"Lady Eronit and Sir Varian," I said. "How nice to see you again." The words might have sounded formal and polite if I hadn't said them with all the elegance of a horse stopping to shit in the middle of the show ring.

Eronit smiled, seemingly amused by my awkwardness. "Would

you care to join us, Your Highness?" she asked. Somehow the angular accent that reminded me of Kriantz and his betrayal sounded much softer and kinder in her mouth. Varian looked at me and Fadeyka, frowning. Apparently we weren't the company he would have preferred.

"How are your studies going?" I asked, setting down my over-burdened plate.

"Oh, quite well!" Eronit said. "It's unfortunate that this region has been experiencing such a drought, but it's provided a good opportunity for us to work with the local horticulturalists to test plants for hardiness."

"That's good," I said. If her interest in plants was only a cover story, she certainly had devoted herself to it with great enthusiasm.

"How is your horse doing? Has it been hard for you to keep him fit here?" I couldn't see even the barest hint of malice or subversiveness in her eyes.

"I haven't been riding as much as I should," I admitted, and immediately felt bad. Flicker was probably perfectly happy to spend his time eating through the Winter Court's entire hay supply, but he was still young. A rising five-year-old should have been drilling in moderately advanced maneuvers by now, but the Winter Court also didn't have all the amenities that I would have had back home in Mynaria—a larger arena, practice dummies, and easily accessible trails for conditioning.

"We find the indoor arena here rather challenging as well," Varian said. "Our desert horses are conditioned for distance, and it's best to condition them on open land."

"That's difficult when riding isn't even permitted in the city." I shook my head and took a bite of apple salad.

"Getting around on foot is quite easy, though," Eronit said.

"Oh, do you spend much time outside court?" I asked. "I haven't explored the city yet." At least I hadn't besides following Alek, which had proven to be monumentally boring.

Varian shot Eronit a cautionary look that she either didn't see or deliberately ignored.

"Our studies have mostly kept us here, but we do occasionally visit friends. It's nice to spend some time speaking our mother language or to have a dish prepared with spices from back home. It must be hard for you to be so far away from yours." Eronit's expression held plenty of misplaced sympathy.

I stopped myself from blurting out the response I would have under other circumstances—that I doubted anyone back home even missed me. "It's very different here," I said.

"But the food is good," Fadeyka chimed in. "Try the fish."

I eyed her suspiciously. "This isn't going to be like those foul cookies, is it?"

Fadeyka widened her eyes in mock offense. "It's not my fault you have terrible taste."

"They really are quite good," Eronit reassured me.

I picked one up on the end of my fork and nibbled it. The flavor was delicate and salty, the crispy golden skin melting in my mouth.

"Are there any places in town you'd recommend visiting?" I asked, curious where their explorations outside the castle had taken them.

"We mostly visit friends—we haven't had much time to explore the city beyond what has been useful to our studies," Varian said.

"There's a lovely botanical garden near the bakers' district," Eronit said.

"Sounds delightful," I said. Clearly they weren't going to be particularly forthcoming about where they were spending their time outside court. And why would they, especially if they had something to hide? It all made me that much more suspicious.

I paid a visit to the clerks first thing the next morning, hoping to catch the records master before the day's paperwork could bury him. The clerks' rooms, deep in the heart of the Winter Court, were windowless, warm, and brightly lit. Ornate wooden cabinets filled with locked drawers lined every wall, and tall shelves containing even more drawers formed mazelike divisions in the room. Clerks sat in nooks among the shelves, working their way through heaping piles of papers. The records master was an older man with fine white hair that wisped around his head like a puff of cotton, and I found him hunched over his own stack of documents, scrutinizing them carefully and making notes in tidy Zumordan script.

"Excuse me," I said.

He paused and looked up at me over the tops of the reading spectacles perched at the end of his nose.

"If you have documents for processing, I begin accepting them one hour prior to lunch and no sooner." He resumed poring over his pages.

"Actually, I just wanted to get a look at the records related to the low-income magic program," I said.

He sighed, then rifled through the large ring of keys on his desk and handed me a simple silver one. "Credentials?"

"I'm Princess Amaranthine of Mynaria," I said, feeling awkward about pulling rank.

"Cabinet forty-eight at the end of the row," he said, oblivious of my discomfort.

"Thank you," I said, and hurried to the cabinet. It opened easily, and everything inside was meticulously organized. However, there was a large gap at the front of the file, and when I found the list, I immediately knew something was wrong. The latest date I saw on the record was in midsummer. That couldn't be right if the largest influx of magic users had happened in the fall. I returned to the records master.

"Did someone borrow the fall records?" I asked.

He sat back, clearly even more annoyed by the second interruption. "Borrowing of the records in this room is not allowed."

"They're missing," I said.

"There's no way they can be missing. I just went over a recent part of the ledger with the grand vizier earlier this week, and those Sonnenborne scholars were here looking at them just yesterday." He shoved his glasses up his nose, succeeding only in making them crooked.

When he mentioned Zhari, I started to doubt myself. Maybe I was just bad at looking for things, or my rudimentary grasp of Zumordan had made me miss a date. But at the mention of Eronit and Varian, my suspicions sharpened.

"Unless one of your clerks has the records out right now, I think they've been stolen," I said.

The records master stood up with an irritated huff and walked slowly to cabinet 48. When we both stood in front of it, I handed the key back to him and he opened the drawer. He pawed through it at a glacial pace while I fidgeted anxiously, finally turning to me with confusion in his rheumy green eyes.

"The fall records are missing," he said.

"So they did get stolen." I hated that my fears had been confirmed.

He hurried off more quickly than I would have expected he could move, and soon the entire room was a flurry of frantic clerks searching everywhere for the lost documents, which failed to materialize. As soon as it became clear that the ledger wasn't going to show up, I slipped back out of the records room, alone with my troubled thoughts.

Zhari wouldn't have a reason to steal records for the program she was proud of, and after that, Eronit and Varian were the only visitors the records master had mentioned. If they had the list, they most certainly had plans for it. I needed to find out what those plans were.

EIGHTEEN  *Dennaleia*

EVERY MORNING I WOKE UP WITH DREAD IN THE PIT OF my stomach and the distance between Mare and me aching like a wound that wouldn't close. Every night I went to bed sore, bruised, or cut—sometimes all three. Even though I'd found my Sight thanks to the queen's help, it still wasn't enough to make me competitive with the other trainees. I did finally learn how to shield, but it didn't come naturally. In spite of several sunlengths of practice each day, I was only able to grow my shields large enough to protect myself from frontal attacks and could still only hold them in place for a short time.

Brynan paired me off mostly with Evie, though I sparred with Tristan a few times, too. I only used my shielding capabilities against them, afraid that if I tried to go on the offense, I might seriously injure someone. They went easy on me, no doubt because I wasn't perceived as a threat to the other competitors. We had all quickly settled into our roles. The clear front-runners who would dominate at the Revel were Ikrie, whose air magic could knock someone flat with a thought, and Eryk, who could turn people's minds against them.

At night I played the harp, letting it be my reprieve from the struggles of the day. It helped me feel in control again and quiet the thoughts of Mare that rose up unbidden to chase me to bed each night. As I played, my Sight sometimes turned inward. There I sensed a deep well of magic I'd never been able to quantify before. Now I could See my own strength, and it surprised me. It was both frightening and comforting to know it was there, even if I didn't know how to unpack the nuances of everything I Saw.

Redemption didn't come until the end of my second week, when the trainees were asked to attend a dinner with the queen. We were given prereading for once—a massive tome on military strategy that I was grateful to have already read in my own language years ago. From what I recalled, the text was incredibly dry, and a lot of the lessons had been better drilled into me through strategy exercises and games played with my family. In Zumorda, I anticipated that any application of those skills would involve magic, so I dreaded the dinner right up until I walked in the door and Saia handed me a card.

"This dinner is to practice your skills of diplomacy as a guardian," she said. "Your card contains information about your region, your holdings, and what you want. Your job during this meal is to protect your holdings and get what you want by building the necessary alliances. The queen plays as herself. Please take your seat."

Beyond Saia, a long table was laid out with a large array of cutlery. I studied my card. I'd gotten Valenko and the surrounding region—not far from Tilium. My holdings were meager, consisting mostly of farmland, more ranch than agriculture. To the east I had Tamers like the ones we'd encountered on our trip between Duvey and Kartasha. My assigned goal was to obtain stone and wood for buildings. I smiled as I took my place at the table. To an amateur, the outlook for my region was bleak, but this was a game I knew how to play. For once I was going to put my princess skills to good use.

"What did you get?" Tristan leaned over.

"I'm Valenko."

"Kartasha," he said. "We're neighbors."

Ten ways to use and abuse that immediately came to mind.

"How about you, Evie?" I asked. She sat across from me, frowning at her card.

"The northwestern hills," she said, clearly at a loss for what she was going to do. Her strongest opportunities were going to involve working with Havemont across the northern border, but I wasn't foolish enough to tip her off to that before the game had even started.

Ikrie sat down with a triumphant look on her face. "I got Corovja," she said. There was an assumption in her voice that it would give her the advantage to have the crown city. It would certainly play well to her tendency to strong-arm opponents, but she had another think coming if she thought it was going to make for an easy game.

Aela and Eryk walked in together, the last two to join us.

"Duvey and the southlands," Eryk announced, sounding annoyed. Ikrie's smugness only grew. I frowned. The southlands were where most of Zumorda's agricultural activity was, which meant I'd need to work with Eryk to get feed for my animals. Having those two as pincers on either side would make my life harder.

"Orzai," Aela said, seeming pleased. I didn't blame her—it would have been my first choice if I'd been given one. The larger city and the central location were trade and resource advantages.

We all stood when the queen entered the room. She wore a long white skirt made of several sheer layers that shimmered and caught the light. Despite a dispassionate expression, her face was still as lovely as if it had been chiseled out of marble. Even the creases of age looked deliberately carved.

"Welcome to your first diplomatic dinner," the queen said. "I expect you all to keep to your roles and work hard to advocate for the interests of your region. This is an important aspect of your training—just as crucial as mastering your magic. If you did the pre-reading, you should be well prepared for this exercise."

The other trainees shared uneasy looks. Hope surged in my breast. Magic wasn't going to be involved tonight, and I'd been coached on diplomatic strategy nearly since birth. None of them had any idea what they were up against. By the end of the first course of our meal, Ikrie and Aela were already deadlocked in a feud about road permits, fighting over whether a new road to the northwest hills could be built in Aela's territory. Evie looked completely lost, far too caught up in what was happening with Aela and Ikrie to realize that her best resources were on the other side of the border. As for me, I was perfectly happy with my position.

"Corovja is going to have a winter food shortage," Ikrie announced. "I need Valenko to send a hundred head of cattle and fifty head of sheep before winter falls."

"What are you offering in exchange?" I asked, keeping my voice pleasant.

Ikrie stared at me like I was stupid, an expression I was very familiar with seeing on her face. "What do you mean, what am I offering? I'm telling you to send them! The crown is here, and I will get orders signed by the queen."

For her part, the queen looked amused but didn't intervene.

"I'll be happy to send you the cattle and sheep if you can set up a discount for this year's purchase from the Orzai quarry," I said. Getting the best of Ikrie would no doubt be the most satisfying part of this game after how many times she'd used her magic to hurt me.

Ikrie scowled at me and then at Aela. "That's not possible. I won't negotiate with Orzai."

"Eryk," I said, "it appears there is a food shortage in Corovja. Perhaps we can use this to our advantage?" The only thing that was going to make Ikrie angrier than me outsmarting her was using Eryk to do it.

His eyes narrowed. We'd never spoken to each other outside of training, and barely even then.

"Valenko has many silos where we can store grains and other durable produce from your farms," I continued. "I'm willing to offer you free storage in exchange for a silo filled with hay. We'll mark up produce prices twenty-five percent and split the profits. The base sale price remains yours, of course."

Eryk opened his mouth, then shut it again. I could tell how badly he wanted to say no to me, but there were no holes in my deal. It was solid, and it benefited both of us. He looked across the table at

Ikrie, whose face was flushed with rage.

"I accept," he said.

I smiled into my next spoonful of soup. Ikrie looked mad enough to spit nails.

"Wait a minute, I want in on this trade deal," Tristan said, and proposed an idea of his own. Soon I had the entire southern half of the kingdom united to supply the northern half with goods at higher prices, all routed through my small city.

When I caught the queen's eye, she gave me a knowing nod of satisfaction. Brynan and Saia simply looked confused. They were accustomed to my defensive strategy in the training room, more often than not peppered with failures, not this sudden monopoly of success. Confidence swelled in my breast. For the first time, I started to believe that maybe I could succeed in training after all. I had strengths—I just needed to play to them.

Across from me, poor Evie looked in a near panic about what to do.

"Evie," I said, "what is it you're hoping to gain this winter?"

"Our crop was poor—we had a late frost in spring and an early frost before harvest," she said, clearly unsure what to do about it. "And our coffers are low—we don't have a lot of resources here. Just goats and silver mines."

"Ah," I said. "I can't seem to negotiate with Corovja or Orzai for the stone I need to build new farm buildings, and it appears we are going to have a need for them this winter. If you might be willing to trade some of your silver across the border to Havemont for stone, I'd be happy to pay you in livestock and a discounted rate on produce."

"Hey!" Eryk said.

"Don't worry—you'll get your full price plus your half of the twenty-five percent tax," I said. "I'm only offering to discount my portion of the tax."

Eryk sat back, mollified. "All right, then."

"Of course, I can definitely talk to the Havemontians," Evie said, relieved to have a plan and grateful for the save from across the table.

"But how are you planning to get your other building materials?" the queen asked. The trainees all stared at me.

"I've arranged a meeting with the Tamers," I said. "I'm concerned that the additional traffic through our region this fall might bother them and that some travelers might be foolish enough to wander into their territory. So I'd like to offer them some reassurance that their lands will be safe and protected and see if there's anything else they want. In exchange, I'm hoping to be able to harvest some deadfall from the outer boundaries of their territory."

The queen chuckled. "Well, aren't you full of surprises."

The stunned expressions on every other face at the table seemed to agree.

"Lia," Ikrie said, sounding tortured, "is there anything you need from Corovja?"

"What?" Aela said indignantly. "You're going to cooperate with her?"

"Ice," I said. "Sell it to me at half price and I'll waive my markup on livestock for you."

"All right," Ikrie said, agreeing in spite of the anger flashing in her eyes.

I wanted to laugh. She hadn't even tried to negotiate—she should have. I would have been willing to take a much smaller discount, but now what I'd make reselling the ice blocks at full price more than made up for the discount I was offering her.

"But I need ice," Tristan cut in.

"I know you do." I smiled. "And I'll be glad to sell it to you at full price."

Tristan groaned, then laughed. "You're evil," he said, but I knew it was a compliment.

By the end of the meal, Valenko was the year's winter trade hub, and my fictional coffers were overflowing. Aela was the only holdout, and Orzai got none of the things it needed. Ikrie suffered almost as much, her only benefits coming from the deal she'd cut with me. But without the ability to sell ice at full price, her coffers suffered.

"Well played, all of you," the queen said, standing up after the last course was served. "You're dismissed, and I hope you'll reflect on the lessons you've learned tonight about what it takes to protect your region and obtain what it needs. We'll play again with different assignments. Perhaps next time I will assign Lia the crown city as the winner and see how she uses that to her advantage."

Ikrie's face was pinched with anger, and Aela shoved away from the table with disgust. We all curtsied and bowed our polite farewells to the queen, including Brynan and Saia, who left murmuring in hushed tones.

"Lia, please stay back a moment," the queen said before I could get more than a few paces away from the table.

I stopped and turned back to face her, feeling a little jolt of nervousness.

"Let's retreat to my study," she said, once more leading the way to the hidden room that had housed the harp.

Somehow, tea service was already waiting for us when we arrived. I expected a servant to appear and serve the queen, but instead she prepared both our cups herself, pouring the hot water over the infusers with only a tiny tremble in her hands. The aromas of cinnamon and cardamom wafted over us.

"What can I do for you, Your Majesty?" I asked. The longer I waited to find out, the more I worried it was going to be something I wouldn't like.

"I usually make a habit of spending some extra time with the top student in each group of elites," the queen said.

"But I'm not the top student." I was confused. Yes, I'd done well in the diplomacy game, but I was far from the best in the training room. I could barely shield myself, much less use any offensive magic, which was all that Brynan and Saia seemed to care about teaching anyway.

"Perhaps not. But I think you are something more than that."

"What do you mean?" I didn't know what to do with my hands, so I bobbed my tea infuser up and down a few times in my cup.

"You have a very strong gift that you don't use to its full extent," she said. "You play the harp well enough that I've had to scold half a dozen servants for dallying in the hall outside your room at night."

My mouth went completely dry.

"You just won a very difficult diplomacy game playing arguably one of the most challenging hands to be dealt." She took her time pulling the tea infusers out of both our cups while panic climbed its way into my throat.

"It must have been beginner's luck," I said, cradling my hands around my warm teacup.

The queen smiled. "Modesty doesn't always become you, Lia. Or shall I say . . . Your Highness?"

Magic and terror sparked through every inch of my body, and for the next few heartbeats I was sure I was about to send the whole place up in flames. How could she know who I was? I'd been so careful not to speak of my past. Other than the harp playing, my few slipups could easily have been attributed to manners and knowledge I'd picked up as Mare's maidservant. The queen reached across the table and laid a gentle, cool hand on mine.

"Don't be frightened," she said, her voice soothing. "I've known who you were since the first time I saw you. Your secret will remain exactly that."

I swallowed hard. "Everyone thinks I'm dead." Even though it was a statement of the obvious, here in Corovja, leagues from anyone who loved or cared about me, it rang true and deep in a way it never had before.

"Perhaps that's how it should remain for now." The queen took a sip of her tea.

"How did you know?" I sat up straighter, dropping my disguise, and immediately felt more like myself than I had in weeks.

"Because we are of the same blood," the queen said.

"What?" My composure fell apart. Her statement made so little sense that I wondered if she was half-mad. I'd expected her to tell me it was because my manners were too good, or that she somehow knew I was a harpist in my old life, or that she'd seen a portrait of my family in Havemont. The Havemontian royal family had no connection to Zumorda other than through my mother. But the woman who had borne her to help out my grandparents was a commoner.

"Hold out your hand," the queen said, producing a small blade.

I did as she asked, reeling with shock as I understood she intended to do something to prove her words to me.

With a swift move, she nicked the tip of one of my fingers and squeezed a drop of blood into what I thought was a small hourglass. Then she sealed the top, flipped it over, and put a drop of her own blood into the other side. The hourglass illuminated with a soft glow, the two drops of blood suspended, one in each chamber. I was hypnotized as they defied gravity, moving toward the neck of the hourglass until they joined together at its center to make the whole thing glow bright red.

"Before I took the throne, I had a son," she said, her voice distant. "But in Zumorda, one cannot be a mother and a queen."

"What happened to him?" I asked softly.

"I don't know," she said. "I gave him to someone I knew in childhood—a demigod. She left Zumorda. I never thought I'd meet someone of my own bloodline, but when I heard about the star fall . . ."

"I thought fire Affinities were common," I said.

"Not ones like yours." She smiled sadly.

"But how did you know?" I asked.

"Your magic feels familiar to me, like an echo or a reflection of my own power," she said. "I don't know that I can explain it any better than that. When Laurenna sent you to me and the verium purged the last of the peaceroot, I knew right away that there was a connection between us. At first I thought it was simply our shared Affinity for fire. It took me a little longer to figure out that it was familial. My parents were killed before I took the throne. It's been a very long time since I've had relatives."

My heart went out to her. She'd ruled longer than many people's lifetimes and yet never had a family.

"I miss my family," I said. "I'm not even sure they know I'm alive." The admission made my chest ache.

"Perhaps you'll see them again someday," the queen said. "But for now I understand the usefulness of keeping your disguise. Your secret won't leave this room."

I exhaled a breath of relief, and as my fears dissipated, questions flooded in to replace them. My mother had only recently told me she had Zumordan blood—did she know it was blood shared by the queen? It didn't seem that she could know, since she said the surrogate who carried her was her mother's maid. That implied that the queen's son and his descendants had been raised as commoners in Havemont. And what had become of the demigod who had raised him? I hadn't even known demigods existed.

"Are there still demigods in Zumorda?" I asked the queen.

"No, child," she said. "They left Zumorda when its people stopped worshipping the gods. The only people who have powers even half as strong are those with multi-Affinities, which are quite rare. In some cases, the gifts of those with multi-Affinities consume them before they can master them. Grand Vizier Zhari is the only one of my guardians who has a multi-Affinity. I was surprised that the cultist we stopped in Tilium had one, though of course his was on a much smaller scale than hers . . . or yours."

I nearly choked on my tea. "I thought my Affinity was for fire."

"There is often an element that comes most easily or appears first, but the ability to touch other kinds of magic at all is unusual. You've definitely used more than one kind, have you not?"

I nodded. I knew the question was rhetorical, but the answer was also obvious. I'd often been able to use both wind and earth. It wasn't as easy as calling on fire, but I could definitely use them to augment my fire magic, sometimes without even meaning to. And the scale of destruction was always much more vast as a result.

"Multi-Affinities are notoriously hard to train. What works for one person won't work for another, and most of us are used to keeping our focus narrowed to the kind of magic we possess. There are too many unknown interactions between different kinds of magic to predict the outcomes of combining them."

Everything made so much more sense. No wonder I'd struggled so much to keep my magic under control. No wonder half the things Brynan and Saia told me to do didn't make sense or felt too volatile to try. But I still needed to learn. Fear crept back in. If I didn't, my gift might consume me—the queen had said as much. But if Zhari and Sigvar were the only people with multi-Affinities the queen was aware of, that meant there was only one person in Corovja I could ask about my powers.

"What happens when someone's gift is stripped away? Can they still use the Sight and can you See vestiges of their magic?" I wanted to know if there was still anything useful I could get out of Sigvar—assuming I could locate him.

The queen frowned. "Yes, the Sight remains, though it may be weaker than it was before. As for vestiges, I've never especially bothered to study that. I doubt they'd look the same as someone who is *vakos*."

"So someone like Sigvar, for example—he'd still be able to use his Sight but not manipulate magic on his own?" I asked tentatively.

One side of the queen's mouth quirked upward. "Prison doesn't seem to be suiting him very well, so I doubt his Sight is at the forefront of his mind."

So, unsurprisingly, he was in prison. At least that meant I knew exactly where to find him.

NINETEEN

✦ *Amaranthine*

STALKING ERONIT AND VARIAN TOOK MORE EFFORT than I anticipated, though it was at least less boring than following Alek. They were elusive in public spaces. Following them to dinner got me nowhere—they often seemed to dine privately rather than attending Winter Court functions. Fortunately, the easiest place to find them was in the salle, so I made a point of timing my sessions to coincide with theirs.

"Watch your feet!" Alek growled in disgust when Kerrick managed to trip me while I was gawking at Fadeyka and the two Sonnenbornes as they came through the door. I used the momentum to feint even farther to the left, just barely blocking the swing of Kerrick's sword.

Alek was right—I did need to watch my feet. Kerrick fought dirty, and I knew it. He made good use of his speed and agility to counteract what he lacked in strength and size. The muscles in my arms strained as I pushed him back, recovering just enough to get my feet back under me. I was going to hurt tomorrow, but I didn't care. I let my concentration narrow to only my opponent and executed the defensive drill Alek was schooling us on with perfect precision. The focus was something I'd quickly come to love about sword fighting—there wasn't time to think about anything else, especially Denna. Whenever I wasn't in the salle, her absence tormented me through the silence of my room, the chill of my lonely bed, and the lack of wise advice and warm laughter whispered in my ear. The worst torture of all was wondering if she'd ever come back.

"Better," Alek said. "Do it five more times. Both of you." Then he stalked off toward Eronit and Varian.

The flat of Kerrick's blade tapped me in the ribs. "Distracted much?"

"No," I said, and went on the offense with a quick parry.

He barely stopped my sword in time, though the smirk didn't vanish until I'd driven him halfway across the salle and nearly into the wall.

"You owe me a drink for that," he said, panting. "I'll be at Morwen's later if you want to come by again. Harian's meeting me for a few."

"Maybe," I said noncommittally. A drink didn't sound bad, but first I had to make another attempt at tracking Eronit and Varian.

I took my time leaving, wiping down a few extra sets of practice leathers until Fadeyka was done with her training as well. As usual, she noticed everything—including my odd behavior.

"Why are you still here?" she asked, curiosity in her brown eyes.

"Waiting for you," I said.

Her expression warmed, and I felt guilty. She'd undoubtedly noticed that I didn't often seek out her company, which was because she had a tendency to attach herself to me like a burr.

"Why'd you come in with them today?" I jerked my chin toward Eronit and Varian, who seemed to be wrapping up their session as well.

Fadeyka shrugged, hanging her practice sword back on the wall with the others. "They had a meeting with my mother before this."

"What kind of meeting?" I asked, trying to sound casual. If they were talking to Laurenna, it had to be about something important.

"Boring stuff," Fadeyka answered. "Business licensing they need to drop off in town for their relatives later."

My eyes narrowed as I glanced at them again. They were chatting with Alek, who had a typically unreadable expression on his face. What kind of business licensing? I wondered if it was a cover for passing the list of magic users off to someone else. If it truly was business licensing, it might provide some insight into what larger-scale plans they might be involved in. Varian gave Alek a respectful nod at the conclusion of their conversation, and he and Eronit headed for the door. Unlike the rest of us, they didn't have swords or armor to pack up, since they fought with staves.

I stood up. "Thanks. I have to go," I said to Fadeyka, and hurried toward the exit.

"Wait a minute." Fadeyka trotted behind me to catch up. "Why are you asking about them?"

"Just curious about what kinds of businesses are common in Kartasha," I said, hoping she'd lose interest. Outside the salle, I skirted the opposite side of the fountain, casting careful glances toward Eronit and Varian to make sure I didn't lose them.

"Then where are you going?" she asked. "I thought you said you were waiting for me." Confusion and disappointment warred in her expression. I felt like a rat.

"Oh, I was going to ask if you wanted to ride tomorrow," I said.

"Really?" She brightened.

"Maybe before lunch?" We exited the hallway and I slowed my steps, letting Eronit and Varian get far enough ahead of us that it wouldn't be obvious that I was trailing them. Just as Fadeyka said, they turned toward the gates to the city instead of back to the Winter Court.

"That should work," Fadeyka said. "I can't wait! Will you teach me to jump?"

"Not until you can post the trot with no stirrups," I said wryly.

"Where are you going now?" she asked. We were getting close to the outer gates.

"To town," I said. Foot traffic was thickening near the gate, and I was getting worried about losing my marks.

"I'd better go with you," she said, with authority belying her age.

I snorted. "I doubt your parents would like that. Don't you need to tell them where you are?"

Fadeyka kicked a rock out of our path. "Mother won't care. She's in meetings with Zhari all afternoon."

"What about your father?" I asked. It occurred to me for the first time that I'd never heard Fadeyka speak of him.

"My father's dead," Fadeyka said, her voice flat.

"I'm sorry," I said quietly. Whatever her feelings were about her father, I could imagine them all too easily. I'd lost so many people before leaving Mynaria, and while I'd managed to put the pain of that aside during my waking hours, grief still haunted my dreams. I'd never been able to prove myself to my father before he died, and that knowledge cut like a sword. Somehow his death had made my mother's memory rise up fresh, and I often lay awake remembering what it had been like to lose her. Even eight years later, I could picture the exact pattern on the edges of her blue funeral shroud. The vigil candles still burned in my mind as they had in my window for months after she died—until I realized that prayer wasn't going to bring her back. Grief never left—it just changed shape and grew with each added loss.

Fadeyka shrugged but for once was silent. She brushed her thumb absently over the back of her seven-pointed star pendant.

I wanted to say something else to let her know I understood, but I didn't know where to begin. I'd dealt with my mother's death by becoming as unlike her as I could, and by boxing her memory into a piece of my life I barely recognized as my own anymore. I was still dealing with the loss of my father. There wasn't anything I could offer Fadeyka.

The city streets sloped downward, providing a staggering view of the fields beyond. Postharvest they were already cut low and brown. Dry, cold air whipped at our cloaks. The crowded streets made it hard to keep an eye on Eronit and Varian ahead, even with the slope working in my favor. What helped even less were the other Sonnenbornes I saw passing by or working at various businesses along the road. Now that we were out in the city, Eronit and Varian didn't stand out the way they did at court. I craned my neck, trying to see over the crowd.

"They took a right on Halvard Street," Fadeyka said.

I looked down at her, surprised she'd so easily picked up on my mission. "How do you know?"

"Sometimes my magic gives me hints," she said.

A little shiver of unease went through me. Grateful as I was for Fadeyka's help, I'd be lying if I didn't admit the mention of magic made me a little nervous, especially knowing she didn't have it fully under control. I knew I was supposed to be working against the stereotypes of my homeland, but the burn on my side was a constant reminder of how dangerous magic could be. Denna hadn't meant to hurt me, but I also couldn't change the fact that she had, or that it was so easy for people like her to hurt those of us who didn't have powers. Guilt nagged on the heels of my thoughts. I couldn't help the way I felt about magic, and I was trying as hard as I could to be accepting and open-minded. But my best efforts weren't enough to keep Denna from feeling like I didn't support her and, ultimately, from leaving. In the end, it was my fault that she had, and I had only myself to blame for destroying the most important relationship in my life.

Fadeyka and I pushed our way past a vendor shouting the prices of fruits and vegetables and took a right on Halvard. Sure enough, I caught a glimpse of Varian's reddish hair several horse lengths ahead of us.

"Is it like your mother's gift?" I asked, remembering that Laurenna could trace magical energy back to its source. "Water magic?"

"It might be, but I'm not sure," Fadeyka said. "Usually you can tell what your Affinity is before you have even ten winters," she said. "My friend Turi always loved the gardens and had a way with plants. Earth Affinity. My mother grew up swimming in Lake Vieri from the time she was small. Her family called her Fish. Water Affinity. Me? I don't know. Sometimes I get a vague sense of where people are. Sometimes I can walk through rain without getting wet. Every once in a while, I think maybe I made the wind blow harder. Then there was that thing that happened in the salle by accident. Mother isn't sure if I have a multi-Affinity or if my magic hasn't settled yet. She thinks once I have my manifes, it will become clearer."

We took a sharp left to continue following Varian and Eronit but had to drop back from them a bit. Traffic was thinning, and our presence would become obvious if we weren't careful. The street we walked on ended in a T facing a small city park. Cobbled pathways meandered between a few tall evergreens, lined with hedges of neatly trimmed holly. Eronit and Varian took a right. I extended my arm to hold Fadeyka back and peered carefully around the corner before following them. Eronit and Varian had stopped at the door of a boardinghouse or residence immediately beyond the turn. I slipped back around the corner quickly, hoping I hadn't been seen.

"Varian, Roni!" a man's voice greeted them enthusiastically. "You have the papers?"

"Yes, everything is in order," Eronit said.

"Praise the sands!" the man inside said. "I've got twenty people waiting for work and a shipment coming in just a few days. Bless you both."

Varian asked a question I couldn't quite make out.

"Yes, of course. The loans are already in order," the other man said. "Come in for a few minutes. Our cousin sent a box of fine mesquite with the last shipment. A bit of ephedra, too." I could hear the sly smile in his voice and knew from his tone that the cousin he spoke of wasn't really family.

Eronit and Varian accepted the invitation, and I heard the door shut behind them. I cursed the cold weather and the fact that no one's windows were open. There was no way to get any idea of the conversation going on inside. What businesses? What shipments?

"Let's cross over to the park," I said. We could hide behind one of the holly hedges and wait for Eronit and Varian to reemerge.

"You're acting very strange, even for someone who's sneaking around after people," Fadeyka said. "What exactly are you trying to do?"

"I need to know what Eronit and Varian are doing at the Winter Court," I said.

"That's simple. They're scholars," Fadeyka said.

"Scholars who obtain business papers for mysterious 'relatives'?" I asked.

"I suppose?" She looked uncertain. "But Eronit is a historian and horticulturist and Varian is an expert on tribal politics in Sonnenborne. I heard them discussing those things with my mother."

"They told me they were studying magic and plants," I said, my mistrust increasing. "Besides, why would an expert on tribal politics come to Kartasha to further his studies?" Everything he needed to know should have been in his homeland. "And why would they also be helping other Sonnenbornes open new businesses here?"

"We've always traded with Sonnenborne and allowed them to operate sanctioned businesses." Fadeyka shrugged. "Kartasha is known for its neutrality."

"I'm all for open markets, but doesn't the attack on Duvey seem like a threat to that?" I said. "Not to mention that they outright took over a city in my homeland—a smaller trade city. What's to say that won't happen again on a larger scale?"

Fadeyka frowned. "Nothing."

"Exactly."

I sat down on the cold stones of one of the paths, where I could peer through the holly to the door of the boardinghouse. The shrubs at least cut the wind a little bit, though the chill of the ground was already working its way into my bones. After at least half a sunlength of sitting on the hard ground until my rear was numb and Fadeyka was fidgety with boredom, Eronit and Varian finally emerged. I sat up in a crouch and leaned forward but couldn't catch any of their parting words to the man at the door. Rather than heading back the way we'd come from the Winter Court, they continued down the street.

"C'mon," I said, pulling Fadeyka to her feet. I put up the hood of my cloak and tried to walk like I wasn't in too much of a hurry. Varian and Eronit kept a quick pace, seemingly headed for a busier street on the other side of the park. We trailed them through a textile district, where shop assistants were pulling in their street displays for the evening. Among those working were many I recognized as Sonnenborne, but a few I wouldn't have if I hadn't heard them speaking to each other in their language. It seemed odd to me that so many strong, young Sonnenborne people were working in a textile district when they surely could have found better jobs. No one was elderly, and there were few children to be seen other than those hand in hand with their parents, who were heading home for the day.

Past the textile district, a street curved sharply to the left. The buildings lining it teemed with activity, and lamps were being lit outside as the overcast sky began to dim. My footsteps slowed as we passed a whitewashed building where a woman was using her fingertip to light the lanterns hanging from the eaves. The flames licked harmlessly at her fingers, reminding me of the way I'd seen Denna touch fire so many times. A confused swell of emotion made it hard for me to breathe. How could something that frightened me remind me of someone I loved so much? The woman caught me staring and smiled. I quickly turned away.

"Can you use that gift of yours again?" I asked Fadeyka.

She took my wrist and pulled me forward, her face scrunching up with concentration. A few blocks later, we stopped in front of a well-kept building. The door swung open every few minutes as someone went in or out, and a sign on the door bore a cracked goblet and the words *The Broken Cup*.

I hesitated. On the one hand, bringing a child into a drinking establishment seemed conspicuous. On the other, I could hardly leave Fadeyka out here by herself in the middle of the city. But before I had a chance to say anything, she was already through the door, leaving me to hurry after her.

"Wait!" I said. The interior was well lit with oil lanterns, but noisy and crowded enough that my grab for her arm went unnoticed. Of course, I missed.

To her credit, Fadeyka kept her hood pulled up and slipped

between people like a shadow. She slowed when she got to the back of the room, waited until Eronit and Varian were preoccupied with settling at a table, then ducked into a nearby alcove that was protected from the rest of the room by a heavy black curtain.

"What are you doing?" I whispered as I slid in behind her. "What is this?"

"The musicians' closet," she said, waving to some large objects behind us. "They don't usually start up until after sunset."

I gave her a suspicious look that she either didn't see or didn't care about. She was obviously no stranger to sneaking about in places she wasn't supposed to be—this clearly wasn't her first time here. We had more in common than I cared to admit. I pushed the curtain aside just enough to let in a touch of light, which hit the pile of neatly stacked instrument cases behind us. A leather cello case leaned in the corner, towering above the other instruments. Other than the light oil finish on the case, it could have been my mother's. My stomach clenched.

"You look like you just saw a sword covered in blood instead of a musical instrument," Fadeyka said.

"I'm fine," I said, turning back to peer out of the curtain and trying to shake off the memories.

"Do you play?" Fadeyka asked.

"My mother did," I said, my voice tight. "She's dead." I didn't want Fadeyka to ask any more questions.

Both of us kept our eyes fixed on the room, but a small hand slipped into mine. Her understanding made my chest constrict as a deep wound reopened inside me. She knew exactly what it was like to lose a parent. So many years ago, my mother and I had visited places like this. Pulled an instrument just like that one out of the case to put on a show. Worn wigs and feathers and peasant clothes of all fashions to look like anything other than what we were—royalty. I could feel the hum of the cello's notes even now, written into some deep place in my bones.

A flash of dark hair at the bar just a few steps away jerked me from the well of memories threatening to drown me. Eronit purchased three drinks. Either she was very thirsty, or someone had joined her and Varian. The barmaid used magic to pour the beverages, teasing liquid from the bottles into the glasses in arching streams that defied gravity. I peered carefully around the curtain to get a better look at the table Eronit and Varian had claimed, which was just barely in earshot. She placed the drinks on the table, temporarily blocking my view, and then slipped into a chair beside Varian, giving his arm a squeeze. Then she smiled warmly at the person sitting across from her, whose familiar face made my blood turn to ice.

Alek.

"What the Six Hells is he doing here?" I murmured. Eronit and Varian had only just talked to him in the salle—why would they be having drinks here now?

"Were you able to get it?" Alek asked, picking up a snifter that was dwarfed by his enormous hand.

Varian nodded, and pulled a sheaf of papers out of his bag and passed them across the table to Alek.

"Thank you," Alek said, with a rare show of earnestness.

"Please don't let this information slip into the wrong hands,"

Eronit said, her voice worried. "If anyone finds out that we took these papers . . ."

". . . it would compromise your position at court," Alek finished. "Don't worry. Trust is key here. I have nothing to gain by turning you in."

"The tribes have a very strong belief that this is the way to revitalize our kingdom," Eronit said. "Reintroducing magic could change everything."

Varian leaned forward and added a comment of his own that I couldn't make out. I looked down at Fadeyka, whose expression seemed to be warring between shock and anger.

"Is Alek conspiring against Zumorda?" Fadeyka whispered.

"It sounds like he's at least been helping the Sonnenbornes," I said grimly. For the first time, I wondered if he'd actually had something to do with the abductions in Duvey. Could he have been the one who tipped off the Sonnenbornes that the keep would be weak on defense after Wymund had sent soldiers to Kartasha for the queen? It all made too much sense.

Fadeyka cursed, using language I dearly hoped she hadn't picked up from me.

"I think your mother is about to have another reason to hate Alek," I said. We were going to have to turn him in.

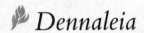 *Dennaleia*

THE ONLY PROBLEM WITH PLANNING TO TRACK DOWN Sigvar was that I needed some time in which to do it, and my grueling training schedule made that impossible for over a week. Finally, without letting myself think about it for long enough to feel guilty, I sent a page to tell Saia and Brynan I was unwell. Then I slipped out of my room and headed straight for the library. The prison had to be on the architectural drawings I'd found there.

The dust and disarray were just as I'd left them previously; I was only about halfway through cleaning and organizing the bottom floor. I immediately went to the trunk full of architectural drawings and laid them all out from oldest to newest. Unfortunately, poring over them revealed nothing—the prison did not appear to be within the castle walls. Disappointment weighed me down as I packed the scrolls back into their trunk. How else was I going to find Sigvar and ask him about multi-Affinities? I hoped he would have some knowledge of how to better use and train mine—he'd seemed to have his well under control until the queen tore his powers away from him.

I left the library and returned to my rooms, deciding to spend some time at the harp honing my Sight. If someone found out I'd been lying about being sick, it would be easier to ask for forgiveness for evading my lessons if I had spent some of the time working on related skills.

I settled on the stool at the harp and set to warming up. At first my fingers were stiff and cold as I worked my way through ascending scales, eventually moving on to arpeggios and chords once I felt myself melting back into the familiarity of the instrument. Every time I flubbed a note, I thought of the disapproving look my harp instructor in Havemont would have given me, and slowly but surely, my accuracy and articulation improved.

A study piece felt like the right choice for working on my Sight, so I began playing a D minor etude. I let my mind empty of everything but the music. When I unfocused my vision and let myself look through objects instead of at them, I could See all kinds of things. A small family of mice scurried through a passage in the wall, and the lamps in my room glittered with the enchantments that kept them bright.

I didn't pause in my playing until something else appeared in my Sight—a human figure with a purple glow I sensed on the other side of the door. I muted the harp strings and sat in silence, my heart pounding, hoping the person would go away. Instead, a knock sounded on the door. I cracked it open to reveal Tristan.

"Abandoning us for a harp, eh?" he said with a wry smile.

I blushed, embarrassed at being caught. Saia or Brynan must have realized I was lying about my reasons for skipping training and sent him to look for me.

"I won't tell," he added. He swept his mop of shaggy black hair out of his eyes. "That you're not sick, I mean. I managed to talk Evie out of checking on you."

"That was kind of Evie, though I appreciate you talking her out of it," I said. "I didn't have training in me today."

Tristan slumped into one of the chairs near the hearth. "I don't have it in me most days."

I shook my head. He seemed to do fine in training, though he didn't have the ambition and ruthlessness of Ikrie or Eryk. "Then why did you sign on for this?"

"Well, I'm not stupid," he said. "Turning down the best education available in Zumorda wouldn't be very smart. Nor would defying the wishes of the queen."

"Fair," I said. He had a point. "How did you find me?"

"My shadow sense," he said.

"I don't know what that is."

"I can sense people who have killed others," he said. "Your shadow is darker than most."

My blood turned to ice in my veins. His gift so easily exposed the darkest part of me. Even if the people I'd killed with my gift had deserved it, thinking about them consumed me with guilt and sorrow. I felt sick.

"I didn't do it on purpose," I said, my voice soft.

"I didn't assume you had," he said. "As for training, don't worry—you didn't miss much. Just Ikrie and Aela showing off for

Saia. I think they're still mad at each other after how badly the diplomacy exercise went for them. The collateral damage wasn't pretty." He held up his arm, which was bandaged just below the elbow.

"Gods, this place is brutal," I said. Everything here was too hard, the people too ruthless. A tiny part of me wondered if Mare was right to suggest that it wouldn't be so bad for me to have my gift stripped, but the thought still made me sick.

"We could get out of here for a while," Tristan said with a sly smile.

"What do you mean?" I said, taken aback.

"I have a way we can leave the castle. Nobody would notice. Probably." Tristan looked preemptively smug.

"Yes, and no one would notice if you killed me and left me in a ditch somewhere," I said. "The other trainees would probably be grateful."

"I don't have any interest in doing them favors," he said. "But I wouldn't mind getting out of here, too."

I thought about what Mare would do in this situation. I'd already skipped my lessons, which was a classic Mare move. And now I was being offered the chance to escape the castle, even though the queen had explicitly forbidden it. I knew exactly what choice Mare would have made and how much regard she had for the rules. Maybe it was time for me to start acting a little less like myself and more like her.

"All right, fine. But if there's a bookshop in Corovja, we have to go." Perhaps the bookstore would have a map of the city that would reveal the location of the prison. I still had a few silver pieces left over from our journey into Zumorda.

Tristan wrinkled his nose. "If we must. And I need to pick up a bottle of ice wine."

"You like ice wine?" I said incredulously. That stuff was too sweet even for me.

"No." He blushed. "Evie does."

I smiled in spite of myself. Apparently Saia was wrong about the trainees not developing friendships—or in this case, maybe something more.

"All right, then. How do we sneak out?" I asked, tugging on my cloak.

"We shadow walk," he said, and held out his hand. "Um, be forewarned that some people find the experience unpleasant."

Whatever he was talking about couldn't be worse than getting beaten up in training every day—or so I thought until I took his hand. Our fingers laced together, and as soon as he had a firm grip on me, the room faded to pitch black. My head spun, and I had no sense of any firm ground beneath my feet. My stomach felt as though I'd been dropped off the side of a mountain. Tristan tugged me forward through the shadows as distant moans reverberated all around me until they seemed to be coming from inside my own mind. Voices whispered the stories of their deaths and how it had felt when their souls had left their bodies.

And as quickly as it started, it ended as we stumbled into the snow and the world came back into focus. Slabs of stone stood up all around us, marked with names and symbols—a graveyard.

"What in the Sixth Hell was that?" I asked, taking deep gulps of icy winter air in hopes of reducing the nausea that still gripped my stomach.

"We took a stroll through the shadowlands," Tristan said. He didn't seem nearly as bothered by the experience as I was.

"You could warn a person!" I said.

"I did!" he said indignantly.

I glanced back, and sure enough the castle wall was visible in the distance. He'd gotten us out.

"Good gods, why did you transport us here?" I asked.

"It's easier to travel to places where the dead rest. The paths are better established."

"It's freezing. C'mon." I started trudging toward the gate, my teeth chattering. As we passed the grave markers, I started to recognize the symbols on them—they looked similar to those sometimes used for the Six Gods. The nicer ones had pellets of colored glass inlaid in them.

"Are these graves marked with Affinities?" I asked.

"It used to be customary to include the symbol of someone's Affinity on their headstone, yes," Tristan said.

"Then what's this symbol?" I stopped in front of one that had a seven-pointed star hanging on to only the last vestiges of silver leaf. The stone was old and crumbling, the name no longer even legible. The grave had to be ancient.

"Dunno." He shrugged.

"What do you mean, you don't know?" I asked.

"In Havemont we don't mark graves this way."

"It doesn't seem like they've done it here for the newer ones, either," I observed. So what did the symbol mean in this context? Tristan hadn't said people could take their manifests with the help of multiple gods, but maybe that was possible. "Could it be symbolic of someone with a multi-Affinity?" That was the only other thing I could think of.

"Doubtful," Tristan said, pointing at an ornate headstone with three different colors of glass embedded in it. "Those are usually marked with some indication of all the person's Affinities."

"Strange." I turned away from the stone and kept walking. My stomach finally settled a little as we made our way down the street toward town.

"I can ask my mother about it when I return home if I get a chance to visit after I'm apprenticed. She might know something."

"Your mother is an expert on ancient graves?" I asked.

"No, but she lived in Zumorda before the queen took her throne. Perhaps she saw something like this before."

"Your mother can't be the queen's age," I said flatly. I couldn't tell how old the queen was, but she was decades past her childbearing years, and I doubted Tristan was any older than me.

Tristan smiled. "My mother's a demigod. I was left on my parents' doorstep as a baby, like many of the other orphans they take in."

I reeled. For some reason, when the queen told me there were no longer demigods in Zumorda, I assumed they'd died out everywhere. "How old is your mother?" As far as I knew, things hadn't changed in Zumorda in at least a hundred years. How old did that make the queen?

"I think about two hundred, give or take a few years. Demigods live much longer than humans."

I nearly choked. "You're telling me the queen is also two hundred years old? How is that possible?"

Tristan laughed at my expression. "Yes. Bonding with a magical creature seems to have dramatically increased the queen's life span. But she's still mortal. She can't live forever."

I had no idea such a thing was even possible. "Are all people's life spans affected by their manifests?" I asked.

Tristan shook his head. "Not really. I think it has to do with the dragon being a magical creature. Choosing a magical creature as one's manifest is fairly rare, if for no other reason than the magical creatures themselves are not very common."

That meant even though we were related, the queen and I were separated by many generations. No wonder my mother had no idea that her lineage could be traced to the Zumordan throne. Then I remembered what the queen had said about people with multi-Affinities being the only ones approaching demigods with the scale of their powers.

"Are the demigods related to people with multi-Affinities?" I asked.

"No," Tristan said. "Demigods can't bear their own children. They usually have powers that correspond to whichever god is their parent, though like our gifts, there is a fair amount of variation among them."

We walked in silence for a few minutes and I took in the city around us. Like Kartasha, the city was laid out on the side of a mountain, but where Kartasha's buildings mostly had gabled or cross-hipped roofs, Corovja's were almost all saltbox style or angled on one side. Snow guards peeked above the dusting of white that had accumulated on many of the buildings.

"It's ridiculous that we're supposed to stay confined to the castle during our training," Tristan remarked. "There's so much to see here."

"I'm sure it's because they don't want us getting distracted," I said. Plenty of the academic communities in Havemont had similar rules, with excursions being tightly controlled.

"I don't think it's a distraction to get to know your kingdom," Tristan said. "Especially if one wants to become a guardian. It's not the same as ruling, but I would think it would take a strong under-standing of the people in your region regardless."

"That's a wise observation," I said. "I'm not very interested in becoming a guardian, though. Not that they'd let me, since I'm without a manifest."

"It's too bad. You certainly have a knack for diplomacy that would give you an advantage. I kept falling asleep over the assigned reading, but it was like you knew it front to back."

I smiled bitterly. If only he knew how many years I'd studied those skills. There was no knack involved—only countless hours of practice. "So where are we going to get this ice wine for Evie?" I asked.

"There's a spirit shop a little ways down the main road," he said, picking up the pace. "If we cut through this alley, we can get there faster." He led me into an alley that took a sharp left turn and was so steep it had stairs.

"When will you give it to her?" I asked.

"I'm not sure," Tristan mumbled.

I almost laughed. He liked her but couldn't have been more awkward about it if he tried. "You could invite her over to share it with you," I said.

"It's supposed to be a gift!" He seemed confused.

"But if you invite her to share it with you, you'll get a chance to talk to her outside of training," I pointed out.

He blushed. "I wouldn't know what to say."

"If you don't know what to say, make the other person do the talking," I said, reciting the advice of my etiquette tutor. "Questions are a way to engage your subjects and show that you care about their concerns and are willing to listen to them."

Tristan gave me a puzzled look. "Subjects?"

"People," I hastily said. "I used to be a princess's maid. One picks things up."

Tristan smirked. "No wonder you got mixed up in all this. Powerful magic, and secondhand princess manners to boot. You know what's funny? You look a lot like Princess Dennaleia of Havemont. Maybe I should start calling you Princess."

"Oh gods, please don't," I said. A jolt of panic stabbed me in the gut that he'd so easily stumbled over the truth. "There's enough of a target on my back already as far as Ikrie and Eryk are concerned."

"As you wish, Lady Lia," he said with false formality.

I glared at him, which only made him laugh.

A little farther down the road, he led me through a door nestled in a narrow storefront. The walls inside were lined from floor to ceiling with bottles in every conceivable shape and size. In the far back was a shelf stacked several bottles deep with various kinds of ice wine, many of them local, but a fair number also imported from Havemont. Seeing the labels I recognized filled me with homesickness. I'd seen other vintages and more exclusive bottles in my parents' collection back home.

"So, uh, you don't happen to know anything about ice wine, do you?" he asked.

"Only what I saw the royalty drinking sometimes," I lied. I was familiar with almost all the northern vintners of good reputation.

"Do they have any of those here?" he asked, his voice eager.

"You must really want to impress Evie," I teased him.

"I just want to get her something good," he said, flushing a little.

"This one," I said, reaching for a bottle with a glittery purple label. I recognized it as a much less expensive version of one of my parents' favorites. They often served the rarer vintages during meetings with high-ranking merchants or other people who were hard to impress. They'd claimed it wasn't easy to find outside Havemont.

"Why that one?" he said, taking the bottle from me and turning it over in his hand.

"It's from your homeland, which means it has special meaning and shows that you selected it thoughtfully," I said. "Also, it's at a middling price, which means it probably isn't cheap wine with sugar added, so it'll be the real deal without being ungodly expensive."

"I'm impressed. You sure think things through," Tristan said with admiration in his voice.

"If you don't trust me, ask the shopkeeper." I gestured to the man behind the counter near the front of the store. "They're usually familiar with everything they stock. I think this might be one that is hard to find outside Havemont."

Another customer burst through the door, setting the bell jangling. The man's rumpled clothes hung on him like trash sacks and his stubble looked more than a few days old.

"Ay, got out of prison again, Lestkar?" the shopkeeper called.

"I haven't been there for ten years, you old coot!" Lestkar said, shuffling over to a shelf filled with magnums of cheap clear spirits. I wrinkled my nose. They were barely nicer than the alcohols the medics used as antiseptics—hardly worth drinking.

"You'd best have enough coin to pay for that," the shopkeeper said, a firm edge to his teasing tone.

Lestkar waved him off and kept browsing.

Tristan and I went to the front of the store to make our purchase, though I kept a careful eye on Lestkar, who made his way over to the counter just as Tristan was wrapping up his transaction.

"That's twenty," the shopkeeper said to Lestkar, tying the last knot of twine over the brown paper he'd wrapped Tristan's ice wine in.

"Fifteen!" Lestkar roared.

The shopkeeper sighed. "It was fifteen before you got thrown in prison the first time—ten years ago."

Tristan started to edge toward the door, but I grabbed his arm to stop him.

"I've only got fifteen." Lestkar slapped his coins down on the shopkeeper's counter.

"Actually, that's thirteen," the shopkeeper said.

"Excuse me, sir," I said to Lestkar. "Is it true you went to prison?"

The man turned and looked down at me with a distrusting expression. "Who wants to know?"

"I'm just a servant, sir. Someone I used to work for got taken to the prison, and I want to see if he's all right."

Tristan looked at me as though I'd lost my mind.

"Haven't been there in years," Lestkar said. "Never going back, no sir."

"The bottle is still twenty," the shopkeeper said, clearly losing patience.

I pulled seven coins out of my pocket. "I'll pay for the rest of your bottle if you show us the way there," I said.

The shopkeeper eyed my coins greedily, and Lestkar looked back and forth between me and the bottle. Eventually, he decided the bottle was worth the trouble.

"All right. Pay up and I'll show you," he said. "But I'm not going within sight of the guards, and I'm not sharing my drink."

"Everyone has their limits," I said, smiling politely.

The shopkeeper took my money, seemingly relieved when we all left the building. Lestkar had his bottle open barely three steps outside the store.

"So, where is it?" I asked Lestkar.

"We'll follow the main road to the crystal shop, turn left on the mining route, and when the buildings all turn to warehouses, it'll be at the end of the block across from the tanner's. Now hurry up, because I have other business to attend to." Lestkar took another swig of his drink and shuffled toward the main road at a surprisingly quick pace.

"Wait, slow down," Tristan said to me as I trotted after Lestkar. "Why the Sixth Hell are you wanting to go to the prison?"

"Sigvar," I said, keeping an eye on Lestkar to make sure he didn't take off in a random direction. "I need information from him."

"What kind of information could possibly be worth seven coins and trusting a drunken criminal?" Tristan asked, his voice rising.

"Sigvar has—well, had—a multi-Affinity. I think he might know something that would help me figure out how to master my own powers," I said. "It would make a big difference for me in training."

"But how are you going to get in? You can't just walk in there," Tristan pointed out.

"You're right. I can't." That hadn't occurred to me. As a princess, I wouldn't have had trouble gaining permission to enter the prison. No one would have questioned me. Here that wouldn't be the case. Also, if there was some kind of visitor ledger or magical means of keeping track of who went in and out, that meant the queen could find out where I'd been. I couldn't risk it. I cursed colorfully enough to make Mare proud. "Six Hells, why is every piece of information so hard to get in this sarding place?"

Tristan pondered this information for a moment. "Maybe there's another way."

I turned to look at him. "Like what?"

"A lot of people die in prison," Tristan said, leaving me to fill in the rest of the blanks.

"Are you saying we could shadow walk there?" My stomach turned at the thought, but I could already see the potential. We could go at night, get inside the building without ever having to speak to a guard, and escape at a moment's notice with no one the wiser.

"I'm saying it's not impossible," Tristan said. "But I worry about where we'd land. I'm not familiar with the building, so there's no saying whether we'd come out of the shadowlands in the right location or somewhere problematic. And there's only so many times I can go in or out quickly—it does use a fair amount of power."

Up ahead, Lestkar took a sudden left, forcing us to hurry to follow him.

"I have an idea," I said. "We'll still go to the prison, but we won't try to get in today. I just need to get a sense of the layout first." I'd have to count on my Sight cooperating, but I felt more confident about it now.

"You're more trouble than I would have guessed." Tristan smiled.

"Not all the time," I said. I felt a little bad about involving him in my schemes, but not bad enough to disinvite him. I needed all the help I could get, and in truth, it felt good to have a friend by my side.

"If helping you with this will prevent me from getting blown off my feet in training by another one of your firestorms, you can count me in," he said.

"I make no promises," I said wryly. "Midwinter is less than a moon away, and I get the impression that Brynan and Saia are expecting us to fight ruthlessly for the honor of the best apprentice-ship."

"I'll take my chances," Tristan said, and offered me his arm.

I laughed and took it, and we hustled down the mining road with the wind at our backs.

TWENTY-ONE

✦ *Amaranthine*

AFTER MY DISCOVERY AT THE BROKEN CUP, THERE WAS
no time to waste before talking to Laurenna. I sent Fadeyka home to
give Laurenna an overview of what we'd discovered and was unsur-
prised when my summons came for that very same evening.

We gathered in Zhari's receiving room, an opulent affair decorated with gilded floral furniture. Her staff sat in one corner, the
gems embedded in its curved top winking back at me as I took my
seat.

"You have quite a collection," I said to Zhari. Tables and shelves
throughout the room held precious artifacts that looked more like
they belonged in a museum than in someone's home.

"It tends to happen as one ages," she said, her tone wry. "I've
lived in Kartasha since long before you were born." She settled carefully into her own chair, the heavy fabric of her gray robes pooling
around her feet.

"Let's get to the point." Laurenna picked up a glass of wine from the small table beside her chair. "Faye said you had evidence of Alek conspiring with the Sonnenbornes."

I nodded. "I'm sure you're aware that several pages of the ledger for Zhari's program were stolen from the records master."

Zhari put a hand to her temple. "They haven't had any luck tracking them down yet, either."

"That's because Eronit and Varian stole them and gave them to Alek." I explained everything I'd discovered—seeing Alek talk to Eronit and Varian at the Broken Cup, the handover of the papers, the strange business loan requests, and how I'd noticed so many able-bodied Sonnenbornes in town. "This is much bigger and more involved than we realized. I'm concerned that Alek may even have had something to do with the abductions in Duvey, or at least tipped off the Sonnenbornes that Duvey's defenses would be weak after sending soldiers to Kartasha. I wish we knew more about what happened with Zephyr Landing, because I fear the Sonnenbornes may be setting up the same thing to happen here. I don't know why I'm the only gods-damned one who seems to see it," I finished.

"You're absolutely certain you saw them give the papers to Alek?" Laurenna asked, her hand white-knuckle tight on her wine-glass.

I nodded.

Zhari frowned deeply. "I'm very upset to think records from my program might be getting used to help the Sonnenbornes target vulnerable young magic users for abduction."

"Protecting our young people is of the utmost priority," Laurenna said. "But I don't know if we could afford to shut the program down. Just this past year we found two guardian candidates through the program. They're training in Corovja now. If we started losing trainees of that caliber, it could have a devastating long-term impact on our kingdom."

"So what are we going to do about this?" I asked. "Surely what I've been seeing isn't isolated. This warrants investigation by the Winter Court. Eronit, Varian, and Alek need to be questioned. We have to get that list back before it can be used as a weapon against your people."

Laurenna nodded her agreement. "We'll need to see to it immediately. In the meantime, it's important that you keep yourself safe. I know you've been spending a lot of time at the salle. I have a gift that may help you with your training." She stepped over to a trunk in the corner of the room that showed no signs of a lock, hinges, or seams. "Zhari, do you mind?"

Zhari smiled. "I haven't minded storing it for you, but it's about time you passed that thing along."

"I agree," Laurenna said. At a hissing word and a wave of her hand, the top separated from the bottom and lifted away.

She returned with a long object wrapped in faded blue fabric and set it on the low table at the center of where we were gathered.

"I think this will help you," she said. "Unwrap it."

I pulled away the fabric carefully, revealing a stiff leather scabbard that looked old but barely used. The hilt of the cutlass gleamed in the low light. It had an ornate guard of twisting silver and a line of blue gems inlaid in the ricasso.

"You can't be giving this to me," I said. Even without taking it out of the scabbard, I could tell the sword was of incredibly fine make. At some point I'd planned to buy a sword of my own, since I had the means, but this was far too much as a gift.

"Draw it and see how it feels," Laurenna said, her voice encouraging.

I stood up and cautiously drew the sword from its sheath. It wasn't overly heavy, and from what little I knew, it was balanced. The grip felt as if it had been made for my hand, and though the curve of the foible would take a little getting used to, I could tell it would make the weapon that much more lethal in a situation where it needed to be.

"Why would you give this to me?" I asked. It looked like an heirloom or a custom weapon—not some generic item she'd pass off to a foreigner without a thought.

"Consider it a reward for the quality of the information you've gathered," she said. "It will be of much more use to you than me—I have plenty of other blades to choose from should I need one."

"Thank you. I'm honored," I said, sheathing the weapon and placing it reverently back on the table. "What can I do to help with the next steps?"

"Continue to keep your ears open, first and foremost," she said. "You did right by reporting this to me immediately. I'll see that Alek and the Sonnenbornes are questioned, and this information will all be passed to the queen."

"We shouldn't expect too much help from the north, though," Zhari said gently. "The queen will be focused on training her elites. We must do everything we can to handle the problems here ourselves so that she has room to do that."

"Of course," Laurenna agreed.

"There might be something else I can do to help," I said.

Laurenna raised an eyebrow.

"My brother has offered his cavalry should it be needed," I said. "Of course we would never send in any fighters without your explicit welcome. But with a threat looming, it might be good to have them on reserve, either in Duvey or here in Kartasha if you don't think they'd cause too much disruption. That would also spare the queen from having to try and coordinate any support from the north."

"That's a very generous offer," Laurenna said. "I'll keep that in mind once we know more. Let's plan to meet again just after Midwinter to go over any new information you've gleaned."

"I'll do that," I said. "Thank you for listening."

"At least we may have some help coming from the north in spring," Zhari said. "After Midwinter, the ranking of the queen's elites will be determined. I'm open for an apprenticeship, and it isn't uncommon for a winner to choose to come here."

She spoke with quiet modesty, but I knew what the implications were—another of the most powerful magic users in Zumorda might soon be here to assist us. I couldn't help but think of Denna, and the agony was almost more than I could take.

"Do you know how the trainees are doing?" I asked tentatively.

"No," Laurenna said. "It's an isolated environment. We are not likely to hear stories of any injuries or deaths until the elites have battled at Midwinter. That's the first time their abilities will be put on display for the public."

"Battle?" I barely kept the note of panic out of my voice. "Deaths?"

"Don't fret," Zhari reassured me. "The Midwinter Revel is not what it once was. I can't recall the last time a trainee was mortally injured."

"Did that happen often?" I asked.

"Oh, of course," Zhari said. "Back when I became guardian, Queen Invasya was still reinventing the government after over-throwing the boar king—finding new ways to ensure that her eyes and ears could be everywhere in the kingdom. The quickest way to identify the strongest magic users was to pit us against one another in battle."

"But to the death?" I asked.

"From what I know of the history, the first Midwinter Revel was a bloodbath," Laurenna said, her voice casual. "They've toned it down since then—now the competitors just have to defeat their opponents instead of killing them, but accidents do still happen."

"The training itself is fairly brutal," Zhari said. "Occasionally there's an elite who doesn't even make it to the Revel."

Had Denna known what she was getting into when she agreed to go with the queen? She wasn't a fighter—or at least I didn't think she was. Her powers were formidable, if uncontrolled, but how would she fare against a bunch of ruthless magic users who'd had proper training from the first time their gifts showed themselves?

My mind churned with worries after I left Laurenna and Zhari. On one hand, Laurenna had taken me seriously. Real progress was going to be made with investigating what the Sonnenbornes were doing, and I'd gotten important information to people who mattered. I'd even managed to bring my brother's offer of cavalry to the table as a strong show of support for everything we were trying to do. Yet in spite of all that, unease plagued me. Zhari and Laurenna's description of the elites' training frightened me, and for the first time it occurred to me that Denna might already have suffered some kind of injury. She could even have died, and I wouldn't know—and the mere idea of that crushed the breath from my lungs.

Instead of going back to my rooms as I probably should have, I headed into town to Morwen's in search of Kerrick, hoping he was still planning to meet Harian there as he'd told me. He might have more information that would help flesh out the Sonnenbornes' plan if he'd been able to find out more about the business loans they'd been taking out. More important, I had an idea about how I might be able to get in contact with Denna. If there was even the slightest chance she didn't know how much danger she was in, it was my responsibility to let her know.

I hurried out the gates of the Winter Court and into the city. It was early enough that people were only just heading for drinks or dinner, looking for an escape from the dry, chilly wind that swept through the streets and kicked dead leaves past their feet. The burst of heat that hit me when I entered Morwen's was a welcome reprieve. I didn't see Kerrick right away, but Harian leaned up against the bar, easily recognizable since he stood half a head taller than anyone else. I hurried over to greet him, finally spotting Kerrick as I drew closer.

"You came!" Kerrick said, looking pleased.

"Nice to see you again," Harian said, always polite.

"Let's get a table," I suggested, pointing to an empty booth not far from the bar. The two men picked up their drinks and we settled in.

"Did you find out anything about the loans?" I asked Kerrick after asking the server for a barleywine.

"Yes, but I don't think it's going to be particularly helpful," he said.

"Why's that?" I asked. Surely there had to be some pattern in what the Sonnenbornes were asking for in their loans, some sign of connections to weapons or military action—maybe even the abductions.

"About half of them were for the usual businesses—imported goods, gift shops, spirit shops, cobblers. General tradespeople. The only odd thing was that fifteen loans were requested for animal kennels."

"Animal kennels?" I stared at him in disbelief. That seemed very odd, and I couldn't fathom a single connection that made any sense.

He shrugged. "Strange, right? There can't be that many people in need of somewhere to keep their animals while they're away on holiday. The wealthy have servants, and the poor have families and neighbors. It's not like the Tamers are moving in."

"You're sure it wasn't for stockyards or livery stables?" I asked. Those things made more sense. Merchants almost always had animals in need of boarding, and the demand for meat meant there would always be stockyards.

"The applications said 'animal kennels.' I saw them myself."

A pretty server set down my barleywine with a wink.

"I should have ordered a stronger drink," I said.

"There's plenty of the night left," Kerrick said, raising his glass in a toast.

I raised my glass to his and Harian's, feeling glum and afraid, only half listening as they chatted about training and a handsome man who'd recently caught Harian's eye. I should have been trying to untangle the strangeness of the Sonnenbornes and their animal kennels, but all I could think about was Denna—how angry I was that she'd left, how heartbroken I was that she'd done so without saying good-bye, and how terrified I was that something could have happened to her and I wouldn't even know. I needed her advice more than ever now that pieces of the Sonnenborne plot were coming to light. Was I trusting the right people? I didn't even know. I needed a way to talk to her—and that meant magic.

Wymund had said the ability to Farspeak was rare, but also that his previous Farspeaker, Tum Hornblatt, had settled in Kartasha. Cockroach and drinking problems aside, if he was still here, surely I could bribe him to help me reach out to Denna. As for tracking him down, I knew where the records were kept. Only one piece of the equation was missing.

"Do either of you know where I can buy a bottle of honey-shine?" I asked.

Harian and Kerrick both grinned.

Unfortunately, the best time to track down Hornblatt was during Fadeyka's usual late-morning riding lesson, since it meant no one would be looking for me, which meant I ended up with company.

"Are you sure you have the right address?" Fadeyka asked as we entered an alley that zigzagged at odd angles.

"I'm sure, or else I spent two hours talking to the records master about ice fishing for nothing," I said.

"Better you than me," Fadeyka said, making a face.

I was grateful for the drought and the lack of snow, because the alley wasn't very well maintained. Piles of trash sat outside the wooden doors we passed, one containing a tailless orange cat who dashed away when we walked by. "Do you see numbers on any of these doors?"

"That one said five twenty-two," Fadeyka said, jerking her thumb behind us. The doors were all made of the same disintegrating wood. Perhaps once they'd been as colorful as the other doors in Kartasha, but their paint had long since worn to nothing.

"We're close," I said, slowing down. Rusting metal numbers on the next door gave the address as 536, and a mailbox hanging crookedly by one nail had the name *T. Hornblatt* inscribed on it. Bless that ice-fishing crab of a records master. "Here goes nothing." I gave the door a firm knock. For a long few seconds, nothing happened, and then a crash sounded from inside.

"Fiddleshits," someone said.

Fadeyka giggled as crunching footsteps approached. The door swung open to reveal an older man with a wild gray beard and red-rimmed blue eyes. The tassel at the end of his stocking cap looked like he'd managed to dunk it in his tea several times over.

"Who are you and what do you want?" the man barked.

"You must be Tum Hornblatt. I'm Mare and this is Faye. We need help your help talking to someone."

"I don't do commissions anymore." He moved to shut the door.

"We have this," I said, pulling the bottle of honeyshine out from beneath my cloak. It wasn't a terribly common spirit, but Kerrick and Harian had known just the supplier to get it from.

The door stopped. "How much do you want for that?" His tone was wheedling, as though he intended to bargain with us, but I could see the thirst in his eyes.

"A conversation with a friend in Corovja," I said.

He muttered something I couldn't quite make out, but I was pretty sure profanity was involved. "How about a conversation with a friend in Valenko?"

"I don't have any friends there. We can leave if you're not interested in the honeyshine, though." I started to tuck the bottle back into my cloak.

"No, no!" Hornblatt opened the door and beckoned us in. "Don't be numbskulls. Mind your step."

We entered the house, which was even less clean than the alley. Piles of books, papers, tools, and dirty dishes sat on every surface. I sidestepped a small gray cat on the floor that was licking the remains of some porridge out of a bowl that did not look as though it had originally been meant for her.

"Jingles, stop it!" Hornblatt shouted from the next room, ostensibly at the cat we'd already passed.

I glanced back to see her still rhythmically licking, completely unperturbed by the reprimand. I shook my head. Cats.

"You can sit over here." Hornblatt swept a pile of papers splattered with brown spots off a bench covered with fabric that was equally stained. Fadeyka sat down gingerly, and I was suddenly rather grateful for the time I'd spent in seedy drinking holes in Mynaria. I'd seen worse.

"We brought this for you to work with," I said, handing him a long, dark strand of Denna's hair that I'd pulled out of the hairbrush we'd been sharing on our trip.

"Let me see the honeyshine," he said.

I held up the bottle and he reached for it.

"Not until we come to an agreement." I pulled it back.

"Fine, fine." He huffed impatiently. "I use the mirror for you, you give me the honeyshine. Simple."

"What happens if we can't get hold of her?"

"I never fail to reach my targets." He thumped his fist on the table for emphasis, sending an empty bamboo birdcage clattering to the floor. "Whether they want to speak to the person contacting them is their business."

"You make it so I can see her face and talk to her, and then I'll hand you the bottle," I said.

The gray cat trotted into the room, leaped onto Hornblatt's desk, and head-butted him fondly.

"These kids drive a hard bargain, don't they, Jingles?" He scratched behind her ears and was rewarded with another thump to the face. "Fine. I'll do it." He pushed the cat aside and unearthed a small mirror from beneath one of the mountains of stuff on his table.

Fadeyka leaned forward, and I put my hand on her arm to stop the stream of questions I could see about to explode out of her mouth.

Hornblatt murmured some words over Denna's strand of hair, which took on a silvery glow. Then he wrapped it around the handle of the mirror and passed it to me. "Speak her name three times," he instructed.

I looked at Fadeyka. "I need you to swear on your mother's life that you will never speak of or repeat anything you're about to hear."

"All right," she said, looking a bit confused.

"I'm serious," I said.

"I swear on my mother's life that I will never speak of or repeat anything I hear today," Fadeyka said.

"Dennaleia. Dennaleia. Dennaleia." Her name felt like a prayer on my lips every time I spoke it. Every muscle in my body tensed at the thought of seeing her face for the first time since she'd left me behind. The mirror swirled with white and silver as though clouds were parting in the glass. When the vision came clear, I appeared to be staring up Denna's nose. Fadeyka craned her head over my shoulder, trying to get a look.

"Denna?" I said. I could hardly believe it was her.

She looked down, and then visibly spooked at what she saw. The sight of her face made a tangle of emotions well up, but before I could say another word, the mirror went black as her hand covered up my view.

"Wait!" I said, panicked at the thought that she might refuse to talk to me at all.

Across the table, Hornblatt was gesturing for the honeyshine.

"She hasn't even spoken to me yet!" I said. Despair was already rising in me. What if she didn't come back?

The mirror cleared again, and I saw Denna's face, directly this time, in much dimmer light. "Mare?" she said incredulously.

Hearing my name on her lips made my heart feel like it was going to stop.

I passed the honeyshine to Fadeyka, who smugly gave it to Hornblatt. He wasted no time uncorking it and taking a sip straight from the bottle, his expression instantly giving way to rapture. My view in the mirror rippled a little.

"You can't get drunk yet!" I scolded him.

"I must be losing my mind," Denna said. "Or this is one of Eryk's mind games."

"Who is Eryk?" I asked.

Her expression stayed tense and dubious. "One of the other trainees. Tell me something only you would know about me. Or us."

I glanced up to see both Fadeyka and Hornblatt staring at me expectantly. My cheeks burned as I went through possible things I could say. Most of them weren't appropriate for my current company, or any company, in fact.

"The first time we met, my horse knocked the wind out of you and I reminded you how to breathe," I finally said. The memory ached now. I hadn't known her then, and I feared I didn't know who she'd become since she left me.

Her eyebrows drew together, and I could see that the memory had gutted her, too. I just hoped it wasn't because she wanted to forget our time together.

"It really is you," she said, her voice soft.

"It is," I said, a little of my uncertainty slipping through. "I may not be able to speak long. Are you somewhere safe?"

"Yes," she said. "I was at lunch with the other trainees, and I've stepped out to the toilets. I don't think anyone can hear us. Just to confirm something, though . . . you're not really *in* my wineglass, are you?"

I smacked my free hand on my forehead. "It figures he'd manage to connect with a glass of wine."

"For what it's worth, I wasn't planning to drink it." Denna smiled. "These Zumordans keep strange drinking hours."

Hornblatt took another swig of honeyshine as if to prove her point.

"How is your training going?" I asked, feeling awkward. I barely knew where to start after all that had transpired in the weeks since we'd last seen each other.

"It's going well," she said. "I struggled at first, but the queen has been a real help to me. She's gone out of her way to help me feel at home here. Of course, there's still a lot to learn."

She felt at home? My worst fears were coming true. I wanted to apologize to her for the fight we'd had before she left, but didn't she owe me an apology for leaving without really saying good-bye? A heavy pause drew out between us.

"Zhari and Laurenna told me that the training you're doing can be dangerous and that you have to compete at Midwinter. Fight each other." I waited to see what she would say.

"That's true," she said. "And it has been hard—at least learning to use my magic. I never set out wanting to hurt people."

"I know you didn't," I said. She'd never been that kind of person.

"But it turns out I think I have a multi-Affinity. I still need more information, but it would make a lot of sense and explain some of why my magic has been particularly hard to train or control."

"I've heard of that," I said. "Fadeyka might have one, too, but they aren't sure yet."

Fadeyka popped her head into the frame, making Denna smile.

"Hi, Faye," Denna said, earning a warm smile and an excited bounce from Fadeyka in return. "Back in Mynaria there was a book I read that mentioned the possibility of using more than one kind of magic, but it sounded more like the stuff of legends than reality."

"It's just uncommon," Fadeyka said.

Denna nodded. "The queen told me Zhari is the only guardian who has one."

"Then you should come back here to train with her," I blurted out.

Denna's expression went flat and unreadable. "Why?"

"Because this training you're in—it's too dangerous. People have died battling each other at the Midwinter Revel. This isn't worth your life, you have to understand—"

"No, *you* have to understand," Denna said, her voice firm. "This is my Affinity, and learning to master it is the only important thing. I'm finally getting some control over my powers thanks to the queen's help, and you just want me to leave all that behind because it's too dangerous? Do you see me as someone who quits? Do you think I'm a weakling?"

The mirror rippled again, for longer this time. Hornblatt had already put back a sixth of the bottle of honeyshine.

"No, I—"

"It's like you didn't listen to anything I said. You'd be perfectly happy for me to pose as your maid forever and never embrace my powers." Her agitation grew.

"That's not true!" I was frantic for her to understand. "I want you to be powerful, but I also want you to be safe, and I want your help with everything that's going on here—so much has happened."

"I left because I wanted to be worthy of you. I wanted to be your protector, not your liability. Your equal, not your maid. Do you even understand that?"

"No, I don't understand," I said, my voice breaking. "I don't understand why you left without even saying good-bye. I don't understand why you couldn't have told me what you needed. I wouldn't have held you back if this was what you thought was right for you. We could have gone to Corovja together. You're the only reason I came to this sarding kingdom in the first place."

"Well, I don't want to be the only reason," she said. "Your kingdom is depending on you. Doesn't that matter?"

I tried to blink back the sting of her words, not to hear them as a rejection, but that was exactly what they were. At some point, she'd decided she was better off without me, and I was the last to know.

"Of course," I said softly. "But I also wanted us to be together. To be safe."

"I can't live my life in fear, waiting for the world to be safe," she said, her expression hardening in an unfamiliar way. Training was already changing her—I could tell. "I will complete my training and participate in the Revel, and if the gods see fit, I'll return to Kartasha as Zhari's apprentice."

The mirror flickered dramatically, and we lost contact for a moment.

"But what if you don't win at the battle?" I could barely choke out the words. "What if you die?"

"I need you to trust me to take care of myself," she said. "Think of your kingdom for once. Think of the hundreds of thousands of people depending on you."

The image in the mirror tilted at a wild angle. I opened my mouth to shout at Hornblatt, only to realize that it wasn't him.

Denna had poured out her wine. The mirror went milky and didn't come back.

I set the mirror back on the table. My throat felt tight with emotion. No matter what I said, it was always the wrong thing. Instead of talking her into coming back to me, all I'd succeeded in doing was pushing her further away. I wished I could have had even five more minutes to explain that I still wanted a life with her, and to figure out if she still wanted a life with me. Instead she'd cut me off at the worst part of our conversation.

"When can we reach her again?" I asked Hornblatt, who was swaying in his chair to music only he could hear. His eyes wandered in my general direction, but didn't focus at all. He muttered some nonsense to himself, then took another sip of honeyshine, spilling some of it down the front of his shirt. I glanced at Fadeyka, who simply gave me a nervous shrug and kept dangling a piece of string for Jingles to swat.

"Six sarding arses," I swore. It was useless trying to talk to him right now. I'd have to wait until he ran through this supply, and then bring more to bribe him again. At the rate he drank, it shouldn't take too long.

"We'll show ourselves out, then." I stood up, and Fadeyka followed me.

We picked our way through the mess and back out the front door. I couldn't help but observe that the horrible disaster of Hornblatt's house strongly resembled the shambles of my own life.

"Why were you calling Lia 'Dennaleia'?" Fadeyka asked as soon as we were out in the alley.

"I thought we agreed we weren't going to speak about any of this again," I said, feeling sour.

"You didn't say I couldn't ask questions," she pointed out.

"You are definitely a politician's daughter," I grumbled.

"Fiddleshits!" Fadeyka exclaimed.

"I'm not sure that's the right way to use that curse—" I started.

"The only Dennaleia I know of was Princess Dennaleia of Havemont," Fadeyka interrupted. Her small body looked about ready to explode with excitement.

"Never heard of her," I said unconvincingly.

Fadeyka squeaked loudly enough startle a man passing on the other side of the street. "You abducted a princess of Havemont!" She was far too gleeful about this news. "She's alive!"

"That's not what happened," I said. "Not at all."

"You're in love with a princess of Havemont!"

"Stop!" I mock-swatted at her, but the taunts continued all the way back to the Winter Court, and the barn, where she fortunately got her wits back about her long enough to help me brush Flicker.

I'd hoped that talking to Denna would leave me feeling more certain about our separation, but instead I felt more frightened and lost than ever. She'd basically placed the burdens of my kingdom on my shoulders, and now I felt like the only way to win her back was to succeed at the mission I'd never wanted in the first place. I thought we were working toward the same future, but what was that future? I didn't know.

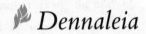 *Dennaleia*

TALKING TO MARE IN THE WINEGLASS HAD BEEN SO brief and surreal that sometimes I thought it was a dream. In some ways, I wished it had been. Her words haunted me, digging deep under my skin and burrowing into my heart. It didn't make sense to me that she couldn't see my side of things, that she didn't seem to care if I was her equal or not. By choosing her over her brother, I'd already given up everything for her once. How could she be asking me to consider doing that again? She had seemingly accepted my gift back in Mynaria, but now it felt conditional. When I failed to keep my magic under control, suddenly it wasn't all right for it to be part of me anymore. I tried to think about it as little as possible, focusing my energy on the Midwinter Revel instead.

In spite of my confidence when talking to Mare, outright winning the competition at Midwinter seemed impossible. Eryk and

Ikrie would fight ruthlessly, and as fond as I'd come to be of Evie and Tristan, their powers were also formidable. The only person who might have the answers I needed to master my abilities was Sigvar, and I also still wanted to know how the boy from Duvey had ended up in his cult. I needed to get to the prison as soon as I could. However, it turned out to be more complex than I expected.

"Are you sure this is going to work?" I asked, shivering in my black cloak. Powdery snowflakes fell from the night sky to sting my face. Tristan, Evie, and I stood in the middle of the Grand Temple ruins with only a small mage light to see by.

"It should," Tristan said. "I can try pulling us back into the shadowlands if we end up in the wrong place."

Casing the prison the week before had been less helpful than I'd hoped. The building was embedded in the side of the mountain, meaning most of the cells were deep underground, with no windows or other ways to get a sense of the layout from the outside. The front of the building seemed to contain mostly administrative offices, processing rooms, and temporary holding cells for criminals who had committed only minor infractions.

"I don't know why you question me about the layout," Evie said. "I'm telling you I can feel it, and it looks just like this." She gestured to the slip of paper in front of us.

After his ice wine had gone over very well, Tristan had talked me into letting Evie in on the plan. Her earth magic let her sense the structures underground that we couldn't see, and she'd managed to draw us a crude map based on what she could tell from how the building was built into the mountain.

"We can do this if we all trust each other," I said. My role was to provide Tristan with a little extra magic to help make our shadow walk easier.

"Then let's go. It's colder than the balls on a brass horse out here," Evie said. "Aim for this area." She pointed to a stairwell on the map that we'd agreed was the best place point of entry. It led between two floors of cells—the ones we thought were most likely to be housing Sigvar. Above were larger cells that seemed likely to have multiple occupants. Below, smaller cells for solitary confinement.

"Take my hands," Tristan said, holding out one to each of us. We accepted them, and the now-familiar feeling of the ground dropping out from beneath my feet hit. In spite of its being my third journey with Tristan, the whispered voices still made my skin crawl with dread. The shadowlands were no warmer than the frigid air outside. Instead of relying on my senses, I called up my Sight, which made the shadowlands take more form around me. Sparks of light in many colors drifted all around us as we pressed forward. Evie was a silver form in the lead, directing Tristan, who glowed purple.

We dropped out of the shadowlands into a narrow stairwell. I barely caught myself against the wall, my stomach still doing somersaults from our journey. The stone was cool against my palms, but the stagnant air in the prison felt warm after the Grand Temple. The reek of urine and unwashed bodies hung heavy in the air. All three of us froze, waiting to see if we heard any sounds. Dim light glowed from the bottom of the stairwell, barely enough to see by.

"There's no one down there but the prisoners," Evie whispered, "but there's a guard on the next floor up."

I silently blessed Tristan for roping Evie into this. We'd surely get caught without her earth sense. I pointed down the stairs, indicating that we should go that way first. The other two nodded their agreement, and we carefully descended to the lower level. The reek of body odor intensified as we drew closer to where the prisoners were being held.

The stairs opened into a narrow hallway lined with about two dozen tiny cells. Each one was barely wider than the cots inside them, and the only light was from dim mage lights at either end of the hall. A few occupants of the cells pressed their faces against the bars with hollow and haunted stares. I shrank away in fear but forced myself to look for Sigvar. I worried that the other prisoners would start screaming and reveal our presence, but every time one of them caught a glimpse of Tristan, they scurried away from the bars, whimpering.

"What are you doing to them?" I asked him in a whisper.

"When they look at me, they see the face of someone they know who died," he whispered.

I shuddered. "Isn't that rather cruel?"

"Better they think they've seen a ghost than alert the guards to our presence," Tristan said.

"You ever do that to me and I'll turn you into stone and then pound you into gravel," Evie threatened.

"Noted," Tristan said, looking a little alarmed.

At the dead end of the hallway was a prisoner who didn't move from his bed when we approached. One arm hung off the edge of his cot, the symbols inked on his skin blending into the shadows in the cell.

"That's him," I said. "Tristan, can you keep the other prisoners distracted?"

He nodded, and paced back the way we'd come to make sure everyone was too frightened to be curious about what we were doing.

"And Evie, can you make sure no one comes down here?"

"I'll go back over by the stairs. Worst-case scenario, I can avalanche some rocks to block the stairwell."

I paled at the thought of being trapped in this airless cave with no escape, even though I knew we could shadow walk out again. I tried to still my thoughts and open myself to the Sight, relieved when it came to me with only a few flickers.

"Sigvar?" I spoke softly.

He looked up suddenly, as though I'd startled him. I barely kept myself from recoiling when I saw his face. Gouges only recently scabbed over laced through his beard. His brown eyes no longer held false warmth—only fear. Though Queen Invasya had been ruthlessly efficient when she stripped him of his gift and ordered his capture, I hadn't expected to find him like this. His condition spoke of far more than simple imprisonment. The queen seemed prone to swift punishments when she deemed them necessary, but she didn't strike me as someone who would favor torture.

"Who are you?" he asked, squinting out of his cell.

"My name is Lia," I told him. The lie had become so familiar, it almost felt real. "I have some questions."

He sat up on his cot and drew his thin blanket around his shoulders. Even without him standing up, I could tell he'd lost a dramatic amount of weight since I'd seen him in Tilium. His once-muscular body was now lean and wiry, his sun-kissed skin paler thanks to being underground.

"Kill me and you can ask me whatever you want," he said, then laughed. It was a strange, pinched sound that sent a shiver racing through me.

"I don't want to hurt you," I said, showing him my open palms.

"I'll die if I see her face again. I'll die," he babbled.

"Who?" I asked.

He scooted farther forward on the cot until he was only a few feet away from me. The gashes on his face were even more terrifying up close. Dried blood and scabs crusted the jagged edges, a few of them green and yellow with infection.

"What do you want?" he asked.

"I need to know about your cult," I said. "There was a blond boy from Duvey who had joined your flock. Do you remember him?"

"There were three," Sigvar said with a choked laugh.

"Three what?" I pressed.

"Three I was given for safekeeping," he said. "Three from the south."

"And one of them was the boy from Duvey?" I asked, trying to get him to make some sense. "How did he get to you? Were you working with the Sonnenbornes?"

"I am no betrayer!" He pounded on the bars of his cell, making me jump back. "I was the one who was betrayed."

"By the boy from Duvey?" I was confused.

"He was just like the others," Sigvar said. "They were all there to be neutralized. No one was supposed to know we were in Tilium. She promised me. She promised!"

"Who promised?" I asked. "Who betrayed you?"

"I was supposed to keep the people calm, take them from Karta-sha. Protect them until the Sonnenbornes come." He raked his hands through his hair in agitation.

"What do you mean? When are the Sonnenbornes coming?" I asked, frightened. Mare had said the Sonnenbornes were plotting something. Was it possible Sigvar had been working for them and knew what it was?

"They'll ride for Kartasha at Midwinter," he said. "All the pieces are in place. Even without me, there's no way to stop them now."

Alarm made my throat dry, and I swallowed hard. Midwinter wasn't that far away, and I had no way to reach Mare to warn her. I shouldn't have cut off our conversation the other day without finding out how to reconnect.

"What pieces are in place?" I asked.

"There is no magic left." Sigvar hung his head in his hands, muttering to himself. He ran his nails over his face over and over again until one of the gashes tore open and started to bleed. Drops of blood splattered onto his blanket, the red spreading to join the brown stains already there.

Bile rose in my throat, and guilt twisted in my stomach. Even though I hadn't intended it, I felt like I was contributing to his torture. "I'm sorry for what you lost." Although he'd been doing something that was objectively wrong, I couldn't imagine how it would feel to have had my magic stripped away and be trapped in this dark hole.

"You have to get me out." He lunged forward suddenly, pressing his face to the bars.

I yelped and jumped back.

"I have to stop her. She doesn't know the cost of what she's trying to do." He wailed, a sound that made Evie turn to me in alarm from her place at the far end of the cell block.

"Who? A Sonnenborne?" I asked, leaning forward. If I could get a name, that was something I could take to the queen. Unfortunately, his answer was random and unhelpful.

"I thought she loved me," he said, his voice fading into petulance. "I would have done anything for her."

"The queen?" I hazarded.

He shook his head until I thought it was going to fall off.

"What can you tell me about how to use a multi-Affinity?" I switched topics, hoping it would help him regain some clarity. Anything he could tell me about multi-Affinities might be useful.

He slid down the bars and rocked back and forth on the ground. "We are channels, we are convergents," he muttered.

"What does that mean?" I felt like he was right at the edge of telling me something important.

"The magic comes from different sources, and you are where it is channeled and then released. You can do one at a time, or you can do both. One or both, one or both, one or both . . ." He devolved into nonsense again.

"I think I understand," I said. The times I'd used more than one kind of magic at once, I'd pulled in each element separately and then combined them into something greater. The problem was that I hadn't really been thinking about what I was creating. I was just opening myself to the powers and hoping that something would happen. I'd called on fire, earth, and air when I'd summoned the star fall, and I'd managed to absorb Evie's earth magic into my fiery shield on my ill-fated first day of training.

"One gift at a time," he said. "Just one. Use one. But the power that isn't yours is also yours if you reach for it. Be the convergent." He laughed again, that same weird, strangled sound.

"Someone's coming!" Evie raced to my side at the same time I heard voices echoing in the stairwell.

"Sig's talking to himself again," one of the prison guards said in a bored tone.

"Give him the poppy juice. It'll shut him up till morning," another said. Their footsteps echoed down the stairwell.

I swore. With all the nonsense Sigvar was talking, I hadn't been able to get nearly as much information out of him as I wanted to, but we needed to escape. Causing a scene wasn't something we'd been counting on.

"Quick!" Tristan said, extending his hand.

I took it, and the three of us were plunged into darkness again. When we came out of the shadowlands, I clutched my stomach as my vision cleared, confused when I wasn't assaulted by the icy wind that had been sweeping through the Grand Temple when we'd left.

"Six Hells," Tristan said.

We hadn't landed in the Grand Temple at all. We were in the queen's study, and she sat at her desk across from us, wearing a furious expression.

"I seem to recall giving explicit instructions that none of you were to leave the castle grounds," she said, her voice even colder than the winter air outside.

"It was my idea," I said quickly, hoping I could protect Tristan and Evie. My chest tightened with guilt. What was she going to do to us?

"I don't especially care whose idea it was." She stood up and came closer to us, stopping in front of Tristan. "Your gift isn't a ticket to go wherever you please."

"Of course, Your Majesty," he said, but in spite of his repentant tone, the muscles in his jaw stayed tight.

"And you might be better off taking your brother's approach to climbing the ranks here," the queen said to Evie. "If your magic isn't powerful enough to serve you, you have to make the best of your other skills."

"Yes, Your Majesty." Evie's voice was barely more than a whisper, and she looked like she was about to cry.

"As punishment, neither of you will be allowed to compete in the Midwinter Revel. You will have last choice of apprenticeships."

Evie's tears spilled over.

"Please don't punish them for something that was my idea—" I started.

"You and I will discuss what led to this misadventure," the queen interrupted me. "You two are dismissed." She waved the others out of the room. I could barely stand to see the crushed expressions on their faces as they walked away. Evie glanced back at me with resentment breaking through the sadness. I had a feeling that as soon as she was done crying, I'd be the one to bear the brunt of her anger. Worse, I deserved it. I never should have let them help me—I should have tried to do everything on my own, even if it was more dangerous.

"Sit," the queen commanded, sweeping back to her side of the desk and taking her place.

I sat down gingerly across from her, feeling more like I was about to go to the guillotine than have a conversation.

"Why did you seek out Sigvar?" she asked.

"I thought he might know something about how to control my powers," I said. "Training has still been difficult, and I don't—"

"The only thing making training difficult is your reluctance to hurt anyone," the queen snapped. "It is the other trainees' responsibility to defend themselves. Your only job is to use your powers to the best of your abilities, and instead you're holding yourself back. Sigvar can't help you with that. No one can. You've spent your whole life with other people telling you what to do, and now you're waiting for permission to own what already belongs to you."

Her words cut deeply. I didn't want to hurt anyone, but there was a grain of truth to her words. My life had not been filled with choices about my future. My studies had always been dictated by the plans my parents had mapped out for me. Choosing Mare was the first decision I'd made completely on my own, and since then I'd felt like I was spinning in circles with no idea which way to go. Still, Sigvar had told me much more than the few pieces of information about my Affinity.

"Sigvar said some things you should know about," I said, gathering all the training I'd ever had to keep my voice steady.

"Tell me," the queen ordered.

"The Sonnenbornes must have been giving him some kind of incentive to neutralize magic users in the south," I said. "There was a boy in his cult I recognized as one of those abducted from Duvey. I'm not sure how the boy got from Duvey to Tilium, but I do know it was through Kartasha and someone Sigvar was working with there. He said he was betrayed."

"He does love to rant about Kartasha from time to time," she said. "The torture he's endured has probably muddled his memories. He visited there when he was apprenticed to Zhari, but that was years ago."

"Training there for even a season would have given him enough time to make contacts," I said. "But more important, he says that Kartasha is going to be attacked by Sonnenbornes at Midwinter," I said.

The queen leaned back and sighed. "That's impossible. He's too unstable to be a reliable source of information."

"But isn't that still significant enough to warrant investigation?" I asked.

"It would be, except that I just spoke to Laurenna today," she said. "They caught a band of Sonnenbornes responsible for human trafficking and imprisoned them in Kartasha. Now that they've caught them, it's only a matter of time before the rest are rooted out. Laurenna and Zhari have the situation well under control."

"Oh," I said. In the end, the information I'd found out hadn't even mattered. I'd barely gotten anything useful out of Sigvar about the multi-Affinities. I felt doubly bad about Tristan and Evie's punishment. If they knew it had all been for nothing, they'd be twice as upset with me.

"I suggest you stay focused on the Revel," the queen said. "You have very little time left to prepare."

"You're still going to let me compete?" I stared at her in shock. After how Evie and Tristan had been punished, I figured whatever she had planned for me would be far worse. "Why?"

"I can't let my descendant be disqualified from the most important magical competition in Zumorda," she said, her tone filled with derision. "I'd also like to give you a gift that may help." She slipped a necklace off over her head. Instead of a pendant, it bore a small vial that glowed with silvery light.

"What kind of gift?" I didn't understand why she was helping me instead of punishing me, and it filled me with guilt and anxiety.

"A gift that will strengthen our familial bond and help you see more ways to use your powers," she said.

"Is that Sigvar's Affinity?" I asked, gesturing to the vial. I remembered when she had taken his powers in Tilium.

"Not exactly," she said. "It's an essence that will temporarily impart some of his abilities."

"I don't think I need any more magic," I said. I could barely manage what I already had. And perhaps demurring would assuage some of my guilt.

The queen laughed softly. "Don't worry, little bird. I wouldn't want to give you any more of those kinds of gifts. But if you'll accept it, I'd like to give you a blessing of sorts."

"A blessing?" I wasn't familiar with how that would work if not connected to the gods in some way. Back home, I'd only ever heard of clerics giving blessings.

"You'll take a vow to knowledge, and the blessing will help you see more ways to use your gift," the queen said. "Trust me, you'll find it very helpful. Think of it as a way of augmenting your magic rather than receiving something new. It's quite safe."

"I suppose I can take a vow to knowledge," I said. It sounded harmless enough, and my whole life had been dedicated to the pursuit of knowledge anyway.

"Good." She uncorked the vial on her necklace and drank the contents. Silvery light spread over her entire body until she glowed like the moon. She crossed the few paces between us and touched a cool hand to my forehead. "Now repeat after me: I am the learner."

"I am the learner," I said.

"I accept the gift of knowledge so that it may serve my kingdom."

I echoed her again, even as a strange tingling overtook my body.

"I will be with you and you with me so that we will know more, together."

I didn't want to speak the words this time, but my mouth moved against my will. "I will be with you and you with me so that we will know more, together."

The queen withdrew her hand, but my head still buzzed as though it were filled with bees.

"Call a flame to your palm," she said.

I did as she asked, opening my hand and summoning a flame. As usual, it flickered and leaped erratically, but then a sweet calm came over me and steadied the magic.

"Beautiful," the queen said. "Now put up a shield of fire."

I'd practiced the move enough that it came easily to me as I covertly sketched the symbol of the fire god under my cloak. But instead of feeling unstable, as my shields usually did, a gentle guiding hand inside my mind helped feed the flames until the wall grew thick and impenetrable, as if it were made of rock. Not once in training had I been able to create something so perfect.

I released the magic, breathless with the excitement of having gotten something right.

Only later, in my rooms, did the true cost of the queen's gift and my transgression sink in. Evie and Tristan would never forgive me once they found out my punishment had been so light in comparison with theirs. And by letting me compete, the queen had ensured that their resentment would only deepen. I was more powerful than ever—and more alone.

Without friends or distractions, I suddenly had a lot more time to study and practice, so I did just that over the days leading up to the Midwinter Revel. The queen shared occasional updates with me about Kartasha. Her reassurances kept me focused on training, knowing that Mare was all right. In spite of the cold, I took to wearing a white cloak that would disguise me out in the snow and practiced my magic at the Grand Temple ruins. The space kept my magic more measured and even, and prayers to each of the gods whose magic I called on helped me summon my powers. The irony did not escape me that my prayers were as heretical in Zumorda as practicing magic had been in Mynaria. No matter where I went, it seemed I would never be completely on the right side of my kingdom.

With all my practice and the queen's gift, I got hurt less often in training, but it was Sigvar's words that ultimately changed everything. *Be the convergent*, he'd said, and I'd thought of the words often but didn't understand their meaning until I put them to work in training.

I stood across from Ikrie, whose pale blue eyes were filled with hate. We'd moved from training exercises to true combat, and every time I stood across from an opponent, I still felt like an imposter. Ikrie terrified me the most. Her ruthlessness wasn't even the worst thing—it was the way she toyed with her opponents until they were practically begging her to stop.

"And . . . go!" Brynan said.

My shield was only half up when Ikrie went on the offense. She smashed through my shield with a single blow, scattering my fire with her wind. I scurried to the side, narrowly avoiding a gust of air that would have knocked me off my feet. Next she skipped some of the showier spells she often favored, instead choosing to draw the air out of my lungs in the same way I'd seen Karina do to Sigvar in Tilium. But it was one of Ikrie's favorite moves for a quick takedown, and I knew it was coming. I activated my Sight. Threads of magic connected her to me as she beckoned the air from my body. For the first time, it occurred to me that maybe I could use them.

I let Ikrie's magic continue to draw on me even as my shield went up—a shimmering wall of flame that flickered through the air a few feet away from me. I made it weak on purpose, hoping to give her plenty of confidence that she could take me down without a fight.

"Nice shield," she said, her tone biting.

I smiled. "Nice spell," I choked out, and let the little tongues of flame wind themselves around the threads of magic connecting us. Then I drew her power into me. She'd expected me to try to snap the connection between us, but instead I channeled her magic into my own. The pressure on my lungs immediately eased, and my shield grew brighter.

"What are you doing?" she snarled, cutting off her spell.

Giddy with power, I held my shield steady and waited for her next move. I didn't have to go on the offense to defeat her, and I knew it. She threw up her hands and pulled a gust of wind out of nowhere, hurling compacted air at me like a blade. Instead of trying to block it, I let it fuel the flames of my shield and then shoved it back in her direction with a flick of my wrist. She ducked, but the firebomb singed the end of her braid.

I finally understood what convergent meant. It meant that any of the elements I could touch, I could channel. There was almost nothing Ikrie could do to me that I couldn't repurpose into my own powers or use to strengthen myself. Each attack was a gift that I could use. All I had to do was stay collected and calm.

Five minutes later, Ikrie was lying on the floor, and the other trainees were staring at me, openmouthed.

"Aela and Evie, you're up next," Brynan said.

The two moved to the center of the room as Ikrie and I moved aside.

"I don't know how you did that, but I will find out and it will hurt next time you try," Ikrie said to me.

I let her words roll off me like rain. For the first time, I didn't believe there was anything she could do to hurt me.

I was no longer afraid.

TWENTY-THREE

✦ *Amaranthine*

AFTER TALKING TO DENNA, I FELT LIKE I HAD NOTHING left to lose, so I took my new blade to the salle with the notion that I might just have to confront Alek about his involvement with the Sonnenbornes myself. I scanned the room, looking for him, surprised to discover that for once he wasn't there. On top of that, everyone else looked far too advanced for me to spar with. Perhaps it was for the best—I wasn't accustomed to my new weapon yet, and it wouldn't hurt to run through some basic exercises to get the feel of it while I waited for Alek to show up. It had to be only a matter of time. I found an empty corner of the room and practiced basic lunges until the sword felt as familiar as my usual practice weapon. I didn't even notice Alek's approach until he blocked my lunge with his sword.

"Your feet are sloppy," he said. "Fix them."

I adjusted the angle of my stance and practiced the lunge again.

As usual, he was infuriatingly correct. A dangerous white-hot rage ignited in my chest at the thought of his involvement with the Sonnenbornes.

"Lunge, then remise," he said, taking a defensive stance and waiting for my attack.

I let my anger carry me forward, only to be blocked with ease. I'd had plenty of instruction from Alek but had never parried with him before. It felt as productive as fighting a brick wall. He wasn't going to be like Kerrick and make an occasional mistake I could take advantage of. I tried to calm down, reminding myself that I would fight better if I were focused, not angry.

He held up his blade again, and I mirrored his position. The moment I did, something shifted. The sword felt like an extension of my arm, and my feet adjusted themselves of their own accord. When I moved to attack, my body moved with unfamiliar catlike grace. Alek barely had time to block me before my remise. Without thinking, I gave myself over to what felt right, and suddenly Alek and I were locked in true combat. My anger flowed into the weapon and I stabbed at him with a flurry of blows he could barely block, finishing with a low swing that caught him in the leg and ripped a hole in his pants.

His expression changed from surprise to stone, and he launched an assault on me that should have immediately knocked me flat. I dropped to the ground in a controlled tumble, and no one was more surprised than me when I popped back to my feet and straight into an attack. Everyone else in the salle had stopped to stare.

"What are you doing?" Alek asked, his voice dangerous.

"Defending myself," I said.

He attacked again, this time anticipating the low swing of my cutlass. What he wasn't counting on was the thrust of my hilt upward into his jaw on the rebound. He staggered, and I dropped into a defensive position.

"Enough," he said, backing into a surrendering stance. I'd never seen him do that before.

I kept my sword aloft a few moments longer, not sure if he was trying to bait me with a trick. Once I was assured he meant what he said, I carefully lowered my weapon.

"What is that sword?" he asked me, his voice sharp. "Let me see it."

I flipped my grip on the blade and held it up with the blue gems facing Alek.

His expression hardened even further. "Who gave you that?"

"Laurenna," I said, keeping my chin up. He might as well know I was on his kingdom's side even if he wasn't.

"That sword wasn't meant to be yours."

"Well, it is now," I said.

He turned on his heel and stalked off. "Get back to practice!" he barked at the other trainees.

The sight of his retreating backside sparked an uncontrollable wave of anger in me, and I stormed after him.

"Why do you hate me so much?" I accused him.

He turned to face me, his gaze dangerously calm. "I don't hate you."

"I know what you did," I said.

"What in the sarding Hell are you talking about?" he asked. I'd never seen him so furious.

"The list," I said, lowering my voice. "I know Eronit and Varian stole it and gave it to you. Laurenna and Zhari know, and whatever you're plotting is about to be stopped."

He grabbed me by the arm, his grip like steel.

"Get your hands off me!" I said, jerking away.

"Come with me quietly, then," he said. "I didn't do what you think."

"I saw you at the Broken Cup," I said. I knew exactly what I'd seen and heard there.

"Just come with me, will you?" He exited the salle through a back door, and I followed him into a room filled with armor and weapons in various states of repair.

I crossed my arms and stared him down. "What, are you going to kill me in this back room? It's too late. Everyone already knows what you did."

"You shouldn't interfere in things you don't understand," Alek snapped. "This doesn't have anything to do with you."

"It has everything to do with me and my kingdom," I said, my voice rising to match his. "The Sonnenbornes attacked us first, and I tried to warn you Zumorda was next. Too bad I didn't know you were a traitor to your own people."

"I am not a traitor!" He looked like he wanted to smash me through a wall, and I barely cared if he did. "Yes, Eronit and Varian stole the list of names for me since I don't have access to the records room. They did it so I could compare the list with the names of young people who have been reporting missing."

"Sounds likely," I said, my voice heavy with sarcasm.

"My sources let me know there's a slave train departing later today," he said. "I needed the names and Affinities to see if I could determine if anyone outbound there was on the list. If they were, that leads me to believe that Laurenna is giving names away as targets. She's the one evaluating the children—she's the one who would know how powerful their gifts are and who is worth turning over to the Sonnenbornes."

"Why in the Sixth sarding Hell would Eronit and Varian help you work against their people?" I asked. His story didn't add up.

"Because not all tribes believe the same things." He threw up his hands in frustration. "Roni and Varian are opposed to slavery, opposed to the factions of Sonnenbornes who believe reintroducing magic to their kingdom is the way to solve their problems. They want to stop those tribes as badly as I do."

"Prove it, then," I said.

"Fine. Come with me to the city and see for yourself." The challenge and disdain in his gaze said he didn't believe for one moment that I actually would.

"I will," I said.

We stared at each other with pure hostility for a few heartbeats before Alek finally broke away.

"Then let's go." He grabbed a cloak from a hook near the external door, swinging it onto his shoulders on his way out. "Meet me outside the court gates in twenty minutes."

The bustle of the city was just as I remembered it from other times I'd been to town, but instead of heading for the familiar areas I'd been through on my way to get drinks, we walked downhill toward the southern part of the city closer to the trade road and the river.

The modest buildings of merchants and tradespeople gave way to simpler structures, some of which seemed to house goods while others served as residences for many families.

"Pull up your hood," Alek said, and followed his own advice.

I did as he instructed, then nervously touched the hilt of my sword, hoping I wasn't going to have to use it. Whatever magical properties it had, I wasn't sure how to get them to work. I hoped it would defend me against Sonnenbornes as well as it had against Alek in the salle.

Soon the warehouses were interspersed with livestock pens, and the reek of animal excrement gusted over us with every breeze. Alek walked between a fence line and a building toward a warehouse that didn't seem to be in use, but he extended an arm to hold me back from passing around the far end of it. Not far beyond him, the hill dropped off into a cliff. If he was going to kill me, there probably wasn't a more perfect place to do it.

"There," he said, pointing over the cliff.

I leaned forward until what he was pointing at was in my line of sight. The cliff had to be about fifty feet high, tall enough that it was hard to make out the individual features of the people below. However, it was abundantly clear what they were doing. A huge train of covered wagons had been set up along the base of the cliff on a crude road, cleverly concealed by trees that sheltered it from the rest of the city. The wagons were being loaded with people chained to each other who moved slowly, stumbling often, as though they were drugged.

"Are those magic users?" I asked Alek.

He gave a sharp nod.

"We have to tell someone," I said in a panic.

"Who, the people who sanctioned this?" Alek said, his voice mocking.

"It doesn't look like anyone sanctioned this," I said. "Why would they be hiding if it was sanctioned?"

"Because Laurenna isn't stupid," Alek said. "Zhari cares about protecting her kingdom. She would never allow this."

"But why would Laurenna be involved with this in the first place?" I asked. What did she possibly have to gain?

"She's the guardian of a city run on commodities," Alek said. "She's always been ruthless, so it doesn't surprise me that she'd find a way to make her own people the merchandise."

"You have proof of that?" My eyes narrowed. "Transaction records?"

"Eronit and Varian are working on tracking them down now, since they have a place at court," he said.

"If Laurenna was working with the Sonnenbornes, it makes sense that she might open up to them," I said. It made too much sense.

Alek grunted. "You're at least halfway to a right answer for once."

It was probably the closest thing to a compliment I could ever hope to get from him. Perhaps I'd misjudged him all along. He'd had me fooled into thinking his dull life left no room for uncovering schemes or tracking down the missing children of Duvey. I'd seen him as a soldier, not the shrewd tactician that he clearly was. And I'd trusted Laurenna because she'd given me a magic sword and I liked her daughter, but maybe that had been a mistake just as grave as misjudging Alek.

"If your theories are correct, Kartasha could be in immediate danger," I said.

He nodded. "This train looks full. Once it hits the horizon, we could find ourselves bracing for an attack. The Sonnenbornes will take advantage of having purged so many magic users from the city." It was going to be like Zephyr Landing all over again, this time on a catastrophic scale. I wished I'd already called my brother's cavalry, though there wasn't any way I could have done that without alerting Laurenna to what I'd done—and it sounded like that would have been the worst mistake I could have made.

"I have an idea about how we could get this information to the queen," I said, saying a mental prayer to all Six Gods that Hornblatt was sober today and that the honeyshine vendor still had some in stock.

"How?" Alek asked incredulously.

"I know where Hornblatt is."

As we made our way through the city, I worried that we were already too late. People spoke in hushed whispers, and business seemed slow at every shop we passed. We caught the liquor vendor on her way out the door, closing shop early, and were lucky to get a bottle of honeyshine at all. I saw magic used less frequently than I'd become accustomed to, and Alek kept his hand on the hilt of his weapon all the way to Hornblatt's front door.

When a polite knock on Hornblatt's door got no response, I tested the doorknob. It didn't budge, so I banged on the door. "Open up!"

"Quit yer squalling!" someone shouted from a window on the opposite side of the alley.

I ignored them and pounded on the door again.

Finally, it cracked open. I tried to shove my way through, but a chain held the door so that it opened only a sliver.

"What is this fuss about?" Hornblatt asked with great indignation.

I pulled the honeyshine from under my cloak. "I need to talk to Denna. Now. It's urgent."

He eyed the honeyshine. "It's not a good time, but I'll take that honeyshine if you aren't going to need it." His tone grew wheedling.

"You aren't getting this unless you let me speak to Denna right this minute," I said.

"It's too late. It's already begun." He paused for a moment as if listening to something on the wind, then slammed the door in my face.

"Damn you, Hornblatt, open this sarding door!" I unsheathed my sword. I would get him to let me talk to Denna if I had to hack down the door myself.

"Stop," Alek said.

The wind shifted direction, bringing a whiff of smoke. Distantly, I heard a faint roar I didn't know how to decipher. "What the Sixth Hell is that sound?"

"Probably what Hornblatt heard before us, thanks to his Far-hearing," Alek said.

I heard the familiar snap of a bowstring from a nearby roof-top, and then an arrow embedded itself in Hornblatt's door barely six inches from my head. I dropped the honeyshine bottle on Hornblatt's stoop, and it shattered.

"Sard me in half!" I said. Who was shooting at us?

A quick flick of Alek's fingers made a bubble-like shield appear in front of us just in time to stop the next arrow. "Run," he said, and I didn't wait for further instructions.

I half expected our way to be blocked when we exited the alley—the classic move favored by most groups of thugs or would-be assassins. Instead, I was shocked to see that the city had erupted into total anarchy. No one was after me and Alek specifically; all of Kartasha was under attack by Sonnenbornes. Everything I'd feared had come to fruition—this was Zephyr Landing all over again on a much larger scale. If the Sonnenbornes succeded in taking Kartasha, they'd have the largest city in Zumorda under their control, as well as the biggest trading hub in all four Northern Kingdoms.

We hurtled through the streets dodging flying fists and weapons. A building had caught fire near the tower, and the riot intensified the closer we got to the Winter Court. People transformed right and left, trying to escape their attackers by taking their manifest forms. Bears, boars, snakes, rabbits, and all sorts of other animals flooded from every alley, many of them being chased by packs of savage dogs.

"Are these Tamer dogs?" I asked Alek as we hid behind a building, trying to catch our breath.

"Could be." He drew his broadsword and hurried into the fray.

I followed his example, hoping my blade and what training I had would be enough to keep me alive. Now that we were closer to the Winter Court, everywhere I looked there were Sonnenbornes with weapons flying and Zumordans desperately trying to defend themselves. Soon we were in the midst of it. I took out Sonnenbornes left and right, but even with the sword's help, I could feel my body swiftly weakening. There was only so much it could do with exhausted muscles, and the fighting was only getting worse.

A Tamer's dog burst from behind a wagon and went for Alek's throat. I barely caught it with the flat of my sword in time to knock it aside. A crow swooped toward us, and I put my sword up into an overhead defense.

Instead of attacking, the crow landed on a vegetable cart ahead of us and transformed into Kerrick.

"Oh, thank the Six," I said.

"You have to run," Kerrick said, his expression grim.

"But we need to get back to court," I said. "My horse—"

"What of Zhari? Laurenna?" Alek asked sharply.

"Fadeyka?" I added.

"The three of them have been taken hostage and are imprisoned in the tower," Kerrick said. "The Sonnenbornes have already won the city. There are too many of them. We can't fight back."

My stomach churned. Flicker was still trapped at the Winter Court, and so were the people in power. And had we been wrong about Laurenna? It didn't make sense that the Sonnenbornes would take her hostage if she was on their side. I wanted to fight back, but I was already more than half spent. I looked to Alek for guidance, surprised to see an expression of genuine unhappiness on his face.

"I have to warn as many people as I can," Kerrick said. "Go north to the base of the next mountain. We are planning to set up a camp there."

Before I could ask any more questions, he was already a crow and back in the air again.

"We have to keep moving," Alek said, his voice grim.

I nodded my agreement and we turned away from the Winter Court. Half a sunlength later we hit the edge of the city, and the fighting was no longer audible behind us. A plume of smoke rose high over Kartasha behind us, turning the sun an eerie red.

In just one afternoon, the city of Kartasha had been taken.

Once we were outside of town there was no point in hurrying—everyone heading in the same direction as us was equally defeated. People and animals walked with their eyes downcast. Children sobbed in their parents' arms. The Kartashans were refugees in their own kingdom. Our group of a few hundred was growing fast, and curls of dust still rose from the road to the south. How many had escaped the city, and how many were working with the Sonnenbornes? How many had been sent off in the slave caravans now with no one to stop them? There was no way to know.

The camp Kerrick had mentioned was nestled on a slope at the base of a mountain north of Kartasha, atop the remains of an abandoned homestead. Though it was colder there, climbing to the highest foothills put a sheer cliff to our backs that provided both a shield from the northern wind and a preventative against attacks from behind. The house had holes in the roof and a fair few wild animal nests underneath, but it hadn't taken long to fashion it into something resembling a headquarters for our meager camp. And the animal pens around it were easily, if crudely, restored with branches cut from nearby trees, so we had a place to keep the livestock some of the refugees had managed to get out of the city.

My body was shaking with exhaustion by the time Alek left to help chop wood and I sat down to rest, but sitting still didn't last long—I felt like I couldn't. Not with more people coming in, not with shelters to be built and food to hunt for. How long was it going to be sustainable to live here like this? Maybe magic could help in some ways, but it still couldn't nourish a camp of this size. We had a stream nearby, but thousands of people couldn't subsist on what little food there was to hunt. Rations were going to be short, and it wouldn't take long for tempers to shorten with them. The minute we turned against each other, all hope would be lost.

Every muscle in my body protested as I stood up, but I gritted my teeth. There was only one answer: We needed help. And a lot of it. I had to find a way to send word for my brother's cavalry. I started asking around to see if anyone had Farspeech. Mostly I got weary shakes of the head, or the occasional anecdote about a family member who'd had it several generations back.

Down near the stream, several people, including Alek, were splitting logs and passing them to couriers who took them to stoke fires around the camp. As I drew closer, it was easy to see that Alek wasn't the bottomless well of strength I saw him as. From the trembling in his arms, he'd worked his way past the point of exhaustion since we'd fought our way out of the city.

"No fires after dusk," he said, repeating the refrain to every person who took wood from him. Of course he'd thought of that. This wasn't his first time in an encampment or a battle. It was mine.

"Alek," I said, waiting for him to pause in his task long enough for me to interrupt him.

He turned to me, ready to hand me an armload of wood like everyone else.

"Mare." He was clearly surprised to see me. "I thought you were going to rest."

"I can't," I said.

He gave me an appraising look I couldn't quite decipher. "Bethla, can you take over for me?" he asked a woman nearby whose biceps looked like they were up to the task. "I'll be back to relieve you in a little while."

She nodded, took the ax from him, and soon fell into a rhythm like all the others.

Alek walked toward the stream nearby.

I took a deep breath. "I'm sorry I thought you were behind any of this." If we'd ever managed to talk to each other, maybe we could have worked together to stop it instead of being too late. "Eronit and Varian deserved more benefit of the doubt, too."

"Varian and Eronit were at the Winter Court to try to uncover a conspiracy among their own people," Alek said. "They were too late."

"If they were there to stop a conspiracy, why were they getting paperwork for more false Sonnenborne businesses?" I asked. That had always bothered me.

"They were copies of the paperwork, not originals. Evidence, not licensing. Eronit and Varian were working to undermine some of the other tribes that had been participating in human trafficking. They hoped their research would prove to the other tribes that adding Zumordan blood to their tribes was not going to reintroduce magic to their land and reverse the drought."

I swore. "That's what the other tribes believe?" It was even worse than what Kriantz had been planning to do with me.

"A large portion of the kingdom holds that belief. There were already rumors of it back when I worked near the border years ago, but apparently those factions have become louder and more dogmatic. Sonnenborne archeologists apparently discovered evidence that their kingdom wasn't always a desert. This gave rise to theories that something had abruptly shifted and caused magic to vanish from the land. When it did, the desert began to spread. So now they believe the only way to restore magic to the kingdom is to breed it back in."

"That's why they abducted those young people from Duvey," I said, horrified.

Alek nodded. "They took Zephyr Landing for the resources, but they've been moving into Zumorda with the intention of taking its people as well as its resources."

"Why didn't you tell me about this sooner?" I asked.

"What does a Mynarian care about Zumorda?" he scoffed.

"I care about the Sonnenbornes hurting people," I said. "And I care about being on the wrong side of a fight."

He crouched at the edge of the stream and rinsed his hands and arms in the icy water. "I can respect that," he finally said. He eyed my sword and shook his head. "I'm sorry about what happened in the salle with that sword. I shouldn't have attacked you like I did."

"Why would you feel bad for doing that?" I asked. His purpose there had largely been to teach us how to beat the tar out of each other.

"It wasn't constructive. That weapon . . ." He trailed off.

I tilted my head and waited for him to continue.

"I enchanted that weapon to be a teacher," he explained. "It fills in the gaps in a trainee's knowledge and gives its bearer the ability to move like a master sword fighter. I never should have made that cursed thing."

"That's incredible," I said. No wonder the blade behaved like it did. I was about to ask why Laurenna had given it to me, but then an inkling of an idea crept in that Alek confirmed with his next words.

"A long time ago I was in training with Laurenna. Both of us hoped to become guardians." He swirled his hand in the stream, seemingly impervious to the cold. "We grew up in the same slum, fought side by side, and went to Corovja together to train. Before we went, we swore that nothing would ever come between us."

I knew already that this story didn't have a happy ending.

"Laurenna took to Corovja and to politics like a fish to water. I didn't. She tried to help me understand, but I couldn't fathom why people enjoyed talking about things more than they enjoyed doing things. I wanted to get my hands dirty, to make a difference. She grew frustrated." He stood up and started walking back toward the camp.

"So you made this sword?"

"I worried for her—that she spent so much time studying magic and politics that she wouldn't be able to defend herself from physical attacks. So I bought the finest blade I could afford and spent the winter weaving spells into it. I gave it to her the day I asked her to marry me."

My jaw nearly hit the ground. "You were going to marry Laurenna?"

"I asked her to give up training and to go home with me. We were powerful enough to make our own life, or to move through the Winter Court at the lower levels. We could have had influence that way. But she took the sword, and then she said no. Only then did I realize how power hungry she'd become. It was a while longer before the Eusavka battle, when I left guardian training for good, but things had already begun to fall apart before then."

"So she gave this sword to me to hurt you," I said.

"And to make me resent you, and to remind me of my place," he said. "No matter. The past between me and Laurenna is long buried—especially since it appears my theory about her being responsible for the disappearances was wrong. And the sword is yours."

"It saved my life today," I said. I wasn't nearly foolish enough to take credit for half the fighting I'd done getting out of Kartasha.

"I wish we could have saved more," he said, clearly thinking of the wagon trains that were no doubt now bound for Sonnenborne.

"We have to do something about this," I said. "We have to call for reinforcements."

Alek nodded. "You're right."

"What?" I said, confused by his ready agreement.

"Don't make me repeat myself." He put his hand in the water again and breathed a long sigh of relief.

"What are you doing?" I asked.

"Borrowing some energy," he said.

"Ah." No wonder the Zumordans seemed so tireless. Many of them must be doing what he was—borrowing some power from the land.

"Here's how I can help," I said. "My brother offered cavalry to Zumorda for the fight against Sonnenborne long before we knew this was how things would unfold. They're stationed just across the border. We need more bodies. We need cavalry." I couldn't help but think how different the fight would have been today with a hundred riders on our side. "I just need to find a way to send a message."

Alek's lips narrowed into a thin line. I could tell the thought of asking Mynarians for help didn't sit well with him, but he was a shrewd tactician. He wasn't going to be foolish about this. The important thing was to get Kartasha back before the Sonnenbornes' hooks were in so deep it became impossible.

"It seems to be the only choice," he finally said. "I might have a way to reach the cavalry through Wymund. He could send a neutral party across the border to contact them—there are usually a few traveling merchants who winter in Duvey."

"Might he be able to send reinforcements as well?" I asked.

"That's what I'm hoping," Alek said.

"Have you already spoken to Wymund since the riot?" I didn't know Alek had any way of reaching him.

Alek shook his head. "The enchantment I'll use to contact him is for emergencies. It'll work only once."

"If we can get them here, the cavalry will be under my command," I said, and he gave me a sharp look. "But I'll be the first to admit that I'm not the expert. You're the experienced fighter and strategist. We can take back this city, but we are going to have to work together. Help each other."

"The first thing we need to do is rescue Laurenna and Zhari," Alek said. "With their powers on our side, our chances of taking the city back will increase dramatically. If they die, we may have an impossible battle ahead of us."

"We'll get them out of there as soon as we can," I said with more resolve than I felt. "But to do that, we may need backup. If something happens to us, we need to know that more people will be coming to rescue the city."

"I hate it when you're right," he said.

"So do I," I said, and we exchanged grim smiles.

Even with our tentative truce in place, we had a lot of hard work ahead.

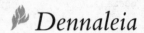 *Dennaleia*

AS MUCH AS I TRIED TO PUT OUT OF MY MIND SIGVAR'S warning about Kartasha being attacked, it nagged at me from the moment I woke up on Midwinter morning. Queen Invasya was busy with final preparations for the Revel, leaving me unable to obtain any reassurance that things were as they should be in the south. I knew my worries were likely due only to nerves about the competition, so I took one final trip to the grand temple to pray and calm myself.

Guests for the Revel began to file in as soon as the sun vanished behind the mountains. They seemed to come from all walks of life, and it was as if the entire city of Corovja had ascended to the palace. I hid in the wings of the stage that had been set up in the throne room and peered out to watch people arrive. They milled about in knots, accepting drinks and food from servers who wound through the room with practiced elegance. This aspect of the party was the same as the other royal functions I'd attended. Yet the room had a sense of restrained energy. I felt it myself, too, along with the nervousness humming in my bones. The Revel would determine the next steps of my future in Zumorda, and though I felt as ready as I could be for the competition itself, thanks to Sigvar's advice and the queen's support, uncertainty nagged at me about what would come after. The influx of guests eventually slowed as the noise level rose and the room filled nearly to capacity.

I walked over to the vanity set up backstage. My hair had been styled into waves and gathered into an ornate knot in the back, as was the Zumordan fashion. I barely recognized myself. The stain on my lips hadn't smudged, but the dark circles under my eyes were not especially becoming. All I could think was that Tristan and Evie should have been there with me, and instead it was my fault that I was alone, again.

"Are all the competitors prepared?" the queen's voice boomed through our small space.

A chorus of yeses answered her, and no one seemed to notice that my voice had not been part of the group. It felt all wrong to be there without Tristan and Evie.

"Eryk and Aela, you will be first," she said. "Now we shall begin." She strode out onto the stage in a sweep of white and silver skirts that trailed along the floor like a river behind her. "Good evening." Her voice carried easily over the crowd. The silence that fell was both complete and energized.

"Tonight the greatest young magic users in Zumorda will compete for your entertainment—and for their fates." She gestured to the center of the stage before leaping off the edge. A shower of sparks trailed behind her, her long skirt shimmering out of existence until a sleek dress was revealed underneath. She alighted in the middle of the floor as the crowd parted around her, and two Swifts moved up to flank her in guard formation.

The audience burst into applause and cheers that died down only as Eryk and Aela took the stage. Almost immediately, Eryk had Aela fighting something that only she could see, and her eyes were wild with fear. Her bubble-like shield of water shrank in on itself until the thin layer hovered barely an inch above her skin. Even though I'd be relieved to have her taken out of the running early, since her gift wasn't one I could channel, it hurt to see someone suffer that way. A body crashed to the floor of the stage and a roar went up from the crowd. Aela had been defeated.

My stomach clenched with nerves. I had to go up against Eryk next.

I was summoned to the stage as soon as the mess from Eryk and Aela's battle had been cleared away. From the opposite wing, Eryk shot me a cruel smile. I hated his magic, the way it could make me feel all inside out and upside down, like I didn't even know my own name. Everything depended on my ability to shield strongly enough to keep him out of my head, since his spirit Affinity also wasn't one I could channel. We took our places several paces away from each other, and Brynan gave us the signal to start.

Eryk sketched a symbol in the air before I could even get a shield up. Immediately my psyche was flooded with memories of those I'd hurt. Tristan and Evie came first, but the memories consuming my mind quickly darkened as I was forced to remember the deaths I'd caused in Duvey and Mynaria. A wave of sadness hit me that was so consuming, it almost brought me to my knees. Defense wasn't going to be enough, and I knew Eryk well enough to know that his psychological attacks would continue. I raised my hands and let magic flow into them, distracting him and the audience with a shield that emitted showers of bright sparks. He laughed at me, clearly assuming I'd forgotten that he rarely used more physical kinds of magic. Then I launched a plume of flame at him that set his jacket on fire—which apparently hadn't been something he'd expected.

Eryk screamed and dropped to the floor to roll, his magic's hold on me fading. I took advantage of the opportunity and reached for earth magic—something else he wouldn't anticipate from me. At my command, the wooden planks of the stage floor bent up and over him, binding him to the floor with his arms by his sides. Without the ability to make eye contact, he couldn't use his gift as powerfully. He thrashed and jerked like a netted fish. I tightened the bonds on him until he could barely breathe and was finally forced to tap out. Even in defeat, his face was twisted in anger, and I knew if he had the opportunity, he'd be sure to make me pay for this later.

I tried not to think about it, instead centering myself to face my final opponent: Ikrie.

The crowd was already roaring when Ikrie faced off against me, creating dull white noise in the background that I tried to tune out. Unlike Eryk, she knew well enough not to attack straight out of the gate. She knew I could channel her powers, and she wasn't going to give me the chance to do it if she could help it.

"I suppose you think you're highborn now that you've got a few wins under your belt," she said, pitching her voice so only I could hear.

I didn't respond, because I knew it was part of her game. She'd picked it up from Eryk—the knack for getting under someone's skin. If she couldn't use magic to do it, she'd use words.

I flicked my hand and sent a shower of sparks cascading over her, hoping to trick her into striking at me. Instead, she just laughed.

"Is that all you have? Has working for someone weak and useless taught you to be the same?" Ikrie circled around me, carefully adding threads of magic to her whirling shield of air and sealing them away from my influence or control.

Her disparaging comment about Mare hit a nerve, as did the reminder of my false station. I tried not to let it show even as the heat of anger burned its way into my cheeks.

Let your anger help you, a voice spoke softly inside my mind.

Ikrie took advantage of my moment of distraction and struck, using her air magic to hurl an ornamental vase from the edge of the stage directly into my head. I barely dodged the blow. In retaliation, I pushed my fire shield away from me in a wide circle, hoping she would run into my defense and hurt herself so that I wouldn't have to hurt her.

Don't hold back, the voice said seductively. It was hard not to listen.

"Is that what you call an attack?" Ikrie said. She launched her own onslaught at me, forcing me to pull my shields in close to protect myself from the blades of air she hurled across the stage. "You're just as useless as any other Mynarian, and too afraid of your powers to even use them."

Anger ate at me, my gift churning through my body, begging to be used.

Do it.

"Why don't you go back to being a maid?" Ikrie said.

My control snapped. But this time it wasn't the control of my powers; it was only the control of my emotions, which demanded that I strike her down for what she was saying. The queen's gift opened up pathways, showing me what I could do to destroy Ikrie. I walked toward her, no longer afraid and no longer trying to hold myself back.

Ikrie flung attacks at me that bounced harmlessly off my fire shield until I got close. Then I started absorbing the magic so that with every blow she landed on me, my strength became greater. Still, she didn't back down, and soon we stood almost nose to nose at the center of the stage.

"You have no idea who I am," I said, and gave myself over to my power.

Fire closed in around Ikrie until she was trapped in an inferno. Her air magic served only to fuel the flames, and soon the heat brought her to her knees.

Hurt her, the voice in my mind said. *Show her your strength.*

I stood over her and reached through the fires I'd constructed around her. They tingled on my skin, harmless to me. I let my hand close around her throat, feeling my palm rage with heat. Ikrie's scream split through the cheers of the audience. Still, she did not tap out. She thrashed in my hand, struggling to get back to her feet. It was futile.

Do to her what she does to you. The voice sounded excited now, which didn't quite fit with the anger I felt. Still, I obeyed. I opened my mouth the barest bit and inhaled deeply. Ikrie's scream stopped, replaced by a gurgling sound as I took away her breath. Moments later, she lay immobile on the floor, a blistering handprint rising on her neck. I stumbled back as bile rose in my throat. The thunder of the audience's cheers increased until it was so staggering I couldn't hear myself think.

I knew I chose the right one. The satisfaction in the voice felt completely at odds with my emotions, and it was then that the horrifying truth struck me: the voice in my mind wasn't my own.

My instinct was to bolt from the stage, but a heavy warmth blossomed in my limbs to root me in place. I hyperventilated like a trapped animal.

Shh, the voice said. *You have nothing to fear.*

I had everything to fear. Someone had manipulated me in battle. If they could take over my mind in the heat of a fight, they'd be able to do it at any time. The implications were terrifying. How much of what was in my mind could they see? What else might they make me do? Fright pulsed through my body as the queen floated onto the stage beside me.

"I now present to you this evening's champion: Lia!" She took my hand and raised it alongside her own. "May Zumorda prosper forever!"

The audience let out a final cheer of joy as servants poured into the room, carrying platters laden with every manner of feasting food.

The queen kept my hand as she led me offstage. I followed her obediently even as panic swirled in my stomach.

"I knew you could do it, little bird," she said once we were in the wings.

"Something is wrong," I managed to choke out. I opened my mouth to explain what had happened in the battle, but before I could, the voice returned.

Don't be frightened. The queen smiled at me. *Isn't this a better way for us to speak?*

The heat of panic swiftly faded as a chill consumed me. She was the one whose voice was in my mind. Her gift had not been to help me with my magic or with learning—it had been to share her consciousness with me and to communicate from mind to mind. She was the one who had helped me, but also the one who had pushed me to defeat Ikrie in a far more brutal way than I would have if left to my own devices. I backed away, reeling at the betrayal.

"This isn't what I agreed to," I said. "You said you'd given me a gift of learning."

"It's a much greater gift," the queen said, reaching out to caress my cheek. "Before you join the celebration of your victory, I have some important news to share with you, since I expect you'll be choosing to apprentice with Zhari. Come with me." She led me away from the party, and I followed. My fear and confusion coalesced into anger as I walked. I did not like Ikrie, but I wouldn't have burned her on purpose like that. The queen had forced my hand, rigged the competition even. Had she done it because I was her blood or because she wanted to use me in some other way I couldn't yet anticipate? By the time we reached her study, I was ready to confront her and demand that she take back her "gift," but before I could, she said something that made the words die on my lips.

"I'm afraid there's been a riot in Kartasha," the queen said as soon as the door was closed and we were sequestered away from curious ears.

My blood ran cold. "What?"

"Kartasha has been taken by the Sonnenbornes. There's been a betrayal." Her demeanor had completely changed from the celebratory mask she'd worn at the Revel. The forbidding expression she wore now indicated that someone would pay for what had happened.

"But there can't be." My hands trembled. "You told me Zhari and Laurenna caught the slavers who were creating problems. You said they were going to use them to trace the Sonnenborne conspiracy back to its source." One question that I knew there was no answer to consumed me—what had happened to Mare? Even if someone knew, the queen would not have cared enough to ask.

"Zhari has served me for over a century and is loyal unto death," the queen said. "She's the one who reached out to me and is still in contact, deploying countermeasures to retaliate against the Sonnenbornes. For something to go this catastrophically wrong, it would have had to be mismanaged locally. Guardian Laurenna has been put in prison on my orders and will be tried for treason."

"But how bad is it?" I asked, still in shock. If Zhari was still in control, it couldn't be a complete takeover, could it? "How could you let the Revel go on with this happening in Kartasha?" If it had been up to me, we would have been on the way south as soon as the news arrived.

"Canceling the Revel would not have had any impact on the situation in the south. It would have only served to upset people in the north, which is the last thing I need. As for the severity of the situation, the last I heard from Zhari, she had barricaded herself in the tower at court. I'll continue to monitor the situation through her."

"But what about Mare?" I blurted.

"What about her?" The queen looked confused.

"Where is she? Is she alive?" Unanswerable as the questions were, they were burning me from the inside out.

"Do you really care for her so much?" the queen asked. "I always thought she was just a means to an end. You got what you wanted—passage to Zumorda and training for your gift. What does she matter?"

Mare was the only thing that mattered. As upset as I'd been with her, the reality of it crushed me with such totality that I couldn't breathe.

"I have to go," I said, my voice hollow. Although I'd needed training for my magic, this wasn't at all what I'd wanted. What good would it do me to be apprenticed in Zumorda if I would never be a guardian? I hadn't come here to ruin Evie's and Tristan's chances to compete, and I had never wanted an unwelcome consciousness sharing my own. The only thing I wanted was to get back to Mare. I could only hope she'd forgive me for leaving in the first place.

You must be tired. Rest now and we'll talk more tomorrow. Emotions flooded into me along with the queen's words. I could feel the way she cared for me, a kind of protectiveness that bordered on possession. I wanted to scream and throw her out of my mind. I wished I knew how.

"You don't understand," I said. "I don't want this. The honors bestowed on me as winner of the Midwinter Revel—they're not for me. I didn't win because I fought well or fairly. I won because you pushed me to use my powers in ways I never would have on my own. That's not who I want to be."

Shock was written on the queen's face. "No one leaves the elites."

"I do," I said.

"But what about me?" the queen said. "You're more than a trainee. You're my blood. My heir."

The word made my breath catch in my throat. "Blood is not the only thing that keeps a heart beating. Please excuse me, Your Majesty." I stood up and walked out of her study, slamming the strongest shield I could manage around my mind in hopes it would keep her out. I needed to leave for Kartasha, and I needed to do it tonight—which meant I needed to get my friends back.

After gathering the few things I wanted to take with me back to Kartasha, I found Tristan and Evie in Tristan's chambers. They hadn't bothered to attend the Revel, and I couldn't blame them.

"Please hear me out before you shut the door," I said hurriedly. Evie already had it half closed again as soon as she saw my face.

"We heard you won," Evie said. "Congratulations. Now leave."

"I'm not taking an apprenticeship," I said.

Tristan snorted. "Really? We lose our opportunity to compete, you somehow escape punishment, and now you're going to turn down the chance of a lifetime like it's nothing?"

"I'm sorry," I said. "I don't have enough words in the world for how sorry I am. I tried to take the blame, but I've made all the wrong choices up to this point. Hurting the two of you was one of the worst of them. I never should have asked you to help me break into the prison. All the benefit was for me and all the risk was to both of you."

Evie and Tristan both frowned at me, clearly undecided about whether to accept the apology. I fidgeted uneasily, worrying that every minute I spent here was a moment that Mare could be in danger, and it would be my fault if something happened to her.

"Why do you look like you've seen one of Tristan's death visions?" Evie said.

"Kartasha has been overtaken by Sonnenbornes," I said numbly. "That's why I'm turning down the apprenticeship. I have to get back there right now."

"My parents and older brother work in Kartasha." Evie looked stricken.

"The person I love most is in Kartasha," I said.

Tristan looked back and forth between us. "How in the Sixth Hell are you planning to get there? There's thigh-deep snow from here halfway to Orzai! No one is maintaining any of the roads."

"I'll just have to do my best," I said, my voice grim. "There are sleds. Perhaps I can use my fire magic to melt the snow."

Tristan sighed. "C'mon, just admit that you need me."

Evie and I stared at him with equally humorless expressions.

"Bad joke," he said. "But I can help you. With enough power, we could shadow walk most of the way there, I think. I just need an anchor."

"My cousin's farm is just north of Kartasha," Evie said. "I know the stone in that region—it might be strong enough to be an anchor for the shadow walk."

"You can't possibly mean to come with me," I said. "Haven't I already ruined your lives enough?"

"We could have said no to helping you break into the prison," Tristan said. "We had that choice."

Evie nodded. "I've been upset about how things worked out, but the real problem was that you didn't come talk to us."

"I'm sorry," I said. "I thought you hated me. I'd understand if you did."

"I was angry," Evie said. "Still am, a little bit. But I don't think it was your intention to hurt us."

"Of course it wasn't," I said.

"Don't get me wrong—good intentions are not a cure-all excuse." Evie pulled her sweater tighter around her shoulders.

"Of course not," I said. "Intentions don't change the fact that I hurt you. And I am so, so sorry for that. You deserved a better friend than I've been."

"Well, we will have lots to talk about on the road." Tristan stood up. "Let's go before the queen decides to stop us."

I nodded my agreement, though a shiver of fear crept down my spine. The queen would probably be able to sense our departure through her bond with me. The thought made my stomach turn.

Tristan and Evie collected a few essentials and then headed for the Grand Temple. But as quickly as we'd made our move, the queen had also made hers to stop us. As we bolted through the gardens, birds swooped down from every side to trail the three of us. I ran until my lungs felt like they were on fire with the icy winter air, until my legs no longer felt attached to my body. I ran until we crossed the bridge to the Grand Temple.

Wind gusted over the crumbling platform of the old temple floor. The Sight came to me so easily I would have wept with gratitude if not for the urgency of our mission. I reached for Evie's and Tristan's hands, letting the familiar tingle rise into my arms and releasing my magic as gently as I could toward Tristan. He jolted with the impact but managed to keep his grip on my hand. Birds screeched overhead as a group of Swifts closed in on us. Still connected, the three of us faced the broken archway that had once been the entrance to the temple. Tristan's magic bound around the empty doorframe like snakes made of shadow until a dark hole opened up where the door had once been. Inside, swirls of blue and purple fog seemed to mix with the shadows. My stomach dropped a little as I remembered what shadow walking had been like before, but there wasn't time for me to hesitate.

Together we stepped into the darkness.

It felt as if the mountain had fallen out from under us and we were lost in a cold tunnel. Whispers caressed my ears, and at one point I could have sworn I felt sharp teeth nibbling at my throat. The walk seemed to last an eternity—an endless span of time in which my heart still raced as if the Nightswifts held knives at my throat. When we dropped out of the shadowlands and onto a patch of dead grass and rocks, nausea rose in me like a tidal wave. Evie and I both clutched our stomachs, gagging.

I tried to slow my breathing and waited for the sickness to fade. The bracing chill of the night air helped quell the nausea. Stars glimmered overhead and a nearly full moon weakly illuminated our surroundings. A herd of sheep regarded us warily from farther up the rocky hill, no doubt startled from their grazing by our sudden appearance. Squinting, I could barely make out the profile of a mountain looming near us, but I didn't recognize it from what I saw.

"Where the Hells are we?" Evie asked, her breath misting.

"Um," Tristan said, eyeballing the sheep warily. "Somewhere near where you were thinking?"

"I thought we were going to end up where I was envisioning. I don't know this place." Evie sounded panicked.

"We're probably within a half day's walk of it," Tristan said. "Shadow walking isn't an exact science. There are probably just more dead things here." He pointed to the left, where a well-picked deer carcass lay draped over a flat rock.

Evie retched again.

I looked up at the sky. "Let's be logical about this. There's the huntress's star." I pointed at a bright star. "That means that way is north."

"And the place I was envisioning was my cousin's farm to the north of Kartasha," Evie managed. "This isn't it, but I doubt we overshot and went too far south. Though it's awfully dry here. This isn't normal for this time of year."

"Look," I said. "The ground slopes downward a little bit here. If we keep traveling downhill, we should eventually reach a river or a road. We're in a sheep pasture, so we've definitely made it to some farmlands. That means we should be near a trade road as well, since farmers need them to get to market."

Evie seemed mollified by this logical information, but she still couldn't resist another jab at Tristan. "I don't suppose you can ask the dead which way we should go?"

"Not at the moment," he said. He was starting to look a little gray in the moonlight. The long shadow walk must have drained him more than he wanted to admit.

"Well, there's no helping this, I suppose. But tell anyone I let you ride me and I'll never heal you again," Evie said. As she finished speaking, her limbs elongated and she transformed into an elegant reindeer. She walked up alongside the fence and gestured for us to get on, or at least I assumed that was what her head toss meant. It was either that or *I'm going to gore Tristan if he doesn't stop fooling around.*

"I guess we get to ride," I said to Tristan.

Evie gave me a unimpressed look and an impatient snort. I climbed onto her back, startled when a small black cat leaped from the fence to sit behind me.

"Tristan?" I asked.

The cat blinked inscrutably. Somehow, his manifest was perfectly appropriate.

We rode south slowly, all of us exhausted from the ordeals of the night. But the important thing was that we were safe, far away from the queen and her dark plans for us. Or so I thought, until her voice echoed inside my mind as clearly as if she stood behind me:

Where did you go, little bird?

TWENTY-FIVE ✦ *Amaranthine*

THE EXODUS TURNED OUT NOT TO BE THE WORST PART of Kartasha's loss. It was the battle that came in the days after, while we waited for the cavalry and Wymund's forces to arrive. Though Alek's message had reached Wymund quickly, it would still take days for the soldiers to travel southeast to us. Those on horseback wouldn't be much faster than those on foot due to the need to keep their mounts fresh for battle.

I stood with a tree at my back, out of breath and with my cutlass up in front of me and Harian and another fighter flanking me on either side. A pack of dogs barked somewhere in the distance, sending shivers of dread down my spine. Every few sunlengths they attacked, just often enough to ensure that no one in our camp got more than a few hours of sleep at a time.

I gazed at the encampment we'd built. Tents and lean-tos were clustered everywhere with little organization. The fighters we had at our disposal ranged from hardened mercenaries to awkward farmers who looked uncomfortable carrying their swords, with the majority being the latter. Those of us who had at least some fighting experience were assigned to the areas near the road as the first line of defense from attackers coming from Kartasha. I tried to stem the rising tide of despair. Even with the help of the cavalry, how were we going to take back the city with nothing but tired and defeated people on our side?

"Look out!" Harian shouted.

I whirled to the right just in time to knock aside a lunging dog with the hilt of my sword. The aching muscles in my arm protested. I'd been on guard duty since the previous night and had no energy reserves left now that the coral light of dawn was blooming over the eastern mountains.

The fighter on my left, a small woman with earth magic named Carys, used her gift to draw vines out of the ground to knot around the legs of another approaching dog. The animal fell in a tangle of limbs, still barking and snapping at us. In the last sunlength or so, I'd started to worry about Carys—exhaustion made a gray mask of her face.

"I curse the day I ever heard of Tamers," I said. After gathering information from throughout the camp, Alek and I had figured out how the Sonnenbornes had staged their coup. Not only had they infiltrated the city with false businesses populated with "workers" who were fighters in disguise, but they'd somehow built an alliance with the Tamers. The loans for animal kennels were for the Tamers' familiars, which had been set loose on the city the day the riot broke out and were the source of our torment now.

"I never would have thought they'd turn against us," Harian said.

"But why wouldn't they?" I asked. "The drought has been eating into their lands. If it was doing damage to the resources they rely on, whatever the Sonnenbornes promised them must have seemed like an attractive offer. I never heard so much as a whisper about the Winter Court doing anything to help them."

"I hadn't thought of that," Harian said, his voice grim.

Another pack of snarling dogs burst out of the underbrush.

"Run!" I shouted. There were too many for the three of us to fend off. Running uphill would slow us too much, so instead we bolted for the road where the next sentry was stationed. Having four of us would give us better odds in spite of our exhaustion.

Trees flashed by as I raced down the hill, just barely outpaced by Harian and his absurdly long legs. When we reached the path where the sentry was supposed to be stationed, all that greeted us was dusty road. We were going to have to fight them on our own.

I slid to a halt in front of a huge rock I could use to defend my back and slashed at the animal closest to me. It dodged my blow with uncanny reflexes and growled, strings of saliva dripping from its snarling jaws. Beside me, Harian breathed hard, his eyes leaping from one dog to the next. There were eight of them surrounding us in a semicircle, now closing in. They knew our weapons were sharp, and they would wait for the right moment to strike.

The first dog lunged, latching onto my boot. I swiped at it with the sword, but my weapon seemed to have given up on me. I was too fatigued to wield it well. When the first dog fell back, another was on me in seconds.

"This is a stupid way to die," Harian said, panting as he struck at another animal. "I like dogs. I don't want to fight them."

A third dog lunged at Carys and she made no move to stop it, forcing me to leap between them and deflect the animal with my sword.

"Not today, Shadow God," I said, and drew on the last of my reserves of energy until we sent the dogs running with their tails tucked between their legs.

"She's going down!" Harian said, and that was all the warning I had before Carys collapsed to the ground, her eyes vacant and pupils rapidly shrinking.

I cursed. We couldn't afford to lose another magic user, but it was happening with increasing frequency. Refugees with the ability to use magic seemed to be falling victim to an illness that rendered them catatonic. Every day there were more cases, and not a single thing anyone did seemed to help. No one could trace the illness to its source, whether magical or physical. With every day that passed I worried more that Alek would be the next one to fall victim to it.

"We have to get help," I said, and raised my fingers to my mouth to blow a piercing whistle.

"Gods, I hope that doesn't draw more dogs," Harian said. "I don't have another round of that in me."

"Me either." I sighed, feeling defeated in spite of our small victory.

As soon as help arrived to carry Carys back to camp, we trudged wearily back up the hill, still keeping an eye out for any more rogue animals. When we arrived back at the homestead, Alek and Kerrick stood up from where they sat around the campfire. I told them about the near miss with the dogs, the missing sentry by the road, and Carys's collapse. In a matter of minutes, Alek had another pair of fighters on their way down there—one to take the post, and the other to search for the missing sentry. To my relief, he still looked clear-eyed.

"Any news from the city?" I asked. I hadn't seen any refugees come in overnight, but that didn't mean new information wasn't bubbling to the surface.

Alek nodded. "A few families that came in yesterday had been dosed with peaceroot. They brought what they had with them to spare others from it." He pointed to a pile of small leather pouches on the table.

Kerrick grimaced. "It's the bad stuff, too—the kind that you don't have to brew into a tea. Inhaling it will take a magic user down in seconds. Applying a little to your gums will keep powers at bay for hours."

Alek eyed the pouches as if they were poisonous snakes. "Apparently the Sonnenbornes require that any Zumordans staying in the city take peaceroot. Any sign of rebellion is a death sentence."

"Everyone has either joined the Sonnenbornes, gone into hiding, died, or come here," Kerrick said. "I doubt we'll be seeing many more refugees from the city after midday today."

"We can't keep fighting these dogs like this," I said. "They're wearing us out on purpose. If all our fighters here are too tired to be of use by the time the cavalry arrives, and we keep losing magic users, we're still going to be short of the power we need to take back the city."

"The fighters we battled in the city were much more than

Sonnenborne's usual bands of raiders," Kerrick said. "These people know how to fight, and more than half the people we have on our side don't. We have merchants and farmers who are little more than warm bodies we can throw at the enemy, hoping to shield ourselves. Frankly, I'm not comfortable doing that. It's an unnecessary loss of life."

"What we need is to get Laurenna and Zhari out," I said. "They may be our only hope. If they're being dosed with peaceroot, they may need some time to recover before they're able to help us take back the city. We have only a few more days until the cavalry arrives. I'd hoped to wait until then, but I don't think we can afford to."

"Agreed," said Alek with his usual grudging tone.

"One thing working in our favor is that the Sonnenbornes are as blind as I am when it comes to magic users," I said. "That means there's no way anyone can detect the presence of active magic users in the city—unless there are a few people in hiding who haven't been dosed with peaceroot. If we make it a covert operation to rescue Laurenna and Zhari, I think our chances are fairly good. The question is, how do we get in?"

"The smaller the group, the easier it will be," Alek said.

"It's still more likely than not to end in death." Kerrick seemed less certain.

"Then Alek and I should go," I said.

"What?" Harian said. "That makes no sense at all! We can't send our two leaders back into the city on the riskiest possible mission."

"Yes, we can," I said, startled that he'd referred to me as one of the leaders. "With every day that passes, the chance of Alek catching whatever this magic plague is increases. And with a little rest and the sword I have, I'm as good a physical fighter as we can get. Besides, I've had a lot of practice at sneaking."

"Then today we rest, and tonight we go in." Alek pulled out a whetstone and began to sharpen his sword.

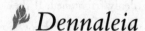 *Dennaleia*

WE MAINTAINED A STEADY PACE, RIDING THROUGH the night and part of the next day until Evie tired of carrying us. After that we walked until evening hovered over the mountains. Fatigue kept us all quiet, though we started to find a little of our rapport again. All of us lived in fear of what we'd find ahead, which made it a little bit easier to put aside thoughts of what we'd left behind.

Even from a distance it wasn't hard to tell that something was wrong in Kartasha. Its white tower gleamed like a beacon, but the city below it seemed strangely dark. We didn't see so much as a single person until we reached the foothills of a mountain to the north of Kartasha.

"You there!" A woman with a sword stepped into the road, her stance defensive.

The three of us stopped abruptly, not wanting to make a scene.

We were too exhausted to fight.

"Oh, you're not Sonnenbornes," she said, her stance immediately relaxing. "Apologies—I wouldn't have drawn my sword if I'd known."

"Have they made it this far north of Kartasha?" I asked, suddenly frightened. If they'd already taken over the region north of the city, I didn't know how we could possibly stop them. The fact that they had the city was bad enough.

"No, but they've been sending out Tamer dogs to attack us. It seemed like only a matter of time before they'd send soldiers." The woman sheathed her weapon.

"The Tamers are involved?" I could hardly believe it. They were Zumordan and shouldn't have had reason to turn against their own countrymen. "How?"

"We don't really know," she said. "Best we can guess, the drought must have been affecting them badly and they made some kind of deal with the Sonnenbornes."

"Who else escaped the city?" Evie asked. Worry for her parents and brother glistened in her eyes.

"There's a huge refugee camp a little deeper into the foothills." She gestured behind her. "I can't say I know everyone by name."

"Do you happen to know what became of Princess Amaranthine or Sir Alek?" I asked. They were both notable enough that surely someone knew if one of them had escaped the city, and as much as they hated each other, I figured they'd each know where the other was.

The swordswoman's expression grew curious. "Are you friends of theirs?"

"Yes," I said, wondering if that was entirely accurate. I didn't know what Mare thought of me right now or if she'd be glad to see me.

"We're here to help," Evie added after I fell silent.

"Then I'd best take you back to camp." The woman sheathed her weapon. "I'm Shazi, by the way."

We introduced ourselves as we followed her to the refugee camp. It was strangely silent for a place with so many people. There were no fires for people to gather around, though I saw a few faces peering curiously out of tents as we passed by. Shazi led us to a ramshackle house overlooking the rest of the tent city the refugees had erected. Even in the dark I could tell the building was in poor repair, though they'd done a good job of putting up curtains to block the faint light emanating from inside.

"I found some help out on the road," Shazi said as she ducked through the blanket serving as a makeshift door. "Kerrick, Harian—meet Lia, Evie, and Tristan."

The two men stood to greet us, the lantern on the table between us casting long shadows over their faces.

"Where are Alek and Mare?" I asked, anxiety starting to break through my exhaustion.

"You just missed them," the shorter man said grimly. "They've gone on a mission to rescue Zhari and Laurenna from the Sonnenbornes."

"What?" Shock made me feel weak. "The queen told me that Zhari had been in communication with her. She told me Laurenna had been imprisoned and was going to be put on trial for treason. Zhari didn't say anything about being held hostage—we were under the impression that she was safe." And surely the Sonnenbornes wouldn't have allowed her to communicate with the queen if she was being held prisoner.

"As of when?" Harian asked.

"Last night," I said. "Midwinter." It already felt like a hundred years had passed since then.

"The city was taken several days ago," Kerrick said. "Zhari was taken hostage by the Sonnenbornes, along with Laurenna and her daughter. I saw it happen as I was fighting my way free of the Winter Court."

"Then how could she have spoken to the queen?" Evie asked.

"Oh gods," I said, dismay crashing over me. "What if their capture was staged? What if one or both of them was lying to the queen?" I racked my brain for any other information the queen had passed to me. "Did the Winter Court ever catch any Sonnenbornes participating in human trafficking?" I asked.

"Not that I heard of," Kerrick said, exchanging glances with the others, who both shook their heads. "But we're fighters, not participants in the political side of things. It's impossible to know everything that goes on at court."

"It seems like stopping a ring of human traffickers would have required a fair number of fighters, though," Tristan pointed out.

"Why do you ask?" Kerrick said.

"It was one of the reassurances passed from Laurenna to the queen—that they'd caught some of the people behind the magical disappearances," I said. "It sounds like that wasn't the case. Perhaps the entire story was a fabrication."

"Do you think Laurenna is behind this?" Shazi asked, her eyes wide. "Alek had that theory for a while but dismissed it once we heard she'd been taken prisoner by the Sonnenbornes."

"Anything is possible," I said. "She or Zhari could be under someone's control, and if we don't know what that person is capable of, we could have an enemy far more dangerous than we're expecting." If I hadn't seen Sigvar ruined and without his Affinity, I might have suspected him. No one had a better motive to get revenge on the queen, and his gift would have given him the ability to control either Zhari or Laurenna—especially if he had a more subtle way to do it than what he'd used on the cultists.

"Speaking of magic users, we should warn you three about the problem we've been having here," Harian said. "Many of those with stronger Affinities are suffering from an illness that's made them unable to speak or function. We've wondered if it might be some kind of spirit magic."

"Is it contagious?" I asked.

Harian shook his head. "It seems to strike at random."

"Show me," I said, an ominous feeling growing in the pit of my stomach.

"I'll come, too," Evie said. "My gift is for healing. Maybe there's something I can do to help those afflicted."

We followed Harian out of the house and to a large neighboring tent.

"See for yourself," he said, pulling back the flap of the tent and holding his lantern aloft. I gagged on the smell that wafted out— clearly the incapacitated people hadn't been able to bathe or make it to the latrine since whatever had happened to them. Inside the tent, a dozen people lay flat on their backs, staring vacantly at the roof.

Someone had bundled them up in blankets to keep them warm in spite of their lack of movement, but even more unnerving than their utter stillness was the look in their eyes. One pair of brown eyes and one pair of blue reflected the lantern's dim light, their pupils barely more than pinpoints.

"I've seen this before," I said.

"The cultist," Evie said. "But he's in prison in Corovja."

But I remembered something Evie didn't know—the person who had trained Sigvar was Zhari. How had I not put the pieces together before? If Zhari had trained him, she no doubt knew the kind of magic he'd used to control the members of his cult. One of her Affinities had to be for spirit. She'd had many more years to hone her skills than Sigvar, and it didn't seem out of the question that she might have the ability to manipulate people's minds from farther away or with more subtlety. I knew how powerful spirit magic could be after seeing Eryk in training and facing him in battle.

"Can we cure it?" Harian asked, closing the tent flap and looking down at me with hope in his expression.

"Only by killing or disabling the person responsible," I said, shuddering as I remembered Sigvar's condition.

"If only we had Laurenna or someone with a gift like hers to help us," Harian said.

"I'm not sure we need that," I said grimly. "And I have a feeling that Zhari isn't under anyone's control. I think she's the one doing this." It was a brilliant way to weaken the refugees and strengthen the Sonnenbornes' hold on the city. But where was she getting the power, and how was her reach so great?

"That can't be," Harian said. "Zhari has been the grand vizier for longer than even my parents can remember. No one is more loyal to Zumorda. She's one of the most powerful magic users in the entire kingdom. . . ." He trailed off as he realized the implications of what he was saying.

"Who better to do this than someone who is the most powerful magic user in the entire kingdom?" I said.

"But why?" he said. "I don't understand why she would turn against her own people."

"Neither do I, but if this theory holds any water, and Mare and Alek just went into Kartasha thinking they were going to rescue her, they could be in terrible danger." My magic swirled restlessly along with my fear. I quieted it with a thought, reinforcing the subtle shields I now knew to maintain to keep it from bursting out of control.

We reentered the ramshackle house to find Kerrick and Tristan taking sips of something from a flask. Tristan sat staring at the fire but looked up when we came in.

"Can you help them?" Tristan asked Evie.

She shook her head, explaining what we'd seen. Kerrick, however, had a hard time swallowing my theory about Zhari.

"You can't assume it was her behind this," Kerrick said. "She has no motive. Nothing about that makes any sense."

"The only thing I know is that the longer we talk about this, the closer Mare and Alek get to danger. Someone has to warn them. Don't we have anyone with Farspeech here?"

"No," Harian said, "and most of the more powerful magic users have already succumbed to the illness you just saw."

"Then our time is probably already running out," I said. My

mouth went dry at the thought of being held prisoner in my own mind the way those people in the tent had been. Even more terrifying was the thought that Zhari might be able to put me under her control. Worse was that I knew the best solution, and the thought of doing it made my skin crawl. I didn't have Farspeech, so I couldn't reach Mare. But I could reach the queen through the bond she'd forced on me—though I'd sworn to myself I wasn't going to let her inside my head again.

"I'm going to go after them," I said.

"What?" Kerrick said.

"You can't." Evie's tone was flat. "We're all exhausted."

"It's not going to get better," I said. "There is not going to be any rest with Tamer dogs attacking the camp and magic users being neutralized by some evil power. Any of us could be next."

"I don't think I can shadow walk without another day's rest," Tristan said, his voice worried.

"If we could just get these damned dogs to stop attacking the camp, we could spare enough people to make a ruckus near the city that would distract the Sonnenborne sentries and fighters," Kerrick said. "That might give you a chance to get in."

"I have an idea about how to stop the dogs," Evie said. "Has the wind been steady out of the north?"

"Sure. It usually is this time of year," Harian said with a puzzled expression.

"That's what I thought," Evie said. "I can bore holes through rocks with my magic and create a chorus of pitched whistles to drive them off. I still have a little energy left."

"I may not have enough energy to shadow walk, but I think I

could help with the distraction," Tristan mused. "Were many people killed in the riot?"

Shazi nodded grimly.

"Then I'll give them a brief second chance at life," Tristan said.

I shuddered at the thought of the dead rising to walk the streets of Kartasha but knew there would be no better distraction. Best of all, it would pose little risk to us.

"Then let's go," I said. "The longer we wait, the more danger Alek and Mare could be in. I have to get to them as soon as possible."

"I don't feel good about you going into the city by yourself," Evie said. Tristan's frown was as deep as hers, and their loyalty warmed me.

"I might be alone in the city, but I won't truly be by myself," I said. "I wouldn't have been able to get this far without both of you." I met their eyes in turn. "But I have to do this. Mare is in danger. It'll be easier to sneak through the city myself than to try to get a group past the Sonnenbornes. If worst comes to worst . . . well, I'm close enough to fluent in their language that I can probably trick them long enough to escape."

"I'll come with you to the edge of the city," Kerrick said. "You need someone who knows a way to get close without being detected."

As tired as I was, having a plan reinvigorated me, and we were back on the road in very little time. We walked toward the city at as brisk a pace as we could manage, and it was there, in the silence of the road, that I quietly let down my shields and cast my mind to the north.

Your Majesty? I projected the thought, wondering how distance would affect our connection.

I knew you'd come back to me. The voice felt too intimate inside my mind, too close to feelings and thoughts I didn't want to share. The physical distance between us apparently meant nothing.

I'm not coming back. I hoped she could feel my certainty as strongly as I did. The only things that mattered were getting to Mare and Alek before Zhari did and letting the queen know the important information before slamming my shields back into place. *Something is wrong in Kartasha. Zhari was lying to you—there are no countermeasures being taken to fight the Sonnenbornes. The city is under their control and everyone here thinks Zhari was taken prisoner. I thought you should know.*

There was a long pause that made me wonder if she'd heard me, or if perhaps I was imagining the conversation entirely. And then a response finally came:

I'm already flying south, little bird. I'll see you soon.

TWENTY-SEVEN ✦ *Amaranthine*

GETTING INTO KARTASHA MADE USE OF EVERY STEALTH skill I'd ever developed and would have been easier if not for Alek, who had the subtlety of a bear crashing through the woods. Fortunately, his magic made up for it. He used it to create distractions and draw enemies out of our path on our way through the city back to the Winter Court. We entered through Alek's childhood slums, which he navigated easily even in the near dark. The area closer to the tower was more difficult to traverse, and somehow the silence of the streets made it seem more sinister than when it had been bustling with people. We got through the walls of the Winter Court thanks to an irrigation canal supplying the horse pastures, which Alek was able to stop with his water magic long enough for us to slip in unde-tected.

My pace quickened as we walked up the pasture hill to the barn. I wiggled open the latch on the back door to the stall where Flicker had been stabled, nearly crying with relief when I saw him crane his neck around to investigate the people intruding upon his nighttime meal.

"Thank the gods," I whispered into his mane. I had hoped the Sonnenbornes would consider him valuable enough to feed and keep safe, and it looked like for now, they had. Unlike before, the stable was full of horses, mostly Sonnenborne desert breds.

"There's someone in the tack room." Alek put a gentle hand on my shoulder and motioned for me to get down behind the stall door, where it would be harder for me to be seen. Then he took Flicker's grain bucket off the hook in the stall and hurled it down the barn aisle. I peered through a narrow gap to see what was happening. Footsteps immediately came racing out of the tack room to reveal a young Sonnenborne man. Alek slipped out of the stall and hit him over the head, dropping him to the ground like a sack of grain.

"There's a servants' tunnel from the barn to the inner court-yard," Alek said.

I followed him to the northernmost end of the barn, which abutted another building, and we entered the passageway. Alek towered ahead of me, blocking most of the light.

When we reached an exit into what appeared to be the kitchen of a residence hall, Alek pushed through the door. A few seconds later came the crash of pots and pans hitting the ground.

"All clear," he said a few moments later.

I crept around the unconscious Sonnenborne cook on the floor. Just past the blisteringly hot ovens, several doors led to different paths into the residential hall.

"Now, there's a problem," Alek said. "There's only one way into the tower—through the front door."

"Then we go through the front door." I drew my sword. In spite of my pretended confidence, my stomach clenched with nerves. To walk through the front door of the Winter Court's tower, we were going to have to take out a lot more Sonnenbornes. It was only a matter of time before someone caught on to our trail of unconscious bodies, and I didn't want to still be there when they did.

Alek drew his weapon and gave me a nod of confirmation before leading the way out of the residence hall. On the opposite side of the courtyard, four guards walked the perimeter of the area in orderly patterns, moving with the grace of trained fighters. There was no way to avoid detection with all four of them on patrol, and I wished like the Sixth Hell I'd brought my bow instead of just my sword. Instead, I was going to have to trust the weapon—and Alek.

Without warning, Alek leaped out of the shadows and took down one of the four fighters with a swift blow. In seconds, the other three soldiers, including one warrior who easily matched him in size and strength, converged on him. I said a silent prayer to the Six and let my sword carry me into battle. Not in a thousand years had I thought I would ever be a warrior, but as I followed the guidance of my blade and knocked another fighter to the ground, I realized that I felt as much like myself as I did on the back of my horse. It wasn't about hurting people—it was about standing up for what was right and doing my small part to protect the people I cared about. A few minutes later, the courtyard was silent again, and the way to enter the tower was clear.

"Where do they keep prisoners?" I asked Alek.

"Tower dungeon," Alek said, as though it was the most logical thing in the world.

"Is that the only place?" I asked, not sure the answer could be that obvious.

"It's the only place secure enough to hold anyone with an Affinity as strong as Laurenna's or Zhari's. The cells are insulated to prevent magic use."

"Great. A magical dungeon." Zumorda would never cease to be full of unpleasant surprises.

Alek opened the tower door. I expected to walk into a room filled with destruction, but the interior of the tower seemed untouched by the riot that had filled Kartasha's streets. Laurenna stood at the center of the grand receiving room with her arms raised. A hailstorm swirled around her to form an icy shield that looked as if it could just as easily be turned into offense.

"I thought you might be coming," she said.

Alek raised his weapon. "Laurenna, what are you doing?"

"Serving my kingdom." She raised her hand and a bubble of water formed around my head.

"Help!" I tried to scream, but only ended up with a mouthful of water. I clawed frantically at my face, but no matter how hard I tried to fight off the water, it re-formed itself around my face. Through vision blurred by the water, I could barely make out Alek and Laurenna fighting. She hurled spell after spell at him while he came relentlessly at her with his sword.

"Where's Fadeyka?" he demanded. His voice sounded like it was coming from underwater, and my vision had begun to swim with dark spots. I fell to my knees.

From behind me, a sudden blast of heat exploded as a wave of flames rushed past me toward Laurenna and Alek. I flattened myself on the ground, certain I was about to die. Instead, the flames parted around Alek and slammed into Laurenna with physical force, knocking her to the ground. The water around my face fell away, and I gasped for breath.

"I suppose it was my turn to help you breathe again," a voice said, and I looked up to see Denna standing over me. How had she gotten to Kartasha? The sight of her was like the first soothing rain after a long, dry summer. Even in her travel-stained cloak, she no longer looked convincingly like a lady's maid. She stood tall, her chin at a proud angle and her eyes gleaming with strength. When her gaze met mine, there was tenderness and worry in it that nearly broke me in half. I had never seen anyone so beautiful. But as swiftly as my joy had risen at the sight of her, our situation shattered it. Laurenna had already nearly killed me, and no matter how powerful Denna had become, both of us were now in mortal danger.

Laurenna had already staggered to her feet, now with an iridescent bubble-like shield of water locked in place around herself. Denna took a defensive stance in front of me and cast another spell, helping Alek hold his ground. I couldn't let them fight alone. I forced myself back to my feet. I didn't have magic, but I did have a secret weapon. I pulled the small pouch of peaceroot that I'd nicked from the homestead out of my pocket and poured the powder into my palm. Then I brandished my sword with the other hand and headed into the fray. I just had to get close enough for one blow.

I made my way around the edge of the room, trying to determine a pattern in the battle that would allow me to get within striking distance of Laurenna. Denna's fireballs dissipated against Laurenna's shields, making hissing clouds of steam billow into the room. Alek's and Laurenna's water magic seemed to have trouble being at odds, instead combining into new shapes. Finally, I got close enough that Laurenna spotted me.

She whirled in my direction. The temperature seemed to drop in the room as her watery shield grew opaque, crackling as ice formed. She shoved it toward me and I raised my sword, knowing it wouldn't be enough to stop her but hoping it would give Alek and Denna enough of an opening to take her down if nothing else. But then my sword lit up with fire as the shield hit it, and Laurenna's defenses shattered into thousands of icy shards. Before I could think about it too hard, I lunged forward and flung the handful of peaceroot powder into her face. She immediately fell to the ground, screaming, the magic in the room seeming to collapse in on itself.

Alek's boots crunched over melting ice shards as he approached.

"What did you do?" he asked me.

"Peaceroot," I said.

Laurenna wheezed and choked, swiping the rust-colored powder out of her face, but it was too late. Her powers had been sealed away from her. Her entire demeanor changed in just a few heartbeats, her viciousness giving way to a growing look of panic. "Fadeyka," she finally murmured.

"Where is she?" I demanded.

Laurenna looked up at me with pure terror in her eyes. "She's not safe."

Denna came up alongside me, and I felt her presence so acutely

I could hardly breathe. She touched my forearm tentatively, almost as if she were checking to make sure my body was real and solid under her hand. I held my breath as a shock traveled through me. I wanted to gather her into my arms right then and there, smother her with kisses until she couldn't breathe. I wanted her to remember all the most amazing moments we'd had together, and felt the need to grovel at her feet to apologize for the ways I'd failed her. I didn't know what it meant that she was here, or that she'd helped save us.

"What do you mean Fadeyka's not safe?" Denna asked.

"Zhari had me under her control with mind magic," Laurenna said. "She has Faye, and we have to get her now!"

Laurenna struggled to get up until Alek held out a hand, which Laurenna regarded with the pleasure most people reserved for an offering of a long-dead fish. Still, she took it and let herself be heaved back to her feet.

"Who's guilty of treason now?" Alek asked.

Laurenna angrily shook her hand free of his. "Zhari," she spat back at him before turning to stalk out the door.

"You can't go after her by yourself," Denna said, hurrying after Laurenna. "Not without your powers!"

"Powers or not, I would do anything for my daughter," she said.

"Then let us help you," I said. "We care about Faye, too."

"And Zhari must be stopped," Alek added, bringing up the rear.

Laurenna didn't slow down. She led us out a side door in the tower and through the halls of the Winter Court at breakneck speed, leaving Alek to knock down the few Sonnenbornes who tried to stop and question us. Without knocking, Laurenna burst through the doors of Zhari's chambers.

"Faye!" Laurenna screamed.

Fadeyka lay on the table at the center of Zhari's receiving room, her expression vacant and glassy. Zhari stood over her, breathing deeply as faint trails of glimmering light rose from Fadeyka to enter Zhari's nose and mouth. The necklace Fadeyka always wore had been torn from her neck, and the broken chain dangled from the edge of the table. I would have thought she was dead except for the way she convulsed when Zhari looked up at us.

Zhari's face was flushed with color, but her normally amber eyes were black as a moonless night. She raised her hand and, with a simple gesture, flung Laurenna into the wall from across the room. Laurenna crumpled to the floor.

"You're too late," Zhari said. "I am fed, and I am whole, and I am ready for the fight." The blackness in her eyes retreated slowly, and Fadeyka's breathing grew shallower.

I swallowed hard. Laurenna had been difficult enough to defeat, and I didn't have any more peaceroot powder.

"We don't have to fight," Alek said, moving slowly toward Fadeyka.

"Don't come any closer!" Zhari snapped. "You fools are inconsequential. Fighting you is not the challenge for which I've been preparing."

"Then what is it?" Denna asked.

"The one in which I destroy Invasya just as she destroyed me," Zhari said.

I glanced at Alek to see if what she was saying made any sense to him, but I might as well have consulted a rock. The only signs that he was reacting in any way to her words were the tension in his jaw and the stance he'd taken with his sword in front of him.

A small moan escaped Fadeyka's lips, and my fear for her rose. Could we even save her, or was she already doomed by whatever Zhari had been doing to her?

"Why don't you attack me?" Zhari asked, her tone teasing. "It may not be particularly difficult to fight you, but it might be entertaining. After I defeat you, you'll make useful reserves of power for me, far more powerful than the weaklings I've drained in your pathetic little camp."

"How could you do that to your own people?" I asked. Apparently it wasn't an illness after all—it was this giant leech draining away their magic to keep them under her control.

"They've done nothing but use their Affinities for the betterment of their families and their kingdom," Alek said.

"You don't know that, you moralistic buffoon," Zhari scoffed. "Now, why don't we fight a little? You go first. It'll be fun."

"You have a multi-Affinity and we're not stupid," Denna said, her stance as defensive as Alek's.

Zhari laughed. "After all this time, even the gods-worshipping Mynarians don't recognize a god when they see one. What a curse it is to live so long."

"A god?" My confusion was absolute.

"Or a demigod," Denna said, her eyes widening.

"I always knew that one was the smartest," Zhari said, nodding at Denna.

"There aren't supposed to be any of you left in Zumorda," Denna said. "The queen said as much."

"The queen doesn't know everything," Zhari said. "For example, she doesn't know that I've been planning this day since she took the throne. She doesn't know that I had almost achieved my goals when her little coup against the boar king ruined everything. I was going to return to the desert. I had the power and the means to free my parent, the god of confluence." She paced around the table to stand between Fadeyka and us. "Fortunately, you lot are not even remotely capable of standing in my way."

Alek traced a symbol, but Zhari only laughed as ice climbed up her robes. With a simple flick of her hand, the ice disappeared, seeming to only give her more strength. She hurled a bolt of raw power at Alek, knocking him to the ground as easily as she would have a green trainee. I screamed as she did the same to Denna, then threw myself in her direction with my sword in front of me. A blast of power smashed into me, tearing the cutlass out of my hands and slamming me to the ground under the table where Fadeyka was lying. The last thing I saw was Faye's hand weakly closing around her star charm, and then my world went dark.

I woke up freezing cold, propped awkwardly in the corner of a stone cell. The chill of the rocks had sunk completely into my bones, and I ached from head to toe. Dim light revealed nothing in the cell but a chamber pot, two narrow cots, and one other person, who was standing up and pressing her face against the bars. Denna. My profound relief at seeing her still alive warred with the rest of the facts, namely, that we were well and truly sarded.

"Denna," I said, barely louder than a whisper.

She turned around and rushed to my side. "You're awake," she said, her voice cracking. She put a tentative hand on my shoulder, and I reached up to clasp it as tears stung the corners of my eyes.

"I'm so sorry," I croaked. "For everything I ever did or said that drove you away. I—"

"Shh," she said, brushing hair off my forehead. "I know you are."

"But how did you get to Kartasha?" I asked. What I really wanted to know was why she'd come. I wanted to believe it was because she was worried about me, but felt guilty for the desire for that to be the truth. Denna had always been someone who put the welfare of her kingdom above her own, and if this was her kingdom now, that could just as easily have been the reason.

"The queen told me about the riot," she said, helping me up onto one of the cots and seating herself across from me. Then she quietly told me the story of how she'd traveled from Corovja to the refugee camp and how her new friends had helped her. "Only to end up here, with a crazed demigod planning to drain my powers to fuel her revenge on the queen."

"And there's no way out of here?" I asked.

"Not that I've been able to discover since I've been awake," she said. "Laurenna and Faye are in the cell on our left, and Alek is across the aisle. Fadeyka is still unconscious—I'm not sure exactly what Zhari did to her. I don't know who's on our other side." She pointed to the high, barred windows between cells that she must have climbed onto her cot to look through. "I can use my magic inside here to some extent, but it's useless to try to use it on the walls or the bars. There's some kind of shield."

Now that I knew she was there, I could hear Laurenna softly singing a lullaby to Faye, her voice trembling with what must have been fatigue and worry. Somewhere else in the windowless dungeon, water dripped from a pipe in a slow, rhythmic accompaniment to Laurenna's song.

"I'm sorry," I repeated. Despair and sorrow welled up, making my throat tighten. "If I hadn't driven you away with my foolish worries . . . if I had figured out what was going on sooner and that Zhari was the one we needed to worry about . . . I've failed you in so many ways." It felt like it was entirely my fault that we'd ended up where we had.

She took a deep breath. "You haven't failed me. And maybe your worries have been justified all along. After all, we're here. This hasn't ended well . . . other than getting to see your face again."

Joy bubbled up but dissipated just as quickly. "No, I did fail you," I said. "Because I should have listened more to what you wanted instead of the fears living in my own head. You deserve the life you want, regardless of whether it's a life I can give you." I could barely keep speaking the words. We'd come to Zumorda for a chance to be together, and somehow all the kingdom had done was drive us apart. The few strides between us in the tiny prison cell felt like an impossible distance to cross, but all I wanted was to feel her in my arms again.

"But I've always wanted the life you can give me." Her sea-green eyes shone. "My life as a princess was planned out almost from the beginning. Lessons. Marriage. Children. Ruling. There was no room for error or deviation. I had to be perfect, and it didn't matter what I wanted or if I fit into the box I was required to. I chose you for a reason. I chose you because in choosing you I was also choosing myself for the first time." She stood up and came closer, extending her hands to me.

My eyes stung as I took them. "And then we came here to get you help, but instead of supporting you, I stood in your way. I thought that keeping you safe was a way to support you. But it was just a different version of putting you in a box you didn't want to be in."

"That was what it felt like. But I still shouldn't have left you without warning," she admitted. "That was wrong, and it was foolish of me not to talk things through with you, to try to understand your perspective or help you understand mine. To at least kiss you good-bye, because not a single day has passed when I haven't missed your touch."

My heart felt like it was pounding out of my chest. "I just want to know that there might be a time when I get to wake up next to you again."

The cot creaked ominously as she sat down next to me. Her eyes flicked over my face, and she brushed away a tear with her finger. I wanted to grab her and never let go, but instead I held still, waiting for what she had to say.

"Now you're a swordswoman," she said.

"I'm learning," I said. "And you have your gift under control."

"I'm working on it," she said.

"I want to do better," I said softly. "I want to support you, not hold you back. I can't promise I'll be perfect, but I'll try."

"I can't promise perfection, either," Denna said. "But I want you."

Those were the only words I needed to hear. I slipped my hands under her cloak and balled the fabric of her shirt in my hands. The heat of her body flooded me with warmth and a sigh escaped my lips as the dreadful tension of our months apart finally fell away. I pulled her close in one fierce gesture, stopping just shy of a kiss, waiting to make sure it was what she wanted. Denna lifted a finger to my cheek and traced it over my lower lip.

"I love you so much," she whispered.

Her words filled all the places in me that had been empty since she disappeared.

"I don't ever want to be without you again," I said. "I love you, too."

She wrapped her arms around me and kissed me until the horror of our situation faded away, until all I could feel was the fire of her lips and the comfort of her arms.

"Fiddleshits," a male voice muttered from another cell.

I pulled away slightly from Denna, my eyes wide. There was only one place I'd heard that word before Fadeyka started using it indiscriminately. "That sounds like Hornblatt."

"Who?" Denna looked confused.

"The Farspeaker who helped me get in touch with you," I explained.

We stood up and walked to the front of the cell, pressing ourselves against the bars. Indignant muttering came from the cell to our right.

"Hornblatt, is that you?" I asked.

The voice stopped its self-involved rambling. "Who wants to know?"

"Mare," I said. "Your favorite honeyshine supplier."

A pair of hands gripped the bars of the cell adjacent to ours.

"The Sonnenbornes got you too, eh?" he asked, though it was more of a statement than a question. "They dragged me out of my house before I could catch my damn cat." He devolved into a rant on porridge and whether the Sonnenbornes who'd taken over the city were going to feed his cat.

"I don't suppose your magic works in here?" I asked.

"It might, if there was someone I could contact who had any hope of getting me out," he grumbled.

"What about your friend?" I asked Denna, feeling a sudden surge of hope. "The one who can walk in the shadows or whatever it's called?"

"Tristan?" she asked, the spark of hope lighting in her eyes, too. "He might be able to get us out, provided he's had enough rest."

"I don't do anything for free," Hornblatt said, his tone haughty.

"You're in *prison*," I said, exasperated. "We're all in prison. Do you want out or don't you?"

A door opened and shut at the end of the hall, accompanied by the sound of squeaking wheels.

"Get back," Hornblatt said, and vanished into the depths of his cell.

A guard walked by with a tray cart covered in small bowls filled with watery gruel that smelled about as appetizing as wet, shredded paper. He slid one for each cell occupant under the doors of the cells, not caring whether half the gruel sloshed out and ended up on the floor.

Before the guard had made it to the far end of the prison hall, slurps echoed from the cell beside us. Apparently Hornblatt wasn't very discerning about his food. Denna and I exchanged grimaces. A few minutes later, we were regaled with the sound of urine being emptied into a chamber pot. I sat back down on the cot, fidgeting impatiently until the guard vanished back the way he'd come.

"You don't happen to have any extra food, do you?" Hornblatt asked from the front of his cell.

"You can't possibly tell me you want it," I said.

"I mean, if you're not going to eat it, why let it go to waste?" He sniffed.

"Because it is waste," I muttered.

"No, wait," Denna said. "You can have both our bowls if you use your powers to contact Tristan. And if he can help get us out, we'll get you out as well."

"I don't have anything reflective to enchant," Hornblatt said, growing impatient.

I glanced over at the chamber pot and winced. "Sure you do. There's a chamber pot in your cell, isn't there?"

"Well, unless you have something of your friend's, it won't matter."

Denna plucked what appeared to be some black cat hairs off her cloak and held them between the front bars of our cell closest to the wall separating our cell from Hornblatt's. She stretched her arm as far as she could in his direction. "Will these do? They're from his manifest."

Hornblatt stretched between the bars of his own cell to pluck the hairs from Denna's fingers. "Your friend's manifest is a cat?" He seemed to perk up at this. "Good people, cats. I'll do it."

I shook my head. The man barely made sense on a good day, much less when we were all sarded up a wall.

I heard a scraping sound and an alarming sloshing as he dragged the chamber pot closer to the cell's door.

A few minutes later, Hornblatt managed to contact Tristan and get through a somewhat confused message about our location and what had happened.

"Tell him I can give him more power if he can get here," Denna said. "I can help us get out."

"The short one says she can power you out," Hornblatt said to Tristan.

Fortunately, Tristan seemed to get enough of the gist, and moments later, he appeared outside our cell, his face drawn with exhaustion.

"Tristan!" Denna raced to the front of the cell.

"How many do we need to get out?" he asked.

"Six," Denna said. "Come closer." She reached between the bars of the cell and gripped his arm at the wrist. He linked his hand with her wrist, and they stood there in silence for a few heartbeats. As I looked on, some color slowly returned to his cheeks until he finally let go.

"That's enough—don't drain yourself too much," he told Denna. "Thank you."

Using magic I couldn't begin to understand, Tristan somehow disappeared and reappeared inside each cell, coming for us last.

"Are you ready?" he asked.

"As ready as I ever am," Denna said. "This might make you feel sick," she told me.

Tristan held out his hands to both of us, and I stepped up to take one, the prison immediately vanishing into darkness.

 *Dennaleia*

WE DROPPED OUT OF THE SHADOWLANDS RIGHT ON the doorstep of the homestead, all of us retching except for Tristan. The full force of my exhaustion hit me as soon as I knew we were safe, and it took all my remaining energy to stay upright. The trip had awakened Fadeyka, who clung to her mother as they both tried to get control of their heaving stomachs. The cold night air was refreshing after the reek of the prison, and I took deep gulps of it to try to settle my own nausea. As soon as Mare stopped gagging, she rushed from my side to Fadeyka's.

"You're all right!" Mare cried.

Fadeyka clumsily embraced Mare, sagging into her arms. "I don't think I want to train with Zhari," she mumbled.

Mare shook her head. "Only you would be thinking about training at a time like this."

The commotion we'd created outside brought Kerrick and Evie out of the homestead. Evie had a restorative tea at Tristan's lips before he so much as had time to speak, and Kerrick strode over to Mare with purpose.

"Thank the queen you're back," Kerrick said to Mare. "We've received word that the cavalry will arrive tomorrow morning. They sent a bird ahead—they've got an auxiliary of Wymund's riding with them from Duvey."

"We have no time to waste," Mare said. "Everything is so much worse than we thought. Zhari is a demigod and was the one behind the Sonnebornes' takeover of Kartasha. Her magic is incredibly powerful—we were lucky to escape her. Luck won't favor us like that again."

"A demigod?" Kerrick stared.

"I didn't think there had been any in Zumorda for centuries." Evie looked equally shocked. "And honestly, I always thought the stories about them might have been made up."

I glanced at Tristan, but his expression didn't give anything away. He must not have told Evie about his parents, and I was touched that he'd trusted me with knowledge of them.

The whole group of us entered the decrepit house, taking seats on the floor or wherever we could cram in close to the lantern.

"How long do you think we have before Zhari figures out we escaped?" I asked.

"I wouldn't be surprised if she already knew," Alek said, absently touching a bruise near his temple.

"Let me help you with that," Evie said. "May I?"

To my surprise, Alek agreed, and at a brush of Evie's fingers the bruise faded to a half-healed yellow.

"Thank you," he said.

"You should all let me look at you," Evie said, her expression concerned. "If we don't have much time, we can't have anyone going into battle weak."

"What about the dogs?" I asked. "Did you have any luck getting rid of them?"

"She did," Kerrick said. "I checked on Harian at his post earlier, and he said it was the quietest sentry shift he's had since we left Kartasha."

Relief flooded through me. At least that meant we'd be able to get some sleep.

Evie made her rounds with all of us, and then we decided to rest until morning and save our strategizing for when the cavalry arrived. But as I curled up next to Mare on a tattered blanket on the floor, I knew I still had one task remaining.

I cautiously dropped my mental shields.

Hello, little one. I was wondering when you'd need me again.

You need to turn back to Corovja. I tried to convey as much danger as I could in the feelings I sent across our connection. *Zhari has betrayed you. She was behind the riot in Kartasha and is responsible for the Sonnenbornes attempting to move into Zumorda.*

All the more reason to come. I don't turn my back on my people, and I don't let traitors go unpunished. There was a strange note of excitement in her voice, as though she looked forward to the battle.

You don't understand. Zhari is a demigod. The daughter of some god I've never heard of—the god of confluence. I shifted restlessly in bed, agitated that she wasn't listening to me. *She nearly killed us.*

She hurt you? The queen's mental tone took on a sharper edge.

We tried to attack her, but it was completely pointless. She turned Alek's and my powers back on us as easily as breathing.

I will kill her. The savageness in her voice frightened me.

Please turn back. You have to keep yourself safe to keep the kingdom safe. Let us try once more to defeat her. Even if we fail, perhaps we will at least weaken her.

It's far too late for that, little bird. Far too late.

The next morning dawned clear, dry, and ice cold, but inside the homestead shack it wasn't the sun that woke us. Outside, voices began shouting to the point that I scrambled out of bed, sure we were under attack. Mare and I hurried out of the small building, squinting into the morning sun, and it was then that I knew why the queen had said my message was far too late.

Queen Invasya flew overhead as a white dragon, sweeping through the pale blue sky with timeless grace. All around us the people cheered, seeing her as the first sign of hope after the terrible ordeal they'd been through. I didn't find the same comfort at the sight of her—just a growing sense of unease. I wanted to go back to trusting her as I had in the earlier days of our training, or thinking of her almost as family as I'd started to before the Revel, but I didn't know if I could.

The dragon circled the camp a few times as if to soak up the applause greeting her, finally banking sharply alongside the peak behind us and releasing a burst of flames from her jaws. While everyone else celebrated, I despaired. She'd walked right into Zhari's trap. Mare saw the expression on my face and put her arm around me.

I wanted to cling to her, but I forced myself to stand up straight. I couldn't let the queen see any weakness in me.

She landed in a clear area not far from us and swiftly took her human form. She walked in our direction and my mind raced with what to say, but before she got within speaking distance, she turned to a random swordsman and followed him away from the gathered crowd. A little stab of unexpected disappointment lodged in my stomach, and I hated myself for it. What she'd done still disgusted me—I didn't want her in my head. But part of me had expected her to come to me first, and I felt lost and confused when she didn't.

She didn't show up at the homestead even when Wymund's foot soldiers and Thandi's cavalry arrived. Seeing the soldiers ride and march in with shining new armor and strong horses made the refugees raise their own weapons in salute, and while it wasn't quite the clamor there had been over the queen, the air of excitement was palpable in the camp. The time had come to take back their city. The head rider and lead soldier came up to the homestead, where I stood waiting with Alek and Mare. Fadeyka hung behind us curiously, though she hadn't strayed too far from Laurenna since they'd been imprisoned.

Wymund himself was the general, his boots as mud-stained as anyone else's.

"Hate to see you again under these circumstances, Mare," he said to her. "But it looks like you've got yourself a fine weapon. I'd like to pledge mine to yours. The cavalry you called in is a fine band of warriors."

"Then pledge your sword to Alek as well," she said. "I couldn't do this without him—he's the one with the experience and the head for strategy. Honestly, we could use some of your wisdom, too."

"I'm more than happy to swear my sword to Alek and help in any way I can," Wymund said, exchanging respectful nods with the other man.

Wymund joined us at the morning's cook fire as we discussed the plan to take back the city. We wouldn't have the element of surprise for long—while the Tamers' familiars had left us alone since Evie's whistle rocks, I knew they still sent spies. Not every familiar was a dog, and it was hard to trust that other animals weren't watching us.

Zhari was the primary concern, though we also didn't have numbers on our side. The cavalry would provide some advantage to a point—provided the Sonnenbornes didn't have an equally large army of their own skirmishers. Mare told them about all the horses she'd seen at the Winter Court's stables, which meant that they likely had at least a few. What concerned me most was Zhari's ability to throw magic back in the face of the most powerful magic users we had left to us—she'd defeated us with no effort at all, and after draining Fadeyka's power, she was as strong as she possibly could be.

But then the queen swept in with ideas of her own.

"If what Zhari wants is to kill me," the queen said, "then we pretend to give her that chance."

"Your Majesty," Wymund said, his expression shocked, "we can't have you risk yourself that way."

"Oh, but we can, and we also need to make use of the few magic users we have left," the queen said. "Zhari is no fool. By now she knows that a few of you have escaped her clutches, and her spies will bring word that I've arrived. It won't take long for her to mount an attack. It wouldn't surprise me if she sent an army of Sonnenbornes and Tamers to destroy this camp before sundown."

I shivered, and it wasn't from the cold.

We talked through all of it and decided to make our move that night. We split up the cavalry into small groups paired with foot soldiers, devising a plan to have them enter the city in small batches that would make it more difficult for the enemy to determine their numbers. The narrow, sloped streets would make for poor fighting grounds for a large force of cavalry anyway. They'd go in and choose their fights carefully until I gave a signal that they were to converge on the Winter Court. Those who weren't fighters would slip into the city in manifest form and disarm as many Sonnenbornes as they could by stealth.

And the strongest magic users remaining would go after Zhari herself.

The stealth contingent left first, just before sundown. Cavalry and foot soldiers followed when the sun hit the horizon, and the queen winged off ahead of them, ready to draw Zhari out of her tower. I watched them go with anxiety drawing its noose ever tighter around my neck. Those of us traveling by magic did so in the cover of darkness. This time, Evie and Tristan came with us—we needed every weapon and Affinity we had at our disposal. Only Laurenna stayed behind, still recovering from her peaceroot exposure and, in my opinion, not entirely to be trusted. When the time came, Alek, Evie, and I pooled our powers to support Tristan as he opened the portal to the shadowlands. I murmured a prayer under my breath as we stepped in. Zumorda might be a godless place, but it still gave me strength to feel like the gods might be watching over me.

There wasn't time to be sick when we dropped from the shadowlands into the Winter Court's mausoleum. I gathered my nerves, trying to focus on the necessity of the battle ahead rather than the fact that people I loved were walking into mortal danger. If we couldn't defeat Zhari, she'd kill Queen Invasya and throw Zumorda into chaos. Defying customs and traditions by choosing an heir, as the queen had once suggested, was one thing; a demigod murdering the monarch for revenge was entirely another. It put all the Northern Kingdoms at risk.

From the mausoleum it was a short walk upstairs to the medics' building, where we encountered the first Sonnenborne sentries outside. Alek and Mare sprang into action in front of us to attack the three fighters. I clenched my fists as the nearest soldier came at Mare with a mace, holding in my magic and the emotions that made me want to rain hell on anyone who tried to hurt her. I needed to reserve my energy for the battle with Zhari. Mare made the sword work look easy, and though she'd said credit was owed to her weapon, I could tell it was more than that. Her dark winter clothes couldn't entirely hide the way her figure and bearing had changed in the moons I'd been away. She fought with the same pride I'd seen her radiate on horseback.

"This is it," I said as soon as the bodies of the sentries had been moved out of easy view, and I lifted my arm to the sky. I shot a beacon into the air, a crackling explosion of flame above the tower that gave our small army the signal to move toward the court. I prayed they would be successful. Everything else relied on us.

I opened the shields on my mind for no more than a heartbeat to share the message: *It's time.*

We rushed through the medics' building as the queen swooped down to the courtyard and landed with white wings outstretched. She unleashed a burst of flame, sweeping it across the area to incinerate at least a dozen Sonnenbornes, some of whom were posted as guards, and others who were attending a few dead bodies I had to surmise had been casualties of Alek and Mare's first trip to the tower. The acrid smell of burning hair and bodies filled the air, making us choke on the smoke. It took everything I had to settle the churning in my stomach enough to keep moving forward.

Several of the dead soldiers lurched to their feet at Tristan's command as we passed their bodies, stiffly hurrying ahead of us to provide a shield. I shuddered involuntarily. As grateful as I was for Tristan's presence, some of his powers were deeply unnerving. I doubted the reanimated fighters would help against Zhari, but at least a moving wall of corpses was likely to slow down any additional Sonnenbornes we encountered inside the tower.

As it turned out, we didn't get a chance to enter the building. The doors opened as we approached. Bright light flooded into the courtyard and Zhari walked out, a wicked smile on her face at the sight of the queen in dragon form. A delicate circlet adorned her brow, and six Sonnenborne soldiers flanked her on all sides. The hairs on the back of my neck stood up at the sight of her.

"Would you like us to dispose of them, my queen?" one of the Sonnenbornes asked.

Queen? I reeled with shock. Her plans went far deeper than killing Invasya. If she was already considered the queen of Sonnenborne, then she must have been also after the crown of Zumorda. It would be the start of an unstoppable empire. Mare glanced at me, and I saw my own love and fear reflected in her expression. I set my jaw and summoned my magic, letting heat flood into my closed fists until I was poised for attack. If Zhari wanted to destroy Zumorda and kill the people I loved, she'd have to get through us first.

"I wouldn't recommend that," Tristan said, launching his undead soldiers at the Sonnenborne guards. The dead men swung their swords wildly, splattering the flagstones with blood as they connected with the enemy and were hacked to pieces.

Zhari raised her hand, and all four of the dead men came to a standstill, then dropped to the ground. She smiled at Tristan, but there was no warmth in her expression. "There is no Affinity or power in the Northern Kingdoms I haven't seen ten times over," she said.

Alek shoved a wave of water toward Zhari. At a small gesture from her, the water surged up and away, evaporating and re-forming overhead as a cloud. With a single breath, she blew on it and it dissipated. My determination faltered. She made it look so easy to counteract every spell, as if it took her no effort. For all I knew, it didn't.

I pulled on everything I could, opening myself fully to what I was capable of. Chunks of stone dislodged from the surrounding buildings, and I ignited them with streams of flame pouring from my hands. With a feral yell, I shoved everything toward Zhari.

Rocks slammed into the tower behind her, shattering the ornate plasterwork that hadn't already been torn up.

When the dust and smoke settled, Zhari stood amidst it with not a single scratch on her. If anything, she looked more powerful and radiant than ever. Fear raced down my spine, and I couldn't help worrying that we were fools for even trying to fight her. With a wave of her hand, Zhari surrounded herself with a silvery bubble of magic. We kept up our onslaught of attacks, but every spell that hit the shield only served to make it glow more brightly. The queen blasted Zhari with power, her anger seeming to override the logic that what she was doing wasn't working. I held back, desperately searching for weaknesses in Zhari's magical shields, but there were none.

Nothing we did had any effect on her.

I leaped out of the way as Zhari reflected back one of Alek's spells to shoot icy missiles in our direction. From the corner of my eye, I caught sight of Mare narrowly avoiding the thrust of one of the soldiers' javelins. Rage blazed through me, and without thinking I launched a series of fireballs at the fighter. He swiftly fell over, blazing like a human torch. Zhari collected some of my flames in her hands, drawing them from the air and the burning man. I watched in horror as the flames turned to sparks, which morphed into bolts of lightning that gathered around her hands. She flung them at me in a killing blow. I tried to run, but the breadth of the magic was far too great for me to escape. Time seemed to slow down as the bolts crackled through the air. Just as the magic was about to hit me and I had resigned myself to my fate, Alek leaped in front of me. His water shield had taken on a glow luminous as the moon, and it hissed when the bolts struck it. Blinding light flashed and the shield collapsed in on itself, then back on him. He fell heavily on the ground. I stumbled out of the way of Zhari's next attack, but when I looked back to check if Alek had stood up to rejoin the battle, he lay as still as the stones beneath him.

TWENTY-NINE ✦ *Amaranthine*

"ALEK!" I SCREAMED, BUT MY VOICE WAS LOST IN THE din of fighting and he didn't respond. I wanted to run to his side, but I'd only make myself an easy target for Zhari or the next round of her Sonnenborne defenders.

I edged along the wall of the medics' building in the shadows as Denna rejoined the fray. Tears glistened on her cheeks as she slung fireballs with what I knew to be deliberately poor aim. We had moved on to our contingency plan, which my uncle Casmiel would have summed up as "if you can't dazzle them with brillance, baffle them with horseshit." Tristan filled the courtyard with illusions of death meant to confuse and distract, and Evie focused on neutralizing anything Zhari attempted rather than casting spells of her own. Zhari stumbled forward, clearly disoriented, her face twisted with anger. I was almost behind her, and Evie stepped in front of me to give me cover. Everything counted on the others keeping Zhari distracted, and I prayed she wouldn't turn and see me behind her.

"Now!" Denna yelled.

I thrust my arm forward, plunging my sword through the bright light surrounding Zhari. As Denna had predicted, Zhari hadn't shielded herself from physical attacks. The sword slid between the woman's ribs and curved out the front, straight through her heart. My blade burst with light and I screamed, stumbling back from Zhari's body as it shattered into sparkling dust.

I dropped my sword on the courtyard's flagstones, cringing because I knew Alek wasn't going to care about my ringing ears— he would still scold me for ever dropping my weapon. But as the last few Sonnenbornes were chased off and the magic users slowly dropped their guard, Alek's reprimand never came.

When my vision cleared, I grabbed my sword and rushed over to where he'd fallen. Evie knelt by his side, her hands on his chest.

"Is he . . ." I didn't get through the rest of the question.

"It's too late," Evie said.

Denna stepped up alongside me with tears pooling in her eyes. "He shouldn't have jumped in front of me like that. I could have shielded."

Tristan joined the circle around Alek. "Not from Zhari, you couldn't. He saved your life."

I put my arm around Denna as a sob racked her body, my own chest tightening with grief. Alek had seemed indomitable, not like someone who could be taken out by a single blow, even if it was dealt by the hands of a demigod. And in spite of our differences and how much I'd hated him for most of our acquaintance, he had always been a steady presence I could count on. His gruffly barked instructions had chased me around the salle even when he wasn't there. The unimpressed expression that never left his face had become so familiar to me that it was as comforting as it was infuriating. There were a hundred more things I'd hoped to learn from him, and another hundred comebacks I'd hoped to dream up to match his barbed comments.

I knelt beside him, ignoring the sound of horseshoes clattering over stone as my cavalry drew closer to us.

I placed a hand on his shoulder and took a deep breath. "May our swords always meet on the same side of the battlefield."

"And may our shields always be side by side," the others said softly.

I stood up and leaned into Denna. Zumorda had lost its greatest warrior, and I had lost someone I never expected to be a mentor—or such a loyal friend.

THIRTY

🔥 *Dennaleia*

WYMUND'S FOOT SOLDIERS POURED INTO THE WINTER Court shortly after Zhari's death, escorted by one of the small bands of Mynarian cavalry. What they found was a small cohort of exhausted magic users huddled around Alek's body, and nothing left of Zhari but the coronet she'd worn during her brief reign as queen of Sonnenborne. I stood beside Mare, clutching her hand. She'd managed to regain some composure. The breakdown would come later, once she had some time to process all we'd been through—especially the loss of Alek. I kept my gaze focused on Mare, letting her be my anchor. My eyes would flood with tears if I let my gaze linger on Alek's body. He'd saved my life at far too high a cost, and though I knew I couldn't have stopped him, guilt racked me to know he'd exchanged his life for mine. As for Queen Invasya, she'd already taken to the skies, swooping over her reclaimed city and looking for stragglers to kill, lest they think about returning to her kingdom.

One representative each from the cavalry and foot soldiers came to us as soon as their people were organized in the courtyard. As they approached, the cavalry rider sat astride her gray mare with the grace I'd witnessed in nearly every Mynarian I'd met, and the tall Zumordan foot soldier beside her recounted a story that involved more gesturing than I would have thought possible wearing relatively heavy armor and carrying a battle ax. There was a surprising ease between the two fighters, no doubt forged in the battle that had taken place in Kartasha's streets.

"The streets are ours, Your Highness," the Mynarian rider reported to Mare.

"Mostly ours," the captain of the foot soldiers corrected the rider. "My people are still purging the last of them from the city. It'll be hard to make sure they're all out until daylight."

"Zhari's quarters and the tower need to be searched immediately," Mare told him. "Do you have enough people to spare?"

"We do," he replied. "When will the refugees be allowed back into the Winter Court—is there a repopulation plan?"

"After we confirm that people can return, we need to make sure they get in safely," Mare said. "Most important, they need to feel safe once they're here. First, let's get soldiers to search the areas where Zhari would most likely have been hiding anything unpleasant. Split them into two groups, and make sure no one goes anywhere alone."

"We'll see to it." The leader of the soldiers saluted. "I'll send you a group to allocate shortly."

"As for the cavalry, please assign a few riders to search the stables and make sure the horses are fed. The Six only know where the usual stable help is in this mess." She cast her eyes toward the barn, and I knew she was thinking of Flicker. I had no doubt she'd be down there to check on him as soon as she was able.

Pride swelled in my chest at Mare's easy command of the fighters. She was making such wise decisions in spite of the tragedy that weighed on all of us. Who knew what else Zhari had lurking in the tower or hidden elsewhere at the Winter Court? There were no guarantees she'd been acting entirely alone. Part of me itched to search buildings with the soldiers, though I wasn't ready to be separated from Mare. I was curious how deep the conspiracy ran between Zhari and the Sonnenbornes, and hoped some of the evidence the soldiers turned up might help explain that. What I longed to know most of all, though, was more about the seventh god. It seemed unfathomable that the religion I'd been raised in was somehow incomplete or wrong. I wanted to seek the truth.

But first, I wanted to be with Mare.

"You've become so strong," I told her when she finally had everyone organized and set off on their tasks.

"I have Alek to thank for that," she said softly.

"I don't just mean that you learned to use a sword," I said. "It's more than that. Command suits you." And it did. As hotheaded as she often was, being in control tempered that, giving her the opportunity to execute her ideas instead of blowing up because no one was listening to her. She was thinking things through and asking more questions.

"I have no idea what I'm doing." She looked out over the courtyard, weariness heavy in her expression. "What I learned in the last two moons . . . it doesn't feel like enough."

"There will always be more to learn," I said. That held true no matter where one was in life. "The important thing is that you are enough."

"What can we do to help?" Evie asked. Both she and Tristan looked exhausted.

"Nothing," Mare replied. "You were both brilliant."

"Find your family," I said softly to Evie.

Mare nodded her agreement.

"I'll go with her if you don't mind," Tristan said.

Evie grabbed his hand and gave him a tired smile that brought a flush to his cheeks.

"We'll catch up with you later," Evie said.

The four of us said our temporary good-byes, and then hand in hand, Mare and I walked toward the wall of the court. We climbed the narrow stairs to the lookout on the wall, and were rewarded with a view of the city.

Outside the wall directly below us, a few soldiers and cavalry riders had Sonnenbornes tied up, and Kerrick and Harian were directing them to be taken to holding cells, where we could deal with them later. Torches and mage lights glimmered to provide a map of streets as people flooded out of hiding. I heard the distant roar as throngs of people celebrated, joyous that their city had been taken back.

But as much a success as the day had been, a creeping voice in my head let me know that it wasn't over yet.

We need to talk, the familiar voice whispered. *Meet me in the library.*

"There's something I need to take care of," I told Mare, giving her hand a squeeze. "Meet me at the stables in twenty minutes?"

"That sounds perfect," she said. "I see Wymund down there—I'd best check with him about plans for repopulation."

I reluctantly parted ways with her at the base of the wall and walked back through the bustling coutyard to enter the chilly library.

When Queen Invasya arrived, she came alone, in human form and dressed in white as always.

Hello, little bird, she said, easing her way around my mental shields.

"Get out of my head." I stood up from the chair I'd been waiting in. My days of referring to her as "Your Majesty" were over. I was my own person, with my own strength, and she couldn't take that from me.

"I can't," she said, stepping closer. "I go wherever you go. You'll hear me if I want to be heard."

"That doesn't mean I have to obey you," I said. I had to believe it for my own sanity.

"No, but it would be nice if you'd consider it," she said, as though I'd be a fool to do anything other than obey her command. "The threat of Sonnenborne may not be completely neutralized. Two powerful magic users are better than one in a battle, and there is only so much danger in which I can put myself."

"Delightful! I've always looked forward to sacrificing myself for someone else's kingdom." My voice dripped with sarcasm. With a pang, I realized I sounded like Mare.

"It's not just Zumorda. If Sonnenborne were to invade, you know it would only be a matter of time before they pushed on into Mynaria and Havemont." Her voice was persuasive. How could she be so calm after everything that had happened?

"I'm not saying that I'm in favor of Sonnenborne taking over," I said. "But you know what would be nice? It would be nice if once in a while someone asked for my help instead of assuming it would be given. Ever since I was a little girl, my life has been mapped out for me. Study, train, practice, then go to Mynaria to marry Thandilimon and become a queen. Once I married, I would produce heirs and take care of the castle. I managed to escape that trap. But what happens? I get sucked into the politics of yet another monarch who sees me the same way—as a pawn. As someone to be used. As someone expendable." The words felt more and more right as I spoke them, and an anger I didn't know I possessed washed over me, white hot.

"You're glowing," the queen said.

She was right. Particles of light danced around me. I pulled them into my shields. Wasting energy wouldn't do right now, not when I was already exhausted.

"I don't see you as expendable," the queen said. "Family is weakness when you're a Zumordan monarch, so I never sought out my descendants. But I watched, and waited, in case a gift like mine should emerge somewhere in the family. And it did. In you."

"That doesn't mean anything," I said. She hadn't cared about any of us until my gift had shown itself. That, more than anything else, showed what truly mattered to her.

"Do you realize how rare it is to have the sort of gift you possess? The strongest of the guardians I've trained would be laid flat by the day you've had."

"Compliments don't mean anything to me when they were given because I've hurt people," I said.

"Perhaps not, but I hope you'll at least consider helping me, little bird. We need you more than you know. Not just Zumorda, but all the Northern Kingdoms. And until you agree, I will go wherever you go. I'll be with you and care for you until the day one of us dies."

"Or you could leave me alone," I said.

"When you're done having your adventures and your friend returns to Mynaria, and the inevitable boredom finds you, when you're itching to do something useful again, you'll find me. And together we will do more than you ever imagined."

She turned and walked away before I could respond, and was immediately swarmed by Swifts and courtiers as soon as she set foot outside the door. All I cared about was getting back to Mare. The queen couldn't dictate my life. I would find a way to remove her voice from my head. I would remember, every day, how her words were a threat, not a promise.

I brushed Flicker in his stall while I waited for Mare, losing myself in the familiar circular motion of the curry comb and the steady sound of him crunching his hay. The stables were quiet by the time Mare walked in—the cavalry riders had completed their check, and all the horses were fed, watered, and blanketed. In all honesty, the Mynarians hadn't had much to do. The only good thing that could be said about the Sonnenbornes who'd captured Kartasha was that they took good care of horses.

"Well, this is a sight to warm my frozen heart," Mare said, letting herself into Flicker's stall with me.

I smiled into her chest as she enfolded me in her arms.

"So what comes next?" I asked.

"Wymund's fighters are going to help escort the refugees back to the city over the next couple of days," she said, releasing our hug but keeping an arm around me while she reached to stroke Flicker's neck.

"That's wonderful news," I said. "What about after that?"

"Well, I have to tell Thandi what happened and give him the good news that we have help lined up to take back Zephyr Landing." She picked up a soft brush from the grooming tote and ran it over Flicker's coat. He sighed, as if rather overburdened by all the attention.

"We do?" I asked. The queen hadn't mentioned it to me.

Mare smiled wickedly. "Even if the queen refuses to give formal help, Wymund has promised me a contingent of his foot soldiers. I think half of them are delighted by the idea of a Mynarian vacation, even if it involves some bloodshed at the outset. They get awfully bored in Duvey during winter with nothing to do but drills and resurfacing roads."

"That's amazing," I said, only half agreeing with my own words. Of course I wanted Zephyr Landing to be taken back as soon as possible, but there was another problem. "Does that mean you're going back to Mynaria?" I had my worries about returning there, even with my powers under control. Most people would still consider me a heretic, dangerous, or both, not to mention that the entire kingdom—including the man I was supposed to marry—thought I was dead.

"Perhaps," she said, dropping the brush back into the grooming tote and turning back to me. "I need to talk to Thandi first, though. I suppose I should make sure he's all right with whatever plan Wymund and I concoct." She rolled her eyes. More tentatively, she asked, "What are your next plans?"

I opened my mouth, then realized I had nothing to say. "I don't know," I admitted.

She smiled. "There's a first time for everything."

I shook my head, bewildered. "I've always known what lay ahead."

"Well." She took both my hands in hers. "There is one part of your future that could be certain—if that's what you want."

"Which part?" I stepped closer to her so that our bodies nearly touched.

"This." She leaned forward to kiss me. When our lips touched, I let them linger, tasting salt and sadness, but also the joy of being close to her again. Now that we were together, we were both finally home.

✦ *Amaranthine*

IN THE MORNING, THE BLOOD IN THE STREETS OF
Kartasha was covered in a fresh blanket of snow. It seemed so much
more innocent now, but I knew the darkness that lurked underneath.

Denna still slept heavily, and I hesitated to wake her yet. I kissed
her on the forehead, strapped on my sword, and left the room. As
I made my way downstairs and exited into the courtyard, people
behaved with strange deference toward me. It made me uncomfortable, until I realized it was just their way of showing gratitude and
respect. It was because of our team of fighters and magic users that
these people had their city and their lives back. I tried to nod to each
of them, at least until my head started feeling like it was going to
fall off.

This early in the morning there were very few people out except
those getting a head start on shoveling snow. As I expected, the snow
in Hornblatt's alley was an untouched sheet of white. I avoided the

piles lurking beneath it, not knowing whether they were garbage or something worse.

I knocked on his door, smiling when I heard the familiar stream of curses from within.

"What do you—oh, it's you." Hornblatt opened the door and let me inside. I stepped into the wreckage, careful not to trip over anything even as Jingles twined herself around my ankles in an extra effort to make sure I face-planted into something.

"I suppose you want to talk to someone," Hornblatt said.

"My brother," I told him.

He held out his hand, and I pressed my brother's seal into it, hoping it would be enough.

"Did you bring me any honeyshine?"

"I brought you my eternal gratitude," I said. "At least for today."

He grumbled and swept one of his haphazard piles of papers off the desk in his little room. The mirror lay underneath, with a stripe of green crust on it. Hornblatt grumbled, then spit on the mirror and wiped off the crust with his sleeve while I watched with mild horror. After a brief incantation, he handed the mirror to me. I stared into it and waited for my brother to appear, hoping I hadn't caught him so early he was in the bath or some other dreadful scenario I wanted no part of.

"Thandi?" I said, hoping he could hear me though the mirror hadn't yet cleared.

His blond hair came into focus first, followed by his blue eyes and a spooked expression. "Mare?" He squinted at me incredulously. "What are you doing in my horse's water bucket?"

I sighed. Hornblatt really needed to work on his choice of vessels.

"Just be glad it's not a chamber pot," I said.

"Disgusting." Thandi smiled. "I suppose it must be you, and I suppose this is some bizarre Zumordan magic that I'm to accept as a matter of course."

Hornblatt huffed indignantly from the other side of the table.

"We took back the city of Kartasha from the Sonnenbornes," I said. "The Zumordans will help us take back Zephyr Landing in the same way, if you'll grant me command. In addition to the cavalry, I now also have a company of foot soldiers at my disposal."

Thandi stared at me like he was seeing me for the first time. "You're commanding an army?"

"Of sorts." I smiled.

"The Havemontians will be so glad to hear this," Thandi said. "I think they were starting to doubt our strength."

I raised an eyebrow. "You're still trying to impress them?"

He glanced down, his neck turning red. "Well, Alisendi, at least," he said.

"I would laugh, but I'm too tired." I grinned. The truth was, whatever it meant for our kingdoms, I was glad he'd found someone else to love. He'd never loved Denna like I had, but he deserved someone who lit him up inside the way she did for me. "Speaking of Havemont, though, there's something very important I need to tell you about the battle and how it was won."

"Is there a chance we could relocate this conversation to somewhere other than my horse's stall?" he asked. "I look like a nutter talking to my horse's water."

I glanced at Hornblatt, who gave a sour shake of his head.

"I'm afraid not," I said. "But just so you know . . ." I took a deep breath, feeling shaky and unsure. I had to tell him the truth, but I wasn't sure how. "There are a few facts I need to clear up with you about what happened when Kriantz abducted me."

Thandi's face twisted with guilt. "I'd rather not talk about that night," he said.

My own guilt doubled in size. "I know, but we must," I said softly. "It's about Denna."

"Nothing I can do will ever make up for losing her," he said. "I don't expect you to forgive me. I won't ever forgive myself."

The moment had come for truth. "But Denna is still alive," I said. "She didn't die in the star fall."

"What?" Thandi looked like he'd taken a hoof to the head.

"Can you hurry up this confession?" Hornblatt interrupted. "Some of us have other things to do. Or drink."

I shot him a dirty look.

"Who is that?" Thandi asked.

"A friend of sorts," I said, to which Hornblatt looked rather pleased in spite of himself.

"So, Denna . . . she lives?" The tentative hope on Thandi's face was almost more than I could bear.

I nodded. "She was part of the team that helped reclaim Karta-sha. She's been here learning to control her magic and use it for the greater good. I'm sorry we didn't tell you sooner. She feared persecution in Mynaria, and desperately needed training for her gift."

Thandi stared at me, looked up for a few long moments, and

then took a deep breath and finally met my gaze in the mirror again. "I don't know what to say," he finally said.

"That's . . . it?" I said incredulously.

"It wasn't that long ago that I got used to knowing she was dead, and now you're telling me she's not. It's a lot to process, Mare."

"Fair," I said. I resisted adding a snide comment that whatever grief he'd felt over Denna's "death" was probably more peaceful than what Denna and I had been through in the last few moons.

"In any case, it sounds like she's succeeded in doing some good," he said. "I'm happy for her that she's found a path that makes use of all her talents. It's what her family would have wanted for her. It's what I would have wanted for her, had I been a wiser man when we first met."

Maybe it wasn't just my brother who didn't recognize me. I barely recognized my own brother, but I liked the person I was getting to know now.

"I think she would appreciate that a lot," I said.

"In any case, please tell her she's free, in case that was something that still concerned her. Alisendi and I have worked out new alliance terms that don't involve marriage but are still productive for both our kingdoms. And I hope to broker one with Zumorda as well."

"It may be a while coming," I said. "The queen is still a difficult person to win over. Anything that could be a threat to her autonomy isn't received well. I have so much to tell you."

"Mare?"

"Hmm?"

"After Zephyr Landing, will you promise me you'll come home?" he asked.

My throat tightened. I'd never thought my brother would want me around. I'd always assumed that just like my father, he'd want me sent off to be married as soon as he could find someone foolish enough to take me.

"I could really use your advice from time to time, you know?"

I nodded, overcome. "Yes. Yes, of course."

Hornblatt made a throat-slashing motion from the other side of the table. He was starting to look a little gray.

"I have to go for now, but I'll send you a pigeon from Zephyr Landing, if that's all right," I said.

"My right to command is passed to you, and I'll see that the paperwork arrives to the auxiliary there," Thandi said.

"Ugh, paperwork," I said. That was one thing I hadn't missed about Mynaria. "Can I just have Denna set it on fire?"

"No." He smiled. "Take care, and may the Six bless you."

"Protocol has gone to your head," I said. "But you take care, too."

The mirror went cloudy, and then dark.

"Now get out of my house," Hornblatt said. "I need to feed Jingles." He stood up and shooed me toward the door.

"I can show myself out," I said, and picked my way through the disaster of a hallway back to the front door. "Thank you for your help, Tum. You helped save your city, you know. And I'm sure Jingles is glad to have you home." I petted the little gray cat, and she squeaked a happy meow and rammed her tiny body into my ankles.

"I did, didn't I?" Hornblatt said, looking pleased and still mildly confused.

I laughed and headed out into the street to make my way back to the Winter Court. The air smelled heavy and metallic in a way I'd come to recognize meant it was probably going to snow again. I pulled my cloak more tightly around my shoulders and walked as quickly as I could to keep warm. When I arrived in my rooms, now at the Winter Court and far finer than those I'd had at the merchants' hall, Denna was waiting for me.

"How did it go?" she asked.

"We have an adventure to plan and our work cut out for us," I said.

She smiled. "Then you'd best come sit with me. Strategizing requires hot chocolate."

I joined her on the plush sofa in front of the windows and reached for the mug she was about to hand me.

"Wait, it's gotten a little cold," she said, and cradled the hot chocolate in her hands. She closed her eyes and murmured something that sounded like a prayer, then gave me the mug. The earthenware cup was nearly too hot to hold, forcing me to transfer it from hand to hand to keep from burning myself.

"Trying to scald my tongue to shut me up?" I teased.

"Hardly!" She feigned offense.

"Well, if I can't use my mouth to drink this chocolate, I suppose I'll have to find another use for it in the meantime." I set down the mug, then leaned over and kissed the side of her neck in the gentle way I knew would send goose bumps down her whole shoulder. She turned toward me and her lips met mine, impossibly soft and sweet. Every time we touched, it felt like a miracle all over again. And now, more than ever, I was grateful that she'd chosen me and I'd chosen her.

I snuggled in next to her and gazed out the window at the tree-tops and valleys below us, strangely content in spite of the challenges I knew lay ahead. Our life together would never be like the fantasies I dreamed up in my mind, because perfection wasn't sustainable. There would always be new obstacles to overcome, new difficulties to face, and ways that Denna and I would change over time. But even if a lifetime of perfection wasn't possible, perfect moments were. Nestled against her and looking out over the mountains with hot chocolate in my hands and the girl I loved beside me—moments didn't get more perfect than that.

Snowflakes began to fall, blurring the outside world with white, so I turned back to Denna for another kiss, knowing that wherever the future took us, we would go together.

ACKNOWLEDGMENTS

Of Ice and Shadows wouldn't be here without the passionate readers who loved *Of Fire and Stars*. You are the ones who made it possible for me to continue Denna and Mare's story. My agent, Alexandra Machinist, and my editor, Kristin Rens, are also owed bottomless debts of thanks for their faith in my writing—I couldn't have two better pillars for my career.

Kristin, thank you for moving mountains for me throughout the writing and publication of this book. Each book has been harder for me than the last, but your dedication and help have always seen me through the storms. Every one of your authors is infinitely lucky to have you. Other team members at Balzer + Bray and the brilliant freelancers they hire are also due great thanks: designer Michelle Taormina and artist Jacob Eisinger for yet another incredible cover; Audrey Diestelkamp and Mitch Thorpe for marketing and publicity support; and Renée Cafiero and Valerie Shea for heroism in copyediting (also known as preventing me from routinely looking like a complete idiot).

My friends and critique partners are owed my gratitude as always, but especially Rebecca Leach, Helen Wiley, Kali Wallace, and Paula Garner. You all helped me with some unspeakably terrible drafts of this book. Rebecca, you in particular are owed a debt I hope I will be able to repay—thank you for Aster, Brynan, and saving me from drowning. Honorable mentions also go to Ben Chiles, Gretchen Flicker, Doug Twisselmann, Adriana Mather, Gretchen Schreiber, Elizabeth Briggs, Rachel Searles, Jessica Love, and Kathryn Rose. Also, welcome to the world, babies Haxtun, Theodore, and Erin!

At the day job Katie Stout, Elisha Walker, Allison Saft, Kia Christian, and Delia Davila are owed my infinite thanks for making sure I maintain a few shreds of sanity in spite of working two difficult jobs.

Charlie—thank you for being a strong, healthy little guy during the writing of this book. You were right there with me through the exhausting days and sleepless nights, but not once did you make me worry about your health or well-being. And now that you're here, you delight me every day with your smiles and the funny way you sleep.

Lastly, I would be completely lost without my wife, Casi Clarkson. Surviving a full-time job, pregnancy, and drafting a book all in the space of a year would have been utterly impossible without your support. Casi, you are the kindest, funniest wife, and I am so thankful for you. None of my success would have been possible without you, and it is such a joy that I have you as a partner in life and parenting. Happy ten-year anniversary—I love you.